I0656227

Ulmarra

A Novel by

Vivienne Makepeace

Copyright © 2013 Vivienne Makepeace
All rights reserved.

ISBN: 0987458612
ISBN-13: 9780987458612

Chapter 1

Ulmarra was so special he defied all unbelief. He was like a new shoot coming up out of a red gravel desert that stretches a million miles to the horizon. He made you wonder how he had come into being, what kept him alive, and why he didn't dry up and become the same color as everything else. Everything he was, and everything he did, made you think his lone, green spear, fighting it out to "be," somehow embodied hope for us all. We, who aren't much more than burnt stones under his bare feet ...

MY NAME IS Wajilla Wilson. I'm a big fulla, but "all muscle," as my nan used to say, but the mirror didn't really agree with her. My family is from the Djabuganjdji tribe. Me mate Jimmy was the last one of his line from the Yidinji tribe of the Mallanburra clan, and there wasn't an ounce of fat on him.

I knew him from when we was fourteen. But before that, I'd been living up at the Mossman Gorge Reserve with mum, who was on her own. She raised my sister and me, and then she hooked up with this guy from the township of Mossman. They met at the old Regent pub on the corner—the one that has the big verandas all around the front and shuttered windows along the street to keep the heat out. It was dark in there, and this guy was like the place: black-skinned and black-natured. She married him apart from our rellies hating him, and they had a kid, my half-brother Juniper.

I ran away at twelve and went down to Cairns, an hour away, and got in with these guys in Manoora. We hung out there like apaches and did a lot of stuff we shouldn't have. Only one of us had a job; the rest of us pitched in getting money any way we could, and we begged for ciggies from the tourists on the esplanade. The house was a really old place and more or less a drop-in center for all of us who had nowhere to go, and even if we did, we didn't want to go to.

Ulmarra was this scrawny kid who came in one day and never left. He was quiet, but I liked him, and we talked a lot about all kinds of things. One day we was walking down the culvert of China man's creek on the way to Earlville shopping center and he told me his story. It didn't seem too different to everyone else's I knew, at least at the beginning of it. I guess he told me 'cause we was close to the street where he had grown up and I found out later, it was where the Ulmarra's began, when his ancestor landed on the mangrove bank in that very place, a hundred and twenty years before.

"Mum told me my birth happened in the back of a taxi on the way to Cairns base hospital. She said my cord was wrapped round my neck and stopped me falling off the seat." I laughed and said it was a lucky break not to land on your head straight away or get strangled by your own mum 'fore you take your first breath.

"My dad said, 'Kid, your mother was screaming some bad fuck'n' language, eh. So bloody loud it near deafened the driver and he was in shock for days! I had to give 'im half me six pack that I grabbed on the way out and we drank it leaning on the bonnet while we waited for the ambo to arrive an' take you an' your mum to the hospital.'" Jimmy looked across the creek and his eyes seemed to reflect the twisted trees like they was the stream below us and all those memories were flowing through them like it was yesterday.

"I don't think I ever saw him without a beer or a whiskey in his hand or without a fag falling out the corner of his mouth." I thought how it was weird that I'd never seen either in Jimmy's hand the whole time I knew him. The rest of us were the same, normal, and would just about kill someone if they got between our booze or cigs and I thought maybe he was a bit embarrassed about where he'd come from and that's why he refused to be like the rest of us—though I don't know why he should be—and I said so. Hell, we abo's got a right to like our booze an' our cigs, no big deal. We got a right to live 'n die like we like, eh? He laughed the way he does, like I'd said a joke, and then changed the subject.

"Guess who I was named after?"

"That skinny cricket in the cartoons?"

"Nah, my real name isn't Jimmy, it's *James*, after the guy on *Star Trek*. Mum and dad always watched it on Thursday night for years. I think mum had the hots for that dude." He looked up at the blue sky over us and said real calmly, "It was almost the only time they weren't fighting about something." He looked across to me and smiled and said, "Beam me up Scotty!" I laughed too, there were more than a few times I'd have liked someone to beam me up outta the way of mum or me stepdad. Ulmarra looked at me and said, "But I guess we all gotta stay put an' be what we are, eh?" The smile dropped off his face and he said, "No one ever called me *James*, or *Jim*, eh—just Jimmy an' I aint no whitey like the ole' Captain, so I guess that explains why I'm still here and no one beamed me up outta there."

"Nah, we aint no whiteys," I said, "We is full on black fullas for sure. Lucky eh? Who want's ta go where no man's been 'afore. Be boring, all that space..."

We walked on down the creek to where there was a pile of crates, supermarket trolleys on their sides, and empty cans scattered on the grass from some night-time camp. He looked across to the mangroves fringing the other side of the creek and said, "You know, in the whole time I had parents, the only thing I will remember about them is they were just fighters, never changing nothing for all that fight. Just staying there, in that shit hole, complaining about anything an' everything. Both of them had long since given up being anything more'n losers, really."

I asked him, how come he didn't have nobody to go to, because even those of us who were living on our own, still knew we had someone, somewhere.

He told me that he'd lost his dad to a heart attack in the welfare office of Centre Link. He said his dad died 'cause someone said they had the air-conditioning up too high and it was too much of a shock or something.

"That day, was a really steamy day in November, and inside they had it going full noise, so it was like a chiller in there." Jimmy shook his head and said, "It was bloody freezing, and they made him wait about four hours. Some of mum's friends reckoned that's what did it but the hospital people said he had the heart attack because he had diabetes and cirrhosis of the liver from all the booze he drank—and he was fat. I reckon he died of going cold turkey, because if he had an appointment with them, he would be shit scared and try to sober up. If you turned up there drunk or smelling of booze, they would threaten to cut off your benefit and arrange an idiot counsellor for you, you know, because abos aren't allowed to buy booze if you're on the benefit. That's probably what did it, lookin' them white fullas in the eye like your life depended on them and hangin' out for a four X for a few hours too long—plus all the rest."

"So where's your mother?" I had asked him, "Still alive?"

"Nah. When he died, me mum didn't do too well and neither did I. Soon as he was gone and she didn't have him to fight with, she started on me. I had to move out just after my thirteenth birthday, because I just couldn't stand it. I used to go round and visit once in a while, then one day, I turned up and the place was empty. She hadn't paid the rent and had buggered off down to Brisbane with some bloke and all our old stuff was out on the street. A cop caught up with me about two months after she left and said she'd died, mixing booze with prescription drugs. He assumed that welfare would be sorting me out, I guess, or I'd just go to someone else in the family but there wasn't anyone. So I just wandered around thinking, "Wow—I'm an orphan.""

I felt sorry for him 'cause he really was an orphan so I hung out with him all the time after that and he stayed permanently with me an' our mates in Manoora, in Cairns all them years ago.

Cairns is the best place ever, far as I've seen. It's the most northern city in Queensland, Australia, and in the wet season hotter than a steam bath, but damn near the most beautiful place anywhere in the world, in the dry. But none of us cared about where we were; we was just getting on with being young guys living in the backwash of the city, having fun and letting time go by. That young kid jimmy was accepted in because he was alone and one of us, and we wouldn't chuck a guy like that out, but that isn't the real reason I befriended him. Even then, he was just straight-out special, and I could feel it right from the start even if he didn't know it.

About three years or so after I met him, Jimmy Ulmarra got a surprise windfall from an ancestor he never knew he had, an English girl named Margaret Stanford, back in the 1870s. She had a fling with this aborigine message man who was a Yidinji from the Mallanburra clan. His name was Mullegadajawara, but Margaret called him 'Mully' 'cause she couldn't say his real name. Seemed Mully saved her from starving on her farm down near Gordon vale when her husband Edward had abandoned her to go dig for gold. Margaret got pregnant with Mully's child and that was pretty serious stuff back then. Jimmy told me that Margaret had the baby, and coincidentally, she named it Jamie, but then Edward came back and killed the abo when he found out, and then died himself. She looked after the kid in secret, even after she married again, a good bloke named Jonathan Stanford. Yeah, she taught the half-cast kids at the mission school, so she could keep an eye on her secret abo baby. Then later, she took him out to live with them at the farm and had three other kids with her new husband. She left a hidden will, which gave a share of her farm to that secret 'creamy' kid. Her white-kid descendants never told Jamie about the will and they couldn't find it to destroy it. When Margaret and Mullegadajawara's son, Jaimie, was long dead, the estate was passed down, and passed down, as a huge cane farm, until the family didn't want to plant cane no more. So they sold it to become a subdivision and were set to pocket a pretty penny from it.

When the old homestead was about to be demolished, one of the descendants found the lost will in Margaret Stanford's old writing desk that had never been moved in all those years and all those generations. If the termites hadn't done a good job on that old desk, it might still be hidden.

There was also a diary with it that told the whole story, and what a story that was. I tried to read it, but got lost about page fifty, 'cause I was more interested in chasing skirt in them days. But for Jimmy Ulmarra, the whole thing turned him around like you wouldn't believe.

Before we knew about it, the old white woman who found it, Aunty Sal, spent six months trying to find the last living descendant of Margaret and Mullegadajawara, who turned out to be our Jimmy. His parents always told him he was a full Yidinji fulla, so it was a surprise to find out he had white fulla in him too. It was an even bigger surprise that his Aunty Sal took him under her wing when she found out he had no one else, even though he was as black as a coal worker, and she was as white as a bottle of milk.

I reckon the genes in him of that first white woman, way back then, was all but washed out of Jimmy by the time he existed, but they was strong in Aunty Sal, and them two clicked like an old rifle. What came about when it fired was the stuff of legends.

"You have Margaret's green eyes," Aunty Sal had told him when she found him, "and now you're going to have some of her money, too." I just looked at Jimmy, blank faced, when he told me all about it. Hell, I wish someone had said that to me but my eyes were just plain brown and no one had left me a cent!

He told me Aunty Sal had sat with him under a large, big-leafed, tree that had a bunch of bats sleeping in it at the Esplanade, and she told him about the will that was never enacted and how her family had decided to put that right. He would be a beneficiary of a trust they had formed for Jamie Ulmarra's descendants and that was going to make our Jimmy pretty rich.

Jimmy was the only one left of the old girl and her message man and for a while, he didn't think it was really happening but when Aunt Sal reassured him, and told him he was 'family now', it all started to sink in that maybe he didn't have to stay where he was after all.

Jimmy said, "I listened to the old girl, eh, and couldn't say a word. When I took Margaret Stanford's diary from her to be polite, she looked at me real strange, and said, 'Read every last word, Jimmy, and you'll see the truth about yourself in there.' Then she said very gently, 'It might give you an idea what direction you should take from here so you can live up to what they hoped for when those two came together. Even way back then, they had hopes for you and your people now...'" Jimmy looked at me kinda strange with them green eyes of his and said, "Mate, she seemed...really genuine, so I took the diary even though I thought it was gonna take me a year to read it. I thought I'd be bored shitless—even if it was the story of a white sheila getting knocked up by one of our fullas."

He took the diary and went to the old farm to take a look at where the story started. He said he climbed the fence that had a sign that read *Trespassers Will Be Prosecuted* hanging from the barbed wire but that was hardly going to stop him, eh. He was 'family' now and better than that, he was still an abo and no sign could keep us out of our own land. He found the big fig tree down the slope towards the overgrown junction of the river and the stream that met down there and decided to sit in the shade of it. There was a broken and rusted grate around the base. Aunty Sal had told him that Margaret Stanford's grave was under that tree so he sat right beside her, the one that had written the diary and started everything off—that's where he began to read it.

"Even from the start, it was like she was sending a message from her to me through that book. It was weird...the diary talked like she had been waiting for me. She kept saying she wanted me to find my purpose and be more than ...you know, a dumb abo. She wanted me to cross the boundary of both races in me, to find the true message of the 'dream time' for both of us. She said I'd find the answers in the rain forest as my ancestors had and that was the only way I'd find out what was really important. She guessed the old Yidinji ways might not be there to teach me the truth in the way they knew it, and as it turned out, she was right, eh. I couldn't even find one Yidinji that could speak our language. She said I'd have to work it all out for myself and I'd have to find a way to save whatever was left. I had to find a way to protect the last remaining shreds of our land before that was gone too—like most of our people are gone or all mixed up. She reckoned I'd have to find and use the spiritual stuff that had guided those old people—and she'd found out that stuff out here with our people. It was special stuff, real special and she wanted me to find it too—but I'd have to do it for myself."

At the end, he looked up at me and said real seriously, "Mate, there was one thing she said that my eyes got stuck on. She said, *'The rainforest must be your cathedral,'* and I realized she wasn't talking about ordinary stuff like religion. She was talking about something that was way bigger than what they was teaching in those church buildings that the old black fullas called, 'houses that can't be moved'. She knew that the real message was in places like that, a natural place. Still, she didn't tell me to throw away everything her people was teaching, but to fill in the missing bits with what our people knew so I could find the *whole* truth, like she had. She said it was way simpler than anyone knew and we just needed both hands to pick up the book and both eyes to read the message. I tell you mate, when I was reading that diary of hers, it made me think I was going to do me best to find what she was talkin' about because the way she wrote, I thought, 'whatever, she knows ... I've got to find it too or I's never going to find out what I'm made for or get outta here.'"

After he read about old Margaret's secret life in her diary, he took off for over a year on walkabout, and when he got back, he was already sounding different to the rest of us.

I stayed his friend even though he was a bit strange. I liked the way he knew stuff and could find anything, no matter how hidden it was. If you threw your car keys into the forest, ten minutes later he would have found them. And animals everywhere seemed to have him pegged as their best mate. If a dog was rabid barking, Jimmy would just walk up to it, and it would lick his hand. Kangaroos just hopped up; birds never flew away. It was weird, but good weird.

Anyway, he inherited all this money, half a million dollars. Back in those days, that was a ton. I didn't know anyone with more than a hundred but Jimmy, even though he had more than any of us would ever see, he never showed it off.

He went back to school and eventually went to James Cook University and became a doctor of environmental studies.

With the rest of the money, he built his own special eco-friendly house up near the Crystal Cascades, and he started a foundation.

The Ulmarra Foundation. Everything began from there. Hell, he became a pretty famous abo, but I didn't care about any of that, and neither did he. He was my friend, that's all. My best mate and about the most amazing person I ever knew.

I guess the best way to tell you about him, really, is to just show you.

I remember this one time: Jimmy was about forty, I think. The foundation had been going for about twenty years, and it was a big deal. So was he, but you would never know it, because he just wore his usual shorts and a T-shirt, if you could get him to wear it. He never wore shoes—almost never, unless Louisa, his right-hand man in the foundation, made him, or I lent him mine if he was somewhere that had a dress code.

This one time, he went missing, which wasn't unusual. Mac, who was one of the crew up at the Sky rail that went all the way up to the tourist town of Kuranda, way over the tops of the rain forest from the flats just north of Cairns city, told me how it happened.

Mac had been on duty that day when this family of Americans came piling out of the cable car very excited.

They were taking the trip together up the mountain. Mum, dad, and their son had been seated in the glass bubble watching the scenery pass beneath them. Mum had apparently swiveled around in the seat and drawn her husband's attention back to the coastal vista that could be seen spreading out north and south. Long stretches of coral sand from the Great Barrier Reef marked the ribbon line of the coast, and inland, brilliant green areas of cane farms fan back to the rainforest jungle at the base of the climb.

She had been commenting on the beauty, when suddenly the dad spied an amethystine python resting on a platform of roots and epiphytes in the shade of an open area of canopy.

"That's a rare sight!" the dad had said to his son. "Look, he's curled up, soaking in the last of the afternoon sun before he begins his night time hunt in the trees looking for birds, I guess."

And it was a rare sight, though I had seen a couple of them over the years up there in them trees.

The little boy was fascinated and began to search each tree, looking for another one as they sailed over the top of the huge canopy of green below them.

Suddenly the boy was pointing some distance into the forest to their left. "Look—there is a man in the tree!"

The father was nonchalant, and the mother was still looking back to the tree with the snake behind them and the coast behind that.

As the boy was more insistent, the father turned to look. He saw the flash of something reflecting between the foliage, and it piqued his curiosity. As they passed by, his son suddenly pointed, "There he is!"

As the tree bows made way, they said they saw a lone aboriginal seated on an epiphyte platform at the top of a giant tree. He was cross-legged, naked from the torso up, with khaki shorts on. He had pulled out his cell phone that was ringing, clicked it off, and put it back in his pocket. He rested his head back against the trunk of the tree and closed his eyes, ignoring the passage of the cable car some distance away.

Old Mac said the bloke told him he had grabbed his wife's arm and said, "Look at this!" She swung around, and the car bobbed a little as they all had their weight on that side. She asked what he might be doing, and the father said he looked like a 'native'. I thought,' you don't know nothin' mate ... we ain't no 'native's no more, we can mostly all read and we even watch the movies over here!'

The son asked, "How did he get up there?" But the dad just shook his head, because it's the kind of question you don't have an answer for and I can understand that, because even I could never quite get how Jimmy managed that feat.

As they passed by, they lost sight of the man in the tree but were excited by the chance observation, and their conversation was full of questions that never stopped, even when they got out and got hold of Mac.

Mac had just laughed and said, "That's just Jimmy Ulmarra; he's often down in one of those trees, and he's a scientist actually." When he told them who he was, they were pretty impressed.

When the Americans finished their conversation and headed off for the tourist township, Mac immediately pulled out his cell phone to call the foundation and tell Louisa Henderson.

The phone engaged, and he said, "Your mate is up in the tree again," and he listened to her going on and then finally said, "Yeah—I know. Want me to go down and get him?" He nodded, saying he would be "just a tick, I need to take a break anyway," and finished the call.

He said he walked to the small office attached to the cable-car platform and his workmate came out. They chatted and laughed about it, and Mac grabbed his lunch box and coffee flask and jumped into one of the empty ascending cable cars, swinging around the central column to head down the mountain. He waved to his mate, who shook his head, because he knew all about Ulmarra, before he sat himself down on a yellow chair to watch Mac go and wait for more tourists to arrive and disembark.

Mac said he had settled into the cab and pulled out his sandwich as the car descended, and the scenery went by beneath him.

As he came down past the second dip in the mountain trip, he stood up, moved to the door, and lifted his hand up and out the small window at the top of the door, feeling for the outside release clip that he knew was there. He unlocked it and slid the door open. Occupational Health and Safety would have had a fit if they knew he did that sort of thing and he'd probably get suspended but he reckoned he loved looking into the forest below and feeling the warm wind as it blew up the mountains. Searching each tree for Ulmarra, he said he had moved from one side of the doorway to the other while he hung on to the opening with one hand and his sandwich with the other.

Suddenly, he said he had spotted him and yelled out. "Oi! Ulmarra! 'The Queen' is looking for you!"

Ulmarra lazily swung his head around, stood up on the platform, and waved out to the man passing thirty yards away in the cable car, still eating his sandwich in the open doorway.

"Want me to tell her at the bottom you're on your way down?"

"Yeah, mate!" Ulmarra yelled back as he watched the cable car disappear, and he heard the other man reply distantly, "See you on the way back..."

Mac said he saw Ulmarra stand up for a moment and survey the peaceful surroundings filled with cicadas rasping all around and an odd parrot screeching somewhere deep in the rain forest. He turned and gathered up a long, woven section of loya cane with loops in each end and slung it around his waist and then looped it around the trunk of the tree.

Mac said he saw Ulmarra tightening the slack loya-cane rope, and then he placed his feet hard up against the trunk and began to walk down it.

I've seen him do that too. Right from the top, you can watch him slide and walk all the way to the bottom and your stomach is in your mouth the whole way even watching him. I tried once, but I couldn't get even six feet up before gravity got the best of me, and I realized if I wanted to survey the world from the perspective of a rain-forest giant, I'd need a winch and a chopper.

When Ulmarra reached the bottom, he would have looked up at the two-hundred-foot descent from the top of the tree and said, "See you, ol' fulla," like he always did. He would have folded up his vine rope and set off, up the incline through the trees toward the station at the top.

I met Mac's cobber by accident at the burger bar on Abbot Street a few days later. His name is Steve but we call him Steve'o in these parts. He said when Ulmarra arrived-not even puffing-he'd jokingly yelled out to him before he walked up the steps of the platform, "You're in trouble again, mate."

Ulmarra had smiled a white-toothed, aborigine smile, and nodded toward the cable cars. "Okay to catch a freebie?" Steve'o had nodded and opened the door of an empty cable car for him. "You owe me a beer, mate," he replied, even though it was common knowledge that Jimmy doesn't drink so it would be a long wait for payment. He closed Ulmarra into the Perspex capsule and away he went.

As he took the trip back down the mountain, Mac said he was in another capsule, on his way back up. The two cars passed each other, some distance apart, and Ulmarra waved out as Mac waved back.

Mac told me as he had passed him, he put his two hands up to his head to make horns and mimicked gouging the air, pointing back down to the bottom to indicate that "the Queen" was as angry as a Black Angus that had just been branded—twice.

He said he saw Ulmarra just shrug it off and salute his thanks to him as he went on down.

Mac said he understood why our Jimmy took time out up there, and he never minded covering for him, but that day he was pretty sure Ulmarra was going to get a good stripping down and he was glad he was going back to work because he reckoned it wouldn't be a pretty sight. Hell, he didn't know Ulmarra. He could charm the birds out of the sky and tame a school of bull sharks in a feeding frenzy. Somehow he always managed to sort the Queen out, even when no one else could.

When Jimmy reached the bottom, he walked through the tourist shop, where all manner of stuffed koala, bat, and kangaroo toys are always stacked up. The shop girls would have smiled and nodded to him, 'cause they all knew who he is, and he would have dodged the odd tourist and passed through.

Outside there is a wide car park. Buses were always arriving, and tourists of many kinds are always disembarking, ready to go up the cable-car attraction pretty much all year round.

Jimmy's not keen on tourism, so he would have skirted around them and headed for a fence he always jumps over and then walked barefoot through the long grass of a wide field ringed with trees on that side.

There are cockatoos in them trees, and, sure as eggs, one of them would have set off and Jimmy would have looked up and wished he was able to do the same because above all else, he likes his freedom.

On the other side, he always jumps the fence, even though you can walk ten feet along and go through the gate. I've seen him pushing through the trees to the footpath beside the road, and I've said many times, "Jimmy, you are just asking to get hit, 'cause them taipans like to go to sleep in the long grass in the shade of the trees." But he never seemed to worry.

He would have walked up the concrete path with his bare aboriginal feet hitting the hot pavement. I swear his feet must be as tough as a dead kangaroo hide dried for a year in the red desert, 'cause he never felt the stones or the heat that even burns through rubber soles on a really hot day.

Finally, he arrived at the front of the James Cook University. Walking into the air-conditioning set at an environmentally friendly, 23 degrees C or 73.4 F, he waved to the reception staff, and one of them said they called to him, "You been AWOL again; she's been looking for you everywhere—those guys from Indonesia are here."

"Shit!"

Old Dulcie on reception told me, "Wajilla, can you believe it? I heard him swear under his breath-but I still heard it!" She was pretty shocked because Jimmy hardly ever loses his cool and I think I could count on one hand the amount of times he has said a curse word but that day, he had forgotten the meeting and it was an important one, according to Louisa. He didn't speed up, though. Instead, he caught a T-shirt that Dulcie, always had tucked away under the counter for him. She said she pulled it out as usual and threw it to him, and he pulled it over his head.

"Thanks, Dulcie. You're looking good today, pretty as a tea-tree flower."

She smiled broadly. She loved him, she reckoned, because he always "remembers the little people"—though she was 'all muscle' like me.

He walked down the corridor and turned at the junction that had a sign and an arrow over the opening that read, *Ulmarra Foundation*. The corridor ended in a large glass door and opened to the outside. A path headed off through tropical gardens toward another smaller building.

As he walked toward it, an attractive, dark-haired woman in her forties rushed up the path.

Yeah, that's Louisa, 'the Queen'. She came from a well-off white family in Sydney and was educated up to the eyeballs, and didn't she let us know it.

That day, she was as mad as a cut snake.

"Where the hell have you been? For god's sake—why won't you wear shoes?" She was struggling not to speak too loudly and grabbed a pair of sandals from behind the door for him to put on. "They've been here an hour! We've been showing them everything but the kitchen sink to keep them occupied, but it's you they want to see."

Ulmarra wasn't moved. He simply walked up the path beside her and said quietly, "You shouldn't get so worked up Lou. By being late, I just saved them from making it to their flight back home on Garuda Airlines—and crashing into the sea off Bali."

"Yeah, right!"

She shook her head, and, even though she was angry, you couldn't possibly miss how fond she was of him. But she always disguised her feelings by chiding him over bloody near everything, and he ignored every bit of it.

"So what did you save *me* from by being this late?" she joked.

He swept his hand through a spider lily flower by the path and caught up a butterfly that had been sitting there, releasing it to the air.

"A life held captive by your ever-increasing need to control everything," he said, looking straight into her. "In other words—yourself, Louisa *Janelle* Henderson."

She smiled, I guess because she knew he was right.

When they entered the door of the new building, she ushered him down another short hallway. Just before they went into the room where the Indonesian dignitaries were waiting, she whispered, "Watch what you say—please—don't get on the subject of palm oil. They are here to learn something from us, not be offended. If you want to change the world, James *Byron* Ulmarra, first you have to get it to listen—and no one listens if they are being criticized."

The doors swung open, and Ulmarra replied, straight as an arrow, "Change comes for two reasons, Lou: at the end of a gun or with a fistful of dollars."

She shook her head. "No," she said right back, "sometimes it comes because people want to do the right thing, so please—*please* give these guys the benefit of the doubt, particularly if you want to see native trees replanted in Indonesian Borneo and a bunch of happy Orang-utans swinging off them. You just remember, those palms that are planted there now, have nothing but little, white, Orang-utan crosses sticking up at the bottom of them, so be good!"

She walked in after Ulmarra, and, when they came into the room, ahead were three overweight men in business suits seated at a table. The men smiled and immediately stood up enthusiastically.

"Gentlemen, may I introduce Dr. James Ulmarra, head of our foundation and visionary for the Rebirth Green Project." She put on her best smile and ushered Jimmy Ulmarra forward to the men who held out their hands to shake his.

Louisa handed them a pamphlet with the new logo on it, a green-skinned face of a smiling kid with white, white, teeth.

"The RGP system is already in five countries, and some pretty distinguished people have realized—"

Jimmy broke in, "Louisa puts a lot of stock in all the letters after someone's name but I don't care about that stuff. It doesn't matter who you are, or what karat gold your watch is made out of. To me, it's just about 'sanity'—getting things right before we got no time to do it."

The first of the Indonesians nodded, smiled, and said glibly, "I have to agree, sir, and that is why we are here to look into your wonderful program for the benefit of future generations."

Jimmy turned to face the man squarely and spoke softly to start with, because that's his way and even though he is quiet most of the time, when he speaks, it's with enough force in the meaning to blow Everest off the face of the earth and leave nothing but a big hole that no one can explain how it got there. "You can't tell me you're gonna rip out palm trees to do what we are doing here if there's nothing in it but a good conscience?"

Then he turned and walked toward the door, and they all followed like wet lambs, with Louisa hurrying after them but she was scowling in Ulmarra's direction like she was gonna burn him good when she got the chance latter.

"What Dr. Ulmarra means," she spluttered as they walked down the hall toward the control room filled with our computers and Matherson seated at an architectural drawing board working on something technical, "is that there are substantial financial benefits to the program in the long term, but we know that's not the prime reason for the interest it's creating."

Jimmy shook his head and replied, "What 'he' means is, you ain't here for the 'good' of it, just the bucks, right?"

The chief Indonesian stuttered and went a light shade of blue under his tan. "I admit that the intensive permaculture and aquaponics developed by the foundation to grow crops less labor-intensively and more productively than traditional palm-oil plantations is a draw card, sir. We are always interested in diversifying so those commodities we currently have to rely on for gross domestic income may not need to be, shall we say, so 'pervasive'. Scientific development like yours offers new options. We can 'pacify our conscience', as you put it, by considering your RGP system while still keeping our business targets intact. I doubt any one with practical considerations would find fault with that, sir."

Louisa said he may as well have read it off a card, it was so practiced, but it wasn't doing nothing to convince our man. No way—but the guy carried on.

"We can 'look into' native reforestation to restore our own rainfall cycles and do our small part to reverse the effects of global warming precisely because your intensive farming towers mean we can produce more economically. Of course, the bi-product is the benefit of a reduction of habitat destruction." She told me he said something about times like these being a time of great scientific opportunities that combine 'economical options and conscience' together. They were very 'gratified' that the RGP plan was so 'cheap' so it made it worth considering—before he was cut off by Jimmy, his green eyes flashing with that weird intelligence behind them that had been there even when he was a kid.

"You know—words are cheap too. Making money is the main motive for all you guys in suits, right? And it has never been any different, has it?" He pointed out the window like he was throwing a spear.

"You see this land? People came here a hundred-and-thirty years ago and ripped out the forest, and my people from it, with nothing but wealth on their minds too. As far as future generations were concerned, they could only see as far as their own kids. They cut us all down and planted crops of sugar cane here, just like you and your palm oil, to put sugar in everything you eat and drink. If you eat enough of it, it'll help you get fat, give you diabetes and cancer, and make it so you can't drink a cup of coffee without it. It's worse than crack and twice as addictive. They took this land away from people that had been here for forty thousand years who had never had one teaspoon of the stuff and who ruled their world and each other with nothing but 'conscience' because they had no 'economy' to get greedy over. Everything was already provided for them, free of charge.

"When the wrong of it started to show up just a hundred or so years down the track, they gave us some of that money they'd made off their 'economy' and said, 'Tell us what to do; we got a problem happening here. We've screwed up the whole cycle, and the crops are being hammered by floods or we got drought and everything is dying or being ripped to shreds by super storms.'

"So we said, 'Put back the forest, and we'll find another way to give you enough to eat and run your cars and make your lipstick!'"

Ulmarra had their attention now, and he went on as though he didn't have to breathe like the rest of us.

"Now, I can see that back then, they didn't know what they were doing. It looked like a big, big world with 'endless everything,' so fixing up what they did when they burned it all away is one thing and maybe they could be forgiven for what they did. But guys like you—living now, when we know so much about what happens if you destroy the natural order. You want me to stroke your egos and say what good guys you are for 'considering' RGP?

"What you're doing to your own country is crazy! It can't be called anything but madness to burn off an area of rainforest about the size of three hundred football fields every hour just in Southeast Asia alone—let alone an area the size of Greece each year worldwide.

"Look—Indonesia and Malaysia alone have got twenty million hectares of *abandoned* land to plant palm trees on—use that and leave your forests intact." He shook his head. "And if it isn't palm-oil plantations someone's clearing rainforest for, you're clearing it to graze the most inefficient source of protein there is for your 'two beef patties and fries.'

"Even you guys have known the science for thirty years, and everyone by now should know without doubt that the world is about to be hot enough to fry a chicken before the bird even gets to the grill—only it will be us who gets fried, and we will be eating each other before long because all the animals will be gone!

"No one would believe you've come over here because of your 'conscience' or that you have any intention of doing the 'right thing' for future generations because you're ruled by the dollar. But I'm telling you, you had better get a conscience—and fast."

The faces of the Indonesians turned to stone with shock. You could almost hear their wallets snap shut even though their mouths had dropped open.

Jimmy turned to the window and said quietly, "You know, when you're an alcoholic, the first thing they tell you to do, is, 'Stop drinking.'"

As quick as the quoll, that is his family's totem, he turned and walked off towards the door, saying as he went, "Louisa can show you how it all works, and how there is 'money in it' for you. The only thing you need to know from me is, stop hacking down what's left of your trees—now! When you have put that kind of law in place over there, then come and talk to me, and I'll be happy to listen to you—hell, I'll even buy you an orange drink made with real oranges and no sugar!"

Louisa, flustered, and tried to save the situation by volunteering to show them our computer program and field science that designed the replanting of forests the way they are meant to be. It's radical science and means that wildlife could be reintroduced almost immediately to the new areas and they grew together, to be as close as possible to the original forests that had once been there. She told them that our latest intensive farming towers were now entirely solar powered, so farmers who bought into the requisition scheme could produce as much as they did before without the use of the large areas of land or toxic fertilizers of the past—and dedicate the rest of their land to the RBG project that restored the land and made it green once more.

The most senior Indonesian delegate was barely listening to her, and, in the middle of what she was saying, he called out after Ulmarra, "So were you an alcoholic, Dr. Ulmarra?"

Jimmy stopped, turned, and said back very quietly, "No, but my father was, and he's dead." He turned to walk away but said clearly before he left through the glass door, "That's the lesson, mate. You've come a long way to learn something really simple— stop or die." The door closed with a *shush* behind him as he disappeared.

Louisa was left, as she always was, to balance the egg in that political spoon of profit versus the environment with people who generally just wanted to grab the egg and sell it. The great Dr. Jimmy Ulmarra and his ideals were often at odds with those realities. Mind you, for all his admonishment of the fat suits, he had long since decided that the money men could make their profits if they had to, as long as there were "profits" to the natural world as well.

But one thing you could always be certain of: Ulmarra would do nothing less than call it as it is, and you had to take that, because he couldn't give it any other way.

Chapter 2

A FEW DAYS AFTER Jimmy had stormed away from the visiting Indonesian businessmen, I saw him for the first time actually showing an interest in a human being beyond what part it was playing in the scheme of saving everything else. We were up in Jalang forest section, number four.

It was strange to see, because he was usually in a different world from all of us, and especially out there, in the wilderness.

I'd seen him many times in the middle of a forest with the sound of a whip bird cracking its distinctive whistle over the valley. The footsteps of that barefooted aboriginal would be threading through the undergrowth, his khaki shorts brushing quietly through the ferns and his feet passing silently over the leaf litter. I can still see him as he might pass a fallen log, and he'd stop and bend low to look. He'd sit down carefully, and then he'd rest his right hand with its open palm up on the log while he'd pick at a tooth with a twig in the other, seemingly minding his own business and just taking a rest.

A few moments would pass by, and then a small snout would poke itself up from around the log. You'd be watching quietly way behind him, waiting for something magical to happen, because this was Jimmy Ulmarra and half the time, what you'd see, was unbelievable. Then, a little creature, maybe a very small marsupial like a kangaroo mouse or a pandemon, would sniff the air and snuffle up gingerly onto the top of the log. It'd hop quietly toward the man's hand, still sniffing furtively, then rest its paws on his palm. Then it would wander about near him, completely unafraid looking for something to eat but really, just hanging out with the man.

Jimmy would watch it, alone and lost in the moment, smiling to himself, forgetting you were even there, stopped in your tracks, hardly daring to breath. Quietly, he'd lift up his hand and gently push the animal off to the side of the log, and you could see that it was utterly tame and unconcerned even when he touched it.

He'd say quietly, "You better head off home, little fulla, before a quoll spots you, and you become 'mouse tartare.'" Then he'd stand up and begin to pad off, and you'd wake up and follow along like you'd been spying on a forest god, wondering what the hell this man had when even wild animals would come out for a visit.

On this occasion up at that section, I saw him as he came through the trees toward us, and that strange calmness was with him but all that was about to change. Something new was about to show up in him. Maybe something a bit more "human."

There were a whole lot of us there doing a field study as he came out of the forest that day.

Two people were setting up one of the tripods and anchoring it to the ground; two others were on their haunches taking samples, and distantly, an open insect-proof tent had been erected. You could see a table with microscopes, a computer, and two people inside moving about like shadows.

Jimmy had appeared like a ghost behind Doug as he walked up to the first of us.

The old bloke jumped and said, "Oh, hi, boss! Just about got this place rigged. Should have some images in about an hour." He pointed to a monitor that was showing red lines crisscrossing the screen. He said, "There are small-animal trails all over the place, so should be some good night scans."

Jimmy pointed to some of the leaf litter and said, "There's been a goanna through there hunting; looks like he got a gecko."

Doug wasn't surprised that Jimmy had already seen, without the aid of high-tech equipment, where the animals had been, as his special talent was something we were all familiar with.

"Are we going to catch anything this time?" Doug asked.

"Nah, no need—done a grid on the far side of the valley. It's pretty much the same there, so we can leave these fullas in peace on this side," Jimmy told him.

He was looking right across the scene where long line wires had already been hoisted from one end to the other of the fifty-meter square, and solar-powered infrared cameras were already sliding silently along them, tracking the ground beneath and the air above.

Jimmy watched a man on the far side of the grid erecting another machine to the wire on that side. Jimmy walked around the outside of the square and headed over to see if he could help.

When he arrived, Matherson—a small white guy from the University of Melbourne—was standing with a young woman. She was a small aboriginal with fuzzy hair tied back in a bun. She had beautiful black, almond-shaped eyes that seemed to flit around like dragonflies, and her black shoulders were shining with a light film of perspiration.

Matherson was telling her how they had created the grid to thermal-image the area and catalogue what life lived in this section of bush, both on the ground and in the trees above. He told her the cameras would slice slowly and effortlessly through the space, capturing the quantity, and behavior of the animals here without disturbing them.

"These machines will also record changes in air temperature, air pressure, and soil moisture," he said, pointing to another section where two men had marked out a separate ten-meter square and were finding and counting various bugs in the debris and soil. They were taking samples and marking lists as they worked, and he told her how everything worked and why we had to do it.

That girl took his instructions very seriously, like it was the very manual needed to breathe, and she never saw Jimmy or me walking up to them.

I noticed that Jimmy watched her with interest almost straightaway, like he hadn't seen a bird before. He tried to look like he was ignoring her, and instead he made a comment as Matherson came to the end of his speech.

"Dreamtime beings taught all this stuff to the people back then; now we have to find out for ourselves with the use of sci-fi gear."

She replied, quite bravely, really, "Makes us the Dreamtime beings now, doesn't it?"

"Maybe," he replied, "but can we turn into animals and live at peace in the land like those Dreamtime beings did? They never hurt nothin' and didn't have to spend mega-bucks to study it so we can put it all back." He had a funny smile on his face as I watched him walk off, and I thought, "He likes her."

She smiled too and turned to her companion, whispering, "If you look around, there are plenty of 'people walking like animals' these days—that one, for a start!"

He grinned back and said, "Sure—not the kind of animals he's talking about, though. More like the kind that have been on the grog all weekend!"

"Yeah, well, who doesn't?"

"You know that one doesn't touch a drop." His eyes followed Ulmarra walking to the tent, and he said, "But if anyone could turn into a real animal, it would be our illustrious leader."

"Oh my god, is that Jimmy Ulmarra?" she asked and her eyes widened so far they we almost as round as a chocolate covered Macadamia nut.

I laughed, and Matherson said, "Yes that's 'the god of the rainforest'; you can call him 'Mr. Inspiration-for-Us-All,' but he will probably tell you just to call him Jimmy.

I was watching Jimmy as he strode away as Matherson went on and said, "Not many people know, the name 'Ulmarra' means 'a change in direction'—or something like that. He likes to think that that is what we are all here for: We are changing the direction for Australia and maybe even the world." He grinned cheekily, "In my case, I'm here to play with this high-tech gear and live in awe of a man who never wears shoes but doesn't ever get a splinter or need a sticking plaster."

When I turned back, I saw her looking at Jimmy disappearing into the tent like she somehow understood the famed man even from the first hello. He was more like a forest spirit than a human being and the way she watched, it was like she knew its secret name, the one that is way deeper than 'a bend in the river', or 'a change in direction' that Ulmarra means.

"I suppose you are going to say next, where *he* walks the flowers bloom," she said as she turned back to us.

Matherson grinned and replied, "No, but you will find the odd fern bowing low."

As Jimmy spread the screen of the tent and walked in, I said good-bye to the new girl and Matherson and followed him.

When I got there, I heard Louisa pipe up, "Ah, you made it—look!' She moved away from a microscope to make room for Jimmy. "I'm not sure, but I think this one is entirely new. I can't identify it. Thought I would catalogue it and see if Mark Robilliard can put a name to it."

"It's a type of carrion beetle," Jimmy said as he looked at the insect.

She laughed, saying, "I know that, idiot!" Then she playfully slapped him and asked did he know what *kind* of carrion beetle. He said, "I've seen it before …"

He was somewhat disinterested in the beetle and made room for me, so I could take a look. He stepped over to the net and stared out, in the direction of the girl and the scene outside.

Louisa spotted him and spoke a little more seriously as her gaze drifted out to the new girl working and laughing at some pathetic joke of Mathieson's. "By the way," she said, interrupting Jimmy's private thoughts, "those Indonesians were impressed with our intensive farming technology, but not so much with your manners."

"That's because they want the IFTs without having to restore their forests," he replied, still looking at the girl in the clearing. He said, somewhat distractedly, that he would just about guarantee they would continue burning virgin forests to plant palms anyway, and they would take on the new methods of growing mass-produced crops in our intensive farming towers just for financial gain. I looked up from the beetle as he said, "Lou…they have to 'stop' before they can 'start'. That's the message we needed to get across, not that we want them to sign a deal."

Louisa shook her head and sighed.

Jimmy never reckoned you could trust an Indonesian in a suit. He had some strong feelings about them after they invaded East Timor in the '80s and annihilated the indigenous people there just to get their hands on the huge oil fields off those islands. They were teaming up with Australian companies to get to it now, so he didn't have a high opinion of them either or half the other giant energy companies all over the world tearing up everything to get the stuff. He thought it was ironic that oil was just a stack of dead animals and vegetation buried for millions of years under pressure and these guys were killing off billions of living things to get to it.

That wasn't the only reason he was a bit cold towards the Indonesians, though. He got scammed in Bali one time and lost a thousand bucks on some time-share con. That really seemed to do it, and after that he was always suspicious.

"They were wasting our time as soon as they stepped off the plane." He shrugged as he watched a rainbow Lorie try to settle on one of the wires before someone chased it off.

"Sure, sure, I've heard all this before," Louisa snapped back. "But let me remind you that all our contracts for the IFT system stipulate that a certain amount of land has to be returned to native use so they would have been locked into doing something for reforestation."

"Policing that is almost impossible, Lou. You know that." He finally turned back to us and said with certainty, "If the heart isn't in it, the fat cats find ways to get around your contracts, and not one blade of native grass will ever be planted."

"It's still worth trying. You could have been a bit more convincing."

"Who is the new girl?" Jimmy ignored her and looked at me.

I noticed Louisa suddenly acted strangely at the mention of her, looking up to see the girl still being shown about the site and turning some heads too.

"Jyly Ungaru," Louisa replied for me with a tinge of sarcasm in her voice. "She's our latest scholarship recipient. By all accounts, she's got a good history of supporting indigenous conservation programs on native title land, and we've awarded her a place at the foundation based on that. She's not got much else going for her— no education to speak of ..."

Ulmarra turned back and stood very close to the net, watching the young woman for a second or two—too long for Louisa's liking, I'd say. She added with false humor, "She's only twenty-two years old, Mr. Ulmarra, and has a long way to go," as though she wanted to counter whatever hidden thoughts he might have about the girl. "She's also a bit of a smart-ass as far as I can tell."

Jimmy smiled and, far from putting him off, I could see that before she'd even started, Jyly had won points in his eyes, because he approved of anyone with spirit. Having got Louisa's disapproval, I guessed she probably had plenty of it and, I admit, if she was upsetting 'the queen' it was a good enough reason for me to like her.

We worked all that day up there in the forest grid copy section, and it seemed like Jyly and Jimmy were always facing each other and stealing a glance or two, but neither ventured close enough to talk, which was good, because Louisa was watching both of them while she pretended to be totally disinterested.

I was watching all three and thinking to myself that something was going on, and it was likely to be explosive or interesting. Either way, that day Ulmarra took his own change of direction and it was going to take us a long way away from where we'd ever been.

When the evening had fallen, the sky turned brilliant red.

Jimmy had walked to the edge of the gorge by himself and was staring out over the precipice to look at the distant horizon, like he often did.

He told me later that he had heard a sound behind him but didn't turn to look, staring down at his feet instead and then back up to the sky, pretending he was preoccupied. He had heard Jyly from the moment she followed him, but she had stopped and was hiding behind a tree, working up the courage to walk forward and introduce herself.

"If you wanna gawk at me just say so, and I'll pose for you," he had said quietly.

"S-s-sorry..." Jyly said, and when she finally spoke, he told me her voice sounded childlike and small. "I followed you up here so I could meet you properly, now that I know who you are, and maybe we can talk about the project and stuff."

"I know—heard you about three minutes after you left the camp. You sound like a cassowary crashing through the bush. Every animal for two kilometers has buggered off."

"S-sorry," she said, stuttering again.

"So what do you want to know?"

Jimmy said she began to ask the usual questions he had heard a million times before, like, how and why he does what he does.

"A gift makes room for itself." He said he replied quietly as he stared into the red of the sky and she walked up beside him.

When she told me the story later from her perspective, she said it seemed like the Universe reverberated with those simple words, and she felt strangely uncomfortable because his voice seemed to have a strange power to make the words come alive. Yeah, I knew what she meant.

While she stood there trying to work out what he might mean by it, he said, pretty sharply, "Is that it?"

She said he had completely ignored all her questions, as though he already knew that they weren't what she really wanted to know. Instead he just sat there, quietly waiting.

She said she finally asked him straight, "Can you feel the animal souls, like some of our people say you can?"

"Ahhh," he replied. Then he looked at the burning sky and the dark landscape resting under it and said to her, "You see this? You think we are separate from it or part of it?"

"Both."

"Good answer," he said. "Deep down, everything is made of the same stuff, just slightly differently organized. Even among living things, it's only a few genes that change you from being human to a chicken." He let the ocean of space in front of them swallow up his words and form a long pause.

"Is that it?" She mimicked his reply to her, because he hadn't given her anything new. She said he turned and looked up at her. A slow smile crept up his face.

"You're a smart-ass alright!" he said and began to get up, humming a tune, and looking over the edge to the sky beyond, still avoiding her direct question.

Suddenly he straightened up and began to sing an aboriginal song at the top of his lungs over the gorge. He began stamping his feet and moving his arms in the traditional dance on the edge of the cliff as she watched on in surprise and then stepped back out of the way.

He flicked his arms and head, mimicking some mythical animal while making strange faces at her.

All at once she realized he was showing off, and she couldn't help but giggle at being the only audience for his show. *The Great Ulmarra show*, on the edge of eternity, just for her.

When he had finished, he seated himself in the grass and indicated she should do the same as the echoes of his song faded away into space.

She sat cross-legged on the edge with him, staring into the darkness taking over the fading red and letting the stars appear like bloody pin pricks struggling to shine under an abos skin.

"Listen," he told her. "Hear the sound of all the things moving and breathing down there. Our people could hear everything—the rocks, the wind, the creatures—and they knew how to understand and interpret what they heard."

"I wish we could go back—we've lost so much."

"Mmm—it's still there. Where do you think they learned it?"

"It was handed down, word of mouth, in stories round the camp fire, how can we get that back now? Can't imagine sitting round the microwave... and the only stories you gonna here in our household is uncle Gunya John bein' arrested again for drunk and disorderly!"

"In the beginning, they learned from all this"—he swept his arm across the abyss—"and we still can."

"So teach me," she said.

He looked across at her, the last light painting her skin with hues of shining blood wiped across her, turning black as it dried. "You begin by understanding what I said before, that we are made up of the same stuff the land is made up of. But even though we got the same materials as the earth itself, the thing that is added, is a single word, *life*. It is the power that organizes atoms. A single, one word, command. I'm not talking about our actual cells being alive either or how they fit together to work. This *word* is more than that. It's extra. Take it out, and we are just living goo; put it in, we start to move."

She looked out at the new stars that were bright now and said, "So you are saying that all the animals and plants, all living beings, including us—are the same because we are alive with this *word* that makes us alive?"

He shook his head. Jimmy was trying to take her further. He was always trying to get us to look past the obvious.

"No, we are different again from the rest of the things with 'life' in them. Whatever this thing is that changes plain matter into something moving and reproducing—it has made humans very different from the rest.

"Our people knew this too. And more than that, they knew this one word could 'speak' by itself to the things it makes alive. You can hear it underneath the sound of all living things. It's a voice that all human beings alone can hear. If you know how to listen, the message carried in the act of 'life' starts to make sense and—it's personal."

"Spiritual stuff, eh? I thought you were a scientist?"

He ignored her. "Science is not an exclusive ideology. It is the business of finding out whatever is there. Someone famous once wrote, 'Science labors up the mountain to discover the truth, only to find that religion is already there.'"

He shook his head and grinned broadly, because that was somehow amusing to him, and she could see his white teeth even in the poor light. "Yeah—my guess is, we are singled out and are able to hear for a reason. Maybe it wants us to know something, maybe to connect with it. Otherwise you and I wouldn't be sitting here, because for mindless survival we would only need to be talking about eating, drinking—maybe, mating. We wouldn't wonder about anything, and there'd be no such thing as scientists or priests." He plucked a grass stem from beside him and threw it out into the night air, and it caught the draft off the cliff and sailed away as he went on.

"A long, long time ago, a white woman named Margaret Stanford learned the secret, and wrote about it because she had heard that voice. She said it was a 'still,' very small, voice. She said our people had been listening for thousands of years, and that's how they knew how to live..." He drifted off a little and said, "Most people nowadays are too busy talking for it to get a word in—but that doesn't mean it doesn't want to."

"I better get back; it's getting really dark."

He just nodded without getting up as she rose to her feet.

She said, almost as an afterthought, "You didn't answer me before, about whether you are in touch with the animals like they say."

He thought about it for a moment and said, "I'm in touch with that word, life, that's all—after that, it's all bullshit, what they say about me."

I know he always denied it, over and over, but I never believed him. He was gifted with animals, all right; I had seen it a thousand times. How he got that way, I don't know, but there was no denying it if you were around him for more'n a minute an' a half.

Jyly said she saw it too, later, but that night she was just taken by the conversation that seemed to be deeper than it should have been and of course—his dancing.

The next day was the start of "the chaos season," as we called it later. If you had to trace back to find the beginning of it, it was there, that day.

It started out all right. The camp was some four kilometers or 2 odd miles, away from the scientific investigations, and it was a fairly relaxed affair. The morning was filled with the smell of cooking bacon and sausages and eggs on the BBQ. The sounds of the tents flapping and movement of waking people filled the air like it does when you are out there, knowing you are doing something important.

I was coughing as I sat down with a plate of food in my hands on a section of eucalyptus log.

Jimmy appeared from the bush, where he'd been walking since before dawn, and grabbed a plate. He helped himself to toast and so on, joking quietly with the camp cook. He walked past some of the other workers where Jyly was seated, and she looked up. He nodded to her, and she nodded back shyly. He walked over to me and seated himself on the log and it rolled a bit, even though he was too light to make it move. I saw Jyly, look up and she seemed to fix her gaze on him a little longer than is normal. The chicks always seemed to go for Jimmy because he was ok looking, I guess. Even so, he had long since given up on Sheilas because none of them quite managed to get him hooked for more'n a month or two and anyway, his first love was out there with something wild. I looked back at my food and thought to myself Jyly had better lock on to that too because our Jimmy was a wasted curiosity in that department. Anyway, I was sure, he'd never escape the queen's clutches long enough to get a life with a chick in it, even one as cute as the newbie.

"Hey up, Wajilla!" He said as he settled beside me, oblivious of Jyly. "Good tucker, eh?"

"Not bad—breaks the fast and gets the gut going." Right at that moment, I had an accidental but very loud 'passing of wind', and he raised his eyebrows.

"Sounds like your gut is makin' a cyclone in there, Mate!"

"Whoops!" I said, and stuffed another mouthful in. "Sorry, might have knocked you off the log, eh?"

"Can't you put a cork in it?"

"Better out than in, mate, better out than in!" I replied like a naughty giggling between my mouthful of egg and toast.

Someone said from some distance away, because it had been loud enough to hear, even from there, "Better go and check your underwear, eh?"

"Fuck off!" I yelled back and everyone laughed.

As we ate, I asked nonchalantly, "What you think of the newbie?"

Ulmarra didn't look up but mumbled. "She's okay."

"Could be a bitch in bed," I said.

"Yeah? How'd you work that out?" Jimmy stole a quick look across to the workers eating some distance away, with the girl sitting among them.

"Just guessing." I also stole a glance at her, and then I said, "Where's Louisa?"

"Gone back to base with a beetle."

"Oh—I feel sorry for the beetle."

"She's pissed, you know."

"Yeah? Why?"

"Indonesians aren't interested in the terms."

"No kidding."

"She don't like the newbie, either," he said, as I swiped a stray fly from my face.

"Why?"

"'Cause she's getting too much attention, I'd say. The boys are being 'polite.'"

"Ahh. What's happening with you 'n' old Louisa?" I moved a leaf at my feet, looking to see if something was under it, and then lit a cigarette.

"Nothing..." Jimmy looked up toward the girl then nodded to the cigarette and said, "That'll kill you."

"Yeah, right!" I rejected Jimmy's comment just as I always did, but came back to the subject of Louisa. "Why don't you get it over with—just do her and make her happy; we'll all be grateful to you."

Jimmy took a deep breath before he said, "Ever been tempted to put your head in a croc's mouth?"

"Nah—but I jumped on one's back once."

Jimmy laughed. "And?"

"And it was a ride to remember."

Jimmy prodded a piece of bacon and picked it up with his fingers to eat it, and as he chewed, he said, "Well, Louisa is one ride that is best not attempted if you want to come away with all your limbs intact and your balls still attached."

I laughed loudly, and some of the others looked up. "Be a good death, though," I said, grinning broadly at the thought, and I bumped Jimmy with my shoulder to make the point.

"Maybe..." Jimmy went silent.

After a minute or two, the conversation turned to more important things as we went on about the science we were working on with the latest grid pattern and also about the other grids we had just completed only thirty kilometers, or 18 miles, north. These new sections were going to be good connections to other farmland closer to the coast that had already been returned to natural forest. End to end, we were creating a corridor for animals to rein habit and a buffer zone for residential growth around the coastal cities.

Jimmy started to rabbit on about how he wanted to acquire land all the way down through New South Wales, so a flora-and-fauna thoroughfare could extend down the coast like a green *Great Wall of China*.

I must have heard the plan a thousand times, and, as we put it together, piece by piece, I never got sick of hearing it and planning the next sections to add to the vision. We all lived for it, and he was the life source of us living it, making it happen, keeping us all on track.

I nodded, and the conversation went on as Jimmy mentioned the opposition we were starting to get against the plans to create the green belt. Every man and his dog seemed to object, as we had more and more land requisitioned and locked off, transforming it into native areas.

"I'm surprised there's so much opposition," he said, "It doesn't make sense. The farmers are compensated for the land and given the new intensive farming technology as well so what has anyone got to lose?"

"I dunno. Seems there is always someone who wants to spoil a good party so they can prove they are just plain, stupid shits." I said and shock my head. It was surprising because it was an amazing scheme. It enabled farmers to continue production of new and profitable crops less labor-intensively while using only ten per-cent of the land area for the same yield. They didn't really lose their land altogether to the forest planting, anyway. They still held the lease for it and collected the carbon credits that, one day, when the trees had matured, add up to a tidy sum.

We—or, rather, Louisa and Samson Donahue, who had been to university with Louisa and was a white, blue-eyed giant of Irish descent—had developed the amazing plan when he hooked up with the foundation and caught hold of Jimmy's vision. Donahue had joined our team almost from the beginning at Louisa's invitation, because he was an engineer of some note, even in those days, and he also knew how to make a dollar or two.

The development of the IFT 'towers' was part of the foundation's scheme to make sure the giving up of the land to replanting would be attractive and profitable for landowners and sure enough, we had been doing it ever since.

The huge Perspex towers rose up like shining beehives, many stories high. Layer upon layer of whatever crops you wanted, grew in the shining pyramids. They were fed at the bottom by an aquaponics pool in the center that was filled with whatever species of fish you wanted to farm. Nutrients produced by the fish were pumped up the layers, and the spent water and condensation was collected and recycled back to the pool. All of it was powered by the free solar energy the structure collected through its skin.

Jimmy told me Donohue had just improved the uptake of solar cells with a new microscopic implant in the clear cladding. It had the effect of transforming the whole structure into a massive collective energy cell, powering not only the pumps for the fish tanks but also feeding power back into the national grid.

Much of the science and engineering for the thing was beyond me, but Jimmy did understand it all, and that was the thing about him: he was utterly simple, naked in his wilderness ways, yet as smart as they come when it came to the mechanics of science.

Even though what we were doing seemed like the most perfect answer to the needs of people and the planet, there were still detractors. That loud-mouthed bitch, Maria Ferris, and the mining giants, unions, and all manner of hungry businesspeople with agendas we could only imagine were beginning to speak out against us as the scheme got going and proved to be a success.

We were talking about this when we were interrupted by one of the crew who said he was going to take the team up to check on the grid and collect the night scans.

"If it's working okay, the rest of you can get back to base," Jimmy said. "But be careful not to be too noisy, or the locals won't settle down to their normal patterns, and the data will be skewed. I'll come up later to clean up and check the power packs on the computer relays, because we're going to leave the grid alone for several days to work on its own so we don't want any cock ups. It's a long way to have to come back out if one fails."

"They won't fail boss, you can get home and just forget it, when has any of my set ups failed?" Mathieson said indignantly.

"Never. I guess I'm just looking for an excuse not to go back." Jimmy laughed and so did they all.

"Hey, Jimmy," I said, "I'm going to walk the ridge on the next section, maybe you should avoid that old croc and come with me?"

The section I was talking about was ear marked for grid copy, as we called it, which means I needed to survey the area so the mapmakers could lay it out accurately. I had learned how to do this over the years while working with Jimmy, and I'd even got certified as a surveyor back in '91 and I admit, it was something I loved doing, even if it meant a hike through some god forsaken piece of wilderness.

This time, I was going to be picked up by helicopter and was to be dropped on this ridge about eight hundred kilometers or 470 miles, south, and then camp for about a week as I surveyed the whole site. All I had to do was create a decent map of each area and make sure there weren't any cultural heritage sites to be preserved. Of course, I had to survive the exercise, which sometimes was no mean feat, considering the country we went into.

"Come on! You know you want to come with me." I pressed, knowing he'd never skip an opportunity to get out into the wild.

"Sounds good," he said enthusiastically.

We finished our breakfast, and then I heard Jimmy on the phone to Louisa telling her our new plan. It sounded like he was having to explain a fair bit. Louisa could be difficult about losing him out there for days at a time, even though they weren't a couple or anything, she definitely acted like they were.

The constant tension between them made me think they should just get together and be done with it, since they were like an old married couple after all these years, anyway so I yelled out to him, "Just promise to grab the damned croc by the tail when you get back, tie her up, and be done with it. Go on, tell her you're gonna taker her out, then she'll let you do whatever you like!"

"Shut up!" He called back and then apologized to her and said he'd see her in a day or two.

Jimmy hung up and sighed deeply.

"I'm telling you, jump 'er, and she'll be putty in your hands."

He shook his head. I guess he knew it couldn't be as simple as that with Louisa.

In the afternoon we were well under way. We had got John'o, the contract helicopter pilot to the foundation, to come and get us. He's a good bloke but a bit of a cowboy, as I soon found out.

When we got into the flight and had been in the air for about an hour, John'o told us that the gully below led to part of the next section. I could see the long expanse of rocky terrain, the valleys of scattered bush, and a massive escarpment of grey rock that was part of an ancient gorge.

I heard John'o say through our earphones, "I've heard that you boys have cracked the mystery of how to make it rain without cloud seeding?"

"We've always known how it worked theoretically, but you gotta have the right geological conditions and the right plantings." Jimmy replied.

I thought I would sound knowledgeable and carried on explaining the natural system through my mouth-piece over the scream of the rotors above us. So, I started telling him how vaporized water, drawn inland by low pressure created by the hotter interior, seeped over the landscape like a sinister mist. Once it hit a formidable rocky boundary that had been reforested with carbon hungry vegetation, the oxygen-laden air would condense and it would rain on the inland plains on the other side. We just needed the right kind of "fortress" and the right planting pattern to make it happen. Where it rained new trees would grow and draw the moisture further and further inland as far as the tree belt could reach.

That was our big plan: By increasing the tree belt, we knew we could draw the rain further inland and reverse relatively recent effects of global warming. The wider the belt, the further in the rain would go, and dust storms would start to be a thing of the past. Soon soil would form, and that would be locked into the undergrowth. Dry, sandy areas might begin to turn into grass plains, appearing where there was desert before.

"This isn't doable," Jimmy broke into my lesson and added, "Unless very large areas can be returned to native ground cover—and in the right areas but theoretically, you could make arid areas go green."

The pattern of planting was crucial, so these were the studies we were completing in this grid because the geology was right. There was a huge rock fortress in this gorge to force the air up and over.

I was staring out at it as we flew over it and I said, "I hope you have a good lot of hours under your belt. This terrain looks pretty wild." I looked down at was still as dry as a paper bark tree, an ancient river at the bottom running with only sand and scattered brush. "Doesn't look that bloody remote on the map 'till you see it from this angle!"

John'o replied, in an understated tone, that there was nothing to worry about concerning his flying. He used to chase camels for culling in Northern territories for the conservation department up there. Before that, he had mustered cattle by helicopter in South Australia. I knew he was ok but somehow, looking down, I didn't feel that reassured.

He swung around and grinned at me, saying, "I'll give you a demonstration, eh?"

Before I could say anything to stop him, the helicopter swooped from the air and dropped low along the ground of the plains above the gorge like it was a dragonfly skimming water.

When John'o suddenly spotted a kangaroo, he honed in on it and began chasing it. Swinging in the air to miss trees, the craft sprayed dust and grass all around, until the kangaroo changed its course to join with others of the group already fleeing. He soon had a small herd and pushed them along as they hopped desperately from his chase. Then he broke off and raised the craft into the air again to continue our journey.

I hardly remember the details. I was in shock! I yelled through my mouthpiece, trying not to throw up, "Cobber, you gonna get my fist when I get off this heap of shit!"

Jimmy just grinned and said to the pilot, "He's gone as white as you, mate!"

"Sorry, mate—thought you might like some fun."

"You call that fun! I need a new pair of jeans, an' I only brought one pair!" I was pretty bloody angry, I can tell you.

"Take 'em off, mate, and go bush!" Jimmy laughed.

"Yeah, right! Just so you know—I'm not that kind of indigenous fulla."

We flew on for another twenty minutes and were almost at our destination, when we saw a huge flock of white corella parrots appearing from over the inland area like a living cloud ahead of us. They began to pour over the rim of the gorge to land at a couple of water pools at the bottom. I watched them stream down the granite cliffs like falling snow that couldn't melt and the sight made me whisper involuntarily, "Wow...", because it was just so beautiful. They were tipping over the gorge edge and swooping down in their hundreds and all three of us watched, mesmerized by the sight. Pink underwings flashed out from their brilliant white plumage, shining like little feathered angels in the sun—but squawking like a few hundred maddened wives, giving it to their husbands who had come back drunk from the pub.

John'o commented on them being of pest proportions nowadays, eating all the farmers' crops like feathery locusts, not like the angels that they looked like.

"I suppose the IFT towers stop all that? They wouldn't have a chance. That must go down well with your "clients" as one more incentive to hook up with the foundation?"

"It isn't the birds' fault that they're breeding like flies," Jimmy said. "The problem started way back when we needed more crops to feed ourselves and to export. Huge areas of grain have gone in where dense bush lands once would have been and that's increased the food supply for the birds as well."

I agreed. Some of the farmers wanted to poison them but even if they were a pest, I didn't think anyone should because I liked them. But just as I said this, we heard a crash against the side of the craft, then several more, and the pilot looked around to see where and what it was that had hit us.

"Some of the late comers are getting blown up by the updraft between the cliff and the chopper!" John'o yelled and there was real concern in his voice. "They're hitting the lower fuselage."

One struck the bubble of the helicopter, and Jimmy yelled out, "They can't get out of the way, mate! Go up!"

As feathers and blood start streaming across the Perspex, a strange sound came from the engines above us, and a heavy jolt made the craft drop. We were suddenly jammed into the top of our seat belts.

"We have to land fast!" John'o yelled.

A bird must have been sucked into the engine inlets. We heard several other bangs and began to descend roughly—very roughly. My stomach felt like it was in my mouth, and I held on to my seat, ready for a grim and violent death.

The rotors screeched above us as we made a haphazard descent to the floor of the canyon and with a loud crash, we hit the ground and rolled, ripping off the blades. I don't remember much accept it was the fastest ride in a washing machine I could ever imagine and when it stopped, I was amazed I was still alive.

The helicopter was a write-off and John'o was injured. We saw right away that his arm was broken: it was sticking out at a really odd angle and was bleeding badly.

He groaned with the pain but managed to croak out, "Well guys...a landing you can walk away from...is still a good landing, everyone still breathing?"

My hands were shaking, and I could hear this buzzing noise in my ears as I pulled myself out of the upturned craft.

"Yeah, I think so, you ok Jimmy?"

"Yeah, give me a hand to get our crash instructor out."

I thought that John'o's remark about it being a good landing, had to be the comment of someone who had crashed-landed on his head a few too many times and I puffed out, "Yeah well, maybe I don't want that kind of lesson mate, might walk in next time, it's a bit safer!"

Jimmy and me helped pull John'o out, and he surveyed the craft as he nursed his broken arm, his face screwed up in an agonized wince.

"Looks like she won't fly again in a hurry. We might have to grant your wish and walk home."

Jimmy and I looked at each other and shook our heads.

"Do you know how far it is?" I said incredulously.

John'o looked at us both and said, "Should be no trouble for you blokes and I thought you said you'd rather walk? Well, now's your chance."

"Just because we are abos doesn't mean we are supermen, you know," I said. "I want me ticket refunded and compensation! I sure didn't sign on for a death march!"

Jimmy said quietly, "You didn't pay for the ticket anyway, so the only compo you got, is you're still alive to walk."

John'o tried to summon up a smile, but he had turned decidedly grey in color and looked as if he might faint.

He sat heavily on the ground and puffed out the words. "I tell you what; I'll shout you a cold Four X beer when you get back...and I'll throw in a free stubby cooler with '*I Survived John'o's Landing*' written on the side. If you can just get me out of here in one piece..."

"Yeah, very tempting offer, but I've still gotta live through the walk out myself to get that beer and your stupid stubby cooler!"

Jimmy patted me on the back and said, "I told you, you should have given up smoking." He went to the crashed craft and tried to radio for help, but the radio wasn't working, just as you might expect.

John'o said that at least the beacon was on, so we should stay with the craft.

I looked at the mangled arm of the pilot and then stared at Jimmy who knew what was on my mind. "Ulmarra, I'd rather try to walk out with you actually, even if it might kill me. Some people have been lost for weeks, even months, out here. By the time anyone finds us, I'll be thin, and you will have grown scales and slithered away and left me with this drongo..." I said only half-jokingly, "...And on top of that, I'll run out of smokes in a day or two and then I'd probably kill John'o anyway."

"What about me?" John'o said. "You gonna leave me here?"

I looked at him shivering on the ground.

"Your arm is going to get like overripe sushi so I guess we'll have to clean you up and take you with us somehow…and if you live, I'm telling you know, I aint never getting in a chopper with you again. You got that, cobber?" John'o laughed shakily. "Yeah right, I know you're joking! You love my flying!"

He was wrong on that one. I wasn't really joking. I walked over and leaned into the wreck and found the emergency medical kit and began to unpack supplies to tend to John'o's arm. I told him I'd have to do a bit of "maintenance" as I brought over some suitable sticks to brace the arm and his face went stiff as I said, "This might tickle a bit so try and keep your laughter down so you don't frighten off them birds and cause an earthquake next!"

Between us, Jimmy and me pulled the arm out straight, and John'o cried out so loud it bounced off the walls of the gorge, and the corellas squawked in unison all around us as we braced his arm over my thigh. "My jeans are totally stuffed now." I said as blood poured down John'o's arm and stained the fabric.

John'o was panting heavily. "Give 'em a good wash— they'll be okay, but I think it's gonna take me a while to get over your 'maintenance', mate." He looked over to the chopper. "I guess I'll be stuffed for a job for a while anyway. There's gonna be an investigation a mile long, 'specially if you tell them about our little roo roundup earlier."

"You'll be okay, John'o, don't worry; we'll blame Ulmarra—he attracts wildlife, so we'll just say them birds couldn't help themselves, and the rest I don't remember, anyway; I was scared shitless and just about comatose from the time we took off!"

I poured disinfectant on the open wounds of the arm. John'o stifled a cry as the stinging liquid entered the raw flesh and I said to Jimmy, "I reckon he's cut something big. It's bleeding like a stuck pig."

Jimmy nodded and then walked across to the overhanging rocks and scanned the area for two or three minutes and then came quickly back to me. He handed me some leaves and said, "Wrap these in the wound too. They'll stop the bleeding—and keep the flies out."

I grinned at John'o, who was looking a bit suspicious as I added white cream from a tube to the leaves and plastered them onto the wound. I comforted him by saying gently, "Never hurts to have a bit of the black fulla's magic mixed in with white man's medicine, eh?"

John'o struggled to smile, looking a bit dizzy from shock but I could see he was relieved the worst was over.

After I had finished tending him, I walked over to the craft and dived into the mangled mess of broken wreckage. I pulled out a toolbox and then began to disassemble the front panels of what was left of the seats.

John'o yelled out, "What are you up to now? I don't think you will be able to fix it, Wajilla!"

"I'm taking the battery and the beacon. If I'm going for a country walk, I'm taking the minder. You think I'm nuts?" I shook my head as I stood up. "I, for one, want to get found out here if anyone is looking. Preferably before I'm dead. Getting lost out here is not a good idea, mate."

John'o smiled. "Thought you guys couldn't get lost."

I laughed and said that I was pretty sure that sort of stuff had been bred out of us these days, and then I said jokingly, "I even have trouble finding my way home from the pub!"

"Me too. Looks like we got the same problem Wajilla." John'o said as he drifted off dizzily.

I pointed to Jimmy, "Don't worry, that one there—he probably wouldn't get lost if you dropped him in the middle of Arnum land, and that wilderness fills the whole north-eastern corner of Australia. I'd bet me balls, he'd come trit-trotting outta there in a month or so." Then I turned back to my task and said, "But me, I'm taking the beacon just in case."

John'o smiled between his grimaces and said, "That's reassuring—we've got the beacon and a genuine abo, so we will be home in no time."

Jimmy was silent; he was looking out over the expanse, and I could see he was working out where we should go. Suddenly he broke into the friendly banter me an' John'o was having and said we should walk out the way we flew in: up the valley, and out the end.

According to my survey map, that was a mere eighty-nine kilometers, or about fifty-five miles to Yarraman as the crow flies. "Jesus!" I said, "That's a fair hike for a fat abo and a broken white fulla!"

Jimmy said we were bound to come across a cow cocky, which is what we call a white guy who has a cattle ranch out here.

"It's all scattered eucalyptus forest till you get to open farmland, so not too hard." Jimmy said as he raised his eyebrows and then looked at the pilot and frowned. "It's a bit of a walk, but we should make it okay if we don't take too long."

I knew what he meant by *if we don't take too long.* John'o would be a dead weight if he couldn't do it on his own, and to leave him anywhere along the way meant we'd be coming back to get him later with a thick rubber body bag. It was a hard ask even if we were led by a barefoot, rainforest deity.

We set off, and after about three hours we had got to the top edge of the end of the gorge. All of us were puffing and straining to walk up the incline by the time we got to the top. John'o was between us, struggling to keep up, but I kept prodding him along. I checked his arm a couple of times, and it had stopped bleeding and though we were swiping away desert flies with the 'Aussie salute', nothing was going near his wound with the leaves all over it.

Jimmy was up ahead and looked across the terrain to decide which way we would go. He stopped for a moment and frowned. He turned to us and said, "Got some big browns in here, so follow me and grab a stick and hit the ground as you go, okay?"

John'o picked up a stick and started to flail the ground rather weakly, and I nodded towards Jimmy and said, "If he says there are snakes in here, there will be, so put a bit of effort into it, and make some noise. The snakes can't hear us, but they will feel the vibrations and bugger off—unless it's a big male and we are in his territory, then he will have a go, in which case, run!"

"Shit, ...snakes—I hate them!" John'o said, and his voice conveyed that he wasn't lying.

We walked through the trees and saw that Jimmy was watching the grass all around us carefully. Suddenly he stopped and said we should go around this section because it was mating time, and there was at least one in there, and it could be aggressive this time of year.

I knew John'o was pretty slow; but I nodded that I agreed we shouldn't risk it even if we'd climbed all this way up and would have to take extra time by another route.

John'o looked left and right, but the grass looked exactly as it had: still and quiet and he whispered, "You sure?"

A bird screeched overhead, and Jimmy looked up. "There's a big one in here, an old fulla."

"Which way should we go—back down the gorge?" the pilot asked breathlessly. We could see he was looking pallid and sweating badly.

Jimmy paused, looking across the grassy area and then back to John'o. I realized we had no choice and I replied for Jimmy and said, "Nah, best we get on, eh—need to get you to a doctor. We can handle a big one if we have to, eh Jimmy?."

Jimmy nodded, but I could see he was a bit worried. A big one was also a fast one and anything could happen even with the great Ulmarra leading the way.

As we walked across, Jimmy suddenly said, "Head for the trees over there!"

I couldn't see what Jimmy had, but he started to smack the ground, and I decided that I wasn't going to question him. I grabbed John'o's arm and helped him as we hurried through the grass.

Jimmy had decided to move too, and he jumped through the undergrowth barefooted, like a big pelican waving his wings and stretching his beak. Behind him, I could see a large snake was slithering through the grass really fast. Jimmy veered off in the hopes that the angry snake would follow him instead of us.

John'o suddenly tripped and fell. The snake immediately noticed us slap-bang in the middle of his territory. I grabbed John'o off the ground and said, "Mate, hey, get up—gotta go!"

The snake was now going full tilt through the grass toward us, and it suddenly appeared behind us, its black eyes frowning; its tongue tasting the air. I froze and whispered very quietly, "Change of plan, mate, don't move a muscle—not a muscle. He's a bad bugger with a hard-on!"

Very slowly, I moved away from John'o, and like a dancing crane I too lifted my arms up with the stick and stepped through the grass, looking, no doubt, like the quintessential aborigine, albeit well-padded and out of step with my ancestors who knew this dance. I had been taught this movement by my granddad when I was a kid, and even though I was rusty it worked.

I watched as the snake moved to the vibration of my feet and away from the fallen pilot. It slithered forward, stopping from time to time, its tail just sliding past the forearm of John'o, who, I was pretty sure, had his eyes closed and was praying.

Jimmy had moved into the center, and we were travelling through the grass in unison with the snake lured to the two of us coming together. As we finally met up, we could see the snake still moving towards us following our vibrations.

Normally, you could just grab even a big one by the tail and use a stick over its neck to sort it out, but this one was really pissed, really hot under the collar, and even Jimmy wasn't going to go near it so when we started to run out of room, I whispered, "What the shit, are we going to do now?"

Jimmy pointed to the higher ground and indicated that he would draw it away from its territory and then it would break off its attack to stay in its own area. Together we stepped back through the trees then split up. I stopped and pointed to the area where I thought the snake was, then again further ahead and shrugged, because we had sort of lost sight of it.

Jimmy began to step through the grass using the old people's movements with his hands, willing the snake to follow him. And sure enough, it appeared again, and he led it, like the pied piper, over the open area and up into the trees.

John'o was watching like a frightened ghost. He waited until Jimmy had disappeared from view and then he stood up and walked to the far side of the clearing, watching carefully in the grass for any further movement. He reached a rocky patch and started to climb, struggling a bit to find the energy to get up, and then he rested on the top of a big boulder looking pretty sick and dejected.

Suddenly, we two aboriginals appeared, and I grinned as though nothing had happened.

"G'dday, mate! Looks like you could do with a taxi!" I said flippantly.

Jimmy walked forward to help him down.

"Where's the snake?" he asked.

"He got distracted by the smell of a bigger one and wasn't quite brave enough to cross out of his territory, so he let us go!" Jimmy replied.

"Jesus! A bigger one? Are we going to make it?" John'o shook his head and was obviously worried.

Jimmy cocked his head to one side. "It's not as bad as it sounds—there's not many of them that big, and mostly you'll never see one unless you happen to step on him. It's just this area has been undisturbed by any big-foot humans for a while, and it's mating season, so now and then a big fulla like that isn't scared of taking someone on." Jimmy started to giggle.

I thought it was pretty funny too, actually, two back fullas dancing through the grass leading a nine-foot brown. I smiled and said, "Mate, there's nothing to worry about. You got the abo Dr. Doolittle here. He can stare them snakes into submission."

"God, you talk a lot of bullshit, drongo!" Jimmy slapped me on my arm because he hated me making out that he was doing anything weird with the wildlife. He looked at John'o and said, completely seriously, "They're deaf and can't see anything too well, so it's obvious he was going to follow our noise out of there. Hard to get hit by one of those blokes if you are sensible."

"Yeah? Well, they must make some lucky strikes now and then, because I heard three to four thousand people get bitten every year in Australia." John'o was puffing as he was speaking, even though he wasn't really doing much. "All I can say is, I'm pleased Dr. Dijeridoo knows a thing or two about them, whether he stares them into submission or dances a jig." John'o sighed as he started to walk very slowly behind Jimmy, and right then I thought, forget the snakes, we gonna be lucky to get this guy out of here alive.

"G'dday. We could do with a lift." Jimmy and me walked forward with John'o, our wounded pilot, dragging as he was held between us. We had walked at least forty kilometers or 24 miles, over three days and had found a farm track.

"What the hell happened to you lot?" exclaimed the man who was sitting on his horse on an overgrown trail we were following.

He climbed off the gelding with his dog at his heel and walked over quickly. The dog immediately licked Jimmy's hand, and he leaned down to pat him.

We told the cow cocky about the accident, and he told us that we were about twenty kilometers or 12 miles from the first station and civilization. He said it was lucky he found us. He had been checking out cattle that had wandered towards the reserve that borders the farm station. He was hoping to find the steers before they found a way into the reserve, because the station could be fined if they let cattle in there. He said he was pretty keen to find them and had been searching all day, because they were worth eight hundred bucks each, so they didn't like to lose any.

I thought to myself, thank god a black angus steer was worth more than a couple of black fullas, because no one had come looking for us. We would have had to walk another couple of days, and John'o was just about had it.

Together, Jimmy, me, and the cow cocky helped John'o up onto the horse, and John'o apologized breathlessly that he didn't think he could stay on.

I told him to just lie on the saddle. "Won't be long, you'll be in a nice hospital bed with a big titty nurse teasing you and be as right as rain in a couple of days."

John'o didn't hear me, as he was already unconscious.

The cow cocky said we had better tie him on because he would be a dead weight to carry if he fell off.

After we did this, we began to walk with the horse back down the trail towards where the cow cocky had parked his four-wheel drive, about a mile away.

We talked along the way, and I told him we were from the Ulmarra Foundation, and I pointed to Jimmy and said, "This is Dr. Ulmarra, the founder." Jimmy definitely didn't look like any kind of doctor at that point, and I saw the Cow Cocky raise his eyebrows.

I didn't look too good, either; I swear I had lost about twenty kilos on three days of Jimmy's gourmet goanna and roast fern root, washed down with the water you find in the trunk of a grass tree at dawn.

The cow cocky had heard of the foundation. Hell, who hadn't? He was quite keen to take advantage of the government grants himself that accompanied returning land to natural use, and he said he wouldn't mind trying the IFTs the foundation had developed instead of cattle. In years to come, the carbon credits would do better than the cattle anyway, even if they did nothing at all with the land. He seemed quite in awe of Jimmy, once he knew he wasn't just a dirty abo walking out of nowhere, and asked him a lot of questions.

"Is it true that wild animals are tame with you?" he got to right away. "And do birds really come to your call?

Ulmarra told him point-blank that those rumors were wildly exaggerated.

I didn't say nothing, but pointed behind us.

The cow cocky turned too to see a small kangaroo sitting in the wake of our trail. It was quietly feeding, even though we had the dog with us. The Cow Cocky wasn't really impressed by the roo sitting there, as he often saw them, so he just nodded politely.

Jimmy turned to see what we were looking at, and he realized, as he looked at me, that I was sort of propagating the myth, so he lifted his arms up and shooed the creature away. It sat bolt upright with an odd look on its face, somewhat ignoring the man and his noise, and this was pretty unusual, as everyone knew a wild roo would normally bolt.

I looked at the cocky and said, "Probably a deaf one, eh, mate?"

The cow cocky nodded as he watched the kangaroo hop a few paces towards us, ignoring the dog that had pricked up his ears and would have loved to chase the marsupial. The kangaroo took a final look, hopped off to the side of the track, and disappeared.

"Me mate here tries to make me out to be Saint Francis of Assisi or something." Jimmy said off-handedly to the cow cocky. "It's simple, really: animals are tame if they don't perceive you as a threat or a meal. If you are quiet and gentle, they will come up to you, just to check you out. That's if you can wait long enough. And I'll tell you something else: if you sleep alongside one, and they sleep too, they will wake up and think you are one of their own. They aren't like us humans; they don't recognize differences in the way things look, just differences in the way things behave. That's the clue for them. Are you eat-able, or are you going to eat them? Act like them, and they will assume you are one of their own kind, and they will ignore that you are three times their size and don't have any fur or feathers."

I broke in and offered my explanation, which I thought was miles better. "He spent a whole lot of time out there on walkabout, so he would know! An' they say he's got a quoll spirit that's doing all the animal talk for him."

"You're full of shit, Wajilla Wilson!" Jimmy punched me on the arm, and I admit he must have meant it, because it actually hurt.

We walked on for another half an hour, I guess, and eventually got to the truck. We loaded our injured man in the back, and Jimmy climbed up and cradled him so he was secure for the ride on the bumpy clay road. The cow cocky's dog jumped up at his master's command and sat by Jimmy, leaning into him heavily. He was looking into the aborigine's eyes and then licked John'o's unconscious face.

"It's okay, fella. You sit still with me." Jimmy said to him gently. The dog immediately returned his attention to the aboriginal like he was his real master and had been his whole life, never taking his eyes off him.

I got in the front. As the truck took off, the cow cocky looked back down the track and saw the kangaroo hop out onto the roadway. He frowned, as it looked like the same kangaroo we saw miles before. He could hardly believe it had followed us, and he pointed it out to me. He shook his head at the highly unlikely possibility, and I said, "Well, he ain't famous for nothing!"

The cow cocky drove us to the station house, and a Westpac rescue chopper came in and picked up John'o and flew him to Brisbane Hospital.

Jimmy and me got to the hospital by late that afternoon. The cow cocky's mate drove us all the way in, so we could stand by and wait for John'o to wake up.

We were waiting in the hallway, and Jimmy and I were discussing whether we should get another pilot and transport ourselves back to the area, since we were still in that neck of the woods and had already walked the gorge and ridge. We could finish off the survey and be ready for the next grid copy if we went back in, and we had more or less decided that was what we would do when Louisa appeared.

She was restraining her emotions but visibly shaken. I'd never seen her really worked up before.

"Thought we might have lost you," she said to Jimmy.

"I'm a bad penny, so I always turn up, you know that Lou."

"More like a weed!" I said, since he looked like he had lost some weight too.

"What is this stuff about a snake?" She said and Jimmy looked at me, and I grinned.

"I rang up Louisa to put her out of her misery," I explained, "and to get her to get me some smokes to put me out of mine!"

Louisa handed over the packet she had in her hands but ignored me.

"How's John'o?"

"He's a bit dehydrated," I answered. "But he was lucky the wound didn't get infected. The doctors are going to reset the arm and clean him up, but otherwise, he's okay."

I could see the woman's eyes were a bit misty, and she didn't take her eyes off Ulmarra, and I knew then that the pilot was the least of her concerns.

I realized that I was the third man out, so I nodded and excused myself, saying, "I can't wait no more for a ciggy, so I gotta to go."

She told me they would catch me up at the hotel that she had booked for us all. She handed me a card and said to put the taxi fare on the foundation's Visa, and I said, could I put another pack of ciggy's on it too?

"No, one packet should do you, you need to give up." She laughed, but she still didn't take her eyes off Ulmarra.

He told me later that for a few moments after I left, she had just stood there quietly, not saying anything. She was just trying to get hold of herself, and that spooked him more than the whole crash. He hadn't seen her so shaken in all the time he had known her, which was something like twenty years.

Suddenly both she and Jimmy spoke at the same time, and that broke the awkward silence.

"I should get you to the hotel," she whispered and he nodded, saying he needed a shower because he must've smelled like a dingo in a rubbish dump.

She agreed that he did, and I can vouch that that was true, because all three of us, including John'o, smelt pretty bad by the time we got back.

They took the Ute truck that had the new Ulmarra Foundation logo of the green-faced kid on the side of it back to the hotel. Louisa had picked it up from the Brisbane wing of the Ulmarra foundation that had only just been set up a month or so before. The 1,700 kilometer, or a 1,056 mile, trip from Cairns to Brisbane takes a few days to drive, so she had flown down and thought she would take a break before we decided whether to go back in or come home.

The two didn't say much in the new, borrowed Ute, Jimmy told me.

When they arrived at the hotel, she let him in and handed him a new towel from the bed.

"I'm number 306, three doors down," she said nervously.

He thanked her and began to head for the shower, but she called after him, "You gave me a fright, you know. I'm not sure if I could do this thing if you weren't around."

He turned, realizing her genuine fears, and walked back to her and kissed her on the forehead, you know, real friendly-like.

"I've known you for years," he said. "You can do anything you want to."

She laughed shakily as he held her shoulders and then she jokingly replied, "You're right; up close you do stink like a dingo in a rubbish dump!"

He grinned and began to walk back to the bathroom. As he reached the door, she called out to him again. "I could wash your back—you know, if you want me to."

He paused for a moment but walked on towards the bathroom door, ignoring her offer like you do if you see a couple of croc eyes appear on the surface, seemingly innocently beckoning you in for a swim.

She shrugged her shoulders with a little embarrassment and turned to leave, but just as she opened the door, she heard him call out.

"Okay."

Of course, she immediately smiled not so innocently, and closed the door quietly. She must have thought all her Christmas' had finally arrived at last.

When she arrived in the small bathroom, he was already in the shower. She slipped off her clothes and opened the shower screen.

For a moment, he looked at her standing naked in front of him. He didn't say anything but leaned forward and pulled her into the water.

Jimmy and I had a way of talking to each other that was pretty plain and to the point, so he told me straight out that Louisa was no tame, innocent, dedicated, scientist that first time! He said that was probably what the attraction was. For once, she just looked like a woman to him and with all the stress of the accident, that's what he needed. Who knows?

He said he clasped her to himself and kissed her without any real tenderness, just getting right to it and pretty roughly too. He pulled her black hair back, and they ferociously made love against the wall of the shower.

When they were finished, he kissed her and she whispered, "I guess you want me to scrub your back now, dingo?"

He grinned and turned around in the water, grabbing the soap and handing it to her behind him. She leaned up against him and washed him like they'd been married for twenty years.

Then he turned and took the soap from her and began to wash her breasts. He said she was still on fire and swallowed hard, and then he turned her around by her shoulders roughly and washed her back just to disappoint her.

"I feel like a child," she gruffly complained.

"You are," he said quietly. "A child that has got too old and should remember she's still a kid on the inside and should let someone else be in control sometimes."

"As long as you stay closer to the office, you can control me all you like." She said softly.

Well, he was right with what he said, I guess, but not much else to do with her, I'd say. And I admit, I was wrong. Some crocs are better left alone and not made into handbags because if they get on to your arm, they can be bloody hard to get off.

We did go back in and finish the survey and chose a site for a grid copy.

Louisa went back to the Cairns office but she wasn't happy about it. Still, considering she had finally hooked up with Jimmy, she didn't protest too much. Actually, she couldn't wipe the smile off her face and pretty much, whatever he said, she was replying, 'Yes and amen' to it.

Back at the base lab in Cairns, Louisa took on young Jyly and no doubt it was about making sure the girl knew who the boss was and she would have been dropping the odd remark in 'female speak' that would tell Jyly, Ulmarra was now *her* Ulmarra.

Jyly told me things were quite peaceful with the Queen up until she went down to Brisbane to make sure Jimmy, John'o and me were all right. When she got back and called her in, it started ok as Jyly happily studied printout sheets and Louisa was telling her how to interpret the data. Jyly had trouble getting it because for some reason, Louisa was deliberately making it hard for the girl to understand what it all meant. I can guess what she was up to.

Feigning frustration at the girl's lack of responsiveness, Louisa told Jyly to go out to reception and see if they had heard from Jimmy and me and to get her a coffee.

Jyly was pretty smart. She knew the instruction to go to reception was a ruse and a way to let her know she was under the older woman's control and was going to be treated like one of the lowly minions if she stayed, and Jyly didn't appreciate it.

She put her fists on her hips and said, "You know, I'm not here just for fun—or to waste my time. I take this research seriously, and I want to know enough to really help with my own people's conservations efforts way above what you people think you're doin'."

Louisa stopped, somewhat put on the spot by the outspoken girl. She dropped her head and said, "That's good—if, in fact, you *are* serious."

Jyly was immediately incensed at the comment and inference that she was not committed to the project.

She said firmly, "What does that mean?" Then she decided to give it to old Louisa, real clear. "Look! I don't have the education nor the degrees after my name like all of you do, but you know, 'a gift makes room for itself,' and I can take in anything you throw at me, because it really matters to me."

Louisa couldn't help soften a bit at the girl's sincerity. She looked up and studied the little aboriginal face, fixed in an angry scowl. Then she said somewhat coolly, "Okay, then—now we have that straight, I guess you should grab a chair, and I'll show you how to work all this data so *we* can save the world." She looked up and stared at Jyly, who seemed on the edge of flying out of the room but wasn't going to give old Louisa an inch.

After a tense pause, the girl took a breath and looked about for a chair while Louisa ignored her. As she sat down, Louisa flattened out the sheet with her hands and without looking up, asked her where Jyly had heard the saying, "A gift makes room for itself."

"Dr. Ulmarra used it to describe something, so I looked it up on the Internet. It's Proverbs 18:16," she said. "And I think he meant that you don't need to be a scientist or a scholar to be in this. You just have to have a passion about it."

"Really?" Louisa replied. "Well, it's good to see you think you have a gift, so I guess we had better exercise it."

The girl ignored her sarcasm and said bluntly, "My gift is, I care so much that I could tell myself to stop breathing if that's what it took to make a difference."

Louisa finally looked up at her and smiled genuinely for the first time. She sighed a little before she replied, "Now that is something I really do understand! I've always felt that way, but I worked out that I needed to keep breathing to do any good." She took a deep breath as though she realized she might have made a mistake about the girl and said quietly, "let's just get on with it."

Jyly reckoned that was what was needed, a sort of female laying down their guns between them and a clearing of the air.

From then on, they had a sort of Mexican standoff, and the two began to work together quite well for a while.

Four days later, Jimmy and I drove back in the Ute. It was way after five when we got back, and most of the university car park was empty. We had made it back this time in one piece. We had led the chopper to the place where we crashed, and some hours later, people came in, hooked it up, and winched it out. Nothing was left on the ground that could start a forest fire, and the only hint that there had been an accident was a big hole and a ton of footprints.

Jimmy was leaning into one of the Ulmarra vehicles and pulling out a laptop and a large map from inside as I strode off. He turned to shut and lock the door when he heard a voice behind him.

"Back from the wilderness?" It was Jyly, not paying much attention to me, just focused on Jimmy.

"Ah—yeah. How's it been going?" he said. "Settling in okay?"

"Had my moments. Me and the Queen have worked it out and seem to be getting along okay."

"Good—she's passionate, so it will rub off on you," he said.

"I got my own passion; don't need anyone else's."

I saw that he couldn't help smiling. He really liked the way Jyly always defended her own opinions and had her own mind.

They talked for a while, and finally he said he would see her up at the new reforestation site if she was going.

She said she was, and carried on walking along the path to go home, because she had finished for the day.

He watched her and said to me, "Nice kid." But I could tell you, she was more than that, even then. Those two recognized their own kind, and I'm not talking about their tribe or their shoe size. Something way deeper than that had already happened.

Louisa was pleased to see him when Jimmy got inside and immediately walked up to give him a kiss. He stiffened a little, and she noticed it, and my eyes just about popped out of their sockets when I saw it.

"I'm so happy we got together at last, I thought you'd never come to your senses." I overheard her whispering to him softly and I was amazed she would say that with me around but I guess she wanted the whole world to know something had happened.

"I'm not sure it's good for either of us." He said and she just about folded up like a crushed paper cup in his hand. I realized I was the third wheel, and it sounded like they had some things they needed to talk about, so I headed off quick smart.

She told me a long time later that she was really hurt, because her feelings for him ran deeper than just a casual physical affair and she had always been sure he had always wanted her.

She said as soon as I went, she asked him outright, "Do I mean anything to you?" and he hadn't answered, and she said, "No reply Ulmarra? Well, that's an answer in itself isn't it?"

He tried to calm her down and said that it was just that they had been friends and colleagues for a long, long time, and he didn't think they should pursue something so emotionally charged.

She told me she had tried to put a brave face on it but was deeply disappointed. She said she knew she'd been the one to offer herself, and he didn't have anything to feel guilty about, but she was sure that they could have a really good relationship, simply because they had always worked well together, and that was half the equation.

She said she walked up to him and tried to excite his interest with an evocative kiss—which he soon responded to, so she reckons there was definitely something there between them.

I didn't have the heart to tell her that a guy will just about respond to anything if he is in the mood, and Jimmy had been ignoring his moods for a long time.

I think that the problem between them ultimately turned out to be, he did actually love her in a special sort of weird, way. She never realized that and it meant the sex part was always going to be the wrong direction. He would have been better to go down to the pub and deal to one of the sheilas hanging around after midnight than get mixed up with the Queen.

Anyway, she told me that he protested a bit more, complaining that he was a man after all, and it wasn't fair for her to cloud his judgment with what she could do. I know what he meant, and I agree, she is attractive if you like that kind of thing. Attractive, like the witch that gave snow white the apple—even though he was as black as a rainforest bush plum. But having protested, he soon asked her to lock the door, which she did as she unbuttoned her blouse.

He gave in, and they soon had sex right there in the office—with Jyly, not more'n five minutes out the door, and me not even out of the building!

It was fast and when it was over, he must have known it was way out of line, because he made an excuse, dressed, and left.

She said she was left leaning on her desk in her office, staring at the door and thinking, "What's going on with us?"

I saw Jimmy as he came down the hall like nothing had happened as I brought the trolley out of the store room to unload the generator off the back of the Ute.

Jyly had just come back in to pick up her folder she'd forgotten, and passed me, and I said, "G'dday, you ever going to get home tonight?" She laughed and skipped into the technical room saying, "If I get any more forgetful, I might not find my way home for sure!"

Donahue, came in behind her and he went into his office for something and when he came out I saw him bump into her as she was coming back out and he stopped her and started chatting to her. I thought, "Typical Donahue!"

When Jimmy turned the corner and saw them standing there, I couldn't work out why he ducked into the alcove by the broom cupboard and started watching them like something untoward was going on, so I stopped and went into the storeroom and watched as well, peering out through the gap.

Donahue was crowding Jyly a bit, and it looked weird, this tiny black girl of about five feet two and this tall white guy of about six feet three.

We both knew Samson Donahue had a reputation for liking the ladies a lot, from way back, and I guess it was obvious he was having a go.

Donahue started telling her about the intensive farming towers, the IFTs and I thought, "Sure make out you're a big deal!"

He was really puffing his chest out and started giving her the run down to impress her.

"...The difficulty was making them cheap enough so that developing countries could afford the construction. Most of the places in the world that are responsible for deforestation now are poor," he said with a little smirk, like he was the one saving the world. "So, I had to look at what materials were readily available and came up with something like tubular scaffolding. Put together in a certain pattern, it is as strong as any solid building. That's where my engineering degree came in handy."

What a blowhard, I was thinking, and I'll bet Jimmy was thinking that too.

"...But the real breakthrough is in the skin. That's the really clever part. It's lightweight, cheap, and clear, of course, letting in light for the plants. I helped develop it with impregnated solar-cell technology. It generates electricity that runs the pumps for the fish tanks below and shutters for ventilation above on each floor. Connect it to a basic computer, run the program I've developed, and you can set this thing up in a month anywhere in the world, as long as there is sunlight and a bit of recycled water." He leaned down and pretended to brush something off her shoulder. "You should come out and visit the three IFT towers we've set up in Port Douglass, and I'll personally show you around one that's actually running. They're growing test crops of soya in those ones up there at the moment."

She replied, "Ahhh—the dreaded modified crops..."

"No, Ulmarra won't have a bar of that." he replied a bit defensively. "But yeah, I've agreed that nothing modified goes into our towers; we don't really need it anyway. We can control the environment in there, and we don't have pests to worry about so everything grows double speed any way and doesn't need genetic enhancement." He looked up for a moment, and I thought he might spot me, but he was too intent on her to notice anyone else.

"If they wanted to use genetically modified crops, they could anyway; it wouldn't matter, because nothing can get out—it's a closed system. Out there in the world, solutions have had to be found like it or not. You have to feed world populations at a reasonable price, and if you have to use GM to do it, well what are you gonna do? If something eats your crop, and it's costing you production, well, just have to modify the plant to resist that. People have to have their beans or cabbages at a price they can afford. You can't have it all ways, I guess." He smiled at her, and I could see his eyes were following the line of her collarbone.

"But isn't there a different kind of price we might have to pay if that stuff gets loose out there?"

He stared at her for a second.

"The horse has already bolted I'm afraid. Huge numbers of genetically modified crops are already loose all over the world. You'd be hard-pressed to find something completely pure in anything you eat, because even organic produce is being polluted with pollen from GM crops somewhere else."

"So maybe the towers are a real alternative then?"

He nodded, cocked his head slightly, and said very sweetly, as if the words he was saying were nothing to do with what he was thinking, "The only other option would be to kill off...let's say, three billion people, so they didn't have to be fed, and then try to get the ones left to keep all the economies in the world going." He said it almost apologetically. "But thanks to us—maybe something like that won't happen and they can quit the GM road."

I'm surprised he didn't say, 'Thanks to *me*.'

"Hmm—this matters to you eh?" she said.

"Yeah, of course. I do whatever I can—so pretty little things like you can live happily ever after in the new world that is going to come about through all of this." He reached out and tapped the end of her nose.

Jimmy's instincts must have been going into overdrive at that point. Something about the way Donahue was flirting all over the tiny aboriginal woman felt wrong, even to me.

He decided to interrupt and finally walked down the hall so they could see him.

"I'll go out with you next week, Jyly, and we can take a look," Jimmy said casually, and then he turned to her and said, "Do you speak abo Kriol?" He had his back facing Donahue, and the big man stepped aside and away from the wall.

She replied that of course she did, and he said back in aboriginal Kriol, "*Getting friendly with the white natives is not a good idea when they are way bigger than you are, and they are obviously horny.*"

She burst out laughing, because it wasn't like she was unaware of Donahue's little show.

Donahue frowned and asked her, "What did he say?" Then he said to Jimmy, without taking his eyes off Jyly, "You got a problem with English Ulmarra?"

Jyly was still grinning broadly, because she could tell Jimmy was being a bit too protective and I guess she thought the whole thing was laughable as the two men stood in front of her.

She turned to Donahue and said that Jimmy had said that with her hair pulled back the way it was, it looked like a bunny tail hanging on for dear life on the back of her head.

Never the less, she looked across at Ulmarra and nodded subtly that she had taken his warning and then lifted her eyebrows at him as if to say, "And you're no better!"

Poor old Donahue shook his head and said, "It's always about some animal thing, isn't it, Ulmarra? You couldn't just say, 'Your hair is cute.'" He smiled mischievously toward Jyly.

Jimmy forced a smile. "Yep—I see animals everywhere."

Jimmy nodded good-bye to Jyly and slipped out into the night past me as I said, "Mate, what was that all about?"

He just shrugged and walked on.

Jyly reckoned it was as obvious as hell that he was just plain jealous, but, as things turned out, maybe the warning was worth taking whether he had started to get a bit possessive over her or not.

A few weeks later, when we were talking about what had happened that night, she said to me real matter of factly, like she had never been someone that got confused over sex and love, "Men are basically just greater apes aren't they? Some of you haven't evolved one bit, have you—and you're not even half as nice, or safe, as apes." She had looked sad when she said that to me. She had added, with enough regret to make me wonder what had happened to the shiny little bird she had been just weeks before, "Yeah, ...I wish I hadn't laughed at the boss that night; if you're female, you can never let down your guard, even if you think you should be able to."

I didn't think women needed to be that worried about it, but I guess Jyly had reason to know what she was talking about better than most, as it turned out.

Chapter 3

AFTER THAT NIGHT, about a week later, Jyly, two members of the horticultural department connected to the university and on loan to the foundation for the latest planting project, and me, headed up to the new Whyalla gorge replant section up towards Port Douglass. We went in one of the foundation's new four-wheel drive Utes. Jimmy was going to join us later, so our little team of four headed up the highway, and then turned off in the direction of the replant area.

The road was as rough as it gets, and we were being knocked about. Jyly was laughing her head off because she was flying up in her seat belt, almost hitting her head on the ceiling a couple of times, and the other two were like Mexican jumping beans in the back. I thought, 'This new Ute is gonna be stuffed!' but I didn't slow down because it was fun.

Finally we made it to our destination, and the road opened out to a clearing of grass and scattered trees. Several other vehicles were already there, and a large truck was unloading right in the middle. We could see hundreds of pots with saplings of all sorts already sitting on the ground.

A few people were milling about: students, volunteers—the usual. A large tent had been set up, and there were benches set out for people to sit on.

Another vehicle arrived behind us, and Louisa stepped out. I grinned and said, "Now the work starts; is it time for a beer?"

Louisa shook her head, ignoring my joke, and headed off to another smaller tent with a pile of sheets in her hands.

"She aint got a sense of humor at the moment, by the looks of it. Come on, let's go and join the party anyway." I opened the Ute's door for Jyly, and the group of us headed over to the smaller tent after Louisa to get our marching orders.

When we arrived, she was scowling and practically growling like a bear at a man who happened to be my nineteen-year-old brother Juniper, who stood with his arms tightly folded across his chest.

"Uh-oh—trouble again," I said under my breath.

Louisa was angry because there were thirty-five volunteers from the local conservation society sitting around ready to help planting, but Juniper hadn't got anything organized for them to start.

"You're asking for it, Juniper," she squawked like a maddened Corella, You haven't even started marking the key plant structures out! As usual, you've wasted everybody's time! You're making us look like a bunch of ...unprofessional, lazy, lay-a-bouts, like you're an... I don't know! Like you don't care at all!" I had a feeling she had only just stopped short of calling Juniper an abo and I felt a twinge of defensiveness crawl over me.

Juniper didn't even reply. He stormed off past us, and, as he went, he said to me under his breath, "I don't need this shit, eh, bro!"

"It'll be okay," I replied. "Just get your team under way; I'll talk to her."

Jyly watched him go with some curiosity because she knew Louisa didn't suffer fools at the best of times and she'd seen her fire guys on the spot for less. She could tell Juniper was being treated lightly but at that stage, couldn't work out why.

We approached Louisa like she could incinerate us at a single glance. She was as angry as a red hot poker, and was jamming her finger down on the map in front of her and was sighing so loudly, that the paper might well have caught fire with her breath fanning her finger where it touched.

"What's up?" I said, and she let out her frustration right at me.

"If you want to keep your brother on the payroll, he's got to do what he's paid to do!"

"It will all get done in the end, Louisa, don't worry about it." I said. But she ignored me and took a long look at Jyly as though she'd done something as well and I thought, 'she's still jealous of this little girl for some reason.'

"He stinks of booze and marijuana—if he comes up here again like that, Wajilla, he's got to go!" She said, still looking hard at Jyly.

'You're right, you're dead right, you don't have to worry about him, he'll kick in." I made an agreeable nod and turned and left before I could say anything that I would regret and I heard her say as we went back outside, "He better!"

Jyly and me headed straight for the lower field of a hundred-acre area up in a wide valley that was allocated for replanting and as we walked, she said, "He's bit of a wild child, is he? Your brother?"

"Yeah, you could say that. He's only my half-brother, eh. We've got different moms. He's not a happy person if you know what I mean. I've been trying to get him to make an effort with his life, but he seems dead set on wrecking it."

"My younger sister is the same, so I know how you feel."

As we walked up the incline, we could see a man with surveying equipment ahead. Another man was spraying pink marker on the ground some distance away.

We walked up to the first man, and he and me, greeted each other, talked about the plan in his hand, and Jyly was put to work with a huge, plastic, hinged-grid marker. She had to put it on the ground, starting at the first survey peg position, corresponding with the map and then spray a mark on the ground to show where certain trees should be planted.

I went back down and brought a wheelbarrow full of trees up and was puffing a bit by the time I got to the top. Jyly looked up to see a tractor towing a tray filled with larger, taller trees up to us and grinned at me as she said, "You should have waited, they're bring up a load with the tractor for this whole side."

"Now you tell me!" I said, and she laughed and said I needed the exercise anyway.

After a few hours, we had marked the whole side of the hill, and I was starving.

When we arrived back at the base center, Louisa was in a better mood. She was talking with the coordinator of the volunteer plant team that had now been organized. She was telling the coordinator what she wanted them to do and explained why the trees were not block-planted as in previous attempts at native replanting. All the Ulmarra foundation plantings were instead, being planted according to the grid copy of natural bush suitable for this area. She pointed out a group of larger trees marked with pink spray on their pots sitting forlornly in the middle of the clearing, and then to the map under her hands, and then to green spot ones, and so on. She was completely absorbed with the conversation that she didn't see me passing the doorway. I yelled out, "Hey, lunch!"

Louisa looked up and smiled almost in surprize and she nodded, grabbed the coordinator by her arm, and they came out and walked with us. We went into the makeshift mess tent and sat at benches before helping ourselves from a buffet table on the left-hand- side.

Someone had organized one of the big hotels to donate the tucker, and it was pretty good too. There were big bowls of prawns and some battered barramundi or coral trout and the usual salads and fresh bread. I spotted a pile of sandwiches and another big tray of sushi that had just about been cleaned up already. A huge bowl of tropical fruit was in the middle, and I grabbed a dragon fruit before anything else.

I said to Louisa that my son was coming up to help out in the afternoon and she nodded and smiled because she likes the kid.

"I didn't know you had children," Jyly said, looking up. I corrected her pretty quick and said, "Child, singular," then told her his name was Amadeus Wilson.

She said, "Amadeus? You're kidding!"

"Yeah," I explained that Amadeus was the result of a lustful month or two when I got on the piss and forgot that in the light of day, I'd be shelling out money for twenty years to someone whose last name I didn't even know.

"So you called him *Amedaus*?"

"Yeah, well, I didn't want him to feel unimportant or like he was just something I wanted to forget, even if his mother was. I thought the kid should at least have a really memorable name and at least know his dad's. So I got the mother to put my name on the birth certificate, and now I have him two weekends a month and holidays, to make sure he is being fed and going to school and stuff like that."

"But—Amadeus?" Jyly asked again. I laughed and said I supposed it was a bit crazy.

"It's all because of the woman next door. She used to play Mozart over and over on her stereo at ten at night, and when I complained, she said I needed culture. But even after I'd complained, after that, she used to come over and give me her cure all drink of god knows what, for my hangovers and she used to talk to me about Mozart and why kids nowadays never knew nothing about stuff like that, and why they should."

I had hardly any European 'culture', as she put it, growing up at the abo reserve at Mossman. We didn't really give a stuff about it but I knew it was always gonna be hard going for my kid, even being half indigenous. I wanted him to have something of it, even if it was in name only, so maybe he could make it better than I did. So, in memory of the old girl, I named him after old Mozart. His mother didn't care one bit what I called him. She was just happy with the money I gave her every week.

Jimmy arrived just as we finished lunch. Jyly and I watched him as he met with Louisa and could see that the two were being very cool with each other. Jimmy barely looked at her. I stood up and yelled out to him, "Oi, Ulmarra, we're going back up the hill." but he yelled back, "Later" and strode away.

Both Jyly and I could see that things were strained between the two and I said,

"The croc is looking pretty hungry for a bite outta our Jimmy, I'd say."

"Ulmarra is as wild as a dingo," Jyly said, "He's not the sort anyone should get attached to, so she's crazy to even try."

I was a bit taken aback and disagreed on behalf of me mate. "Hey! He's far from being a wild dog, eh." I protested. "You won't find a more deep-thinking man anywhere. Most people can't understand him properly anyway. Hell, even I don't, and we've been best buddies since we was young fullas." I shook my head and said quite seriously, "Maybe what he knows and what he is, is just too far ahead. He's always talking about 'the future looking back' at what we are doin' like he is already up there and that don't make him no dog, does it?" Maybe that's why he gets everyone fired up, you know, inspiring all of us! 'Cause he's seen it all ahead of time and he knows we gotta get this done—or else. Nah, he aint no dingo, Jyly, he's way ahead of us." I said it with real conviction as I broke open my dragon fruit and continued, "It's good enough for me to just go along with him," and I looked up at her and smiled, "and I've never seen him being anything but a good bloke to flora, fauna, and friends alike the whole time I've known him so don't you worry, he aint no dingo."

Jyly was silenced by this and ate a whole banana before she replied. "Sometimes I'm amazed that everyone thinks so much of him. Maybe I'm missing something, because he seems just like any other man to me. But I know what you're saying; what he started is pretty important, and he's... interesting, I'll give him that."

I knew she was lying. If not lying, she was covering for the obvious and I started to suspect then, that Louisa might have had a good reason to want to drive this one off.

Late in the afternoon, a minivan of ten people arrived. I saw it drive up the track way below us, and I started to walk down to meet it as it pulled up.

Jyly took a break too and followed me but she hung round where the water station was. I saw her checking us out as me son got out with Donahue behind him and I tousled me son's hair and asked him if he'd got car sick on the way up because sometimes he does. He was about nine at the time, and he used to love to come out when there was a planting going on even if we were in the back of beyond somewhere.

Louisa came straight over and greeted him and if you didn't see by the kid's beaming face that he was fond of her, you would have had to be straight out dumb or blind.

He ran straight to her and showed her something drawn on a sheet of paper. She touched his face as if he were her own and smiled at the kid's drawing and said it was pretty good.

A few minutes later, Jimmy arrived too, and the boy ran up to him, jumping up on him like a puppy.

Jyly was till watching us, and she must have recognized right then, that all of us were not only colleagues but a close-knit family as well. She could have joined in but she told me later that one of the lab guys that had come up to her while he was waiting for a coffee, had said, "Watching the Ulmarra clan in action, are you? They're as tight as a goannas ass that's for sure! None of us got a look in there, we all just follow them like a bunch of awe struck green ants, up the Ulmarra foundation tree of life! There's no denying it, it's bloody amazing what those four have achieved since it started. And you can see Wajilla's kid—young Amy, is the next in line. I guess he'll go out with them on walkabout soon to learn whatever it is they learn out there."

Jyly looked on as our group turned and headed to the main scientific tent with the puppy in the center of us all, and Louisa looking happy at last because Ulmarra was walking alongside her for once.

I looked around once we got to the tent for her, so I could invite her to join us but she had gone off somewhere.

One of the guys said later that Juniper had met up with her and was flirting like hell, and then she'd gone off with him. I smiled when I heard about it because I thought it might solve two problems at once. Maybe if he could find someone like young Jyly, he might settle down and Jimmy would stop stealing glances at her that stirred up the Queen to try and get rid of her.

By the time I was ready to get back to work and had Amy with me, Jyly had already gone back up the hill to the field we had been working on earlier and was hard at work. She stopped and looked down the hill and watched me wheel out a trolley full of small trees, with my boy happily grabbing one side of the barrow. Jimmy was striding alongside, his eyes fixed on her, and I swear a laser beam was connecting the two.

When we arrived, I gave Amy a spade and he started to make a hole on one of the colored spots. Ulmarra said he was a great little digger and the boy smiled shyly while he hacked away at the green spot to make a hole.

"I'm pretty useless at digging, so I hope you can help our team catch up to the others." Jyly said warmly and Amy looked up and grinned at her broadly. I could see he liked her straightaway, as he started trying to dig a second hole on one of the spots we had sprayed earlier with renewed energy.

Jimmy told me he was going to give my brother Juniper a hand and asked if I had seen him. Jyly said brightly, "I left him where the pots are getting marked. But he said he was going to head for the truck and help unload the next batch."

"My god! He's actually working? Seems like he might be showing off to ya Jyly, we'll have to keep you around for the rest of your life, eh?" I replied with a grin.

Jimmy half frowned but he said he'd go down and keep the renegade on the job, and I replied, "Thanks, mate," because I knew Juniper was walking on thin ice even if he was having a spurt of interest with Jyly around. Jimmy headed off down the hill, saying he'd come back later and we carried on.

Jyly, the boy, and me stayed high on the ridge as we started to get some trees in. When I grabbed three saplings and sat them out on the grass ready for the next holes, Jyly looked at the spray marks and said, "Those are the wrong trees."

"What? They match the marks straight off the grid plan."

She looked at them and the larger tree varieties that had already been planted and said again, "The plan is wrong then. I'm telling you they're the wrong ones."

I got a bit annoyed and said, "Who cares anyway; in a hundred years, who is going to know?" Because I really didn't want to have to go back down the hill and change them anyway.

She smiled, mysteriously and said, "The trees will know!" And walked back down the hill to get another variety.

I couldn't believe it, and I called out, "Do what you like, lady. A tree is just a bloody tree."

"No it isn't mate, you know that. Our trees are the first link in a mighty big chain. If it's the wrong link the whole chain's gonna break."

When she returned, Jimmy Ulmarra had come up for some reason and was standing next to Amy. He watched Jyly climb the slope towing a trolley with half a dozen new saplings. He didn't greet her but asked me what the fichus trees on the ground were there for.

"They're the ones that match the grid markings on the plan."

Ulmarra shook his head and said, "It's gotta be wrong."

Young Amy piped up and said, "Why's that uncle?"

Jimmy pointed to the far hillside and the distant horizon and explained that the water vapor was going to go through the gap, and the wind would peak on the far side.

"If we plant fichus here, they'll dominate the lower area and cause the water to condense too early. They'll make this a swamp instead of a running stream."

I just laughed and shook my head at the "reading" of the future effect the trees might have.

Jyly grinned and put the wrong trees back in the trolley without telling me "I told you so," but her face said it anyway. I shrugged, and pretended I didn't care.

Jimmy walked across to her.

"You made a good call," he told her. "How did you know they were wrong?"

"It was a lucky guess."

"There is no guesswork in what we are doing, but some of us have better instincts than others."

I looked up sharply, and he grinned mischievously. He turned back to Jyly and explained that they were planting the big-seed and wild fruit-bearing trees high, where the contours of the land undulate, so that the future fruit and seeds would scatter when they fall, and seedlings would spread out through the new forest naturally. He pointed out certain places on the field where people were planting different species depending on the pattern we found using the grid-copy research on the small patches of natural forest already in that area.

He leaned down and showed her and Amy a bushy plant in a pot and explained that these would cover the ground for about ten years and deny grass and weeds light, which is why they plant them in groups around the seed-bearing trees that take a long time to establish themselves.

She was really interested, and she said, "Won't the small trees need to be weeded to stop them from suffocating?"

"Yeah, a little bit. But we put these little screens around them, and that gives them some wind protection and a bit of breathing space. We will have to maintain the area for about two to five years, but the local conservation community have committed to that upkeep, so the trees we have planted can get a good start."

She was hanging on to every word as he told her that in due course, the taller trees planted on the green spots would kill off the lower scrub we were planting now, as they got above it and eventually denied them light and the big forest giants would one day thin them out too until the whole area was as good as the real thing.

He pointed to the area on the far side almost fully planted with small blue screens, saplings poking their heads out from each one. "We've planted slow-growing hardwood down there," he pointed, "which is shaded strategically by the bigger, leafy trees above them. They like lower light while they are juveniles and work their way up into the canopy after a long time." He showed her several herbaceous plant species and told her these would stop kangaroo coming in and damaging the new shoots of the more important trees that take a while to get tall enough to beat the roos.

Amadeus was listening intently too, and I thought that they were just like sponges, sucking in all this stuff that Jimmy knows and becoming a new generation of people of the land, like our people had been a long, long, time ago.

Jimmy told Jyly and Amy to be careful of the ones in purple pots. "They're gympie-gympie, and they'll give you a nasty sting so be careful, eh." He grinned at me and said, "Your dad can tell you all about what happens if you try to wrestle a gympie-gympie."

I knew what he meant, because I'd encountered a gympie more than once when I was a kid, when we'd go hunting brush turkey up the back of the Mossman reserve. Amy nodded very seriously, listening with bated breath as Ulmarra picked up a pot and menaced me with it.

"Oi! Aint you got better things to do?" I scalded so Jimmy put it down carefully and went on with his lesson.

Jimmy explained to them that the pattern we were following was essential because the wildlife that would come into the forest when it had grown was also "tiered," like the trees.

"Wildlife needs all the different varieties of vegetation to attract all the different insects to live on it. Lots of the animals have to eat those, and that's what makes them healthy. Some of the trees bear seeds and fruit for birds or bats, and the lizards and snakes feed off them and their eggs. Some plants produce special leaves for food, or medicine for the animals, and not one part of the forest can be missing if it is going to be a complete and healthy ecosystem."

He looked at Jyly. "But even though you'll have something that looks like a rainforest in fifty to eighty years, it won't be complete for thousands of years. That's why we have to stop them cutting the real stuff down. There are thousands of interlinked species in real forest. Even us smart-ass scientists can't re-create, it exactly. That, it has to do for itself, but we give it a good start."

He swept his arm over the huge area that 350 people were helping plant. "And all these trees? As they grow, they scrub the atmosphere of carbon and lock it in their wood and transport it back into the earth, where it does no harm. The earth is missing millions and millions of acres of these cleaners. We have to teach people that if they see a spare bit of ground, any spare bit—they gotta want to plant trees back where they belong."

He looked out over the shallow valley and sort of whispered, like none of us were there, "Yeah, we're creating a whole living forest, full of balanced wildlife just like it used to be—not just a 'desert' of trees and one day the world's got a chance to go back into balance."

Jyly broke into his story and said, "It's amazingly complicated—is it worth it to do it like this? I mean if it's just a drop in the ocean, we need millions and millions of them put back"

He looked at her long and hard and said, "Yeah, Rome wasn't built in a day. It took six hundred years to build, and they burned it down in just one night. It's always easier to destroy than to build but they rebuilt Rome and we can do the same."

He smiled at her. "Come back in fifty to eighty years' time Ms. Ungaru—hike through this forest, alive with birds, and animals, and insects. Breath in the fresh oxygen-laden air, and then ask me if it was worth it."

She didn't say anything. She just picked up another tree and grabbed Amy's hand, and the two of them walked to the next spot and started digging.

Several weeks later, it was finally over. Three-hundred-and-twelve acres somewhere between Mareeba and Ravenshoe was now covered in a variety of saplings and plants staked out with small windscreens with the icon of the green-faced kid printed on the side of them. Each one was planted in a scattered pattern, pretty much the way they would have been if they had always been there.

This strip now joined two little islands of wild rain forest left standing in the 1970s by a farmer who cared about a family of agile wallaby and a native pigeon whose numbers had been decimated by the clearing of forests for farmland. He'd have liked what he saw today. A promise to a future looking back, and smiling at all our hard work

I took Jyly down to the huts where people stayed as they did a planting stint of a few days or for some of the more dedicated ones, several weeks. We'd been there from the beginning to the end, and no one could be happier to see that section done than me.

Jyly was hot, sweating, and worn out. She flopped down in a chair of the communal barracks set up at the beginning of the project, and, just as I said good-bye to go and pick up Jimmy and Juniper from the other end, I heard John'o's voice coming in the door. He had come back to get his bags, and I heard him say, "Jesus, I didn't think I was gonna make it, I'm so stuffed but at least one more section is planted!"

He sauntered in, slightly nursing his arm that was now out of its cast, and I said, "Mate! So you came up here and did your bit for posterity even after the accident? How's the arm?"

He said it was aching a bit but otherwise it was ok. He grinned and shook his head, "It got a bit of a workout, I can tell you, along with the rest of me! But I'm glad I was grounded, since I got to see what you guys are doing first hand. Someone should dish out medals: that's bloody hard going to get that many in the ground!"

"There's plenty more you could do if you want to stay earthbound for a while," Jyly said with a grin. "This is just the beginning bit, now we have to monitor this connection to the northern section and keep the plants going until they are properly established." She looked up and her chocolate eyes sparkled. "One day, we can reintroduce lots of species from zoos and breeding sanctuaries as the land returns to its natural state. So there's years of work if you want it."

He smiled and lingered for a moment, considering what she had said and then he looked at me. "She's cute! Well, I guess, to tell you the truth, I think I'd rather just check out its progress from the air."

She grinned and nodded, and I took my opportunity to go and get the boys, because we were all going into town to celebrate, and I was hanging out for a beer. I left Jyly and John'o chatting and a bit of me felt annoyed because it looked like Juniper wasn't going to get a look in after all.

Jimmy arrived at the foundation offices at James Cook University about eight days later. He told me he had met Louisa in the hall, and she was cool but polite.

Louisa said, "The little protégé has gone walkabout. No one has seen her this whole week." She reckoned this bothered Jimmy, and he had asked Lou when Jyly was last seen Louisa looked at me with a certain fire and indignation and said, "The way he asked, it didn't look to me like parental concern!"

Louisa told him that reception had rung Jyly's home and her mobile phone several times, but she hadn't replied or been seen since the last section was finished. Louisa made the comment that maybe the physical work of this was too hard for her, and she had given up.

She turned and looked at me and I half pie thought she was looking to me for some insight into how Jimmy felt about the girl when she said, "When Jimmy looked worried, I said, "Why do you care?"

She said he had rebuked her sharply, saying, "You are going to have to do something about your stone heart, Louisa, because if you go for a swim, you may sink to the bottom and drown!"

She remembered that comment for a long time after, and, I admit she still had a strange look of disbelief on her face that he would ever turn on her.

She said she ignored it and went back to what she was doing, and he just ignored her and left.

However, as soon as he had gone, she told me she walked to the counter and looked up Jyly's mobile phone number herself. When it went on to answerphone, she left a message saying she'd call her back, as she was worried for her so I knew old Lou wasn't quite the stone-hearted bitch we thought she might be.

Something told me things had gone wrong, so I excused myself and went looking for Jimmy.

I guessed he would go up to the Mossman Indigenous Reserve, because Jyly had some close ties up there. I was right; he had taken the foundation Ute and headed for his second home.

Chapter 4

WHEN I CAUGHT up with him, Jimmy told me he had driven down to the small town of Innesfail as soon as Maisey and the guys at the Mossman reserve told him where they thought he should start looking. The town of Innisfail is a couple of hours from Mossman on the main highway, south of Cairns city.

It's small and has old buildings from the days of the settlers. Wide, Iron filigree fringed verandas, and turn-of-the-century buildings made it look like time had stopped and nothing much had changed for the last hundred years. Of course, lots had happened. It had a muddy river through it and a huge croc farm on its banks that had gone through a big cyclone one year, and the crocs had escaped into the swamp and river. Some big ones had a field day terrorizing the locals, and a few dogs went missing, but one by one they collected them up. The locals weren't absolutely sure they got all of them, though, so, if you were going to fish in the river for yabbies or barras, you did it carefully to this day.

Jimmy said he drove around the streets looking for her. The old stone church and wooden buildings towered over the smaller shops and cafés down the main street.

After about an hour, he decided to head for the bridge that crosses the estuary river. There were definitely wild crocodiles in there. A sign had been erected with a warning: *Achtung: Crocodiles May Cause Injury*, which was an understatement, in my opinion.

He left the vehicle and, ignoring the yellow warning sign, walked down to where the mangroves meet the sides of the river.

He said he followed a track, and it soon led him under the bridge.

Jyly appeared around the corner of the bridge just at that moment with two young men in their twenties.

He said, when she saw him, she froze. Her two companions turned sheepishly and headed back up the track, thinking he must be her father, and they obviously didn't want to get involved.

Jimmy said it was a bit tense, and he thought she might bolt. He walked over to her. Standing side on, he looked over her face. He said there were bruises healing on her cheeks and a cut under her nose.

He said quietly, "I'm looking for advice; can you tell me of a good shrink?"

She stuttered, and her eyes were fearful and unsure. "What?"

"I thought I saw a ghost, and she was standing under a bridge. It looked like someone I knew, but I thought it couldn't be, because the one I knew was better looking and was a smart-ass."

She smiled a little.

"Want a burger? McDonalds is up the road," he asked her.

"Yeah—okay," she said and turned to walk with him up the track to the Ute.

He opened the door for her, and, when they had got in, he drove her up the main street to McDonalds. They got a drive-thru burger and fries each, and then Jimmy turned the car and took it back over the bridge and out into the countryside.

"Where are we going?" she asked.

"I know a nice restaurant on Mission Beach."

"We just had McDonalds!"

"Yeah, that was so I can afford the coffee at the restaurant."

She shook her head.

When they got there, they went into a rustic property and were seated by a very friendly woman who ran the place.

I've been there, and it's a cool place. Hung on the walls and even the ceilings are early bits and pieces of historic items of the area. Posters from the war and even a plough had been hung up in the high ceilings that were painted chocolate brown. Sometimes wild cassowary came down out of the forests and begged for food from the tourists just outside.

Small cubicles made private booths, and Ulmarra showed her through to one beside a window looking into a green and flowery garden. He told me he knew she would talk, so he just waited.

A few moments went by, then finally she spoke. "I s'pose you want to know—"

"Nah."

"Why not?"

"Because people tell you what they want to; you don't have to want to know," he said.

"So if I tell you, I don't know if you are interested or not?

"Nah."

They sat in silence for a bit longer. He said it wasn't long before she couldn't stand the silence so started talking. "My dad was a bastard," she said.

"Most of them are, aren't they? I reckon they are only one generation ahead of the rest of us bastards coming up."

"He used to smash my mother a bit, and he liked the booze."

"I don't."

"You don't like booze, or you don't smash women?"

"Both."

"Why not? I thought all blokes did."

"I don't like the booze, because you may as well drink petrol in your fruit juice. Same stuff you pickle dead animals in…" He smiled. "I like my animals alive and me with 'em." More silence filled the space.

The waitress delivered the coffees and left.

"Someone raped me." Jyly looked down at her hands in shame.

"Know who?"

"No. It was dark—he was big. I kicked him in the nuts, and he left."

"Good on you."

"Upset me a bit, so I came down here for a while."

"You coming back?"

"Don't know if the Queen will be pleased with me; she's left about fifty messages."

"I'll deal with her."

Jyly began to struggle not to cry, and he watched her as tears filled her eyes and slid off her brown face.

He almost whispered as he caught her eyes in his gaze. "Animals can't cry—isn't that terrible? Imagine being hurt, afraid, lonely, and not being able to cry." He leaned forward to catch a tear from her face and wipe it away.

"I don't like crying," she said.

"Me neither, but sometimes there is nothing else you can do except wash your eyes out, so you can see properly."

She grinned and said, "Thanks."

"No need—I'm good with kangaroos too."

She laughed, and the two finished their coffee, and Jimmy drove her back to Cairns to her mum's house. She thanked him, and he said he'd call her when he had talked to Louisa. She didn't say anything but just turned and disappeared inside.

She told me that even with Jimmy on her side, she was sure it was over for her at the foundation. She was scared anyway, because until someone was caught, she was pretty sure she would be no use, because she would always be looking over her shoulder.

When Jimmy got back, he found Louisa working at the office, trying to prepare accounts for the annual audit. The foundation was a charitable trust and received donations along with huge government subsidies for the land-requisition projects and the IFTs, so everything had to be shipshape for the once-a-year sign-off.

Jimmy told me he knew it wasn't a good time to go and see her, but he wanted to sort out this thing for Jyly.

I stayed well out of the way when all this went down; in fact, I was on my way to Juniper's place, because Jyly's wasn't the only bit of drama going down at that time.

Jimmy told me how it went with Louisa, because he was pretty upset afterwards, and he just wanted to off-load the whole affair to someone, and that was me.

He walked into the offices, and she looked up a little shyly, as the tension between them was getting beyond a joke.

Coincidentally or not, Louisa had been bitching about people not getting their act together, and she went on to Jimmy about her frustration with my brother Juniper. Jimmy said she thought it was doubtful Juniper had any commitment to the project at all, and he'd not turned up to work for three days.

Jimmy said she then started on Jyly. She said Jyly had been missing for days, and Louisa had left messages, and the girl didn't even have the decency to call back. He said she'd just about had enough.

"If Jyly ever comes back, I'm not going to accept any explanation but just terminate her scholarship.

"Why not wait until you hear what the girl has to say?" Jimmy said softly. "She's worked harder than anyone I've ever seen. Let her tell you what happened."

He said Louisa looked up at him suspiciously. Maybe it was the way he said it or just instinct, but he said Louisa got a clue that something was up, and a frown crossed her face. Maybe she thought he was attracted to Jyly, and that's why he had refused her many attempts to win him over, even after they had had a talk, and he told her he wanted it to go back to what it was with her.

"There's something I don't like about Jyly," Louisa said. "She's a rebel. I can never trust or rely on her," she said with obvious distaste.

"I'm a rebel," Jimmy said, "and you trust me. What you don't like about her is the girl can't be controlled or manipulated. She's her own person, and that means she'll only do what her conscience dictates. She's as reliable as clockwork, on her own terms. Just not on anyone else's."

When he went to leave, Louisa took one step toward him, as though she might have been going to give him a quick peck but decided against it.

He just said good-bye and, according to him, that was the end of it.

I caught up with Jimmy two days later. By this time I'd heard that Jyly was back working, but that Louisa was acting weird about it.

When I finally cornered him, he point-blank refused to tell me anything, but said some stuff had to be sorted out. He hinted that there could be a mongrel in the team, and if he found him, he would drop him out the back of Arnum land without any water and let him try to walk out of there.

This comment didn't do anything except whet my interest. I was worried for Jyly and asked if she was alright, and Jimmy said she would tell me herself if she wanted to.

I went straight to Jyly, who was sorting out some plants in the foundation nursery attached to the back of the university offices. We had taken over an area that had been a spare car park, and now scores of plants were delivered, sorted, and marked ready for the next section plant. She was checking leaves for insects or rust when I found her.

I'm not shy or careful like Jimmy, so I came straight out with it.

"You been in the wars—what happened?"

I could tell she wanted to tell me, but there at work wasn't the right sort of place, so I said, "Come on, we're going down to the beach, and I don't care if we stay there all afternoon, you need to tell me what's going on.

A little shyly, she agreed, and we took off in my Ute.

I walked her to a picnic seat under a couple of coconut trees at Holloways Beach looking out on the top of Trinity inlet.

"Okay, so can you tell me now? I ain't gonna think anything bad of you, Jyly. You're the best kid I've known for years in the scholarship program, and if Jimmy likes you, well, that says it all." She looked up at me when she heard his name, and that was all it took.

She told me about the man who attacked her up at the dongas at the last plant. I pressed her for details, and she answered reluctantly and said Louisa had insisted it be reported to the police, but she didn't want to report it she just wanted to forget it somehow..

"Why not?" I said. "The next woman may not be as lucky as you were."

She looked strangely at me and said, "I wasn't that lucky."

That stopped me in my tracks.

"Any idea who it was?" I asked.

"No, but he would have been pretty scratched up and sore, because I kicked him hard."

I grinned and said, "Good on you! Perhaps that will make him think twice about letting his sick desires out of the box." I asked if there was anything that might give a clue to the man's identity.

She said no, just that he was tall and much stronger than she was. I could see she was trying to muster up the wherewithal to tell me everything she could remember, so I helped her out by reminding her about John'o being there when I left. Just the mention of that night made her look up with fear in her eyes, and she began to breathe quickly.

Suddenly she just let it all out, and she began to tell me what had happened to her, and it was awful, listening, but I knew she had to tell someone or be consumed by it.

She said she had clawed and scratched him as he had surprised her in the shower and forced her small naked form across the floor and over to a couch before rolling her on to floor.

She said she fought with everything she had, kicking and struggling, trying to stop him from holding her down even though she could feel his size and weight on her, and she knew she was going to lose, and he'd have her. She said she was screaming in terror, but the man finally slammed into her and crushed her ribs into her back with every thrust.

Jyly choked as she spilled the humiliation and agony of that crime from the bowl held shakily in her heart and let the putrefied memories pour from it through her lips, mix with her tears, and run clear to the ground. I watched and marveled at her courage. I watched and felt strangely ashamed for my sex.

She said that just when she thought her attacker might release himself into her, and she would be utterly defiled, her sweat allowed one of her legs to slip up under his stomach, and she kicked with all her force at his midriff.

She said the force threw him off, and he groaned, crumpled, and then rolled off her. He pulled himself up on the couch, then staggered across the room, doubled over and winded, until he slammed the door open and fled.

In the darkness, she felt around for the towel and wrapped it around herself, wiping sweat and blood from her face and swallowing fearful tears.

She crept over the floor and shut the door behind him, locking it. Then she went to her room and packed her one bag, carrying it quickly from the empty camp, terrified that he was still out there somewhere, expecting him to grab her again from behind. She jumped into her car parked in the roadway and sped off into town.

"I just screamed and cried the whole way, Wajilla. It was a wonder I didn't have a smash coming down the range. By the time I got to mum's, I just couldn't move for about half an hour. I sat in the drive listening to them inside. I could hear my sister's kid screaming, and I was thinking, 'Why doesn't she pick up that baby?' But I couldn't do anything at all. I was frozen to the steering wheel.

"When the baby stopped crying, I sort of woke up, got out of the car, and went inside. I didn't say anything to anyone. I just went into the bathroom, locked the door, and had a shower for about half an hour until all the hot water had run out."

When she was finished, I sat quietly too. I didn't know what to say. I looked long and hard at her and then nodded and said, "If you need anything at all, call me."

I took her back to her plant inspection and sorting, and she gave me a hug and said she felt better.

I strode off toward Louisa's office. When I got there, I bluntly asked, "You know what happened! What are you doing about Jyly?"

"It's really a matter for the police. We'll have to put in some safety measures for people when they are out on a plant from now on and start screening the volunteers. We'll have to increase security in here too. There's also money missing." She spoke so sourly I knew she meant someone we knew had been in here and knew where she put kept the petty cash tin.

I wanted to know if there were any clues who it could have been, and she told me that when it happened, most people had already gone into town. It could have been the guy who offered her a lift in, "the helicopter pilot; perhaps he could have come back." She said she'd given his name to the police, and they were going to interview him.

"John'o? Nah, it won't be him," I said.

"Well, Donahue was still out there that night, over at the research tent about a kilometer away, because I said good-bye to him at about nine at night. You and Jimmy were out there somewhere; did you see anyone?"

I broke in and said Jimmy and me were on the way to Mareeba to meet up with Juniper to take him home, but he had already got a lift with someone, so we didn't go back to the dongas. "We didn't even get to the pub that night." I said, straining my brain to think of something that might lead us to the mongrel.

"Jyly thinks she scratched him pretty bad, so he should be easy to spot if they get onto it before the scratches heal."

I went still, like a stray bullet had hit me. My stomach turned, and I felt like I was about to have a heart attack. I didn't wait to hear any more but turned on my heel and walked out. I caught a glace of Louisa's frown, probably wondering why I was going so quickly without even saying good-bye, but I didn't care—I just went as fast as a lizard drinking.

The rest of the day was a bit of a blur, 'cause I was so enraged, I could barely think straight. I was amazed I managed to drive at all, but I told Jimmy what I suspected, and we took off to the rental house in Manoora.

We stormed into Juniper's flat, Jimmy behind me. I rushed past the two idiots lounging on the couch and grabbed my half-brother by his shirt and pulled him up.

Juniper yelled, and I screamed over the top of him. *"What the hell have you been doing?"*

The kid looked bewildered but feigned the kind of innocence that's not believable.

"What the bloody hell, are you talking about?"

I started to open his shirt, and he resisted, but I tore it, and there were the tell-tale scratches like a full-sized grizzly bear had mauled him.

Jimmy stood looking on, and the other two men got up hurriedly and left through the front door, not wanting to be involved.

I let go of Juniper and demanded to know where he got the scratches on his neck, shoulders, and chest.

"In the rose garden next door."

Jimmy said, "There are no roses next door."

I asked where he went on the Friday night after they finished the plant when we were supposed to pick him up, but he wasn't there.

Juniper spluttered his apologies and said he was sorry about that, but he got sick of waiting. We both fired a few more questions at him, and he kept staring up at the ceiling, very cocky that we couldn't prove anything.

He maintained he went into Mareeba with "the boys" and then came down to celebrate like everyone else.

I remembered Tony had said he had come in with some guys he didn't know, and, for a second, I thought, "Is he telling the truth?"

"Where did you pick up those bozos? Tony didn't know any of them boys?"

Now the young man started to falter. He said he didn't know—he couldn't remember, he'd had a lot of drink that night, hence his falling in the rose bush...maybe that wasn't next door but up at the pub—or at one of the boys' houses.

I looked at him, and Jimmy scrutinized his face also.

Jimmy shook his head very slowly.

Then I said quietly, "It was you, eh? You mongrel!"

I flew at him, and Juniper ran to escape. I got him around the waist, just as he made it to the door, and we tumbled down the stairs.

Jimmy was behind me, and when we hit the landing, we sort of rolled all the way to the bottom.

He tried to get up, but Jimmy and me wrestled him to the ground.

The kid started to make excuses that it wasn't whatever she had said, that she came on to him.

"She had a few drinks too—and when she gets fired up, she's an abo wildcat!" He said that if she is accusing him of anything else, she's lying and looking for a payout.

I stopped and looked at Jimmy, and then Jimmy very gently shook his head again.

Looking down at my younger half-brother, I felt like I just didn't know him at all, and I started to cry. I stifled it back and asked him what made him become a filthy dog capable of such a shit life. I let him go and looked up at Jimmy.

"What do we do?" I asked my friend.

I answered for him. "Our people would have dealt with this in-house, on our own. She's got a right to be asked what she wants to do."

We gathered Juniper off the ground and threw him in the Ute.

When we arrived at the nursery at the back of the foundation offices, Jyly looked up. She immediately saw Juniper, and something in her face told us she had somehow recognized what we were there for.

"We gotta talk to you."

She replied, "Yeah?"

"This one is marked—is it him?"

She came up to him and stood side on, not looking at him directly. She lifted her face slightly and looked across at his neck and shoulders. "I can smell him," she said. "He's like a dog that's been peeing on himself. I can smell him."

I struck the kid over his head.

Jyly had walked away, and Jimmy had put his arm around her shoulders as she looked at the ground.

"What do you want to do?" I said. "Do you want us to get the police or sort him our way?"

She looked straight into Juniper's eyes that were still defiant and unrepentant, and I was dumbfounded by her courage. "He's wild—he should be treated like he is. Can't blame a dog for being one—but I don't want him around here no more."

I grabbed him and headed back to the vehicle.

Jimmy asked her if she would be okay. She told him she would be, and he lifted his hand and stroked her black cheek, and he said he would be back.

As he left, he called out almost as an afterthought, "We're going out to Frazer Island to look at some animals to be rescued. Department of Environment and Resource Management are willing to get another location going for the last of the pure-blood dingoes—you're coming."

She brightened immediately. She called after him, "What are you gonna do with the mongrel?"

He yelled back as we disappeared, "Wajilla wants to fix him the old way— teach him permanently. It's his call. Don't worry."

Chapter 5

"WHERE ARE YOU taking me?" Juniper was a bit shaky, but his voice had no fear that I would do anything and was bound to go easy on him. Well, he was going to be wrong this time. "Walkabout," I replied, not giving anything away. "Gonna teach you the old way criminals were handled by our people. In them days, not even one per cent reoffended, and you're gonna be no exception, mate. It's about time you learned that you are not immune, and there is a price you're gonna pay for all your shit."

The kid just shook his head, as though he didn't really have that much to be worried about, and my lecture wasn't worth his time. He just replied offhandedly, "Whatever."

We drove almost an hour and a half up to Lake Tinnaroo Reserve, a large catchment area that had rain forest all around it. It was some distance from habitation, and when we pulled up at an open spot, Juniper said, "No way I'm getting out; you can't piss off an' leave me!"

We ignored his protests and pulled him from the vehicle by his shirt. Jimmy slipped a noose around his hands and tied them behind his back. It happened so quickly that Juniper spluttered, "What the—" but couldn't get the rest of his words out before I had stuffed a rag in his mouth and tied a gag around his head. Juniper began to struggle and tried to run, but I simply kicked his feet from under him and he fell to the ground.

"Don't worry," I said to the kid, "we ain't going to kill you, mate, even if that's what you deserve. We just gonna make it so you remember that no matter how horny or stupid you are, you can't touch a woman."

I looped a rope around each foot as he kicked furiously then tied the end to a large tree. Jimmy sat on the kid's hips and held him tight.

I walked to the vehicle and pulled out a long, Phillips head, cross-cut screwdriver. I pulled out a bottle of disinfectant and wiped the tool down the shaft, from end to end, and then I lit a lighter and burnt the length of steel.

Juniper was watching with eyes as big as saucers, and he began to wriggle and struggle against Jimmy holding him.

I looked at the kid and I said, "Count yourself lucky this isn't a hundred years ago, when they would have set you loose and thrown spears at you until one of them fired one through your leg. You'd have a hole the size of a broom handle, and it would fester for months. We're a bit more civilized than that, but you're gonna learn the same lesson, mate." With that, I pulled out a blade and cut his jeans up to the knee.

With one big hand, I grabbed Juniper's calf and pinned it to the ground and raised the screwdriver high in the air. I brought it down fast and speared him through the calf muscle right into the ground underneath.

Juniper screamed under the gag and he stiffened, thrashing with pain, but Jimmy had a good hold of him.

I pulled out the screwdriver, and the bruised and oozing hole let out a little blood. I stood up, and Jimmy released Juniper and stood over him also. Together, we looked at Juniper whimpering and crying on the ground.

Loosening off the ropes, I said, "Hurts me more'n it hurt you—you're gonna limp all the way home, which is about eighty-two kilometers from here to town, but you can pick up a blue bus from Gordon vale, which'll save you twenty-five kilometers." I threw the kid a blue ten-dollar note for the bus fare before going on.

"The whole way, you better think about what you need to do to get on the right track. Your crime has been paid for this time in the old way, an' we're never gonna bring it up again. You're lucky she didn't want to see you put in Lotus Glen prison, and that'd start you off with a record, an' you'd learn nothing 'cept what those bloody evil bastards know in there. You'd only have crim' mates from then on and be in trouble for the rest if your life. You can thank her for letting you off that. But you better head south and start a new life, 'cause I ain't gonna feed you, or bail you out, or let you off if you ever do anything out of the way again. You understand me, mate? Never. My love is too big for that—" My voice brook a little, and I leaned down and pulled the gag from his mouth, and then I turned and walked away.

As I did, Juniper started to swear and throw insults, and he screamed in fury at us as he rubbed his wrists and grabbed for his calf.

I stopped and closed my eyes.

Jimmy walked up and patted me on my shoulder, and I stepped forward and opened the door of the vehicle without looking back.

As we set off, I stole a quick glance at Juniper in the side mirror. He was still lying in the dirt.

"You can only do your best, mate," Jimmy said to me. "In the end, a good tree can't bear bad fruit, and a bad tree never gives you nothin' worth eating."

"I know," I whispered. "It's just that I can't help loving that idiot tree, no matter how crooked it's got."

Jimmy looked out at the road in front of him, and he said, "Well, then, let the shit compost the tree for a few more years and see if one day something good comes off it, but whatever you do—don't do more than you've done. Don't rescue him this time—otherwise, someone is gonna have to chop that one down for good."

I couldn't even speak all the way back. I just kept thinking, I left me kid bother out there. I would have done anything to turn round and go back and get him.

Later that month the trip to Fraser Island was organized.

Louisa was furious that Jimmy was taking Jyly. She stormed across her office and threw a pile of sheets across her desk, and they slid and fell on the floor. She started to pick them up when I came in.

"What do you want?" she snarled.

"Whoa—got your period, or what?"

She shook her head and hid her real feelings by saying the petty cash was definitely two hundred dollars short, so we had a thief and a rapist in our midst. She let off steam by saying that the world had fifty years left if we don't get control of global warming, and the Ulmarra Foundation is showing the world how to do it, and still some asshole thinks she has time to sort out police reports.

I swallowed hard, trying to keep her mind off the petty cash. I said, "People don't think that far ahead, Lou; you can't blame them. They're only interested in what is in their stomach today."

I grinned and said I thought she needed a rest. I pulled her by both her hands towards and through the door and said, "Look, I'd drive you home myself, but I have to finish those orders to the nursery tomorrow for the next grid plant. You get out of here and do your bookkeeping tomorrow. You are overstressed, that's all. Have a good, hot bubble bath and maybe a full-bodied glass of red, and tomorrow will look different."

She smiled and agreed to go.

Just as she got to the car, she stopped, and she said, "You know, Jimmy and I aren't going to go there."

I was surprised she actually said that out loud, and I replied, "Well at least you know that now." I nodded knowingly and said, "Better to have loved and lost..."

She grinned and said, "I'm not sure if that old saying works out to be true. Pandora's box wasn't too successful after it was opened."

I smiled and said, "But that was a box, and you are a fox, and a smart one—Jimmy isn't like any normal guy, and he might never find what he needs, but that should not be important to you. You need someone who will keep a clean house and do as he's told; otherwise, you'll be crazy in a year. The truth is, Lou, if Jimmy had gone on too long, you two would have wrecked a friendship and the foundation."

"You're probably right."

She waved good-bye, and I headed back into the offices.

I took my keys, unlocked the petty cash, and grabbed my wallet from my back pocket. I took out a few notes, counted them, and put them under the receipts in the tin and said quietly to myself, "You owe me big-time, bro—you little shit."

Chapter 6

ETTING THE STORY from Jimmy as to what happened on that Fraser Island trip was like pulling teeth. Jyly had her own version too.

From what I gathered, they took a ferry over in the morning.

Jyly said the water was an amazing color, a brilliant turquoise. The two of them were standing together alongside the deck the whole way, watching as the waves went by.

"How long is the trip going to take?"

"About an hour for the Hervey Bay to Moon Point crossing."

He pointed into the water as a round shadow scooted through the clear sea away from the craft. "Green turtle!" he said, and she watched it disappear.

"They got dugong here too," he said like an excited boy, and she said he never stopped smiling the whole way.

"How big is it?" she asked.

"The island is just over 123 kilometers in length and 22 kilometers at its widest point. It is the largest sand island in the world."

"What—no rocks at all?"

"Nah—just sand. And sand cliffs with colored layers."

When they reached the pier, they grabbed their bags and disembarked. Tourists were moving around them, and Jimmy said quietly, "This is why there is a problem: last population of pure dingoes in the world, and they have to try and share their island with tourists."

They made their way to the Queensland Parks and Wildlife Service offices on the island, where they were expecting them and going to put them up.

When they got there, the head ranger, David Pullman, suggested that they settle into their cabins first, and they could go for a ride into the interior of the island when they were ready, maybe after lunch.

"We're keen to get under way," Jimmy said, and Jyly also had no interest in anything but seeing the controversial dingoes in their natural habitat.

"Let's dump our gear and get going straightaway," she said.

Ranger Pullman was happy to oblige, and he told them to make sure they hadn't got any food on them, because the dogs will seek them out otherwise. "In fact, they're smarter than you would believe, so you have to be careful."

Pullman said they are quite different from a normal dog. Their wrists are capable of rotation, and they can use their paws like hands and turn doorknobs. They are the world's oldest breed of canine and descended from the Indian wolf dog. They have just one litter a year, and all the pack members rear the pups of the dominant female so they stay in families, living for about six years in the wild.

"That's not long," Jyly said. "And not many offspring either."

"That's not the problem; it's interbreeding that is wiping them out. It started back when cattle ranchers created the great Australian cattle dog, because the English imports couldn't handle the conditions; but if they are pure, they can't be domesticated, and they're dangerous.

When they got to the four-wheel drive, he told them they had another attack about three months ago and two dogs had to be destroyed. He said the Department of Environment and Resource Management has dictated that any dogs that develop an attitude of fearlessness or come too close to the area where tourists are camping, fishing, or tramping are to be rounded up and destroyed. So thirty-one others were also destroyed because they had no fear of humans either.

"It's a shame that the message to visitors isn't getting through. People are still feeding them and not being careful to seal rubbish in the waste bins or take it with them."

Jyly told me she listened but had already looked it all up on the Internet and didn't think it was possible for these animals not to interact if they were hungry, but she listened politely because they had only just arrived.

Driving through the island, heading north, Jyly smiled and said, "It's a pretty place."

"Fraser Island is known as being of exceptional beauty; it has long, uninterrupted white beaches and strikingly colored sand cliffs. There are over one hundred freshwater lakes scattered all over the island, some tea-colored and others clear and blue, all ringed by white, sandy beaches." Pullman told her. "Ancient rain forests grow in sand along the banks of fast-flowing, crystal-clear creeks, and it's the only place in the world where tall rain-forest giants are found growing right on sand dunes."

I'd been there in spring and summer, and the low wallum heaths on the island were also an evolutionary and ecological wonder. Magnificent wildflower displays paint the dunes in beautiful colors. The island is unique and, thanks to a special fungus in the sand that enables plants to grow, it supports all kinds of life: goannas, small animals, and of course the infamous dingoes.

Jyly said she couldn't hold it in anymore, so she looked at Ulmarra and began talking back to the ranger. "I read that the dogs are losing their natural food sources because of the pressure the island is under with tourism, and when the dogs are so underfed, they take risks. It's just not big enough for them and people wanting to come and see this jewel island. Is that right?"

Ranger Pullman stuttered a bit and said, "Th-that isn't quite how it is." He said they thought there was still a good population of two hundred dingoes and they were doing okay. He said they were definitely heavier than the mainland ones, at about 18.3 kilos for a male on average, so he reckoned they couldn't be faring too badly.

"My research has conflicting info about them, eh?" Jyly insisted. "What I've found out is that there are probably only 100 to 120 animals left, and most of them are very undernourished."

Ulmarra jumped in and said, "I'm glad a backup population has been approved to be released in our Great Dividing Range reforestation section. That area is nearly twenty years old now, so it's fresh territory; they should do okay in there."

Ranger Pullman asked how they were going to stop cross-breeding with domestic animals on the mainland, and Jimmy said that the area was border-fenced like the dingo fence in New South Wales, to keep them out of the farms down there. But our fence has been built to keep them in, because we want to ensure a closed unit is available and it is geographically remote too.

"The population at the northern end of the reserve is still pure, they think, but so small they need fresh individuals to ensure that the dingo doesn't go extinct, as it's likely to be on Frazer if the park can't manage the problems and the reducing population."

"I'm pretty sure we won't lose them here."

"'Pretty sure' isn't sure enough." Jimmy cut him off quite sharply. "When an animal as uniquely Australian as the dingo is lost, it's like losing all the 'Caucasians' of the world in one hit, and who would want that to happen?" He grinned at Jyly and said, "I supposes life would go on without the blondes—but the human population would be missing something, and that would be bad for 'diversity,' don't you think?"

Ranger Pullman looked at him and said, "I don't think that's a good example, mate." And his tone was quite flat, probably because he was blonde and blue-eyed.

Jimmy was watching Jyly, and I would bet he was really talking to her when he went on to say, "Sure, there are lots of 'dogs' in the world, but the dingo is the only one that can never be truly tamed. It's been cut off and separate from all other dogs for five thousand years, like an evolutionary time capsule. A dog is not just a dog if it's a dingo, you know. It's a small wolf, and it needs its space."

Jyly agreed. "Maybe they would have been treated more seriously if they weren't seen as 'vermin' as they were in the '60s and '70s by farmers and landholders all over Australia and wouldn't be down to the last few hundred purebred ones."

"We have to 'guarantee' they're saved, or be the first modern country in the world that was well able to protect its most unique inhabitants and didn't. And if the most unique resident of Australia is a wild dog, we have to fight to save it, because a lot of people just won't care, because they have their prized poodle, and that's all that matters to them. Dingoes might not be cute, or sweet, but they are priceless. I'd even try to save the 'blondes' if they were that endangered!"

When they arrived in a sandy and tree-ringed clearing, the ranger got out of the vehicle and whispered that they should bring the binoculars. He said there was a group of about twelve that live in this area, and they had seven pups this season.

Jyly asked how many survived, and he said that about four had made it to nine months and were ear-tagged, but about 80 per cent are lost by twelve months due to population pressures.

Jyly said that was pretty poor, since 90 per cent of the wolves in Yellowstone survive to maturity. She asked him point-blank, what did he think was going wrong?

He didn't reply but whispered and pointed, "There they are."

Rolling in sand, the dusty, yellow-colored dogs were playing, and among them were two mid-sized juveniles, a bitch, and some smaller puppies.

"They look okay," Jimmy says.

"Yes, they're doing fine," Ranger Pullman said. "The really lightweight ones tend to show up later in the season as the pups get older and food is scarce because of available food having to go around more dogs." He told them how you could tell a dingo was 'pure' by the white tip on their tail, white hair on their paws, and sometimes a chest spot.

"There's a few other unique characteristics like the rotating wrists and webbed paws." He told them how the dingoes didn't bark like modern dogs but howl at night instead. This 'singing' was to stay in touch with each other.

"They've developed totally different hunting tactics on the island due to their lack of prey. On the mainland they'll take down things as big as a full-grown, six-foot red kangaroo and eat anything from coconut to carrion. Here they get small stuff on the beach and sometimes team up together in big mixed packs to hunt anything going, and that's when they can get dangerous," he whispered.

They watched the dogs play.

"We have six animals further inland that have been getting too bold and will be trapped, and would have been destroyed if it were not for your foundation."

Jyly smiled. She said Jimmy patted her on her shoulder, and they returned to the vehicle quite happy that they had seen some of the dingoes and excited that a new pack would soon be ranging through one of their replanted areas.

The following morning, Jyly said Jimmy knocked on her door just before dawn.

"Come with me; we are going to take a look for ourselves at the wild dingoes of Frazer Island." She was a bit unsure but got dressed and followed him out.

Jimmy took her to where the conservation jeeps were parked and jumped into one of them.

"Did you nick the keys?"

"No," he said, and started fiddling under the dash, then the vehicle started.

"You're pretty good at doing that."

"A leftover from what I learned as a kid."

They drove miles down the long island to reach an area of sand dunes and brush beyond the tourist camping areas. He stopped on the flat, and they got out and walked for another kilometer or more.

"Is there a reason we are walking to the ends of the earth?" she asked, and Jimmy explained that he didn't want the dingoes to know they were coming for a visit.

As they walked into the brush, she said to him, "Isn't this dangerous?"

"Yep," he said, "but there is only one way to really find out what the truth is, and that is to get out on foot and get some real data."

Perhaps to keep her from thinking it, Jimmy asked her, "Do you know how the island got its name?"

"No."

"They called the place K'gari after a beautiful spirit who helped Yindingie, messenger of the great god Beeral, creator of the land. As a reward to K'gari for her help, Beeral changed her into an idyllic island with trees, flowers, and lakes. He put birds, animals, and people on the island just to keep her company.

"She probably got quite upset when they closed the Bogimbah mission down, and the people got taken away—those who survived disease or trouble, that is. They were shifted to Yarrabah near Cairns and Durundur near Caboolture. Some of my ancestors would have been there at Yarrabah when the islanders from here were dumped there."

"So that is its real name, K'gari?"

"Yeah but it's called 'Fraser Island' because of Eliza."

"Who is Eliza?"

"Ahh, the story of Eliza Frazer...

"Back in the early 1800s, she was married to an old captain out from England, Captain Fraser. But their ship was wrecked at Swain's Reef, north of Fraser Island, that way." He pointed into the clear ocean-scape stretching out north from them.

"The survivors floated south in lifeboats but lost each other and eventually found themselves marooned on K'gari on the other side.

"Poor old Eliza had a rough time. She had been pregnant and almost full-term when they grounded, and she gave birth to a baby a few days after the wreck. It died but they eventually made it to this island too.

"On the island, the Butchulla bama stripped them all naked and separated the men to do work, and the aboriginal women healed Eliza's badly sunburned body with sand and rubbed it with charcoal and grease and decorated it with colors and feathers like she was one of their own.

"She was made to nurse their kids 'cause she had milk, dig fern roots, and rob bees' nests, but she wasn't too good at anything and had a bad attitude, so they hassled her for years. She saw the death of her husband after he was speared because he wasn't doing too well either, so she was all alone after that and lived with them here.

"A few of the others who had been marooned made it off the island and got back. They told stories of her living out here, and Lieutenant Otter rescued her. Yeah, life after the island must have been interesting, and she got a dollar or two out of it—"

Suddenly he had stopped and pointed over the ridge, and she said she saw a lone dog skirting over the sand dunes to catch something small in the grasses and swallow it quickly.

Ulmarra lifted his head and then looked to the south. He sniffed the air a little, and he said, "We should skirt round before our scent upsets the six or so dogs that are on the low side where we can't see."

After a few minutes, he showed her a few tracks in the sand. He pointed at one and just touched the edge of the print to see if the sand held together or not. He whispered to her, "They been hunting since before the light. If we go down that way, we'll see them come out on the beach."

They skirted around and started to walk down the slope when a big male, who must have been shadowing them just out of range, suddenly appeared.

"Told you they were smart." Jyly stopped and Jimmy smiled. "Hello fella, you out-dingo'd me." Ulmarra put his hands out and stood up tall to his full height. The dog growled, and Jimmy made an odd movement, and the dog momentarily hunched, and his ears pricked up.

"What do I do?" Jyly stood still, terrified.

"First, don't let that fear I can smell on you get the better of you. Stand up tall and walk behind me and a bit to my left, like we are a team."

As she did this, several other dogs appeared in the scrub, and they moved about, shifting positions nervously.

"They are really thin," Jyly commented, and Jimmy says that is why they are interested in them. Jyly started to stutter a little, "Th-there are dozens of them—I thought they were supposed to be in packs of four or five."

"Their new hunting tactic might be a problem," Jimmy said to her softly. "Stay close to me no matter what happens. The big one is not going to attack if he thinks we're dominant, and neither will the others.

Jimmy said he was going to yell at her, and he wanted her to shy away a bit but stay close to his back, so that he looked as if he was the top dog. She nodded, with her eyes firmly fixed on the three or four bigger dogs circling.

Jimmy growled and moved at her sharply, then she cowered obediently.

The big dog's eyes were watching.

"Stay with me, I'm going to charge." She dutifully obeyed as he charged at the leader. The dog flashed away into the bush but was soon back.

Jimmy stalked to the left and right, as though he was sizing up the leader, and then paused.

All the dogs were silent and stopped moving for a moment.

Jimmy put out his hand and stared at the big dog. He stepped to the side and forward towards him, leaving Jyly standing behind.

The lead dog froze, recognizing Jimmy as the leader of a pack of his own and who was preparing to make contact.

Just as Ulmarra came close, the big dog dropped down a little and backed a step or two away, his eyes riveted on Jimmy.

Jimmy stood quietly, the dog in front of him, still and quiet, and then suddenly Jyly realized the other dogs had disappeared, perhaps hiding in the scrub behind their leader.

"Okay, big fulla—it's okay." Jimmy walked forward another step, and the big dog circled a little and raised his snout in the air, sniffing for the aborigine, and decided to leave this new "dingo" alone. He turned and bounded for the bush. But just as Jyly thought she could start breathing again—a shot rang out.

The ranger had appeared down on the beach in a four-wheel drive. The sand flew up close to the departing dog, but the shot missed him.

Jimmy swung around quickly and yelled, "Oi! Put that rifle away!" faster than the departing dingoes.

Jimmy ran, with Jyly following, down the dunes to the beach and up to the vehicle.

"Lucky we came along; had a feeling you would head up this way—Bob counted thirty-four in the dunes all looking at you as bush tucker." The ranger yelled out to them as they arrived, his companion Bob with him sporting the rifle across his lap.

"Mate, what the hell were you doing? You could have hit us!" Ulmarra said incredulously.

"Nah, I was aiming miles away—the dingoes were the only thing in our sights, and we don't really want to have to shoot them either." He frowned slightly. "If people didn't encourage them to interact, we wouldn't have to." He pointed up to the bush that now seemed empty again. "We been watching that bugger; the bigger bloke is getting too bold. He's earmarked for destruction. He's got the others in tow, so we might have to shoot the lead six or seven."

"No way!" Jyly said.

"Trap 'em, and we'll take him as the sire for relocation," Jimmy replied calmly.

"You don't want one like that, man; he's likely to follow you out and take up residence near human habitation, then anything from tins cans in the rubbish to a sleeping baby is likely to go missing."

"Nah, he's strong, and he will hunt first, and that is what we want—survivors."

She said he turned away without even waiting for a response and said under his breath, "Looks like he'll be lucky to be alive if we leave him here with you lot."

Jyly couldn't help thinking about what had just happened and asked, "You know those attacks? And the fatal one—did they eat the bodies?"

The ranger looked a bit quizzical and said, "No—the victims were just mauled."

Jimmy answered her, "They don't see humans as their food source—they're hungry enough to overcome their fear to attack, but they don't know what to do with us, really."

He walked away from the vehicle down the beach, and as he went the ranger yelled out, "Hey, you better come with us!"

Jimmy ignored them and kept walking.

Jyly said to them stiffly, "We'll be alright—we'll be back for breakfast."

The ranger shook his head and lifted up the rifle to give her. "You'd better take it 'in case.'"

She looked at the gun, and her stomach turned like a huge step of faith had to be crossed. She shook her head and replied, "No—I've got something better than a rifle: somebody who really knows about dingoes."

The ranger sniffed at the subtle insult, and the vehicle revved up before they drove away in a wide circle around the two walkers, then headed off down the beach.

The two then walked silently together down the beach, beside the tire tracks.

"You seemed to have a connection with that big dingo."

"No, it's just understanding and mimicking animal behavior."

"There's something almost 'spiritual' about the way you are with things. Do you think animals have a spirit?"

"Everything has one. Anything that is living, that is."

"How do you know that for sure; where's your proof?"

Jimmy stopped, and when she turned, he had already laid down on the flat sand.

She stood there looking at him in surprise, and he popped his head up and smiled, "Come on—you want to find out?"

She lay down on the sand beside him. She looked up at the open sky, utterly blue in every direction, and waited.

He told her to shut her eyes and listen.

"To hear the voice of the Spirit, first you have to hear 'nothing.'"

"Nothing? How can you hear nothing?"

He told her that to start with, you could think about it like when you first hear a guitar, or the piano, or the drum separate from the music you are listening to. You don't hear the rest of the tune if you just concentrate on that one instrument playing some totally different melody. If you concentrated, you could tune out one and move on to next. Sometimes you could get to a place where you're so lost in it, you suddenly come to, to find the whole song has gone by, and all you're left with is the message of it, something you can hardly put your finger on, but it feels good, and you know something about that music that you didn't know before. You've actually heard what the composer was trying to get across using his collection of notes.

"To get to the place where you can hear 'life' speaking, you need to start by listening to the separate voices of creation first, so you can get to that silent place." He looked across at her and said cheekily, "There is a lot to be said for silence, Jyly."

I knew what he was doing with her, because he had done this lesson with me too, but not on a sunny beach: mine was in a scrub clearing at the top of a gorge, about a thirty-hour walk from a burger.

"Listen to the sound of the waves, then that sea gull," she said he had told her. "Hear the click of the clams in the sand closing, the wind up over the sand dunes, the crash of that big wave—me telling you all this.

"Then, just like you do for music, start to hear them all together—nothing distinct, the whole piece, the movement—so you can get lost in it."

Jyly concentrated and merged all the sounds together and listened hard.

"If you don't focus on any one thing, it all sounds like nothing." He paused. "It's real quiet out here, eh, even though it's filled with all those sounds."

She didn't know how much time went by, but they lay on the sand in silence. She broke the mood by whispering, "So what—now I know how to lie in the sand and listen to nothing."

He sat up and looked down on her with her eyes shut.

What he said next may have changed her whole idea of everything.

"You know, when you think about all the music you have ever listened to, you know that 'someone' out there made it, because the unthinking random sound of a drum or a reed can't form a string of notes that make sense by themselves. The composer or the leader of the band, someone, 'organizes' it all—same with the painter: he takes red, yellow, green, and blue, puts them together so you see something else. The picture.

"But what makes the picture and the music 'art,' and carries a message instead of just being something flat and lifeless, is what the painter or the musician puts 'inside' the work. That's what really gets us. You can hear 'him' thinking, hear 'him' speaking to you through the music or the art that he has made.

"Same with all of this creation. If you are looking to see the art of this and the message behind it, first you learn to listen to the silence of the whole thing, ignore everything—then you'll see and you'll learn to hear through and behind the silence, to the guy who made it."

He grinned as she lay quietly thinking, engrossed in the exercise.

Moments went by as though years had come and gone and waited behind her like a crouching servant, ready to yell at her slightest understanding, "Ah ha!"

The thought scared her because of the encounter with the dingoes.

"I am for you..." Her eyes opened instantly.

She said she had looked up and seen Ulmarra standing a little distance away; she had not heard him get up and leave her alone. He turned and smiled subtly, as though he might have known she would hear something, and began to walk toward her. He held out his hand to her, and she reached up and grasped it to lift up from the sand.

"I think I heard something... Is that really possible, Wajilla?"

She turned as she told the story and looked in my eyes.

I nodded and whispered. "I heard it say 'Friend, I saw you.' And I can tell you, I knew exactly what he saw, and I can also tell you he's never seen me like that again."

She said she had asked Jimmy the same question, but Jimmy had ignored her, just as he wouldn't tell me what he'd heard.

She said they began to walk down the beach towards the jeep in the distance, and she frowned as she thought of the disconcerting moment she had experienced while Jimmy seemed happy to say nothing at all about it or anything.

Some ten minutes later he looked out to sea and finally said, "Go looking, and you are bound to find something."

"I never realized you were religious," she said.

"I'm not, I'm just a realist, and it isn't hard to work this out as soon as you look out there..."

"Just because 'this' is here doesn't mean something, someone, made it."

"Whether you want to believe it or not, it's still here." He smiled at her.

"You know that it's unlikely that Amy would be called 'Amy' if Mozart didn't create his special string of chords. You could listen to the wind for a trillion years; those notes would never happen without Mozart. He was the specific personality and cause; the music was just the effect of his expression." He swept his hand out to sea. "When you see all this, or even if you look in the mirror, you have no excuse not to realize that this is the effect of something planned, something executed, and you have been made to understand it."

"I don't have your—faith."

He looked across to her and grinned. "People struggled to believe the world wasn't flat too. Someone in 1969 had to get off the planet to find out it really was round, which was what a group of so-called nutters a thousands of years before had believed was true but just couldn't prove."

He knocked into her shoulder with his own and whispered, "An' people still think you are nuts if you 'believe but can't prove' that unorganized matter can't organize itself, so there *has* to be an orchestrator. And if you tell them to lie in the sand and 'listen for nothing,' so you can hear that orchestrator 'speak,' they want to lock you up somewhere or feed you drugs so you think it was just your imagination!" He had winked at her.

She looked me in the eye again and said, "I guess you don't think it was just your imagination, Wajilla?"

I said no, then said, "Best we don't tell anyone."

She went on telling me that she had asked Jimmy how he learned all this, and he had said he took the advice of his great, great, great grandmother, who learned it from the first Yidinji, one of which was Jimmy's great, great, great grandfather and a Yidinji message man.

He paused and somewhat shyly, offered, "If you are interested, I'll give you Margaret Stanford's diary to read."

"And she was who?"

"My ancestor, and the woman who made the foundation possible, and she also gave my family their name, Ulmarra. She wrote of her life with the Yidinji and the secrets she discovered from them. She had a pretty interesting life."

Jyly said she had realized this was a very great honor and thanked him saying, "I'd like to read it."

"She was a white, English woman."

"No kidding! White? Pure white?" It seemed odd to hear that as she walked along with him, his black hair and black skin sparkling with the light salt film all around them. "I don't think I've got anything else in me, just different tribes all mixed up, but I think we are just abos." She grinned and said her granddad used to say they were "purebred, mongrel abos."

He laughed, and then he said, "You wanna come on walk-about up in the Daintree at Cape York with me—an' Wajilla an' Amy?"

"Yeah, I guess so, if I'm not imposing."

"I wouldn't have asked if you were."

They made it back to the jeep, but when Jimmy tried to start it by hot-wiring it again, it wouldn't start.

"It's out of petrol."

"It's too far to walk!"

He looked serious.

"We can walk about fifteen kilometers a day, so we'll be back in about three days.

The thought scared her because of the encounter with the dingoes. She grimaced and slapped her thigh, and stifled an expletive.

Then he grinned broadly and pulled a cell phone out of his pocket. "That is, if we didn't have this."

She leaned over and slapped his shoulder.

Jimmy took a deep breath in and smiled as he looked into her face. The playful moment stopped for a moment as they looked at each other with a certain recognition of tenderness.

"Of course, I could drop the phone in the sea accidently, if you like."

Awakened to the meaning of the suggestion, she frowned slightly, not knowing how to reply. She might have considered it, but suddenly some internal thought about being out there alone with the much older and famous man broke her momentary pause, and she turned away saying, "Nah, I want bacon and eggs for breakfast, not something only a dingo would eat."

Jimmy nodded and phoned the ranger to tell them to come back with a can of petrol and a spare set of keys, as they seemed to have lost them.

Jyly sat down by the vehicle and leaned up against the wheel. Putting some distance between her and Jimmy seemed like the right thing to do.

Jimmy must have felt that she wanted to be alone and decided to walk up into the dunes.

He told me that he had also got a bit of a scare by the moment of attraction between them, and he felt oddly conscious of the 'wrong' of it, because he was so much older than the fresh, young woman.

He said he had called back to her, "Give me a yell if the rangers arrive or if you need me."

She nodded, the odd morning experiences obviously upsetting her slightly. She said she had watched him walk up the dunes and thought that if it was dangerous for two of them in the scrub with the dingoes, she wondered why he had no fear on his own.

She said she didn't stop him, though, and was left alone, staring out to the ocean. She had whispered to herself, "I am for you, eh?" and now she looked up at me, and an angry expression passed over her face.

"I was bloody confused by whatever it was I heard, and all I could think was, 'What the hell does that mean?'"

Chapter 7

JIMMY, JYLY, AND me all appeared through the door of the Ulmarra Foundation offices, where Louisa and Samson Donahue were staring at a newspaper.

Louisa looked up with concern on her face, but, as she saw Jyly standing near Jimmy, the look changed to utter distaste.

"Have you got any idea how bad this is for us?" She bit like a hungry shark at all of us.

I walked forward to take a look. The headlines of the paper read, Corruption Allegations in Scientific Conservation Foundation.

We talked back and forth about it and how this had come about. Louisa held up an official-looking letter and explained it was a legal demand for an audit, and that all the foundation accounts had been frozen until further notice.

"I didn't know about it until I went to pay this month's outstanding creditors, and none of the bank payments would go through."

I thought I might know what it was all about and sheepishly turned to Jimmy and whispered, "This could be something to do with Juniper."

Jimmy nodded.

Louisa saw us.

"What are you two talking about?" she demanded.

"Don't worry; we'll sort it out," I said.

She blew up in our faces with an angry outburst. "What 'we' are doing in this foundation is so important as to be lifesaving for the world, and nothing should put it in jeopardy! Nothing! The way you go on, you would think it is some 'indigenous only' mystery, and the rest of us are outside the circle. But when it comes to the work, we still have to be willing to give it everything we've got while you lot sort some secret thing out."

She used the, them-and-us line and slammed her hand down on the desk, making Donahue jump. Jimmy had a sad expression on his face, like she was a cat with her tail caught in the door, and, even though someone might be willing to save her, she was so tormented, no one could get near her to relieve her of whatever it was that was causing so much pain.

"Just because you all have the same kind of genes, you can't just shut the rest of us out as if you know something, and we don't belong in your special little world. You can't assume that we couldn't possibly understand because we didn't 'grow out of the land' like a bloody mushroom in some Dreamtime landscape."

That was about as much as I wanted to listen to, and right before I was ready to blast forth myself and storm out, Jimmy stopped her and said very quietly, "That isn't how it is, Lou."

"That *is* how it is!" she yelled at him. She turned to us almost in tears. "I have never once put a racial slant on anything you do. Never once have I not treated you as my own body, my own flesh—family. I never once referred to you in any way other than as human beings first, but right here, and right now, your silence is making me feel as though I am the one left out, because I have different genes, and that it isn't safe to tell me your little secrets. Because I'm not a precious indigenous person like you, I just work here—"

I began to get angry and started to give her a piece of my mind. "You shouldn't go there, 'Ms. Boss of All You Survey'! Hell, you make us feel like we are your little black fulla mates who give the right kind of credentials to all those government departments, and high flyers who don't mind donating their money, just so long as it looks like they are supporting their indigenous pets. We don't need that shit or your support; we got brains of our own. And this 'secret' you don't like being left out of—that's about family, not race. If you had one of your own, maybe you would understand."

That shut her up. Jimmy shook his head, and I realized I might have gone a bit far.

"Well—you're right. I don't have a 'family,'" she said quietly. "I've given up that option to put my life into this, and I thought—I would have a 'family' out of the people who felt like I did about it. I was wrong." She turned her back on us, and I heard her voice break, and her hand quickly swept up to her face to wipe it, and then she said, "I don't believe this is just about 'your family,'" and she turned sharply and looked squarely at Jyly.

The look was so obvious, it prompted an angry reply from the small woman. "Maybe if your lot hadn't stolen everything from us and destroyed the bloody world for us, you would understand why we don't want to be 'one of you,' and we wanna be our own people! That ain't no secret, lady—we been yelling it from the mountains since you lot first arrived!"

Louisa slammed her palms on the table and screamed, *"How dare you!"* Almost spitting in anger, she said, "You can't hold me responsible for a crime that happened a hundred years ago or make us hang our heads in shame for things we haven't done today. That is the ultimate race card in reverse! And anyway, hasn't every last Australian paid out for those crimes fifty times over and still can't get free of it?" She yelled, " *When is it going to be over? When is everyone just going to drop it and become 'Australian?' What color is that? Purple, green, something with stripes, perhaps?* She wouldn't stop. "When is the 'National Sorry Day' going to mean, 'Okay, it's over, we forgive you, your children, your children's children, and hell, we'll even forgive the kids who haven't even been thought of yet in a hundred years' time. Or are you going to hold out your hand even then, way out in that future, and try to ram those past crimes down those future innocent babies throats and tax them too?"

I saw red, and Jyly erupted. The fight accelerated with Samson getting his boot in too, siding with Louisa. The four of us threw insults back and forth—crime and counter-crime, justice denied, justice defended—for a good five minutes. Every one of Louisa's tears dried up, and there was only steam 'n' brimstone coming out of her, and flamethrowers coming out of our mouths!

Jimmy, who had been silent, finally stepped in. He picked up a chair and placed it in the center of the room under the light and stood up on it. He lifted up his arms and shifted the clear ceiling panel and then started to unscrew the fluorescent light.

We all stopped, one by one, and watched him.

"What the hell are you doing?" Louisa asked sharply, and he said very calmly, as the light went off, "Letting you stand here in darkness, so you know how you all sound to me when you speak that crap that belongs in the Dark Ages." He got down from the chair and walked out.

We watched his silhouette as he passed out of the room, with one tube under his arm and the other in his fist, and closed the door behind him.

I stood in the pitch-black office, and I could hear the shuffling of the others as they moved about.

Suddenly Louisa's voice broke the silence right opposite me. "Alright—I'm sorry."

Jyly replied from somewhere a bit further away. "I am too, I guess."

Sam said quietly, "It's always just under the surface, even with us—we need to get rid of it."

I was last, and I couldn't quite say how I felt, so I volunteered, "How 'bout a beer; it's bloody hot in here."

One by one, we left the room and headed off to the bottle store, with Louisa, Donahue, and Jyly saying they'd go and get some meat and salads, and we'd have a BBQ.

I said I'd find Ulmarra and drag him along too—after I'd groveled at his feet for a while and apologized for all of us.

We set up a BBQ at the botanical gardens. It had rained earlier, but the sky was peacock blue and the few fluffy clouds were rising over the range to the west to escape after dumping the load they'd picked up over the Coral Sea.

The scene was casual, and behind us in the parklands was a huge lake flowering with white, pink, and purple lilies. Smoke and the smell of meat on the fire swirled around us lazily, and we were feeling happier than the hour before.

Louisa was mixing salad on the picnic table, Sam and Amy were walking near the lake, and Jimmy and Jyly were holding Crown lagers and watching as they sat on the edge of the picnic table.

I was poking the meat as it cooked. The atmosphere had calmed, and Jyly volunteered her feelings of sorrow that things don't always go smoothly when pressure is put on, and she asked what they could do about the legal events against the foundation.

Louisa said that what was likely to happen was an audit, and that the matter shouldn't be too difficult or take too long, because every cent was accounted for and always had been. She laughed and said, "Right down to the two hundred dollars I thought had been missing but was there after all; I just hadn't seen it in the bottom of the cash tin."

I looked up sheepishly and said, "We are going to have to do something to make sure the findings of the inquiry are published everywhere, and they should get in touch with every supporter to make sure everyone knows it is just negative publicity because of some disgruntled person."

Louisa took the comment as an opportunity to ask, "So—are you going to tell me now?"

Jimmy looked up, and he paused, deciding whether he should keep it from her or not, considering what was said before.

I looked at Jimmy, and I spoke to Louisa without taking my eyes off him. "I was not having you on, Lou, when I said it was a family thing." I didn't want to reveal the matter fully, because I didn't want to upset Jyly by revealing her part in it.

Jyly looked up sternly. But then she surprised me before I had a chance to say anything more. "It was Juniper who raped me. I scratched him, and they found out, and they took him away..."

I smiled at her and said, "Good on you, Jilly Bird!" Then I turned to Louisa. "He deserved what we did to him, Lou."

Louisa angrily blurted out, "You mean all that work and time wasted with the police and all that checking and interviewing, and you knew all along who it was!"

We all discussed it and why we didn't tell her, and she seemed to accept it.

I suddenly saw my son and Sam walking towards the lake edge, and I jumped up and yelled out, "Hey—don't get near the water; there's supposed to be a croc in there."

Louisa looked up with interest. "Really?"

"Yeah, a taxi driver I know said he and his kid saw it out on the island in the middle, but the council haven't been able to catch it. It comes up from the sea, because this creek meets up with a tidal creek up past the airport." We all fell silent, as though the momentary distraction hadn't worked and we knew it.

Louisa spoke up. "So what did you do with him?"

Jimmy looked at me and nodded. I told her about 'the ancient punishment' we gave Juniper.

Louisa erupted when she heard about it. She broke into a flurry of disapproval. "You just can't do that sort of thing as though aboriginal law is higher than the law of the land!" She ended the tirade with a desperate, almost pleading, comment: "You have got to understand. You are not separate."

Jimmy surprised her by saying, "You are right, Lou, absolutely right. But how can I explain without you getting all defensive—"

I broke in. "We are all the same but—"

Jyly whispered beside me, "But we are different."

Louisa looked down at her hands. "Well, maybe Juniper's different, because he is indigenous, but he's the same where it counts. And now he's bloody pissed off, and he is going to be a thorn in our side, because he thinks he deserves justice for himself, because of what you did to him, and he can't get it without incriminating himself."

I said, "Maybe—but he ain't gonna hurt a woman again, because the Yidinji way works."

"So what—he's going to hurt us instead! He'll be the one that has stirred up all this stuff about the foundation being corrupt." She slapped her thigh, almost talking to herself. "Of course it's him that's started this; it's too obvious for words!"

Louisa angrily looked up at me and returned to my remark. "And what does it mean to be Yidinji, anyway? No one is full Yidinji anymore, and there are only eleven people left who can even speak the language! The only thing you can be sure of is the cops are going to turn up sometime and charge you with assault!"

I answered shyly, "Na, he won't say anything—we don't say nothing about that stuff."

She shook her head and said sarcastically, "Typical—even now, the 'secret squirrel' society. Well, whatever you think, he's saying something to someone! And now the news is spreading crap about us, and we got a pile of questioning coming our way. Even when they find out it's all groundless, there will still be people out there who believe there's something crooked about us—and all because you got some half-baked brat stirred up by your ancient code that no one understands the sense of anymore."

Jyly broke in and said, "Nah. If they believe there is something going on, it's *because* we are black fullas—not counting you an' Sam."

Jimmy spoke up. "There might be some fullas that think like that, Jyly, but it isn't about what color we are—it's because people, black and white, enjoy thinking the worst about each other. If there is a rumor or hint of something bad, people clan together and start stoning whoever stands still to get hit, innocent or guilty."

Louisa nodded. "Well, you are right about that—now we have to make sure we aren't 'standing still' about this. I'm going to see our lawyers tomorrow."

After the BBQ, and most all of us, having returned to a team and a family of sorts, had gone off separately to our own homes, I said I'd see Louisa home, because she had come with us and left her car behind at her apartment.

I saw her inside, and she said, "Stay for ten minutes, Wajilla, so I don't feel so damned lonely up here tonight."

I knew Lou well, and I could see she was more upset by the 'upset' than she had let on. Louisa sat in her lounge room alone, while I got her a glass of wine and put it in her hand. She was looking very defeated and depressed.

"Lou, you know I didn't really mean that shot I said to you earlier. I know what you've given up—and hell, I think of you as my sister, especially since my one's an idiot. See, I'm like you! I don't have everything. No wife, no one to stick by me, just a crazy for a sister and a mongrel of a half-brother. So I really mean it when I say I think of you as someone real close—not like a wife, of course, but definitely a sister. Hell, you're the kind of sister any man would be proud to have, eh? You're smart, bloody smart—beautiful, wise—an' you've got good legs!"

"Okay, that's enough; I get the picture."

"So are we okay again?"

"If you can just forget it and be normal again and don't notice my legs too often."

"Ah—okay, you're on!" I looked at her, and even though the words had come out of her mouth, I wasn't convinced she was feeling any better, because the only one who could say anything that would really make her feel good was Jimmy, and he wasn't here, for good reason.

"Do you want to watch the TV?" I asked gently.

"Yeah, okay." I turned it on for her and took off to raid her fridge.

As she watched TV, she saw a newscast story, and she leaned forward, wide-eyed, to listen as they recounted the famous activities of the foundation planting huge areas of Australian farmland and wasteland back into forests.

She yelled out to me, "Wajilla—there's something on about us. Come out here!"

The story went on to list the accusations that "insiders" of the foundation had supposedly raised of corrupt practices, bullying of farmers to get land, and money being skimmed off government grants to give foundation members free travel and luxury properties.

I said, "Bullshit!"

And Louisa said, "Shah!"

The face of a woman, introduced as Maria Ferris, came on the screen. She strongly argued that the hype about global warming was politically motivated and that there was little or no proof that the phenomenon was anything but natural and would right itself with fluctuating cycles of the earth cooling itself anyway.

"I agree reducing carbon and so on is not a bad idea, but wholesale hysteria is worthless! Humans have rights too, and farmers are entitled to earn a living without this dramatized rhetoric ruining their chances of supporting their families."

Louisa and I watched with increasing distress as this woman said that communities rely on mining and farms to feed their families, buy houses, and afford imports from overseas from countries that were doing almost nothing to stem their own emissions.

When she was asked about the intensive farming towers being created to compensate farmers in this country for the traditional incomes they used to get from their land, she responded fiercely. "Conservationists continually flog this argument for a return to 'responsible natural practices,' but these towers are using crop seed that is nothing like natural! They conveniently ignore what effects this kind of 'genetically modified' material grown in these huge sci-fi towers springing up all over the place will also do to the environment if it gets out, or anyone who eats what they grow in there. I mean, I wouldn't want my children to be fed anything that came out of those IFT towers—"

The interviewer interrupted her to say, "Surely, if there are good regulations to protect the public, the pluses must outweigh the negatives."

Maria outmaneuvered the question and simply said, "This minority movement must be stopped one way or another. It's a corrupt organization, and there will be nothing but disaster if it's allowed to continue."

Louisa spoke to the screen, "How can they say this rubbish?" Then she put her hand to her temple and whispered to herself, "God—the knives are well and truly out now. They say they have evidence from 'insiders! That's got to be Juniper. You and bloody Jimmy—you should have left him to the police. What have you done to us?"

I didn't say anything back. I could see what we had done, so I just moved off behind her and slid out the door and went home.

Chapter 8

S AM AND I came into the offices and approached Louisa. She was on the phone and speaking earnestly to someone about what could be done about the false accusations leveled at the foundation. We could hear her telling the other person that she was not really keen to be on camera, but for the sake of the foundation she knew that the accusations had to be answered.

We heard her say, "No, he will never agree to that," and we could easily deduce that they must have been asking if they could interview Jimmy Ulmarra. She repeated it again and said that the foundation is not "Jimmy Ulmarra" alone but a group of dedicated people all working together on a common goal, which is restoration of the natural rhythms of the planet's climate by replanting huge areas of cleared land.

Sam whispers in her ear, "And we find alternative methods of feeding the ever-growing population, so land isn't cleared in the first place." She looked at him and shooed him away.

When she finished the call, Donahue asked her what that was all about, she told him Channel Nine was going to run a piece on the foundation's work on *A Current Affair*. She told him they were going to interview her.

He asked her if she thought that might be a bit risky, and that he didn't think that they should be drawing the spotlight on themselves until they were "out of the woods, so to speak." He said he thought it would be better to just ignore it and hope the whole thing goes away.

"No, it's time people knew the scientific facts about global warming, and this will give us a chance to show that. It might drum up support and drown out the negative rubbish, when people see how important our work is."

"I don't think it will work," Sam said.

"Look, the most important thing is to use the opportunity to make more people aware," Louisa insisted. "Eventually everyone will know we're innocent anyway, so I want to make sure the real issues are heard. I'm not going to let the chance to get some free airtime slip past us. Someone out there thinks they have got us; now we can turn it back to the facts."

As she was talking, Jimmy and Jyly appeared.

Louisa was a bit cool towards them, but Sam was far warmer and asked Jimmy, "How's the dingo transfer going? Are you still going to be able to go ahead?"

"We are. The dogs are coming up from Frazer Island, then we'll go up and release them, after they've been through their quarantine period. We're going up end of the week to see if the quarantine center is ready and make sure they arrive safely. Some of the animal-rescue people are coming up to volunteer and keep an eye on the wild pack: feed them and look after security. You wanna come up and take a look too?"

"Sorry, mate, I got a fish tank to fill Thursday."

"Mate, you don't know what you're missing! While we are up there, we are going take a trek into the reserve and check the fencing that will keep 'em inside the park. Hopefully, we can identify where the native pack are and mark out any changes to their range, so we can find the best location for the release of the new animals."

Jimmy moved across to Louisa, and, as she looked through some papers, he told her Jyly would be accompanying himself and me on the trip up there.

Louisa looked up and sarcastically said, "The three musketeers."

Jimmy took a deep breath in and said, "Four—we're taking Amy up too. It's time he had a bit of a walkabout."

Louisa looked up and asked, "Isn't he a bit young for that?"

"If he was born a hundred years ago, he would have been out on his own at about seven and know how to look after himself by now—and there was no helicopters to rescue you back then!"

She laughed and said jokingly, "You and helicopters don't go too well together, anyway."

He grinned.

Louisa finally addressed Jyly. "You better keep an eye on that kid; he's a mate of mine, and I won't be pleased if he's eaten by something."

Jyly smiled, as the banter had relieved the tension in the room. ' I'll be in good company, so I guess me and Amy will be safe enough."

"Yeah—well, you make sure you are; I don't want only two or three musketeers to come back—it's got to be a full hand."

Jimmy said good-bye and told her he would see her on Sunday when they got back.

Louisa just nodded.

We left the office and walked out to the car park to get organized. Jimmy said to wait for him; he had forgotten something. He turned on his heel and skipped back inside the building.

Jyly watched him go, and, I don't know why, but I suddenly felt like I should keep her occupied and distracted from his going.

Louisa told me a long time later, after all the trouble was finished, he had come back into the office when he left us out in the car park and walked up to her as she sat at her desk.

"Lou—it'll be all right. You are doing good, and you'll be great with Channel Nine."

She said he had put his palms around her face and kissed her on the forehead.

"Jimmy," she whispered, but he didn't say any more, nor did he wait but turned and left again, calling back, "The foundation and what it is doing is all that matters, Lou. Keep your eye on that for me—keep your eye on that."

We got up to the quarantine station in time to see the choppers flying in with the dogs crated up in individual boxes, all joined in a long train. They were suspended in the air and had had to be flown in because the road was too difficult and the stress on the animals would have been too great to bring them all the way from Fraser Island by road transport.

The location was remote, beyond the mountains to the northeast, where a large area had been enclosed with tall, double, dingo-proof fences. The area had sparse vegetation and was not the lush rain forest of the coastal belt. The reforestation reserve was twenty kilometers from the quarantine station to ensure that any native dingoes could not be cross-contaminated and to let the new dogs settle without hearing their cousins howling in the autumn evenings.

When Jimmy and our team arrived, the dogs landed in a swirl of dust, and several keepers unhooked the chains they were attached to, and the chopper sailed up like a balloon that had been let go. The quarantine keepers looked quietly around each box.

We attached a purpose-built funnel arrangement, so the dogs could be released from the crates and encouraged to enter their open pen without being anesthetized, or stressed by human contact. We could hear them inside their crates, thumping from time to time, even though they had been fed sedatives before being trapped and flown up very early that morning.

When we opened the first slide door, we were all hiding behind brush screens, and the first dog didn't come out. I had the horrible feeling that maybe something had gone wrong.

Ulmarra peered out from his screen, and he walked a little way out along the link-chain funnel and peered into the door. The dark shadow of the interior meant he couldn't see much. He stood up and shrugged. Just as he did, a sandy snout appeared low in the doorway. Jimmy quietly stepped back and watched from afar with his hands on his hips.

Suddenly the dog shot forward, slamming into the fence. Not sure where it was or what direction to run, it spun around, and might have run back into the box.

Jimmy rushed forward and placed his hand on the top of the mesh, and the dog turned again and bolted forward. When it saw the opening toward what looked like freedom, it raced so fast to the opening that a trail of dust wafted up in the slight breeze from its frantic paws.

"We need to put hessian on the lower parts of the race, so they move towards the cage and don't hit the wire." Jimmy quietly spoke to the keepers behind the screens. For the next twenty minutes, we rigged that along the race and got ready for the next one.

"Could be a long day," I said to Jyly and Amy, who was watching with wide eyes.

"Well, we got one in," Amy said brightly.

"Only five to go." Jyly smiled.

The second dog took off fast from her crate too but wouldn't go through into the cage. We waited a good ten minutes before one of the keepers walked out. Before he had got three feet towards the mesh, she saw him approaching from inside the crate and turned and fled towards the pen. The problem was, she kept on going, and very soon we heard a crash on the fence on the far side of the enclosure.

Dogs three and four could smell the trail of their mates, so they trotted quickly into the enclosure without mishap.

The big male was the last to go. He stopped a couple of times and looked around but trotted into the enclosure and spent the next hour shifting position, sniffing every blade of grass and searching out the perimeter of his cage.

We shut the door and erected the last brush screen, so they were enclosed.

The three younger dogs raced desperately toward one section of fence or another, some slamming into it with, looking up and around, trying to find a way to escape. Some of them let out their fear on each other, and a few small pecking-order fights broke out. We could hear occasional yelps, so we knew that they were terribly distressed, even though they had had minimum human contact and couldn't see us.

We all remained hidden behind brush fences and watched to see that the wild dogs were all right.

Jyly said she thought they had been sedated, and Jimmy replied, "They still are."

The dogs flashed about, searching, then Jimmy spied the top dog through a tiny gap in the brush. He was the big one they had first seen in the dunes of Frazer Island. He pointed it out to me and Jyly, and we all watched as the big dog also dashed about, searching for escape.

In the center of the enclosure, he suddenly paused and took a glance at the brush fence where we were hidden. Jyly noticed the behavior and said, "They know we are here."

"Of course they do," I replied. "The question is, Will they settle down, or kill themselves on those fences!"

Jimmy watched the leader and said, "They'll settle. The big fulla has already decided he will take it in stride, and the others will follow suit." He smiled at me and said, "You know that people always think that dogs are man's best friend because they fit in with our way of doing things, but, really, it is the other way around. Humans are very like dogs in their behavior, and if a strong leader shows himself, everyone else follows, no matter if the direction is good or bad."

"Yep," I agreed, "we call that 'government.'"

Jimmy looked across at them and whispered, "Well, I hope Louisa can handle the dogs we are up against down south on her own. It's bad timing, us being here."

"Yeah, but she's the Queen, mate—she'll eat that bitch Maria Ferris for breakfast, don't worry about that!"

I excused myself and said I was going to the huts. They were a kilometer away from the pens to keep human scents away. I took hold of Amy's hand and said, "We'll leave you to it. I gotta see to Amy's lunch." It was well after three, and the kid looked tired. I was starving too.

Jimmy and Jyly were left together alone behind the fence. They watched as the top dog lay down on a slightly higher mound, and Jimmy whispered, "Good boy—you show 'em."

Jyly told me later he had quietly collected her hand, and, for a moment, she turned, and they looked at each other. He stuttered slightly, as though he wanted to say something other than what he did. "Come on—they will be okay. Best thing for them is for us to get out of here." He pointed up to the security cameras placed on poles and on the fences in various positions to observe the animals without disturbing them and said, "Big Brother is on guard, anyway."

Back at the huts, Amy and me had "lunch" at almost four in the afternoon, and then we organized packs and gear for the trek into the mountain area, where the reserve hides its deepest secrets.

Jimmy strode toward us with Jyly alongside and commented on the size of the packs. He laughed and said, "Why do we need all that stuff? I thought we were going on walkabout to teach Amy how to survive the old way!"

I replied, "They are exactly the size they need to be! I'm too soft now to be without some civilized comforts: things like, something to sleep on, some chocolate—the important stuff."

Jimmy shook his head and said the boy had better go with him, or he was never going to learn anything out there.

Amy immediately perked up and said that he wanted to go with Jimmy.

But I shook my head and said, "I'd rather you be only half Yidinji and fully alive at the end of this, than be all 'wild' like this bloke." I pointed to Ulmarra. "I'd never be sure where you were or even if you were still alive."

"Dad—you are a real scaredy cat. Uncle Jimmy knows everything about out there. He'll look after me."

I was sure that was true, actually, but I wasn't going to admit that I liked being with my son and didn't really want to share him on his first walkabout.

Jyly appeared, and the young boy greeted her affectionately as Jimmy and me discussed when we would set out. We decided that we would leave in the morning before dawn and try to make it up to the ravine on the south side of the reserve and make camp at the billabong we knew was there.

Amadeus was excited, and he pulled out his phone and started texting someone.

Jimmy shook his head as he started to walk away, and the boy looked up to me and said, "Hey, I can't get reception!"

I laughed and told him, "That would be right, mate, and there is no pizza delivery out here either."

Jyly grinned and told him he would have to go cold turkey and leave the phone behind. The kid shook his head and said, "I still have games, Aunty, so I gotta take it, or I'll get bored."

She laughed and nodded towards me and said, "I guess that's life as a modern kid."

"No kidding."

One of the quarantine keepers walked across the compound and waved out to us before meeting us. "They are going to try and feed the dingoes this evening. Do you want to go up and watch?" she asked.

"Yeah, Dad, I wanna go, can we?"

"I want to go up too." Jyly smiled, and her eyes were as wide as my young boy's.

"I don't really want to go; I'm stuffed."

"Jyly can take me, Dad!"

"Can I?" she said.

"Okay, if you want to, but stick close to Jyly. And don't do anything to upset them blokes."

The keeper said she was going to walk up after she had something to eat first, so Amy and Jyly trotted along beside her, and I headed off for the kitchen.

About two hours later, Jimmy, Jyly, and Amy all arrived back. The kid was quiet, and he said he was going to our hut.

I looked at Jyly and said, "What's wrong with the boy?"

"We had a bit of a reality check." Jyly sucked in a deep breath. "It was a bit rough for me too."

"What happened?" I turned and looked across at Jimmy.

"They fed them live wallaby."

"What?"

"Well, they're wild dingoes, so they gave them natural prey." Jimmy looked up from his coffee.

Jyly cut in, "Yes, but it turned out that Amy wasn't quite ready for what dingoes do with 'natural prey.' When they let three wallaby into the cage, the dogs just sprang to life, and it took about a minute and a half, and they had corralled them up against the fences, strangled them, and torn them to pieces." Jyly looked at me and said, "I think it is safe to say that I have a new respect for dingoes. And there ain't no way I'm going to walk into that reserve without Dr. Ulmarra with me, because those dogs know how to kill."

"You worry over nothing." Jimmy took a deep breath. "I'm going to ring Louisa and see if she's got everything under control, then I'm going to have a shower and go to bed."

"I guess I had better see to the boy." I looked across at Jyly.

"I'll go and check on him if you like?"

Just at that moment, one of the animal-rescue people shuffled into the room. She had been caring for a distressed fruit-bat baby. It had been clinging to its mother when she had accidentally flown into a power line in the city and died. The animal-rescue girl couldn't leave it back in Cairns, because she was having to feed it four times hourly. It was wrapped in a small towel, and she had been carrying it everywhere.

Jyly took a look and was immediately in love.

"We should show her to Amy; that would cheer him up," she said with great enthusiasm.

I said that was a good idea, and they trotted off, crooning over the bat baby and taking it over to where our cabins were, on the other side of the compound.

The story of the dogs "doing what they do naturally" made me somehow curious, so I decided to call in at the surveillance control room before turning in.

"G'dday; is there room for a small one in here?" I opened the door and shuffled into the small office. There were three screens flicking from one shot to another of the cage and its surrounds.

"G'dday, Wajilla; you've missed all the action."

"I heard about it. How are they now? Have they settled down?"

"One of them has regurgitated his dinner and buried it down by that bush." His finger pointed to a fence post hidden with a round brush plant.

Watching with the two volunteers on the closed circuit screens, I suddenly spotted Ulmarra.

He had not gone to bed after all. Instead, he had disappeared up the one-kilometer track that led to the dingo pens. It must have been pitch-black when he got there, but somehow he could see, and he crept up through the undergrowth, downwind of the fences. He was looking like a pretty skilled abo tracker as he came on camera, and it looked like the dogs didn't know he was there. He squatted down on his haunches and watched.

The guy turned and smiled at me and said, "Ulmarra is doing his own checking—look at that, the dogs haven't changed their behavior at all; they don't know he is there."

I replied, "I doubt that—these are dingoes; nothing gets past them."

In answer to my comment, we watched the screen and saw the big dog look over his shoulder and stand up. He trotted left, then right, and headed towards the fence, stopping some eight feet from where Jimmy was seated. We saw the dog drop his head and sniff ahead of him, seemingly curious and unafraid.

The other bloke watching said, "I hope that one hasn't already become too casual about humans."

The first guy nodded, saying, "It will be the death of him if he has."

I stayed quiet for once. I watched as Jimmy stood, and the dog instantly flashed away into the interior of the pen. My crazy friend walked off camera, I guess to head back towards the camp.

"Well, looks like everything is okay, so I'm going to bed. We gotta get going before dawn tomorrow. We are going to walk into the reserve and find the native pack in there, with any luck."

"Good luck," the first man said, without shifting his eyes off the now-empty screens. "Just keep in mind there won't be a fence between you and them."

"Thanks!" I said.

I headed off to Amy's and my cabin, and the whole way I fought with myself as to whether I had done the right thing by bringing him up here for his first walkabout. While I was thinking about it, my mind kept replaying the sight of Ulmarra, squatting on his haunches with the big dingo standing in the dark, sniffing and watching.

By the time I got to my door, I was saying to myself, "It'll be okay..."

Chapter 9

IN THE EARLY morning light, the four of us were threading our way through the undergrowth, following animal trails. We had already been walking about an hour and a half. We had started in the dark and watched the warm light of dawn turn the night callers into the morning chorus and the trees from specters to reverent worshipers of the sun.

Jimmy was leading our troupe. Amy followed him; a little way behind was Jyly, and I was making up the rear. The odd fly buzzed around us, and I swept one away from my face. The air was clean and clear, and the sky blazing with gold and mauve hues.

My legs had already warmed up and settled into the rhythm of the walk, as I followed the bent grasses of the three in front of me and sucked in that air and the scene around us. I had a feeling as close to joy as I could imagine joy being.

Jimmy suddenly stopped, and the boy quickly came alongside. Jimmy rested his hand on the boy's shoulder and pointed ahead with his other.

Stalking through the undergrowth some way ahead was a tall cassowary bird a little shorter than an ostrich, but his high comb of bone and blue-flushed face and throat could be clearly seen as he pecked off leaves and seeds.

Some twenty yards behind was another one, which stopped and looked about cautiously. Suddenly realizing they were not alone in the thickening forest of the upcoming ravine, the first bird dashed forward and crashed through the brush to escape. The other one did likewise but stopped and looked around quickly, trying to discern what manner of animal was there with them.

Jimmy lifted up his hands, caped them over his mouth, and made an odd noise. The cassowary looked in the direction of the sound, stood dead-still for a moment or two, then, reassured by the call Jimmy had made, it sauntered away, clearly not interested in us after all.

I said to Amy, "That was good, eh—wild ones, you don't see them much now."

"That's because they're so dumb they were easily caught and eaten in the old days, and these days there isn't enough land left wild for them."

The boy piped up and said, "But we are doing something about that, eh, Uncle?"

"Yes—come back in a hundred years, and you might see lots of them."

We walked on and headed towards high buttresses up ahead. Beautiful granite cliffs, carved and weathered, rose up from the trees.

Jimmy stopped occasionally to show Amy some plant or other, pointing to the ground or to some insect that was needed by the plant or vice versa.

Above us, bird sounds pierced the air at odd intervals, and the scent of green bush and eucalyptus groves filled the air.

We climbed up into the gorge and finally came upon a green water hole captured in the cleft of the huge rock formations. Making camp, we settled down to eat, and I broke into my pack for much-needed supplies, because, by the time we had walked that far, I was feeling like I was running on empty.

Jimmy, however, told Amy to follow him, and they disappeared.

They returned sometime later, maybe half an hour, and young Amy was running towards Jyly and me, carrying a large, dead goanna, and Jimmy was grinning from behind with a pile of various greens in his hand.

I inspected the monster, and Jyly commended the boy as he excitedly and knowledgeably told us where to find the lizards and how to catch one without being bitten by the poisonous creature.

Jimmy called the boy aside and showed him how, with the aid of a stone, he could pierce the tough skin and pull it off and then gut it and stuff it with the greens. He tied the carcass together with a thick grass twine and covered it in mud that he had found near the water hole. Then he showed Amy how to start a fire and what wood to use that would make good embers.

I was munching on my chocolate bar and watching on, glad I had thought to bring decent food with me.

Jimmy laid the clay cocoon in the heat of the ashes to roast.

When it was cooked, we all had some, and I had to admit, it was pretty good.

We settled down to rest for a while, then Amy and Jyly decided to take a swim, not even bothering to take off their clothes. Jimmy and me got roped into it too, and we all splashed and lazed in the cool water while the heat of the day ascended overhead.

In the afternoon, Jimmy showed Amy how to make a buru while I fought with a light pup tent and Jyly quickly erected hers.

By the end of the day, Amy was tired and fell asleep inside his buru hut as soon as he hit his pile of leaves. Jyly was really tired after our trek and the first day in the reserve and adjourned to her tent to sleep on top of her sleeping bag, because it was warm that evening.

Only Jimmy and I remained awake.

I said I was going to take a leak, and when I came back, he was gone. He had left our impromptu "village" and climbed up in the dark to the edge of a precipice to listen to the night.

I thought I'd go up and keep him company and followed him, even though my legs ached, but the call of the night compelled me, and I clambered up to find him.

"Thought you'd never get up here, mate," Jimmy greeted me, when I finally caught up with him. "You climb like a girl, and you sound like a grunting bandicoot." He appeared like a ghost out of the black sky and held out his hand to pull me up the last step.

"It's the chocolate."

"Yeah—listen!" he said, mesmerized by evening sounds. Soon I could hear the familiar notes of howling far in the distance, and we waited, unmoving, to hear them again. Finally he whispered to himself, "See you tomorrow, guys." He took a step forward as though he might just transform into one of them and run off into the dark and leave me there, but turned and said, "Come on, mate, need to get your soft bones into that comfy bed." By that point I couldn't have agreed more, so we climbed down in the dark to the camp below, and I crawled into my tent and went out like a light.

Daybreak, we made breakfast and cleaned up the camp. Amy had a few things to say about various insects that seemed to seek shelter in his buru during the night, and he was a bit sore from walking the day before and sleeping on the ground.

I said, "Toughen up, boy!" and Jimmy said, "It won't take long, and you will feel like you lived your whole life out here." The kid nodded, but I don't think he believed him.

We set off up the ravine, because it ascended to a tight point and then tipped up and over to a higher plateau. Jimmy explained that he knew the small dingo pack we wanted to find was ranging far to the east side of the gorge, so we would have to pick our way around the edge to take note of their territory marks and roughly work out where the dogs were operating.

When we reached the top and walked along the edge for a while, observing the beautiful views of the blue hazy cliffs on the other side, I spoke to Jimmy about how I could see a way down and up the other side that would shorten our distance across by hours. Jimmy agreed, but he pointed out that he was pretty sure the dog's territory included the apex of the curve around to our left in front of us, and he'd like to find out how far around this side they were hunting. He suggested we split up. He said he and Amy could go the long way around alone, since it would be safer than the climb up the other side.

I laughed and said, "Jimmy, mate—you just want time to convert my son into a native!"

Jimmy grinned and replied, "It won't hurt him, mate—you don't want him to turn out like you, do ya?"

I laughed, and the truth was, I didn't want him to turn out like me—at least, I didn't want him to end up with my waistline, so I said, "Your call, mate—just keep him out of the way of them dingoes."

So Jyly and me headed off towards a downward incline that would take us to the floor of the gorge. And Jimmy yelled out as we went, "See you in a couple of days."

Amy later told me how that little private walk went, and when he did, I admit I was happy they went together and slightly envious too. It's one thing to know about your roots and your culture and the Dreamtime you belong to—but to have it "in" you, and to live it like it was real, was something few of my family had experienced. Jimmy reckoned that was because you learned it from your elders, but you practiced it in the silence of the land itself. Jimmy was the only abo I knew who had done that. Everyone else watched TV, ate burgers, and drank Four X or Jack and had a Camel hanging off his mouth.

Amy said they had walked a long way. The day moved on, and the boy and his elder stalked through the trees around the top of the gorge's rim.

Jimmy told the boy they should stop for lunch. He pointed Amy to a large log and showed him how to roll it over and start stripping off sections of rotting, dry wood. As the tree opened up, he found the long tunnels of white grubs the size of a man's thumb, and he pulled one out, held its black head in his fingers, and told the boy, "Always eat them this way, Amy, so the 'crunchy bits' don't get stuck in your teeth."

Amy told me he had thought it was pretty gross but gingerly did likewise. He said he had struggled to bite into one, and he told me very brightly, "It popped, Dad! And squirted all down my chin!"

Jimmy had exclaimed, "Not like that! Put the whole thing in your mouth." He smiled as he demonstrated with a second one. "Mmmm"—he grinned—"tastes like chicken."

The boy summoned up the courage to follow suit and gingerly chewed the thick, white morsel. Jimmy said he nearly choked with laughter as the boy's expression changed slowly from horror to acceptance, and he declared very proudly, "It does taste like chicken—with that peanut sauce Dad likes."

Jimmy's eyes rested on the boy for a moment, then he said, "Come on, let's take a detour—I know somewhere you should see.

Jimmy later said the boy had been dragging his feet a bit as they walked through the bush by the afternoon, but they made it to the secret place. Ahead, a rocky outcrop and a few scraggy trees appeared in a clearing. A small pool was caught in rocks that had been worn smooth, sloping down to show where an ancient watercourse had flowed. Twisted formations showed where the water had poured over various escarpments and left the sculpture.

"Dad, I asked Uncle Jimmy what that place was. And he smiled and said to me, "It's a Dreamtime place, son.""

The boy had cocked his head on its side, because he still didn't understand the Dreamtime, and he looked around the area. "How do you know this place, Uncle ..." Amy had asked.

Jimmy puffed a little as he climbed up one level and turned back to look down at Amy standing below him and then he looked around, surveying the vista. "Was an old voice I heard while I was on walkabout when I was only a bit older than you. That voice told me where this place was."

"You came out here by yourself, Uncle?"

Jimmy turned and disappeared into a bushy crevice, then reappeared below. "Take off your shirt," he told the young boy, "and your shoes, 'cause this place is a sacred place."

The boy did as he was told.

Jimmy gathered up water in his open palms and spread it over the boy's head, and he did the same to himself. Then he started to sing an aboriginal chant. The boy listened and watched wide eyed. When Jimmy was finished, he said, "It's okay now—them spirits know who we are and what we are here for, so they not gonna hurt us. I'll teach you that song, so you don't ever get trouble, no matter where you go in life—it even works with white man's stuff too."

"How did you learn it?" Amy asked, and Jimmy told him, "I 'knowed it' in my heart all along, but the elders at Yarabah showed me the right language to sing in, so I didn't look like an uneducated drongo to them spirits that listen out for us." Jimmy turned and climbed back up the rocks.

The boy hurried up behind him. As he followed, the rock ledge led to a section of semi-open cave.

I can bet that's one amazing place, wherever it is. A surreal place but to this day I don't know where it is. As far as I know, no one does. Yeah, what

I would have given to be there with them but some moments are special and don't belong to you, they're a gift just to the person they are meant for.

My boy described it like it was a box office movie, his arms flying all around and his eyes flicking as though he could see it all again. He said sections of roof had showed the sky as the river had carved the rock away. And when the two dropped down into the cave, a dusty floor spread out under a low section of roof. In the powdery dust, a set of young footprints wandered about and led to the end of the first section.

Jimmy looked at them. "Someone's been here, Uncle, look!"

"Me, boy—only me, long time ago." He looked at them intently and smiled as he showed Amy into the cave.

As they walked forward, Jimmy pointed up at a ceiling covered in ancient aboriginal paintings, some vivid, others faded and worn. The red, white, and black outlines showed animals and hunting scenes.

Amy whispered, "Wow!"

Jimmy showed him around the whole cave system and explained what different paintings might mean, and how they hadn't been touched for thousands of years. He showed Amy how some of the pictures were "wishing" pictures. "They used to bring into being the thing the picture is saying. See this one? This one tells the Dreamtime spirits that they should make this man have a good hunt, and he's gonna catch a big roo. An' this one here—it's saying that this man and this one here, they are going fishin', but that big ol' croc is sitting over here on the bank an' it's not going to come in the water and get them, see? They are over here now, all safe, with plenty of fat fish."

"So is what they painted going to be what comes true?"

"Yep. They know they can make it happen by starting it in the other world, then they put it here on these rocks, so it'll come out in this world."

I watched my son as he told the story. His face was animated, and his hands swept over the air like he was repainting the scene and his time with his pseudo-uncle, his respected elder and teacher.

He looked up at me and said, "And Dad—Uncle Jimmy told me real strong, 'Amy, stuff comes in by speaking too, so be very careful what you say over yourself and over other people, 'cause our old people knew they could change things just by speaking an' singing and drawing these pictures. Nothing has changed—it's still a strong magic."

I looked at my son, wide-eyed and moved, and I thought, "This kid is not going to be like his mates at school; he's going to be deeper, and a deep rock is a solid one."

Ulmarra had told him that no one knew about that place, and I wondered where it was. Jimmy said it isn't even on the national list of protected sites, because it used to be closed up, until the side of the cave collapsed and Jimmy found it, but he still didn't tell me how to find it.

Amy had asked him how none of the old people knew about it, and Jimmy told him the people who used to know about it were chased out of that land, and the ones who were left had forgotten. Ulmarra had looked at the boy and said, "But now there are just two of us who remember." And I thought, okay, it's something special for Amy, and I wished I had had an uncle like Jimmy to walk me into the secrets of the past and illuminate the wonders of that time, but I guess I was glad that something wonderful was given to my boy that day, and I was glad I had brought him.

Finally, Jimmy had led him to a lower wall and pointed to where the ancient artist had chewed charcoal and ochre and spat it around his hand and fingers to leave a silhouette on the cave wall.

I could almost see Jimmy thinking about this for a minute, then nodding for Amy to follow as he walked out the far side of the cave. Amy said he showed him where to find some white lime clay embedded on the banks outside the cave, and he found a smooth rock and showed the boy how to grind it up. He scraped it up onto a bark platter and took it into the cave.

Next to the ancient signature they had found earlier, he put the powder in his mouth and swirled it around with his saliva. Then he placed his hand flat against the wall and began spitting the white liquid out over his hand, just as they would have a long, long time ago.

The boy told me he realized he should do the same, so he too took a mouthful of the lime clay and screwed up his face with the taste. Then he put his hand against the wall to follow his uncle.

I could imagine those two Yidinji, the taller man and the boy, as they marked the cave so many thousands of years after our first ancestors once did, but, even today, having every right to do so.

When they were finished, they smiled at each other, with white "paint" dribbling around their mouths. Jimmy rubbed his fist against the boy's mouth as he told him that he looked like a clown, and Amy said, "You look like a vampire that's been sucking someone with white blood!"

"We all got red blood, Amy—don't never forget that," Jimmy said.

Then they left the cave and set off back into the bush to search for the dingo-territory markers.

Just before he followed Jimmy, Amy said he had turned and looked back at the cave and waved to some invisible personality who might be there watching them leave, and then he had turned and skipped after his elder.

"Them Dreamtime spirits were really happy with us, Dad—I could tell."

"I'm sure they were, son," I said. "I'm sure they were."

Amy said they had camped that evening almost at the apex of the gorge, while Jyly and me, meantime, had almost made it across the bottom of the gorge and camped at the base of the other side, ready to make the ascent the following morning.

The two of them had been lying under the stars on mats of leaves with a lean-to behind them. Jimmy began to tell Amy a story about the stars and the ancient Dreamtime people who lived there. Amy said Jimmy began to sing, and the boy giggled and made a playful expression, and he said, "Don't give up your day job, Uncle!"

Jimmy shook his head and grinned as he fell silent. Then he told the boy to copy him, and he taught him the ancient song, correcting him as they went.

When they told me about it, I said to Jimmy, "How come you never taught me half this stuff, an' you never sing with me?"

Jimmy looked a bit sheepish and said, "Mate—you can't hold a tune!"

Amy excitedly told me that their singing lesson had been interrupted by the distant sound of the dingoes singing themselves from one side of the gorge to the other, which Jimmy said proved they were definitely hunting right round.

We could hear them too at our camp, and I spent a fitful night, never quite letting myself go to sleep fully, in case they came down and visited us.

The boy told me he had been secretly quite scared too, but Jimmy had said, "They are just singing to each other and saying, 'Mate—I'll go round and visit that hot little girl dingo, and I'll catch you later for a bite of bandicoot or potaroo at the Mickey Dingo joint!'"

Amy had asked, "Is that really what they are saying, Uncle?"

Jimmy whispered, "Maybe—in the morning, we will go see what they've been up to. Better sleep now, eh?"

Amy said he hadn't wanted to shut his eyes, because he hadn't felt sleepy at all, so he had stared at the stars and listened to the other sounds of the night.

Jimmy reckoned he was quiet for about three minutes, and then he said, "Am I a real Yidinji, Uncle? Even if Mum is, you know—is a white fulla?"

Jimmy said he hadn't replied for some moments, because he was thinking about the question, and then he said clearly, "Yep. If you love this land, and you have it in your bones—you are Yidinji."

"What do you mean, 'have it in my bones,' Uncle?"

"Well, them research people who check things out say every man and woman eats about twenty kilos of dirt every year."

"No way!"

"Yep. That dirt goes into you from the dust an' the stuff left on lettuce and potatoes and stuff."

"Wow. You know, I used to eat dirt when I was a baby, Uncle."

"Yeah, I know—I saw you. Anyway, that dirt has special things like 'isotopes' 'n' stuff in it, and they go into your bones. That stuff stays in there your whole life."

"Yeah?"

"Yeah. Means no matter where you go, that land you been born in is going with you."

"Does it matter that I got blue eyes like me mum?"

Jimmy grinned and said, "No—you're the 'new Yidinji.' As long as you got 'eyes' in your heart that are good, that's all the Dreamtime spirits care about; they won't chuck you out if your other eyes are blue or green or brown, only if you don't want to see. They're all the same color when you're dead for a while, anyway."

Amy was quiet for another three minutes, then he said, "It was good being with our ancestors and the Dreamtime spirits today."

"Mmm—now go to sleep!" Jimmy had said quite firmly, because even if the boy could walk all day and talk all night, he was tired.

When I woke in the morning, I felt like I hadn't slept for a month.

At the same time as Jimmy and Amy were having their close encounters with Dreamtime spirits and each other, I was about to have a near-death experience of my own.

Jyly and me had started up the gorge and followed the faults and crevices almost to the top. We made good time, but I had a mind to reach the top edge by lunchtime, so I could have a snooze and wait for Jimmy and Amy to catch up around the long way. I took what looked like a shortcut up from the flat ledge we had discovered about fifty feet from the top.

I would have been okay if it hadn't been for a gnarled little shrub that caught the cuff of my jean and tripped me up. I lost my footing and half slid, half tumbled through the cleft in the rocks, catching my leg on the way. It snapped like a twig, and, when I finally landed on the ledge that I'd just climbed up from, I knew I had gone and done it, good and proper.

Jyly yelled and rushed over to me. She could see I was in agony, and there wasn't much she could do except gently help me shuffle back to rest against the wall of the rocks towering above us.

"Looks like this is the end of our walkabout!" she mused nervously, and I said, "Sorry, mate."

She used the UHF radio in my pack and radioed the quarantine station to get an evac. organized. I felt like shit. Partly from the pain and partly from what an idiot I had been trying it when I was so tired.

After she had made me as comfortable as she could and then radioed Jimmy, her voice couldn't disguise how worried she was.

Jimmy immediately answered, "What's happened?"

Jyly told him that I had slipped and fallen and I'd broken my leg. She said she'd radioed the quarantine base for help already, and made me comfortable.

"Where are you and Amy, Jimmy? How far away are you?" she asked with a certain urgency.

"Where are you and Wajilla now?" Jimmy asked back.

"We're on the other side near where that little creek tips over into the gorge. I got some water to wash Wajilla's hands and face, and there are dingo tracks and marks not far away. Should I be worried about that?"

I heard my son in the background asking Jimmy, "Is Dad going to be okay, Uncle?" and I knew he'd be worried after seeing what the dingoes had done two nights before when they killed the wallabies.

"Don't worry, Amy," Jimmy reassured the boy, and then spoke to Jyly over the UHF. "The dingoes won't come near, because it's broad daylight and they are very shy anyway. Remember, these dogs out here have had no contact with humans, so they'll be wary."

"I'm glad about that," Jyly said, "but you guys had better get here as quick as you can, because the chopper can pick us all up and take us back as soon as they arrive."

"Okay, we're on the way."

Jimmy told me that when they came to the edge of the ravine, there was a rocky pathway down about halfway and across. Now, when Jimmy says a "rocky pathway," he really means a few rocks occasionally lined up on a three-hundred-meter drop to the bottom.

He said to Amy, "You be okay to go this way?"

The boy looked up bravely and said, "Anything you can do, I can too, Uncle. We are the 'new Yidinji,' remember? You told me."

Jimmy grinned and started to climb along the ledges and steep pathways of the upper end of the area. He said they stopped as a flare suddenly shot up, and they realized Jyly had set that off so they knew where to find us.

Jimmy said he turned to the boy and said, "We gotta go round that way 'cause it's quicker, so watch your step."

The two climbed down and headed towards the flare. When they reached the fault line, they skirted along the cliff above the floor of the gorge below, and my boy was puffing hard but never paused for a moment in his efforts to get to me. When he saw me, he rushed to where I was lying, my leg trussed in the splint Jyly had made, and grabbed me round my neck.

I greeted my son and said, "I'm okay, just a few scratches. It's not an open wound, so it just means six weeks in a cast, and I'll be back to fighting fit in no time."

Jimmy shook his head. "Too many takeaways and ciggies to call yourself fighting fit, mate!"

"And no more chocolate, Dad—you're too fat! That's why you're no good climbing up this stuff anymore."

I laughed. He was sounding like Jimmy.

I grimaced a little as I readjusted my position.

"How long until the chopper gets here?" Jimmy asked.

"It's left already," Jyly said. "It should be here within an hour. All we have to do is wait."

Jimmy asked her where we had seen the dingo signs, and she pointed higher on the rock line. "See where that water is coming down there? Well, just above is a marshy bit either side of some scrub. There's a big tree that has been scratched and scented, and around the water are prints. We climbed up from the bottom that way and then came along there to get to this flat bit, but this mountain goat decided to take a shortcut straight up—and straight back down again!"

I said he should go and take a quick look, because we had come all this way, and we needed to know what was going on with them if we wanted to drop the new dingoes in this range.

Jimmy said he would, so he left the three of us waiting for the chopper and headed up the tree line towards the distant creek.

When he came back, he said that he had found the marks and prints and followed the trail up over the top to the plateau. He said there were six or seven, including two juveniles, and he had seen in the distance a rise and a pile of boulders. He knew this would be where the pack had their lair. Then he thought the chopper might come, so he took a look at the sun to gauge the time, and skirted back to where we three were waiting below on the ledge under the cliffs.

While he was standing with his fists on his hips telling us what he'd seen, we heard a noise, and suddenly a golden-colored dog dived from the undergrowth and grabbed me by my jeans.

I hardly had time to be shocked.

Jyly quickly picked up a tree branch and flailed it in the air, whacking it on the ground to frighten off another dog that had appeared in an instant and was growling and menacing Amy and herself. Amy had fallen backwards, because he got such a fright and was terrified, scuttling back on his ass to the rocks at his back.

Three dingoes darted through the trees with their teeth drawn, and dust whirled up in the air as Ulmarra spun round to try and get the dog off me.

I screamed as it tugged at my leg with the splint on it. I tried to kick it with my good leg and leaned forward to punch it hard, but it wasn't gonna let go.

Jimmy dived forward and whacked the dog on his back, and it let go at last and then rounded on his attacker, growling loudly. I thought Jimmy was gonna be bitten for sure.

Behind us, Jyly screamed as a second dog leapt from the rocks and grabbed Amy by the arm. She beat the animal with her stick, and it yelped, but didn't let go of him, dragging my boy across the ground as he screamed. She yelled and hit it again until it released him, only to turn and have a go at her.

Then Jimmy did something weird. He stepped back and faced the dogs. He put his hands above his head and made some sounds like a howl crossed with a growling camel.

Instantly, the dogs stopped. They started flicking their eyes around and crouching before they turned and fled. They stopped a little way off, looking back at us and then finally flashed away up the incline. The younger dogs that had been hovering in the brush line watching also bolted with the adults, and we were alone again.

Amy sat up holding his wounded arm. His face was screwed up like he wanted to cry, but not a single sound came out of him. Struggling to contain tears of shock and pain and shaking like a leaf, he shuffled back to the rocks and sat up against them.

Jyly rushed forward to look at him and his arm. It was already swelling, and bright red puncture wounds were weeping blood. A long, deep scratch showed where a canine had gored his under-forearm before sinking in further up.

"It hasn't snapped—it's not broken," she gasped, and gave Amy a big hug. Then she rushed over and dove into one of the packs, pulled out the first aid kit, washed the wounds, and wrapped them up tightly as my boy started to perk up and recount the ordeal bravely.

"That dingo was biting hard, Dad; felt like he was gonna bite it right off!"

Jimmy turned to me sadly and stared at me. I could see he was blaming himself for our close call and the harm to Amy.

I was panting a bit and asked, "Why did they attack? It's broad daylight!"

Jyly stood and walked over to me, squatting down to take a look at my leg before Jimmy answered. "Good question," she said, as I grimaced and adjusted my position and said, "That's another pair of jeans wrecked!"

Jimmy looked up the rocky cliff toward the opening above the water falling down the escarpment. "Their den is about one kilometer over that way, and they've got two pups—they probably came looking 'cause we're in their territory, and they were protecting their young. They attacked 'cause you looked weak and—they can smell that food." He pointed towards the remains of lunch and the cold embers of the fire.

I looked across to Jyly and asked a little nervously, "How far away do you think that chopper is? We need to be outta here before dusk, 'cause they'll be back, eh?"

Amy got up and came over to sit beside me. He leaned his head on my shoulder, and I patted the side of his face.

"They could really do some damage if they attacked again, now that they knew there's two of us down," Jyly said.

"Are they gonna come back, Uncle?" Amy asked Jimmy.

"Yep—when it starts to get dark. At least they aren't hunting like the Frazer Island dingoes; there's only a small pack here," Jimmy said quietly, without hiding anything from the boy. "Still, we need to be gone as soon as."

Jyly went to the boy and sat down beside him, resting her arm around his shoulder. She looked up at Jimmy. "Don't worry, Amy, your uncle knows how to deal to a dingo, so we will be okay."

Amy nodded and looked relieved and went back to nursing his war wounds bravely.

I said, "How come people didn't think a dingo could take Lindy Chamberlain's baby out of their tent down in Uluru and take it away after what we just saw? How many attacks have there been now? And now there's one more to add to their rap sheet!"

Jyly replied wistfully, "They just are what they are; you can't blame them for it. Anyway, when they put poor Lindy away for murdering her baby instead of giving her some sympathy for losing it that way—that just showed we are what we are, and are a dammed site worse than any dingo."

Just as she finished speaking, the distant thump, thump, thump sounds of the chopper at the end of the gorge drifted in to us. The small dot of the craft slowly made its way towards us.

"Ah, thank god for that!" I sighed in relief as Jyly scrambled in the pack and pulled out a flare, lit it, and it shot up in the air above us.

When the chopper arrived overhead, a winch brought down a rescue man who introduced himself with, "I'm Rob. Looks like you're in a spot of bother, mate. Who's hurt?"

Jimmy pointed to me on the ground with Amy beside me, his arm still cradled like a newborn.

Rob walked over to Amy and me and smiled reassuringly, "Looks like you two could do with a lift."

"Yeah—can you knock me out before you winch me up, though? I'm afraid of heights," I said.

The man laughed. "I'm gonna tie you in to a cradle stretcher solidly, and that winch can handle a two-thousand-kilo steer, so you're as safe as houses, mate." He was yelling over the sound of the hovering helicopter thudding above and swirling dust against the cliffs.

Soon the stretcher was lowered, and I was lifted into it, wrapped, strapped in, and shaking like a leaf. Rob had undone a bag of items lowered with the stretcher and found a harness that he began to fit it to Amy.

Finally, the winch started to haul me up, and I shut my eyes and tried not to think about throwing up while Amy and Rob waited below with Jimmy and Jyly.

It seemed to take forever. When I got to the top, another rescue guy pulled me aboard. After he had unhooked me, the winch was lowered again.

I was lying in the cradle in the chopper and couldn't move to see anything. I could only hear the booming sound of the big rotors whooping around and feel the wind blowing in on my face. It seemed like an eternity passed while I waited for Amy to appear, trussed up in a sling with Rob hooked on to him. They fumbled over the side and came in to the craft. Rob strapped Amy into a seat and turned and closed the slide door.

"What about Jimmy and Jyly?" I yelled over the noise.

"They're not coming," Amy yelled.

Rob leaned over to me and said he had spoken to Jimmy and Jyly and told them he'd take the boy up and then the lady could go next and then finally, Jimmy.

But Jimmy told him he was going to stay to finish the job and would walk back out as planned.

When I heard this, I thought, "Typical! Ulmarra waits until I'm hovering a hundred feet above him and can't argue the toss, and then decides to change the plan."

Rob said that Jyly had immediately volunteered she'd go with him.

"I asked them if they were sure about it, but that bloke Ulmarra just looked at her, and she looked at him, and that was it." He leaned over to me and said, "Is there something going on with them two?"

Amy yelled, "No!" And then he looked over to me and said, "I tried to get them to come, Dad. I said, 'You *have* to come, or the dingoes will get you!'"

He pulled his arm in close to his chest and looked down at it. "Uncle Jimmy just said that the dogs wouldn't attack them again, because they would be far away from there by nightfall. I argued with him, Dad, but you know Uncle Jimmy..."

I could see Amy was quite distressed by the idea that they would be left behind, and his voice caught as he said, "When the winch came back down for me, he grabbed me by my shoulders and said, 'You have to be with your father—I know this land; I'll see you in a few days. It'll be okay—don't worry.'"

Rob nodded and smiled at the boy reassuringly. "It's true, he did try. Dr. Ulmarra gave Ms. Jyly the option to go too. He said, 'You sure? Now or never—you can save yourself a long walk if you go with them.'" Rob shook his head and continued, "She looked like she was pretty serious when she said, 'You're kidding; someone has to look after you!'"

I thought, "Well, that's true—he does need looking after, but maybe not the way you think, young lady."

After we all made it back, Jimmy told me he was surprised she had wanted to stay with him, but even though no one said anything, it wasn't really that surprising, because they were already so far down the track with each other, they were probably ready to just let it happen or go mad with the tension.

He said he had smiled at her and gently swept his finger along her jaw, and she put her head down shyly as they let the last rescue guy be winched up to the chopper.

He said he somehow knew something special was happening.

They watched the chopper fly out of sight with us safely on board, and they were left alone with the gorge, the dingoes, and each other.

Chapter 10

AFTER WE WERE evac'd out, I spent a day in Cairns base hospital, and we waited for Jimmy and Jyly to come home.

Both of them were different when they got back, and both of them had slightly different stories, which they must have wanted to offload somewhere, and the somewhere was me.

Jimmy said he had led Jyly up toward the lair of the dingoes, because he wanted to know if the attack and the chopper had disturbed them and whether they would abandon the pups for a while.

When they were close, he bobbed down, and the two of them approached downwind and very quietly. He said they saw three adult dogs sitting under the shade of some scrub panting, and the young pups darting in and out of the entrance of the lair, playing, and occasionally biting the face of one dog or another.

The alpha female was looking about from the top of the highest rock, but the heat was enough to drive even her off, so, when she was sure there was nothing of danger out there, she climbed off, and the pups grabbed an impromptu feed by nipping at her muzzle until she regurgitated a small morsel. Two younger dogs were hidden somewhere beyond the humans' sight, but Jimmy knew they would be close by, because this was a family that stayed together.

Jyly smiled at the sight, and then they backed away.

She told me that when they had reached the marsh, Jimmy pointed along the top edge of the gorge and indicated that they would go along that way. Looking into the dry ground, he followed the invisible tracks of the dogs and showed Jyly various signs that showed the territory where the dogs normally frequented.

When they had gone about five kilometers, the trail began to disappear, and the gorge tipped down onto a long plain of uninterrupted trees.

"They probably don't go much further than this except in the long dry, when food is scarce. Best place to release the new dogs will be up over there in the distance about twenty kilometers, so they don't interact too closely. Otherwise, our big fulla will kill those pups and take over.

"There's good water over there too, but the young dogs of each pack will mix here in the middle, and they will begin to interbreed and refresh the gene pool." He looked far ahead toward where he had pointed. "You see, along there—that ridge. That's where we first started planting. All that is our forest over there, that valley and way over to that distant hill. Took us five years to get it all in, and it meant that this reserve and the piece on the bottom of the range join up into one long stretch."

He looked at her and said, "I was a kid then, with big ideas."

"How old were you?"

"Never mind; it was a while ago."

I knew how old he was when we started that block. He was twenty-three, and I was about the same. We used to go out every weekend after we got that first approval from the big guns in Canberra to "create an extension to the reserve." Now you couldn't see where the original ended and our bit began.

Jyly was feeling the heat and exertion, and Jimmy noticed her struggling and said, "Do you wanna stop now?"

She shook her head, but he could see she was suffering. "Can you manage another kilometer? We can make camp in a place I know."

"No dingoes there, I hope."

He laughed and shook his head. "Not yet, there isn't. Anyway, how come you got no faith in me, even if there were?"

"I've got all the faith in the world in you," she whispered to herself. "It's me I've got no faith in."

"Why?"

She replied a little shyly, because she said she hadn't thought he'd heard her, "Because I'm only twenty-two, and I got scared during that attack." She paused then stuttered a little to reveal what she was really thinking. "And... and...I'm in the company of 'this guy' who is gonna change the world, and that is scarier to me than the damned dingoes!"

He walked back to her. "I didn't start out to change the world; no one does. I just am who I am. Anyway, it's the real world, the natural world, that's making its own cure for itself by having some of us born to do this, so it can get back to a safe balance."

She told me he had started talking as they walked. "We don't decide nothin', you know. In the end, we two are the product of the whole system looking after itself. After all, it's got billions of years up its sleeve. You an' me are just part of its plan. You aren't just here with me learning how this recovery can be done, and you're not just a twenty-two-year-old nobody. You were made exactly as you are to be part of the answer, according to the plan."

"That's a bit far-fetched, wouldn't you say? People helping out the whole of nature by its own design? I mean, I can almost understand that might be true about you—"

"No," he interrupted, "the plan is for both of us together."

Jyly looked up with surprise. "Together," she whispered.

"Yep." He smiled a bit shyly and said, "When you have to go on a long journey in life, it's better to go with other people, so that what you lack is filled in by the others."

"Oh, I see. But what do you lack? You have it all: no one knows more than you about what this land is and what it needs."

"Nah—I don't have it all. I'm missing lots of things."

"What? I don't know what I can add to help you with this thing!"

He had stopped suddenly and looked down at his feet. "You're an echo for my soul."

She paused on the moment and then whispered, "I know what you mean—I understand. Lots of people do. We maybe don't have it as strong as you, but—"

"Not talking 'bout that—"

"What, then?" She was beginning to shiver slightly, because something they had been feeling was about to get a voice, and there would be no going back after that.

"Now I'm the scared one." He laughed and walked on more quickly, and nothing more was said.

Fifteen minutes went by, and finally they reached an area that had a tall rock-face and a wide waterfall spilling over several steps to a green pool carved from solid rock. It tipped again over a rocky edge and disappeared into the undergrowth.

"Oh, wow!" Jyly exclaimed as the water and misty air cooled the area.

Without saying anything, Jimmy stripped off down to his underwear and jumped into the pool.

"Wait for me," she laughed and dropped her pack, pulled off her clothes, and, in her underwear, dived in. She said the place had overcome whatever shyness she might have once had in the presence of her illustrious leader, and she wouldn't have cared if he was the king of England; she needed that water to cool off, and it was wonderful.

Jimmy came up to her in the water. She smiled gently as he approached and didn't say anything, but their eyes caught each other, and, for a moment, they seemed to lose sight of the surrounding view as the soothing sound of the waterfall behind the pair engulfed them with its music, and the mystery between a man and a woman blinded them to everything but each other.

"You look like you belong here," Jimmy whispered,

"You do belong here."

"Come with me. I want to show you a little secret."

He turned and swam across to the rocks near the waterfall.

She climbed up behind him as he leaned back and grasped her hand to help her. They climbed along the rock face carefully. "It's back here; take a deep breath..." He let go of her and disappeared into the falling water.

She put her hand under the fall but felt only rock. Leaning back, she frowned, wondering how he had disappeared.

Seconds later, his head popped out with a spray of water around it. *"Just dive in."* he yelled.

She took a deep breath and put her face into the water, clinging to the rocks as she stepped along in a spray of droplets. Sure enough, the rocks curved inwards, and she found herself on the other side in a low cave undercut by eons of floods.

Jimmy's voice echoed from ahead, "Come over here."

She walked along and realized the rocks had given way to a sloping sandy beach trapped by boulders in front of a sheet of water falling from above.

She saw Ulmarra had already seated himself and, with his forearms locked over his knees, was looking out at the water. Ahead of the silver sheath, the distorted scene of green apparitions hovered in the falling water, lit brilliantly by the afternoon sun.

"Wow," she said, as she sat down beside him. "How did you find out about this place?"

"I'm like a quoll: I put my nose into everything, and sometimes I find something like this."

They sat together, quietly watching the falling water.

Suddenly, he put his hand across and picked up hers. There was no denying it then; each was clearly aware of the other's feelings.

Then he spoke. "I'm not worried about you being twenty-two but of me being forty-two."

"Why?"

"Because I will go to be with my ancestors twenty years before you do."

"So you'll have to fit those lost years into the time we have now." The smile dropped from her face as she realized for the first time that she was serious. She whispered and smiled again mischievously, "That could be interesting, you know. It could get quite busy..."

He looked at her and smiled. "Wanna start now?"

She grinned and leaned over as he did and their lips met.

Before either of them could think about anything that might stop it, they were quickly locked in a passionate embrace. She was glad they were behind the falls as the water splashed on their skins, and she reckoned it must have looked very strange from the outside when it got to its crescendo, because she couldn't resist reaching out and sliding her hand over the surface of the waterfall, skimming a path down the silver screen as they were engulfed in ecstasy.

When it was over, she said they had lain in each other's arms in the cool of the secret place and were entirely peaceful. She stroked his chest and fingered the leather string around his neck with the small kangaroo skin pouch tied to it.

"What you got hidden in here?" she said she asked him.

"Old magic that I never take off."

"Lucky roo foot?"

"No luck in a dead thing. Nah—it's something been in our family since long, long time ago. It was made by a healing spirit, and it has a message in it."

"So you're a message man?"

"S'pose so." But she said he wouldn't elaborate.

Finally, Jimmy whispered, "Come on, let's get something to eat."

She said they sat up and climbed to their feet. He picked up their underwear strewn on the sand and said with a grin, "Shall we take a look out?"

She nodded.

Jimmy forced his head through the water and focused on the pool below, then he ducked his head back in, stood back, and then ran out through the water to jump into the water. He surfaced and looked up at the falls waiting for her dive out from behind it too, and when she did, her sleek body fizzed with bubbles in the clear water.

He threw the wet underwear up onto the bank, and she said she swam lazily up to him and they linked hands and twirled around for one last time.

"You know—I don't care about how old you are, just that I won't be good enough for you."

He ignored her comment and simply pulled her in and kissed her, and then he said, "I'm hungry—come on, I gotta catch a decent dinner after that."

They dressed, and Jyly hung their wet underclothes on various branches, and Jimmy made a fire. She said he had kissed her good-bye and went off hunting for something to add to their packaged supplies.

Jyly told me she had pulled out the pup tent from her pack and set up a campsite before he returned with a small wallaby over his shoulder. He butchered it and cleaned it in the stream below the pool. He showed her how to skewer pieces of meat on sticks he had soaked in the water and laced it with wild herbs and salt, leaving it to cook over the coals.

Seated in the falling darkness after they had eaten, they had held hands, Jyly said, and enjoyed the time together as though they were the very first people on the earth.

When she told me all this, I thought, this is what it probably should be like to be in love and to be right for one another. But Jyly said it wasn't completely perfect, and I asked her why.

She said she had been watching the fire lick away the last of the juice and fat of what they had cooked when she revealed her hidden concerns.

"What are we gonna tell everyone? People are gonna think it's pretty weird, you with me."

"Yeah?" Jimmy fell silent as he thought about it. "I don't want you to get any flak, with me looking like a cradle snatcher..."

"Let's just play it by ear—no one needs to know just yet, anyway, eh?"

"Yeah..." But when he said that, she said she had the feeling that he was just agreeing with her for her sake, and that he was disappointed with her.

They fell silent. After a little while, Jyly whispered, "I'm going to turn in." She said she got up and disappeared into her tent.

Lying in the darkness, she said she watched the light of the moon play the shadows of tree bows over the nylon covering and thought about how great it would have been to just disappear with Jimmy and not have to worry about anyone. As she watched, Ulmarra's shadow passed by, and she heard the zip open. She said she smiled to herself.

He came in and lay down beside her. She felt his lips on her neck, and she turned to respond to him, and again they locked together in natural passion. When it was over, she said they had fallen asleep in each other's arms, and her worries seemed to sleep too.

A day later, they had made it almost all the way back to the quarantine station.

Ulmarra had a tinge of sadness in his voice when he declared, "Back to civilization!"

"Damn," Jyly replied. "I could get used to just walking around."

I knew what she had meant. For me, however, I always had enough after about a week, because I had people to come back for: Amy and my job and stuff like that. Those two might have been better if they had just disappeared in the mist and walked their way into the Dreamtime place on their own. But like the fools we all are, they walked back into the world, and their destiny kept on its course.

Meantime, I was taking Amy back to his mother's back in Cairns. I hated going there, and when that bloody, pain-in-the-ass woman saw Amy trussed up and in a sling, she let me have it. Amy just shook his head as he pushed past her, because he'd heard it all before, and he headed for his PlayStation that I'd got him for Christmas.

I told her if she didn't wind her head in, I'd see the magistrate and tell them she was an unfit mother. That shut her up, because, in actual fact, she was. If it wasn't for the fact that a kid loves his mother no matter what, I'd have taken Amy full-time and worked it out somehow, but I knew he still needed her. I just made sure I kept a close watch, and I looked forward to having him every chance I got, and, for all her protestations about him being with me, she was quick to get me to take him if she wanted to go to some party or just "had" to go with some mate to Brisbane.

When I'd dropped him off, I hobbled back to the car on my crutches, bloody furious with myself for letting her stir me up, but I headed to the foundation anyway.

Louisa was there of course, still working. She said the girl from wild rescue had come back to Cairns early with her bat baby and was told that Jimmy and

Jyly had made it back alive. I was pleased to hear that, not that I was worried. They were said to be heading back in the foundation Ute.

Louisa rang to see how long Jimmy thought he would be, but the guys at the quarantine station said the pair had looked in at the Fraser Island dingoes that had settled in quite well, passed on valuable information of the range and territory of the native pack on the first part of the gorge, and had already left. The reserve ranger told her where it had been decided the new dogs would be released, so Louisa and I planned out when we would go back, because Jimmy and me wanted to be there for their relocation.

We were expecting them back the following day, and, I tell you, Louisa was like one of those Fraser dingoes when she realized they had been alone on walkabout and were coming back in the Ute together.

I already had a pretty good idea that it didn't matter anymore what she thought, because nature was going to take its course one way or the other.

Jimmy must have had some kind of sixth sense that whatever was happening between them needed more time, so, on the way back, he suggested they stop at Cook Town to get some lunch and have a look around.

He told me they had driven into the small town at about two thirty. As they arrived, they called in to the local IGA store in the main street to pick up some food and drink. They were stopped at the door by a large, fat, aborigine with an Akubra hat on who jokingly said, "Looks like we gonna have a big blow, eh mate—shelves are cleaned out."

Jyly stopped to talk to him and said, "We've only just arrived, so we haven't heard anything about the weather."

He replied, "A cat three cyclone is on its way in, and they say it will hit direct on Cook Town. It's about a hundred kilometers out to sea at the moment but heading right for us!"

Jyly turned to Jimmy and said, "We better get going!"

"You can't," the man quickly interjected. "They is closing the road south, 'cause it floods."

"What are we going to do?"

"Nothing to do but bunk down in a motel and...and stay, you know, occupied!" he said with a grin.

She slapped Jimmy, and they carried on into the IGA. There was a rush of people getting supplies, all right, but the two managed to get a few things and went back to the vehicle.

Jyly looked worried. She said in a flustered voice, "Maybe the man was just being dramatic, because there's nothing on the radio about it, and no sign of wind or rain. Maybe we can still make a dash back to Cairns."

When they pulled into the BP to fill up, Jimmy told the attendant that they might carry on to Cairns.

"You won't be able to," the guy said firmly. "The main highway has already closed. My mate is stuck on the wrong side and can't get home to his wife and kids. You'll just have wait it out."

"What are we gonna do?" Jyly was obviously getting worked up.

"Try the motel at the end of the peninsular under the rock, and just stay tight there until it's over."

"There's nothing we can do, Jyly. We'll have to spend the day in a motel. How bad can that be?"

"But what if the motel blows away?"

"Nah, what's here now has been blown about a lot of times before. This town is over a hundred years old; it's not going anywhere."

They drove down to the end of the street to a motel that was almost in the shelter of the huge hill at the head of the river. They passed turn-of-the-century buildings that had been restored, but were largely untouched from their long years planted on the edge of Charlotte Street.

"We should take a walk up here before the storm hits," Jimmy said as they passed.

"Sightseeing, before we get blown to hell? Don't you ever get scared?"

"Yep—the first time I looked at you! That's when I realized I was in serious trouble."

She had smiled, he told me, but something about her wasn't convincing. He put it down to the fear of the storm but thought to himself that maybe the fling in the waterfall didn't mean too much to her after all. He said it had made him feel strangely unsettled.

They pulled up and parked in the street, and Jimmy went in to get a room, and Jyly followed up the steps, pulling her jacket around her, because the wind was coming through the Endeavour River mouth from the sea, and it was unusually cold.

Jimmy went into the office, and the manager told him he'd have to pay cash, because the EFTPOS was down. "It went down about an hour ago," she said, but didn't look at him. He pulled out his wallet and, luckily, still had some cash left.

After they had paid and been shown in by the somewhat curious motel lady, they spent an hour resting and enjoying each other's company. Jyly showered, and they sat together in each other's arms to watch TV.

Jyly said the wind was only moderate at that stage and, apart from the odd leaf blowing into the windows, it was just like an impromptu holiday.

The news came on TV, and an update showed the progress of the storm coming in from the Coral Sea.

"There are these blokes that chase storms," Jimmy said casually. "They drive all the way up from Sydney or Brisbane just to see one in action, and here we are right in the middle of it for free!"

Jyly pulled in under his arm more tightly, and he told me that all he had wanted to do was hold her and protect her.

Suddenly the weather report was over, and there was the face of Louisa being interviewed.

Jimmy sat up and leaned forward to stare at the screen.

I saw that report on us too, at home. They'd shot the interview while we were up north.

Louisa was commenting about "false and scurrilous victimization" against the foundation. The in-depth news story flicked away from her to that poisonous woman, Maria Ferris, who began to argue that the global warming crisis was being falsely "talked up" by organizations and individuals like the Ulmarra Foundation who were "taking advantage," wanting to make big money out of new, "scenically groundless theories."

"These organizations make a lot of money for themselves by claiming farmers and landowners need to replant forests on their land in some bent scheme that only has one winner: them!" She spoke with all the force of a pit bull barking, "Traditional farmers have rights to do whatever they want with their land, including clear it, crop it, or graze it!"

She went on to say that fifty thousand Australian jobs were on the line because of this "utter rubbish." She claimed that "even scientists" couldn't agree that it was human activities that were responsible for global warming—even if it was happening at all.

The story skipped back to Louisa, who answered the comments calmly but firmly. "There is no 'debate' among scientists. Humans are responsible for global warming. The evidence is irrefutable. This confusion is being spread around by people who don't have any connection to the scientific community, and they have created a counter-rumor that there is some 'debate' about it. It's a tactic from people who are shortsighted and who can't see the wood for the trees. Before long, there won't be a tree left, because that kind of person has been hacking them down from the beginning!'"

Ulmarra watched her face as she explained that the earth had begun to warm when humans first started to flourish. Even from the beginning of civilization, we were burning huge areas of forest off and planting all kinds of crops. "Century by century, more and more of the earth's cloak of trees has been removed. Population increases have driven a greater need for food supplies, fueling higher populations. The Industrial Age added huge amounts of carbon and greenhouse gasses to the atmosphere, and now we have a runaway train. Ms. Ferris and people like her continue to deny the obvious, while organizations like the Ulmarra Foundation are working to address it in our part of the world with practical solutions."

Jimmy was fused on the screen as Louisa's eyes flashed with complete conviction.

"Apart from reducing emissions, the most effective answer now is to replant the forests wherever we can. It is an immediate action that can 'scrub' from the atmosphere huge quantities of carbon even before changes take effect in the way people will have to live in the future."

Jimmy was listening to every word, and a very subtle smile had grown on his face as he watched her passion and sincerity showing in every flick of her eyes and every word she spoke.

"These are facts we are dealing with." Louisa had said. "We know that soil temperatures fall by some three degrees under trees. The airspace between the canopy and the roots acts a bit like cooling insulation does, and that stops evaporation of precious water from the ground. And the trees suck in all that dangerous carbon dioxide and pump out our precious oxygen. What could be better?

"The foundation and its activities put practical solutions in the hands of ordinary people and make it possible to stop talking and do something to reverse the disaster that is going to unfold in perhaps a mere fifty years or less."

The screen flicked back to the journalist. She was convinced, even if she didn't say it outright. She pointed out that accusations of corruption and profiteering by the foundation might nullify support for them, even if what we were doing had a beneficial effect on the future Australian climate and was an example for other nations to follow.

The story flipped next to a man dressed in a suit who said, "Investigations are essential to put an end to this movement of histrionics and the whole dubious case for global warming. This kind of scheme does irreparable damage to farming as a whole and the economy of Australia, and there are many other ways to tackle these ecological issues." But when he asked what they might be, he simply repeated himself, and, as I had watched, I thought he looked smug and arrogant, as though we were just a fly to be swept aside, and he didn't have to have an answer for anything.

"The Australian public needed to be warned that prices for basic foods will rise by some forty percent. This fanatical idea will hurt everyone unnecessarily." He hammered on without any facts.

"What a load of crap!" Jyly said Jimmy had whispered.

Another scientist came into the debate and brought things back to sanity and gave some pretty good statistics to prove our case. He showed a graph that showed rising temperatures, and snapshots of storms and huge waves sweeping across coastlines punctuated his information.

Jyly looked out the window and began to shiver, because the pictures reminded her of what they were about to go through. She looked back to the screen to listen to his final words.

He had looked into the camera very seriously and said calmly, "Unless mankind masters this damage he's done to the natural world, nature will fix it for us. The price of food will be a moot point if we ignore this. There's likely to be huge shortages worldwide, and people will die off in the millions. Eventually, when fossil fuels finally stop being burnt because our societies will have fallen apart, and all this devastation causes world populations to normalize back to about one hundred million, the planet will slowly cool—but not many of us will have descendants enjoying that world. We and our kids will have suffered and died as part of the process of nature's own correction."

The announcer's face came back on their screen. She finished with her own sum-up. "Regardless of the accusations now leveled at the Ulmarra Foundation of financial impropriety and the case for or against global warming, I, for one, would rather err on the side of caution. Some would say, What harm is there in doing the right thing by our environment anyway, even if global warming turns out to be a natural event and nothing to do with us? Isn't it better to be safe—than sorry? Perhaps cleaning up our act now means future generations will benefit from our care of the environment and will be here to comment about what the facts were from their position of hindsight.

"The Ulmarra Foundation seems to spearhead that care. Whether the foundation is guilty of racketeering, the principles of what they are doing—transforming the Australian landscape back to green—is as ambitious as it is enlightening. Only time will tell if the public will sanction the cause."

I must admit, the journ'os were pretty fair to us in how they had presented the story.

Jimmy had stared at the screen as the broadcast went on to an advertisement.

Jyly felt very insignificant in the face of Louisa doing such a good job fronting for the foundation and arguing the case. She kept her eyes on the screen and said, "She looks good on telly."

Jimmy didn't reply.

She pushed him a bit and said, "You two had a thing going, eh?"

Jimmy turned and looked at her a bit shyly. "Louisa had a thing going—but she's smarter than almost anyone I know..."

"So she broke it off?"

"We decided it would be like a quoll pairing with a bandicoot—one of us would end up dead."

"Bad luck."

"Nah—good luck, because things are better this way. For a start, I don't feel like I'm an endangered species with you."

"Really..." Jyly grinned and leaned back to gather a pillow and hit him.

He managed to catch the small woman in his arms and disarm her. They made love again and, when it was over, lay together staring into each other's eyes.

"So are you the quoll or the bandicoot? Maybe I have to look out for my safety too," she said.

"Neither—we are *Ulmarra*."

She swallowed hard and blinked in surprise. He was hinting at something she was not ready to even dare to think.

Breaking the moment, she swung up from his arms and sat on the edge of the bed. "We should go and see what's happening. It doesn't look that bad to me out there." She said she had been so shaken by what he had said and what it implied that she dressed without looking at him, and he did likewise, feeling her reluctance and sudden distance.

They ventured outside and, in the light wind blowing in from the coast, walked down the length of Charlotte Street.

Jimmy paused outside the Cook Town Hotel, still standing where it had 120 years earlier. She said she hadn't been as interested as he was, and wanted to walk on. The place looked like it had traded on its history a good deal, but today, no one was around, because they had already scuttled into their homes to wait for the storm, so the old building seemed forlorn and abandoned.

"It seems weird," Jimmy said, shaking his head, "but I can almost see my ancestor Margaret Stanford hiding on the corner of that deck listening to her husband's plans for them through the window. At that moment they couldn't have known *I* would be the result, so many generations later, standing in the roadway waiting for a storm and watching them take a different direction, just like the surname she gave us."

Jyly told me she had watched his face as he stood there, looking at the old hotel, and he went on: "It was at that very moment that the path headed towards my great, great, great grandfather, the message man, and the rest became my history. The Ulmarra Foundation wouldn't exist if that one meeting over a beer in that hotel hadn't happened. She might just as easily have ended up on another piece of land in the area, had a few white kids, and they would have been a farming family near this town. Mrs. Birmingham's ancestors might have just served us at the BP or the IGA or even run the motel we are staying in.

"Instead, 'Ulmarra,' 'a change in direction,' started right there in that hotel, and it's like I'm watching it happen right now, in this time."

Jyly could only frown, as she hadn't read the diary and didn't know what he was talking about.

He looked at her and said somewhat shyly, "I wonder who will stand and watch us one day, only separated by time, but existing entirely because of us."

Jyly laughed and said, "We've only just met—not sure if there will be anyone watching us."

He frowned. Her words had broken the spell he was in. He turned away from the old hotel, and they walked on without speaking, until they got about halfway down the main street and turned back.

When they arrived at the motel, the storm was starting to blow, and the manager rushed out and handed them a printout of the storm's course from a meteorological website. "Better stay inside," she warned. "It'll be here in just a few hours."

The wind had definitely gotten more severe as the two headed into their room and locked the door. Outside the window, the haze of salt-laden gusts began to batter the panes with sticks and sand, and the waves in the river mouth began to appear over the rocky edge of the roadway. All the mangroves were bent over in the same direction, away from the sea.

They closed the curtains and curled up on the bed to watch TV. They waited almost in silence until the TV reception stopped, and only the howling of the wind could be heard. At five, Jimmy went out to see the manager only to return minutes later with news that the storm had taken a swing south as it came in contact with the outer reef and had hit Port Douglass instead. The damage was minimal, as it had more or less lost its power.

TV came on again by itself about an hour later, because they hadn't switched it off, and they watched the news to see that only a few trees were blown over. The news said it had rained heavily, however, and there had been localized flooding. A storm chaser came on and grumbled that they had driven all the way from Brisbane to experience it, only to have it evaporate.

"I told you!" Jimmy laughed.

"We could have got back after all."

Jimmy grinned and said, "I'm not sure I would have wanted to," and he leaned over to kiss her.

She nodded and moved slightly away, saying, "I guess we can get going tonight and be back by about nine."

"You want to go now?" He looked up in surprise, but before she could answer, he said, "We can't get back anyway; the motel lady said the main highway is flooded at Jacobs Creek crossing, and no one can get through."

In the morning the day was overcast but still. Jimmy went to pay for breakfast, and the motel manager told him again that the EFTPOS was still down, so he used the last of his cash.

They finally got going about nine o'clock, driving on the road that took them through the black mountains and down the long stretch of highway south.

They were talking quietly when a sudden flash of grey shot in front of them. Jimmy swerved, but a dull thud told them they had hit a wallaby.

"Shit!" Jimmy jumped out and ran back with Jyly following. They found the animal, but it was dead.

Jyly told me Ulmarra had a pained expression on his face as he sat on his haunches and stroked the animal.

She had stood there watching and didn't know if she should say anything or not. "I was wanting him to hurry up so we could get back, but while I was watching him, I realized this guy was not like a normal person would be when you accidentally hit a roo or something. He was connected to the animal, and

I suddenly felt really out of place, like I didn't understand what he did or who he was at all." She said she had walked back to the Ute, because it didn't mean that much to her, and she couldn't help saying over her shoulder, "Lucky they aren't endangered, eh?"

"This one was," he had called out, and she said his tone was slightly angry.

"It's only a roo!"

"You don't understand." He got up and walked quickly to catch her and then whispered, "This morning when the dawn came, and you looked out on it, she did too." He pointed to the small animal lying on the roadside. "She wiped her paws and licked the dew off her hind coat and chewed some of the new shoots that had come up last night. She hopped through the quiet bush and headed our way. She didn't know when she woke up on just another perfect day, this would be the last time she would see it. Some human driving a hunk of metal too fast to be natural was gonna meet her at"—he looked up at the sun overhead— "ten-forty and would take her out, because that idiot took his eyes off the road and was looking at you."

"So it's our fault, then?"

"Nah..." Jimmy said. He walked back, picked up the dead animal, and carried it off the roadside and into the grassy bush land.

"Where are you going with it?"

"I'm putting her in the ground that was her own."

Jyly looked at me sadly as she told me the story. "I was really annoyed, because all I wanted to do was get back, and I yelled out, 'Well, whatever—it doesn't need a state funeral, you know!'"

Her eyes showed how little she understood Ulmarra, and she said, "I sat down on the side of the road and just waited—what else could I do?"

I raised my eyebrows, because I knew him, and burying her was exactly what he would do.

When he had come back, she said she tried to take him by the hand, but he wouldn't let her, and they walked back to the Ute separately. She said Jimmy was quiet for some time. She had tried to make conversation, but he remained silent, until they stopped behind a long queue of cars in front of them.

"The river is up over the road," Jimmy said and hopped out, heading for some people waiting on the other side of the road. She hopped out too, and when he came back to the Ute where she was standing, he told her it would be hours before they could get through.

"Surely we can make it across; it's not that deep." They watched as someone on the far side started walking across, obviously testing out the idea of risking it also.

Jimmy walked forward to the water's edge. He waded in up to his thighs and then put his hand down to feel the speed that the river was going across the roadway.

When he came back, he leaned on the windowsill, shook his head, and said, "Nah; good chance of being swept off the concrete and into the river." He smiled at her for the first time since the wallaby incident, and she was relieved the mood he had been in had passed. He slapped the bonnet of the Ute as he turned and walked around it, saying, "I'd have to go bush for life to escape the displeasure of Louisa if I wrecked this Ute."

She got back in and sat in the front seat for ages while Jimmy, chewing on a grass stem, sat in the grass beside the Ute.

Finally, a large truck towing a car trailer appeared. They watched as an enterprising man jumped out and yelled, "I'll take anyone across for forty dollars."

Several cars lined up, and Jimmy stood up to watch as a car was winched up the trailer and was soon driven across. "Have you got any cash left?" he asked her. "I got nothing left, because the EFTPOS was down, and I paid for the motel out of what I had."

She looked in her wallet and found twenty-two dollars.

Jimmy took it and approached the man. She watched the two and realized that the man was not keen to do it for what they had. She looked around in the back of the Ute. Suddenly she saw a partly used six-pack of Crown lagers of mine. She grabbed them and yelled from the window, "Hey—can you get us across for what we got and this?"

The man roared with laughter, slapped Jimmy on the back, and said, "Your missus has swung the deal for ya."

Jyly was a bit embarrassed by that, but watched as the man told Jimmy to bring the Ute around, skipped back across the road, and jumped in the driver's seat.

"Was lucky Wajilla got evac'd out, or that wouldn't have been there!" Jimmy said, and grinned.

Jyly said they took the vehicle over, hooked it onto the winch, and it was hauled up. They sat inside it as the man towed them into the river, and the water sprayed up as they crossed safely up on top of the trailer. They drove off on the other side and carried on home.

When they got back to Cairns, Jimmy dropped her off at her mum's house. She gave him a quick peck on the cheek as she left. He backed out straightaway, and she said she had turned to watch him go. She said he had driven very slowly for a few meters and then put his foot down and was gone.

"It was like the whole thing had never happened." She looked at me strangely and then looked at her hands. It was hard to say whether they revealed sadness or relief.

The following day, they arrived at the Ulmarra Foundation offices at about the same time. I was hobbling on crutches and plastered up to my knee, because I had been released from the orthopedics department of the hospital the afternoon before.

When they appeared separately in the main office where Louisa was working, things looked a little strained.

"Ah, you made it back," Louisa said. "I thought we would have to send the troops out to look for you two."

I nodded hello to them both and kept my mouth shut.

"We got stuck in Cook Town because of the cyclone—it was a false alarm," Ulmarra replied quietly.

"Why did you go there? That's bloody miles out of the way!"

"Thought I'd show Jyly some history, and then the storm came up, and we had to stay."

"Well, while you were looking into the past, I was trying to secure the future."

"We saw you doing it on Channel Nine—you looked good."

Louisa smiled, somewhat pleased, and looked up at the remark.

Jyly looked toward Ulmarra and then turned away.

"I gotta go," she said, and walked toward the door without looking back. "I'll leave you with the 'past' and the 'future,' because my life is all about the present—and I'm late for it. I only came in to tell you I was going to have some time off because my phone had no money on it, and I couldn't ring. See you."

Jimmy frowned and turned to watch her go.

Louisa noticed the look on his face. "Looks like your little protégé isn't as sold on walkabout as you are." She walked around the side of the desk and stood beside him, looking toward the girl striding off down the hall. "I know how you must feel, when people just don't 'get it' like you and I do."

Jimmy ignored her and started to walk away. "Sorry, can't stay; I got things to do too."

I followed him out, hobbling fast to catch up, but he didn't wait for me or even seem to notice I was there. When I reached him I said, "What's going on, mate?" but he didn't reply; his eyes were firmly fixed on Jyly.

When we reached her, she didn't slow down, so he must have known something serious was up with her.

"I could have given you a lift home," he said, but she didn't reply.

He grabbed her arm and pulled her to a stop, and I was surprised to see him so aggressive. "What's your problem?" he said, frowning.

She refused to turn to him, so he came around to face her. "You okay?" he asked, tenderly this time.

"Of course I am—I got to get back home, that's all! My sister has been on her own... I've been away three days longer than I was supposed to be. My mum is pissed at me, because I didn't keep an eye on my sis—she's fifteen, and god knows what she will have been up to, and she has to go to Center Link today for her benefit review."

Jimmy swallowed. "Sorry, I didn't know."

She took a deep breath and looked at him. "Yeah, well, there are lots of things you don't know—including the obvious."

"Tell me."

"You...got a life that is single, and you don't have to think about other people like I do."

"You think I don't think about anyone else?"

"We got different lives; you and her"—she pointed behind her to the university buildings— "you been living the way you do, for the foundation and saving the planet and all that—for years. The problem for us is gonna be the things you belong to, against the things that I belong to."

"Didn't seem like we were too different back there in the reserve or in Cook Town." Jimmy dropped his head sadly.

About then, I realized it was about to get private, so I said, "I'll wait for you, mate," and hobbled to the Ute, leaning up against the bonnet. Unfortunately, those two didn't seem to notice I was there at all, being so completely in their own little drama, and I thought, "Shit, he's gone from the frying pan straight into the fire!"

She was looking very embarrassed and shy with him, and I heard her say, "Well, everyone is like that, you know—in the heat of it."

When Jimmy came over, and we drove home, he told me he felt totally confused. He said he had looked across the road, totally disappointed, and tried to work out what was happening. "So what are you saying?" he had said.

"Look at us! I'm not going to be able to catch up to you, so I will always be connected to the normal world. You need someone...like her, someone who understands all this stuff."

"No need to be jealous of her, and don't tell me what I need—I'll tell you what I need, and you just tell me what you need. That's all we should be saying."

"Jealous! You wish! But you wanna know what I need? Okay—I need someone *less*!"

"Less?"

"Less." She touched his hand and whispered, "Look, get real and smell the dingo shit—I'm nothing compared to you; I come from a normal abo family. I got no special feeling for this big wild stuff you are all into. I just have normal thoughts, about what we gonna get for dinner, what we gonna watch on TV, what my mates are gonna do on Friday night. I go to the supermarket to get what I want; I get to know people, not kangaroos and dingoes and whatever else there is out there. We got no money and no future people of any importance watching us. We're not connected to the Dreamtime anymore. When we die, we go in a grave with a white cross and no name written on it to show where we are and who we were. No-name crosses—you get it? You have to do what you got to do, and I have to go back to what I have to. You can't just ignore things like that."

She had walked past him and strode away from us. I knew it was like she had rammed a spear into his back, and it had gone right through.

"What about your scholarship?" Jimmy called after her.

"What about it? Give it to someone else—I don't want it no more!"

"You're wrong..." he yelled after her. "You don't know what you want, or you wouldn't let anything stop you!"

He said to me very quietly as he held on to the steering wheel, "She don't know what I need either, but I'm pretty sure I know what I need—and it's her."

Three months went by after Jyly walked out on the foundation and Jimmy Ulmarra.

He told me she hadn't contacted him and had laid low. He knew she had a part-time job at Cole's supermarket, but she had been avoiding everyone remotely connected to him. He felt lost and blamed himself for even daring to look at her as anything more than just a student.

Louisa was curious at his quiet mood, but he stayed busy elsewhere, arranging new grid copies, liaising with volunteer conservation efforts for the sections ready to plant, and keeping a watchful eye on anything that came up in the papers or in the news about the foundation, so she wasn't the only one handling everything, but mostly so she couldn't get her hopes up that it was her he was pining for.

I didn't let him know that I had kept in touch with Jyly. Hell, I had been worried about her. She was a smart girl but disadvantaged, and I was worried that she would sink lower and lower after the rape and then her and Jimmy's fling.

She would come out with me to the night market for a meal or I'd buy her an ice cream, and we'd walk along the esplanade and watch the pelicans and the spoonbills wading in the tide pools. She was always sad and in a mess, and there was nothing I could do for her except be there.

Then one day, things suddenly changed, and I noticed it immediately. I had picked her up from Redlynch, and she surprised me with a look of excitement on her face.

"Is something up, Jilly Bird?" I asked, knowing nothing good generally happened if you worked at Coles and lived with your mother and sisters in a dump in Mununda.

I'd been away all week doing a survey on a piece of farmland south of Townsville and hadn't even caught up with Jimmy yet; if I had, I would have already known that the rains and the heat of the suicide months were over and the beautiful dry season had begun for them.

She jumped in and said breathlessly, before we even started moving, "You won't believe how this week has been. Everything is different now."

"Well, go on, girl, tell me! You know my life is as boring as a fat croc on the day the tourists have all gone home."

Jyly said she had come home on Monday night and been watching TV, seated on a threadbare couch in her mother's rented home. At her feet, her younger sister's baby had been crawling around on the floor between a bunch of dirty, soft toys. A half-empty can of Blackadder was propped up against the leg of the opposing chair, and she saw the baby head for it and tip it slightly as it grasped it in its hands and mouthed the top.

"No, baby—don't do that! You will cut your mouth!" She jumped up and yelled out to her sister. "Danielle! What did you leave this crap here for? Your kid has spilt it on the carpet!"

She told me her sister had come in and grabbed up the child and wiped its mouth with the edge of a faded and grubby bib that hung limply around the baby's neck.

"Bloody Tania left that there, not me."

"Well, take it away! And you should put this other stuff away too!" Jyly said she got up and grabbed a half-eaten bag of crisps from the low coffee table

172

that came secondhand from Lifeline. "I don't have time for all that; me mates are gonna pick me up, 'cause we gonna go into Cairns central."

"I ain't babysitting for you again—don't even think about it!" Jyly had snapped back.

"Awww—why not! I never get any time off from baby." She took a step towards her sister with the child squirming slightly to escape. "Can't you just this once?"

Jyly said she had had just about had enough of her sister, who was always foisting little Sheri on her. She told me she almost screamed at her. "*No way*—you had her, *you* can bloody well look after her! It's about time you grew up and started to do what you should. Look at this shit! You've done nothing but spend the baby bonus on crap, and you got nothing to show for it, and you want to go out with that mob of idiots!"

Jyly said it didn't do any good; her sister just whined, "Grow up, save money, be good!" She bounced the baby a bit and went on, "You do nothing but whinge at me—why don't you try and help me?"

Jyly said she feigned a false tear and mimicked how her sister must have looked, and I could picture it perfectly.

Jyly looked up to me and said, "I said, 'I am helping you. I'm resisting kicking your ass!'" She said she had turned and strode around her sister before she could use some other trick to get her to take the baby.

She said she stormed into her room with Danielle following, grabbed a fresh top, and pulled it on while her sister continued her barrage.

"But what about me? I wanna go out!"

"Lock up after me, Danielle, 'cause you're not going nowhere." She said she headed for the door and yelled back, "'Bye—I'm outta here!"

Jyly said she had left the house and strode away down the street and had soon walked off her anger, but what was eating her was far deeper than a spoilt brat like her sister.

She said she caught the bus, and, in the light of the interior, she said she must have looked like a bloke on death row, because she was so sad inside.

She got off at Palm Beach and walked three or four streets until she had reached the ocean. Looking down the coral sand arc under the swaying coconut trees, she said she could hear the sounds of people laughing at the café on the corner. She decided to walk the length of the beach to get away from the noise and spend some time on her own.

Eventually, she stopped and sat in the cooling sand and stared out to sea. Even though it was very soothing with the light breeze wafting around her, she said she still started to cry.

I put my hand on her shoulder as she stared at me thoughtfully, and she said, "I looked up and muttered to myself, 'Why is it so hard?'"

"I know it can look like that sometimes, Jilly Bird..." She smiled and then continued, almost as though I wasn't there. She said after that wave of misery eased, she wiped her tears from her face and looked up at the sky, envisioning the day she had with him at Frazer Island. Every moment of their time there seemed to reply before her.

Gradually, she began feel curious again about "listening to creation" as he had taught her, as though an answer was knocking on her heart. She said she lay back in the sand and started to ignore all the sounds around her. The sounds of the water died away, and the falling darkness seemed to muffle everything else. She said she drifted, waiting, wondering—

Suddenly, she was interrupted with a loud toot from the end of the beach, and she sat up.

"I knew it—it's just bullshit!" she had said to herself, as the minutes ticked by, and the car disappeared, and things went quiet again.

Suddenly she spotted something dark and moving at the water's edge. Frowning, she leaned forward and squinted into the dark water trimmed with grey wave froth. For a moment, she was utterly focused on the spot, and then she said a gentle voice clearly whispered in her ear, *"My timing is perfect."*

The sound made her jump to her feet and look about her in the dark. "Who's there?" She said she had actually called out, because it sounded so real, but only the silence of the darkening evening returned to her.

She looked at me quizzically. "Wajilla, I thought I must have imagined it, or maybe I was going mad, so I shrugged it off, and I turned back to the beach and the water's edge where I was looking before. Still—I swear, I had heard that voice."

She said she stood up and took a step toward the water, and she pointed in front of her as she relived the story for me. "When I decided it was not a croc, I walked toward it, and found it was a green turtle hauling itself up on the sand. Looking down, I could see it had a spear firmly lodged in the back of its shell."

"Oh, god, poor old fulla—look what someone's done to you."

She had leaned down and picked the thing up with her hands linked under its shell on either side. She said the animal was heavy—almost too heavy for her small frame—but she managed to carry it and walked up the beach until she reached the first set of lights. When she saw a man walking to his letter box at the front of his property under the streetlights, she yelled out, "Hey, mate, you got a phone? I need to ring someone."

"My god, what have you got there?" He leaned forward to help lift the heavy reptile in the small woman's arms.

"Green turtle, I think, and someone has speared it. It will have air in its shell and not be able to swim."

"We'd better ring a vet or the animal-rescue people."

"Yeah. You got a box I can put him in?" She said she put the turtle down and saw a hose wound up at the side of the property, and she ran over to it, yelling behind her, "Is it okay if I use the hose? It might need a drink."

A muffled voice replied, "Go ahead if you think it will help, but don't they drink salt water?"

She pulled the hose along the manicured grass and turned the tap on. Pouring the water over its shell and over its face, she saw the turtle had drawn its head into its shell very slowly, and she said she realized that it was pretty sick.

"I got a box right here in the garage; hang on a minute, and I'll get it," the man called from inside.

Together they put the turtle in the box, and the man rang the after-hours number for animal rescue and offered to drive Jyly and the turtle into the depot.

They set off with the turtle propped up in the box on the backseat with Jyly in the front, leaning over to check on it from time to time. She told me that on the way, they talked about how it might have happened, and the man made a remark that maybe it was a local spear fisherman who had lost control of his weapon.

Jyly said she replied a little defensively. "I suppose you mean an 'indigenous fulla' filling his quota, eh?"

She said it was obvious the man recognized her sensitivity and quietly changed the subject.

He asked her who she worked for, and she said she told him she was at Coles now, but she used to work for the Ulmarra Foundation. He immediately showed some interest and asked her if that was the place that was being closed down because of fraud allegations.

She looked at me and said, "I was shocked when I heard that, and I couldn't believe that would be true."

"It's a mess, that's for sure," I said. "But we ain't been closed down as far as I know, and the Queen wouldn't let it happen, you can be sure."

She said when they got to the depot, an animal-care person inspected the turtle and said that it needed urgent attention. She took all the details from Jyly and told her that the turtle was lucky to have been found, as it would soon have dried out and died because it was so weak with infection and was starving. "This probably happened three months ago, by the look of its condition," the woman said, and Jyly shook her head as she told her story.

Jyly told me she wasn't sure why she said it, but she replied, "Yeah, a lot happened back then for me too. It's strange how this poor old fulla's been struggling and being sick for so long and no one found him. You have to be in the right place at the right time—and tonight was the right time for the turtle to be saved, I guess."

The woman nodded knowingly and laughed, "Well that's right—we all end up meeting our 'appointments' in the end, but some of them aren't so nice, are they? And finally, one day you have to get brave to haul yourself up from whatever sea you have found yourself in and present yourself for rescue!"

Jyly said the man who had helped her was stroking the shell of the turtle lightly with the back of his finger and said wistfully, "Well, luck aside—is he going to live?"

"Not sure, I'm afraid—we will keep him comfortable."

"And he won't be alone," Jyly said she had whispered, and she tightened her lips as though the conversation had answered something in the depths of her soul.

The lady thanked them for bringing the turtle in and told them they could come back to check on it or give them a call. "So we left, and the guy asked me if I wanted him to drop me off home, but I smiled a little, because I knew what it was all about now. I shook my head, eh, and I said, 'Thanks, but I have an appointment of my own.'"

She said the man nodded and left her in the car park. She started to walk off in the direction of the bus stop, even though it was getting late.

When she told me where her "appointment" was, I grinned broadly and had to stop myself from yelling out, "I knew it!"

Shyly, she began to tell me what happened that night when the "timing was perfect."

When she got to her destination, the darkness was broken only by light oozing from a top story window of Ulmarra's house. She hadn't been there before, but I had, many times; hell, I helped build it!

The property was stacked up against the rain forest behind it. The dense trees climb away to a high rain-forest peak against the sky. Below the house, the road curves down to meet the Crystal Cascades roadway leading up to the falls. The distant sound of the river, winding down through the granite boulders, would have drifted up to the home where Jyly knocked on the front door and waited.

She said the outside light was not on, and she wondered if anyone was at home.

The walls are made from cedar, and the entire building is designed to ensure the lowest carbon footprint. It was one of the first homes to be entirely solar powered, as I remember, with water storage underneath and a biodegradable system for waste. Jimmy loved building that place, and, I admit, I loved it too.

Jyly told me she had leaned back and looked along the street. Most of the houses couldn't be seen, as they were also tucked into the surrounding trees. She walked back down the steps and along the road, thinking, "So much for my timing."

"Trying to make a decision?" A cool voice came up silently beside her, and she jumped.

She said she took a deep breath in and calmed her nerves. "I've already made one."

"Yeah? Which way are you going?"

"Um—whichever way you are."

She said Jimmy had grabbed her tiny hand and said quietly, "I was in the bath and didn't hear you. You wanna join me? Can always heat the water up again."

She turned to look at him and sure enough, he was standing in a towel, and his skin was wet under the moonlight that had risen above the street.

"You're a wild man—not much between you and an arrest warrant!" she had said, looking at the towel.

"Enough is all you gotta have—just enough!"

"So are you going to take me in?"

"Yep—you can join me python named Roger; we can be one big, happy family."

They began to walk up the street towards his home. She said they were talking rubbish like no one dared stop talking, in case it all got too serious.

"Roger! Why the hell did you call your snake that?"

"Because he didn't suit Fred."

"I see..."

She said the two stepped into the house that had polished bare boards, and she could see Ulmarra's wet footprints where he had walked out to find her.

"Couldn't you have picked an abo name for it?" she had kept talking.

"Nah, he's deaf, so it wouldn't matter what I called him—actually, I never say anything to him: just 'G'dday, snake, here's your rat for this week.' He don't care what I say, long as he gets his rat an' I let him out for a walk round the house now and then."

"I suppose you are surprised to see me after three months." He didn't reply, and she turned in the hall to see if he was following her.

As soon as she did, he reached forward and grasped her in his arms, locking a long kiss on her willing lips. He pressed her against the door, and it closed with a click.

Together they wrapped together like the python they had been talking about, making up for lost time. He pulled her clothes from her, swinging her in his arms and carrying her into the lounge room. There he laid her on a wide, Balinese-style couch with huge, soft cushions covered in a leaf-design fabric. As he put her down and rolled himself over her, she whispered, "I can't explain; I just knew I had to..."

"You don't have to explain—I know you, and you know me; it's a Dreamtime thing. Somehow planned. Whatever it is—I can't tell you why I feel like electricity is running through my stomach right now, and I feel like I'm gonna cry when I'm with you like this—"

She pressed a kiss on his lips to stop him, and she whispered back, "Someone famous once told me that sometimes you just have to cry to clear your eyes—so your heart can see the way out of its cage."

He shook his head, and the mop of curls tousled to find a position. Then he looked down at her. "Thank you—that's better than I said it."

"Yeah, right—I just added a bit to improve it."

"That's what you do: you improve me."

"And you make me someone I wanted to be.

"And who is that?"

"Someone free."

"Free?"

"I'm not what someone thinks about me when I am with you. I'm not someone who just lives where they started. I'm the 'me' I thought I should've been. When I was six, I used to think I could be anything, and, by the time

I got to thirteen, I thought, 'You liar, you were never going to be anyone at all, just an abo chick—a nobody.' Just some meaningless, breathing, bag of flesh looking at the world and never being in it. But you make me feel like I've added up to something. I'm the real me, and all the other crap, is just that: meaningless crap. You make me think that if I wanna walk out on that road right now, naked, and pick that flower growing on the curb, I can do that—"

"Mmmm—naked!"

"Stop it—you know what I mean. I feel like I am free with you. It's so easy, I don't have to try to be anything. I can think what I like—say what I like."

"What do you want to say?"

"Nothing, really."

"That's good," he whispered. "Best language is the silent one."

He kissed her, and they fell into "the embrace of oneness" like they had never been apart, and the waterfall was all around them again, and time had got caught up in it and stopped.

I'm not sure what she meant by that, but I can guess that these two really knew what it meant to be "one flesh."

She told me that afterwards, they ate and sat in the room arm in arm and watched the moon playing with the trees through windows that were cut in the shape of huge glass leaves in the wall.

Jimmy had cut every one of those leaf windows by hand and fitted them into their frames. He probably broke twice as many as the ones that ended up in the wall. Every part of that house said something about Jimmy, but it had never been complete until she got there.

She said that eventually they had gotten tired, and he took her up the wooden staircase cut into a whole tree log that led to the upper part of the house.

I knew that staircase. We spent weeks cutting the steps out, and when you walked up them, you walked up the tree into the sky. They took you to a loft master bedroom, where a low bed of carved timber was attached to the ceiling by trunks that had been carved in the shape of vines and leaves, twisting up to the ceiling where it flowed into a curved timber roof. Across the ceiling, colorful dotted panels of aboriginal art spanned the smooth, arched timber and led to an opening where the painted creatures appeared to leap out into the night sky.

"Wow—who did this?"

"Me—took me ten years, and it isn't finished."

"What does it mean?"

"It means, start here—end there." He pointed from the bed close to the floor, and then to the images funneling out of the opening on the roof.

"That's not very deep."

"Yeah, it is—it's a miracle."

"Yeah? How do you work that out?"

"To be here at the bottom, someone before you had to survive, and before them, and back. If you look back to all them people, hundreds of thousands of people born—millions never made it. Millions of all them humans never moved forward to the next generation; they were cut off. But one by one, each generation of your ancestors survived—and they made the rungs of the ladder of who you are.

"See, this branch here goes up to this next one there, see?" He pointed to a tiny snout hiding in the vines. "And up there..." She could see another quoll's head peered from his vantage point further up.

"Now, thanks to each one of their stories, here you are. You're the 'rung' in this generation. That's the miracle.

"But up there on the ceiling—that's what our people become when they leave and look back at us. See, they jump off there and go out to their freedom through that window." He pulled her in close as they stood and stared at the work.

"All of them rungs on the ladder you're on, are looking back too, and they're saying, 'Go for it—survive! We're singing for you to be what you were chosen for—before you go on to the Dreamtime place.'"

He leaned down and pulled the covers back, while she traced the beautiful carvings with her fingers.

"What most people don't understand about themselves, is they are sifted out. They are special individuals. They're made from all the sifted-out, chosen individuals of the past, and they're on the rung that everyone ahead counts on."

"One sperm that made it, you reckon. That's what makes me special?"

"More than that. That's just the beginning of your survival story. You didn't die of whooping cough, or fall off your bike and smash your head open; you didn't have a car accident, you didn't choke on a chicken bone, you didn't drown… Most of our people back in my ancestors' day were killed; they were shot like kangaroos and left to rot. But out of all those Yidinji, my ancestor *lived*, and our ladder of people moved forward, step by step. You don't realize the odds beaten to be alive right now."

"Okay, okay! So, I am still alive. I'm lucky, so far."

"Nah, you're not just lucky: you've got a purpose."

"Nah, just lucky," she said, because she had never thought her life had amounted to enough to be any more than just that.

She told me Jimmy had pushed her towards the low bed amid the carved wooden vines and painted leaves.

"What is luck?" he whispered into her neck as he clasped his arms around her small body.

"I dunno. Chance, I guess—something random?"

"What happens to the atoms of a star when it heats up and the pressure gets so great that it explodes?"

"It shoots off in all directions, I guess."

"Random chaos, right?" She told me she was being distracted by his kisses but nodded as she knelt down on the bed before him.

"Some hit each other, some smash into the next star—some fly off into space, never to be seen again?"

"Yeah."

"No plan—just wherever, right? 'Luck' in motion. What if all the stars of the very first energy ball just blew up, and everything just randomly spun off into oblivion in a big bang? What would you have?"

"A mess."

"Right—that's my point. After matter explodes in all directions, it doesn't gather and organize itself if the rule working is luck or chaos."

"I guess so."

"When I look at everything, *order* is the rule—not chaos. So I reckon that all the life in the universe isn't random, either." He had turned and stared into her eyes, and she said she might just as well have been looking into the stars deep inside him, and then he had said, "And that means, neither are we."

"Okay, so there is a plan. So what's my purpose?"

"Whatever fits with the big purpose."

"What?"

"Only you can find that out—if you are looking for it. Right now, I would guess it's being with me."

"I like that purpose."

"That is the first hint that you are in your purpose."

"Hey?"

"There's always a draw card, something that leads you on in a direction. The draw card, it's like the drag of the moon, the tide, the deep water under the earth shifting." She turned on her side, ready for sleep, and he curved around her back and kissed her shoulder. In the light of the moon shuddering through the opening in the roof, they lay still and peaceful.

"Tomorrow I wanna take you to see a good place," he said gently.

She whispered, "Okay," and began to fall into the daze before sleep. As she did, she told me she saw the creatures seem to come to life, and she watched them crawl up the vines, passing each other and scrambling along the pathways, clambering over the ceiling towards the opening. She watched dreamily as they climbed out into the night and instantly dissolved as they hit the moonlight and became free spirits to mix with the forest above.

If creation had a purpose, she said she had suddenly realized that she had found hers. And I thought, "Yeah—them two were on the 'Ulmarra ladder,' and they were going to climb it together."

Chapter 11

I WAS HAPPY FOR them both. I don't think anyone, except maybe Louisa, wouldn't have been. It really looked like two people who were made exactly for each other.

That day I sat there with Jyly, she drinking tomato juice and me a Crownie, she looked like she'd swallowed a star or something, and every time she opened her mouth, her heart just glowed from between her white teeth.

She said that in the morning he had driven her to Gordon Vale. She'd been looking quietly out the window to the pyramid mountain. She said it stood alone, fringed with forest, and the township of Gordon Vale at its feet looked as though the mountain was the mother of a myriad of children buzzing around her skirts.

"Where are we going?" she had asked him.

He didn't answer her but pulled off, taking a road that headed down to the river. A few tire tracks showed where teenage drivers had carved out circles for their fast evening play, probably in beaten-up Holdens, the first all-Australian cars. Jyly wondered what could be here that was worth the trip.

When he stopped and parked under a huge tree fringed with long rhino grass waving in the breeze, she said she shook her head and, curious, looked out the window to the place he had brought her.

He stepped out and looked across the wild fringe to the river, and then he put his hands in his pockets and walked ahead of her. She followed quietly, looking about at the scene.

Eventually, he walked them towards the end of a field planted in sugar cane that stopped at the river boundary. It curved up to the base of low hills that eventually would be cut by the Gillies Gorge road that headed up into the mountains of the range.

Suddenly he looked toward the upper end of the field. She said she stopped beside him. The tall, six-feet-high cane fanned out in its rows ahead of them.

"Over there." Jimmy pointed to the distant trees at the end.

"What is it?"

"That's where the last of my people, my blood—that's where they lived. That was their dry-season camp."

"Really?"

"Come on."

"No way—there will be taipans in there."

He stopped, looked back at her, and then looked out across the field.

"Nah—they sleep up in that clay bit over there." But he picked up a stick and whacked the cane before walking in and disappearing.

"How do you know that—" She told me she had stood considering whether she would follow him, because a cane field was bound to be full of poisonous snakes. His muffled voice came from somewhere ahead. "You coming?"

She dived into the tall cane spears, looking down the rows and back to her feet. She said she knew she didn't need to be scared with him around, but she was still worried about the deadly local reptile and hurried to catch him.

After ten minutes, they reached the upper end of the field. In front of them were a few straggling eucalyptus trees and long grass. A kookaburra flew into the branches nearby and sat looking down at them.

"Is this where they lived?" she said.

He looked around as though he was seeing the village, the people sitting under the trees, and the children playing with sticks. "This is it."

She said he took a few steps towards the trees. "Not a single sign of them now. Not even one thing—"

"Wait," Jyly had said. "Look at these—quite a few have got curved sides." She picked up a heavy stone that was weathered like it was just a river stone."

Ulmarra frowned and picked up two for himself and fitted the curves together. Another stone, thrown up under the trees and buried in grass, was found, and between them, they started to rebuild a circle.

"Looks like these could have been a fire circle," Jyly said. "Maybe they weren't lost when they cultivated the field."

He smiled as he put his arm around her shoulder.

"Yeah—could just be a pile of stones left over from a flood, too!"

"You got no imagination!" She smacked his chest and pointed to the cut-out chinks in the rocks that seemed to fit together so well. She scowled at him and said, "You might not want to believe it, Ulmarra, but the land doesn't deny they were here, even if all the people who have ever owned this field do. Don't you know, the land pushes the stones up to the top and says, 'See? They used to eat my children's meat here and talk and laugh while they lived on me.'" She said he paused, a look of admiration and amazement on his face.

"You might be right." He looked at her and then walked away into the trees and bobbed down on his haunches, linking his fingers together and looking into the surrounding soil.

She said she had walked quietly up to him.

"Most of them died here," he whispered. "My white ancestor Margaret wrote it in her book—she sat here for a whole day holding the hand of her dead friend. Nearly all of them had been murdered by a mob of drunken vigilante settlers led by Margaret's jealous husband."

Then, as he said that very phrase, a huge white cockatoo sailed overhead effortlessly. It headed for the trees at the fringe of the river and landed heavily in the canopy.

Jimmy stood up and watched it like he had gone back a hundred-and-thirty years to the day, remembering something in the diary. "Those that escaped, went up there into the forest. Margaret's own half-cast baby survived and was taken back to the town. If he hadn't been found...if she had died of starvation... if she hadn't met—"

"I get it." Jyly told me she had smiled and walked up to him, resting her hand on his shoulder. "So what do you think the purpose was for your ladder surviving?" She thought he might say it was to meet her, but he didn't. It was far deeper than that.

"To heal."

"Yeah?"

"To take us back, so we can go forward."

"Something is pulling you?"

"Yeah, that's what it feels like. The foundation is just the frills— underneath is what I am." He picked up a seed from the base of the tree and walked out toward the edge of the field. She said he dug a small hole and buried it as though wherever he walked, the reason for the foundation walked with him.

Standing up, he smiled, she told me, and he had said, "Come on." He strode over and collected her hand as they walked down toward the river.

They picked their way along the edge of the river stones until they reached some huge boulders. Behind them, the trunk of a massive fichus tree spread its canopy out over the rocks and the water. "This is the mother tree. This tree would have been here from when they were first here. It's about three hundred years old, at least. It's lived here through floods and fires and watched the clouds go by while good and bad things happened all around here.

"The first Ulmarra took a bit off it and put it where the old woman is buried." He looked at Jyly. "See, he didn't know, but the *pull* made him come out here and get it, even though he didn't know what this tree meant to her." He looked up at it and then smiled at Jyly. "Come on, I'll show you."

They headed to the vehicle and drove back through Gordon Vale, turning off at the junction of a large subdivision where new, plastered houses with fences and steel roofs blanketed the land.

She told me they had wound their way through the roadways and finally reached the lower section of the estate, where a green, mowed area met the road, and the land tipped down in a small park that had two creeks that met and formed the boundary of the whole estate.

Jimmy stopped the car. "I haven't been here for a while." He smiled, and, as Jyly stepped around the car and onto the grass, he grabbed her hand, and they walked towards a huge tree.

When they arrived, he pointed to a new concrete wall with sections of iron grid built into it. It surrounded a section that had been concreted over, and a bronze plaque was fixed in the center. The plaque told a brief history of the settlers of the area and announced that Margret Stanford founded the original farm of the estate and renamed it Ulmarra for the Mallanburra people who were the traditional owners of the land from here to the boundaries of the Mulgrave River.

Jimmy looked at the plaque and shook his head. "This is supposed to honor her—look at how they have sealed her under there with concrete, just so they don't have to clean up the weeds or the grass."

But Jyly said to him, "Hey, mate—look up, she ain't under there anymore. She came up in the sap of this tree, and she is waving her arms up into the sunlight."

He understood.

"Yeah—you're right. This tree came off that big one I showed you, and I took a bit off this one when I went on my first walkabout—I planted it for my own time, so there are three from the same root. The Mallanburra people, Margret and Mullegadajawara's, and me."

"Where?" Jyly told me she had perked up, and her eyes had sparkled with interest.

"Up there —in the Rainforest Cathedral."

"Take me; I wanna see."

"Okay—but not today; it's a long walk up there."

"Take me." She said she had reached over and grasped his forearm. "I can do it—take me now."

He smiled and shook his head, and then nodded. "We'll have to camp up there overnight."

"That's okay, I love camping—makes me feel like a genuine abo!"

The two walked back to the car, and Ulmarra drove towards the base of White Rock, stopping at Mt Sheridan Dairy, where they bought some water bottles, a loaf of bread, and a tin of baked beans.

They drove up to the base of the mountain, finally parking in a turning area at the end of the road where the last houses are built up against the range. Together they got out of the Ute, and Jimmy grabbed the bag that had the bottles of water and supplies in it, and they disappeared into the undergrowth.

When they found themselves under the canopy of the first trees, a few wrappers showed where local kids had explored the trees at the mountain base and, no doubt, had built secret huts and played the games of wilder times.

The rainforest closed around them as they walked on, and the ground began to rise up in a steep slope. They climbed up through dense jungle, getting higher and higher. They were following an overgrown path that seemed to be no path at all, but Jimmy knew where he was going.

Nearly an hour-and-a-half later, they reached a steep plateau strewn with huge boulders pressed into the earth of the mountainside like sweets in some ancient icing made from green palms and grass ferns. They reached an area between a cleft in two massive rock escarpments that looked as though a scoop of earth had been taken from the mountainside to create a small, almost flattened canyon. It was fringed with rain forest and scattered with rocks. A huge fichus stood alone, steeped in copper shadows covering the whole back area, with the mountain climbing straight up behind it. It was beautiful and felt secret.

"Well, this is it." Jimmy indicated the big tree and knelt down on his knees, panting slightly."

"What made you put it here?"

"Something she said in her journal. Mullegadajawara brought her up here to see a quoll, and they slept somewhere on the edge of here looking out at that." He turned to walk through the undergrowth to the edge, and Jyly looked about also. "Old Margaret told her son to find this place because the "author of the Dreamtime" made his own cathedrals and didn't think much of the man-made ones. This is one of his."

Before them, the coastal inlet spread out in front of the mountain. The city of Cairns, with its few high-rise buildings facing the sea, sparkled white and glistened, in the dusk light that was beginning to end the afternoon.

"The buildings look like a coral-shell necklace in this light."

Jimmy began to look around for some long sticks to begin to build a shelter for them. "I stayed up here about a week," he said quietly.

"A week! Bet you needed a shower when you came down."

"I didn't go down—I kept walking up over that peak past Tinnaroo and out to Mareeba and hitched my way over to Kakadu."

"So that is how the great Ulmarra began his journey."

"Yep, it began right here under that third tree, but it was just a foot-high sapling in those days."

She told me they had made a camp, ate the tin of baked beans on bread, and watched the dusk go down over the sea, until it was dark, and the sparkling city lights of Cairns spread out like a starry shawl. She said the light of the small fire bounced off their faces, and Ulmarra began to sing some ancient song he had learned from Willy's old mother.

When he stopped, Jyly told me she had asked him to teach her and, line, by line, she learned the song under the stars in the Rainforest Cathedral and felt as if she had finally come home.

When they were finished, they stared at each other, and a long moment went by.

Finally, he undid his leather necklace and pulled it out from under his singlet.

"Long time ago, a man gave a woman this. He had a spirit knitted into the skin of it, so that it glowed for the one he wanted to give it to, and his magic would never leave her. I've got the feeling that it is glowing now, so that means it is time to give it to someone."

Jyly said she frowned slightly, not sure what he was doing. He untied the small kangaroo-skin pouch tied fast to the leather and tipped the contents into his hand. The gold chain spilled into his palm and, in the center, a natural, peach-colored pearl sat reflecting its light on his skin. He handed it to her.

For a moment, she said she was unsure what she should do. Then she quietly took it from him, looked at it carefully, pulled the gold chain over her small head, negotiating around her bunny tail at the back, and let it fall to her breast.

"Wherever I am—I got your magic on me when I wear this."

"Yep." She told me he had simply leaned over and kissed her. "Time to sleep, eh?"

She said to me she had smiled and stood. Holding the pearl tight in her small hand, she had stepped forward and bowed low to enter the buru he had made.

Jimmy dug up some of the soil around the fire with a flat stone and scooped it over the embers until its light and heat was extinguished, and then he crawled over the grass and into the shelter.

Under the leaves of their makeshift buru, she said they began to doze in each other's arms. Jyly's voice broke the silence of the darkness. "I want the words that's gonna join us, said here."

"You think I can get them fat elders to hike up here?"

"If you ask them, they will come. If they won't, we will say our own words, and that will do."

"Okay, Guba-Guba—go to sleep now."

"Guba-Guba?"

"You're named for the pearl now, but one day you'll be Guli."

"Guli?"

"The Yidinji name for mother-of-pearl, so one day, when there is a little Ulmarra, you'll be named for that."

"I like that. I want you to teach me everything."

"No need—the land does it, the rainforest, the sea, the wind... And everything alive says it aloud. I can only teach you how to listen."

"Okay."

"So, first lesson..."

"Yeah?"

"Shut up and go to sleep."

Jyly told me she had smiled in the darkness and slipped into a deep sleep to the sound of the night birds sounding out and the rustle of the last of the quoll, seeking out his evening meal.

Chapter 12

S HE TOLD ME that when she woke, the morning was bathed in fingers of gold light welling up from the lowland of cane fields and habitation below them and reflecting off the turquoise Pacific rolling over the Great Barrier Reef.

Jyly stretched in the buru as spears of light darted through small openings between the leaves and bark covering above her. She said she suddenly realized she was alone. She said that she quickly rose and crawled from the entrance.

She looked about and, seeing some disturbance in the otherwise untouched grasses of the plateau, she followed a trail up the side of it. As she began to puff a little, she looked about her for some sign of Jimmy.

She said she finally saw a glimpse of his shiny black back, hunched in the undergrowth.

Not sure what he was looking at, she walked up cautiously. With a mischievous grin on her face, she said she planned to surprise him, but as she peered around a huge boulder cemented in the hillside, she paused.

Watching on, she said she saw Ulmarra seated on his haunches with his hands resting in the grass and an animal, spotted and long-tailed, was sniffing up his forearms.

She watched as the creature continued to sniff about the aborigine and began licking the salt off his skin.

She shifted her position slightly, and she said, as she did it, a dry eucalyptus leaf was crushed slightly under her feet. The sound was minimal, but the quoll froze and looked up in her direction and then turned hastily and hopped over the grass, standing for a moment to stare down the slope, and then it hurriedly darted into the undergrowth.

Jimmy dropped his head and shook it.

"Sorry," she said she had called out.

She walked up to him and forced herself into his chest, resting her head on his skin, breathing in his scent, and stroking his neck with her small, brown hand.

"But you love me, right?"

"I dunno..."

"What?"

"I mean, Mr. and Mrs. Quoll get together because they are perfect for each other; you think that's love or just a good pairing?"

"Nah, I know what love is. For one thing, Mr. Quoll would soon run away in a forest fire to save himself. But not us, right? I'd give up everything for you."

"Yeah—me too."

"Now you know what love is. It's when you can sacrifice all—including your wallet and the TV remote."

"What you're telling me is, it is going to cost, and it's going to hurt."

"Yeah—but what a lovely way to die!"

"That's your opinion!"

She kissed him and pulled him down to the grass.

She told me they made love up there, in the Rainforest Cathedral, and when they were finished, they lay in each other's arms.

Jyly said the sight of the quoll with him had made her very curious, and she asked him, "How did you find the quoll?"

"It found me."

"I can't get over how nothing is afraid of you."

She said Ulmarra didn't answer.

"Is it some kind of power?"

"Nah..."

"Tell me—please, I want to know everything."

"When I was young, I went on walkabout from here, and out in it, I got time to think. I just learned to be part of the same world they are."

"You should have been a Buddhist."

"Nah—the Buddha is dead; no man should follow another man unless he wants to end up where the first one is, in the ground."

"I'd follow you."

"Never do that— I guarantee I got no answers to escape what every man has to face."

She said they lay in silence for a few minutes watching the leaves of the trees shimmering and the morning rise.

"So tell me, why did you start the foundation?"

"Someone has to walk."

"Walk?"

"When the dry used to come, our people would pack up and follow the rains. And when the rains came, they would pack up again and go to a dry place."

"I don't get it."

"Needs, sense, and survival."

"No one is going to pack up and leave the cities."

"Can you imagine that day when one of our tribe looked up at the sky, not having a calendar nor one rain cloud as a clue, but knowing that when the figs start to drop their fruit and the wallaby start to disappear from the plain, it was time to move.

"That man was reading the signs of the times, but that wasn't the clever bit. That guy would pack up his stuff and put it on his back and start walking, 'cause he knew what was coming next. The others would see him doing it and, one by one, they started to do the same, even if they hadn't been out on the plains or up where the figs grow."

She said he touched her nose playfully with the tip of a grass stem. "The clever bit of being made a human being, is, after you have seen the signs—being able to do something about it."

She said Jimmy Ulmarra lifted himself up onto his knees and then pulled himself up to his feet.

"If one man 'walks'—some of the rest will follow, and that is all it takes to shift a village to a better future."

"That's only if the village has got enough brains to follow."

"That is what the foundation is about. It's a signpost. It says, 'Look, we gotta be part of the landscape. We gotta get our hands back into the rhythm of the soil and the pattern of the rains. We gotta move our lives *around* the natural order, not the other way around.'"

"But what about all this stuff happening to stop it?"

"We just keep going." She said he got up and started to walk back toward the edge of the mountain and the path back to their buru.

"How, if they find a way to shut it down?"

"One foot after another. That's how," he said as they walked back. "It doesn't take a 'foundation' to plant a tree. Ideas live on, with or without us. If we get taken out and can't walk, someone else will—because, like it or not, the dry season is coming, and they'll die if they don't move."

Listening to Jyly's story, I would bet that quoll would have gingerly poked its nose out and wondered at the two as they left his sanctuary, not knowing that his life was wrapped up in Jimmy's story too. Maybe we all were.

Chapter 13

WHILE JIMMY AND Jyly were up on the mountain, Louisa was at the foundation offices early that Saturday. I had called in to make sure the chopper had been organized for the Fraser Island dingo transfer, and she had told me she was on her own again, because Jimmy hadn't turned up, and she was snowed under.

Amy was supposed to be at his mother's that weekend, and he wasn't too pleased about that. His dingo bites had healed, and he wasn't getting everyone's attention, so he was looking for new adventures and causing his mum some trouble, so I'd picked him up. I was going to take him up to Port Douglass to do some fishing, but, since no one knew where Jimmy was, I came in to give Lou a hand instead, and Amy had to tag along.

She was at her desk, and she was busier than ever. There had been a desperate flurry of legal appointments, letters, and requests for interviews just that week, like everything was coming to a head. She should have been having time off, too, but was at her desk as though it was just another day.

She was deep in matching invoices with projects when suddenly, footsteps came clumping down the hall, and she lifted her head, and so did I, because I thought it might have been Jimmy, and Amy and I could get going.

Samson opened the door instead and saw her.

"Oh—Louisa." He stuttered, slightly taken aback then caught himself. "D-don't you go home?"

"Yes, sometimes; I don't sleep here, you know, even if I could get more done if I did.

He walked over to a set of filing cabinets and began looking inside when he noticed my boy and me.

"Oh, hey, mate, glad to see you up and about already. How's the kid there?"

"What are you doing up so early, Samson?" Louisa asked. "I thought you took weekends off." She had interrupted before Amy could say a word, and he looked at me and made a face.

Samson started looking in a set of cupboards distractedly. "I have lost—my notebook, with all the carry-over invoice info in it. I could have sworn I had it in my briefcase, but it isn't there, and I don't know where I could have left it. I never let that thing out of my sight."

"Well, why did you think it would be here?"

"Goddamn it! I have to find it…" He'd begun to fluster, and we all jumped with surprise. "I've got part payments on three projects and about seven others all ready mapped out, and I need that notebook! Not only that, but I've already applied for grant money, so I won't know what it belongs to!"

"Why did you do that?" Louisa dropped what she was doing. "What do you mean, you have already applied? You know we can't do that till we supply an invoice."

"Shit—'cause it's easier to write up a dummy invoice and apply than fill out fifty submissions for one damned project. Where the hell could this thing be?"

Louisa looked to me like she was getting a bit worried about what he had said. "When did you start doing this?"

He skirted her question. "Never mind the paperwork, Lou—I've got it all under control if I can just find my notebook!"

"I can ask the boys if they've seen—"

"What am I going to do now?" He slammed the cupboard door, and all three of us jumped with surprise. He turned and flew out like a skinned lizard, without saying good-bye, and didn't even close the door behind him.

Louisa frowned heavily. "That was odd."

I replied, "He's normally a real friendly bloke. That missing book's got him rattled, that's for sure."

"I've never seen him like that," she said, quietly wondering.

Suddenly we heard the sound of footsteps again and, for a second, thought he had returned to maybe apologize or something.

Louisa didn't look up from what she was writing, but just started saying, "So you're back to say good-bye after all—and maybe you can explain to me how I'm going to fix up some new muck up you've created."

"Ms. Louisa Henderson?"

We all heard an unfamiliar voice. It wasn't Sam, after all.

It was some kind of a uniformed police officer standing in the doorway, and behind him were two other officers and a man in a suit.

"Yes—what is this about?" Louisa said.

The three officers came lumbering into the room, filling up the space nearly entirely, and stood in their spit-and-polished brass-button big boots, with the suit guy close behind.

Amy looked at me with eyes as big as saucers, since he'd seen a few cops in his time, and he must have thought I had got up to something, because his mum often threatened me with some bogus garbage.

The first one must have been a sergeant or something and he spoke again. "You are hereby placed under arrest for unlawful intent to gain personal advantage and thereby commit fraud against the state of Queensland."

"What!" I got up as quick as I could and hobbled over to confront the bloke. "Are you kidding?"

He ignored me, and I noticed Amy got up too and walked over to Louisa and hung onto her arm defensively.

"Ms. Henderson, I am obliged to tell you your rights."

"No way," I insisted, "What are you talking about? I don't know what this is about, but it's utter rubbish!" Louisa just stood there dead still, like a roo caught in the headlights of a Kenworth.

The man in the suit stepped forward. "Ms. Henderson, we have substantial evidence against you, so I would suggest you utilize the opportunity to hear your rights."

"I know my rights!" She snapped back. "This has to be some kind of joke. Whatever 'evidence' you've got has to be fabricated, and that is going to be found out in due course. The most you are going to achieve by arresting me is to waste my valuable time!"

The policeman quietly took a step towards her and began to read her rights to her from a beaten-up card clutched in his hands. She sighed heavily and shook her head, like she could deny what was happening. Amy looked up at her scowling face and then turned and scowled the men watching her.

When the young officer was finished, he asked her to follow him from the room and accompany him to the Cairns police station.

She nodded, turned to Amy, and smiled weakly. "It'll be okay, Amy—don't worry, I'll be back soon, I guess."

"I'll ring Jimmy, and we'll come down and sort it out."

"Sure—if you can find him!" she whispered before picking up her handbag angrily from the desk.

As she began to walk forward, the man in the suit moved quickly to meet her.

"Ms. Henderson, if you don't mind..." He leaned forward and pointed to her bag. "We will need to search that before you leave."

"My God—what do you think I have?"

"I'm sorry, but we will need to." The young man held out his hand to collect the bag.

She paused for a few moments and then thrust the bag to him.

He opened the bag and emptied the contents on the desk, placing each item back in it one at a time, including a small silk container containing tampons, and I looked away quickly and grabbed my boy and pulled him to the side of the room with me.

The sergeant hurriedly dropped them back in the case, and Louisa's eyes begin to flash with utter shame and fury. He handed her the bag and, with his head bowed a little, he said, "Sorry—it's just procedure."

"I'm surprised you didn't search me for a concealed bomb in my underwear. I am, after all, an environmental terrorist, am I not?"

The suit shook his head and indicated to the other two officers that they should start to search the rest of the office.

Louisa stepped into the hall with her escort, and, as she did, she yelled over her shoulder, "You won't find anything. We store all our really *incriminating* documents up a dingo's ass, and I dare you to try and find anything even there!"

I followed close behind, with Amadeus right beside me, saying, 'Dad, where's Uncle Jimmy? He can fix it, eh?"

"Yeah, son—it'll be okay." But I had this sick feeling in my stomach that was warning me something pretty bad was going down.

Louisa just walked with the officer with her head held high like the nickname we had for her behind her back. She went out of the building in silence, and, as she saw the three police cars in the foundation's parking area, she whispered, "I'm honored to require so much attention."

Amy ran around me to give her a big hug as she stood still for a moment, waiting.

"So," she said to the cop who was opening the door of the first vehicle, "do you think I'm going to need a lawyer, or is this just one of those 'procedure'-type arrests that wastes everyone's time and comes to nothing?"

He didn't look at her but said, "If I was you, Louisa, I would get the best one you can afford."

She looked at him quickly, and I saw a moment of fear pass over her face, and then she bent low and got into the car, and the cop shut her in.

"I'll find Ulmarra—we gonna come sort this out okay?" I knocked on the window to get her attention and yelled through the glass. "Don't worry, Lou, we'll work it out!" She never turned her head to look at me, and the police sergeant seated himself in the front and started the vehicle.

As she realized she was about to be taken, she finally turned and looked at Amy, smiling shyly. He put his hand up and pressed it flat on the glass, and she put her own up against it on the other side.

At that moment I saw, for the first time, the cracks of her painful world: Jimmy rejecting her and the strain of holding the foundation together had a part to play, but the humiliation of being unjustly arrested seemed to shatter her inside, and the break crackled across her eyes like an earthquake through concrete. From within, a spring of crystal-clear tears shuddered on the brink of those delicate rims like faithful soldiers waiting for her command to fall with abandon at last. I saw her holding it all back, but Louisa was human, after all, and they fell, and Amy choked back tears of his own.

"It's okay, mate—I cry heaps, and it don't do me no harm." I patted his back as he dropped his hand and held tightly on to mine.

Louisa picked up the corner or her skirt, because she didn't have a handkerchief, and dried her eyes as the cop lowered the window so she could say good-bye. "Sorry, you'd think someone had just died," she said, collecting her composure.

"It's okay, mate—everybody's human."

"Well, I'm not, Wajilla—I can't afford to be human."

"Why not?"

"Because—you know why."

I wasn't sure, actually, but I knew she had her own set of rules and would stick to them no matter what. We watched her as the three cop cars pulled away onto the highway, and as she went I thought, "We're in deep shit without her."

As soon as the cop cars had gone, Amy and me jumped in the Ute, and I took him down to the Hangars at Areoglen where John'o worked, because he was the nearest and only person I could think of who could mind Amy.

He was in the office having a coffee.

"Can you mind Amy, mate? Lou's been arrested. I gotta find Jimmy and sort out what's happening."

"What? Arrested? What for?"

"Mate, I don't understand it. It's gotta be a mistake, but I dunno, the cops said they had 'evidence' of something—god knows what's going on."

"Bloody hell! Sure, I can mind the kid. He can give me a hand washing the chopper—eh, boy?"

Amy smiled, but I could see he would have rather gone with me.

"I'll be back soon, mate; Jimmy and me will get her out, and things'll be just like normal." Amy nodded, and John'o walked me out to the Ute.

"Keep me posted, mate. If there's anything I can do—"

"You're doing it by keeping an eye on my boy; I'll ring you later."

I headed over to Jimmy's place about eleven that morning to see if he was there. To my surprise, he was, and I wondered why he hadn't come in as expected.

"You were supposed to help Lou out this morning!" I said a bit sharply, and he frowned at me.

"Oh shit! I forgot—I'll have to say I'm sorry, I guess."

I saw Jyly was sitting on the big couch and drinking a big cup of coffee, and I got the shock of my life.

"I suppose you want to know—"

"Tell me later!" I said, and she looked up at Jimmy with a worried look on her face, because I was her best mate, and she probably got a surprise by my attitude.

"All hell has broken loose."

"What?" Jimmy followed me in.

"Lou's been arrested while me an Amy were there giving her a hand. Because you 'forgot'!"

"Arrested for what?"

"Something about money missing, I think—and I don't think they're talking about a few hundred out of petty cash. They came in and started searching the place and took her away. We gotta get to the bottom of it." I looked at him closely. "Mate, she's pretty upset—I mean, really upset."

"What did they take?"

"I dunno—how would I know?"

"We better go and take a look on the way to the cop shop an' see if we can find out what they might have on her."

"Yeah—I guess so."

Jimmy walked over to Jyly and kissed her and then stroked her shoulder. "You wait here. Better to stay out of sight for now, until we figure out what's really happening and what we need to do."

She didn't smile but got up and walked to the door with us. "God, I hope it's going to be alright..." she said aimlessly.

"Don't worry —I'll be back later," he said as we both skipped down the path and jumped in the Ute to drive off with a screech of tires.

We arrived at the university but didn't go straight in. Jimmy drove past the entrance to the car park, and we saw a van parked in the driveway. Jimmy looked at it and frowned.

I said, "Let's take a look on the back from the cops, so anyone watching the place or still inside won't see us."

Jimmy trolled past slowly, and he turned left along the boundary of the property instead of right toward the highway.

"Where are ya going?" I said as he stopped beneath a huge overhanging tree planted on the inside of the high, wire fence that contains the university property. He stepped out of the vehicle and looked down the length of the road.

"What you gonna do, mate?" I said.

He didn't say anything back but stepped up to the tree. Jumping up, he grabbed a low branch and pulled it down, then, using it, he levered himself up the fence, grabbing the bows to climb up into the tree.

"Jimmy! There's no way I can do that with this bum leg, mate," I called from the passenger seat of the Ute.

"Get out and walk along, and I'll open the back delivery gate for you."

He walked through the branches and along the bows until he was over the other side. Climbing down, he eventually dropped on all fours to the ground, and I lost sight of him for a moment.

I leaned around and grabbed a few essentials and got out of the vehicle, looked around to make sure no one was watching, and then hobbled down the sidewalk until I got to the car park entrance we used for our plant deliveries. I looked through and couldn't see him, and I thought, "Bastard's gone in without me!"

Suddenly his face appeared, and he said, "Couldn't leave you out there in the cold."

"Yeah, especially since I brought the tools!" I thrust out my hand with a small pinch bar that I always had on the floor of the backseat for emergencies. I guess we're all creatures of habit.

We stepped over a bark garden, through the plantings of native flowers and low shrubs, and came out on a path that skirts the buildings at the back. He stopped outside a low back window, walked over the garden, and tried to pull the screen off. It was locked fast.

"Try this one," I said. "It's got a bend in it."

He stepped along until he found a second window, and, sure enough, that one could be removed.

"Someone's already had a go at it," I said in a whisper, and he nodded.

I thrust out my trusty pinch bar and handed it to him. Soon the window was slightly ajar, enough for us to get our fingernails in, and together we broke the safety catch and forced it open.

Climbing up and in, he disappeared into the opening.

"You'll have to open a door for me. I can't get in with my leg."

"Shhh—we ain't alone, mate. You'll have to give it a go."

I struggled to get my legs in and awkwardly managed to slide ass-first in the window, my bum leg catching on the sill as I squeezed through. Jimmy grabbed it and lowered it to the ground as I sat heavily in a heap below the opening.

"Should have come back later," I whispered, but Jimmy just put his fingers to his lips and pointed two fingers at the door. I struggled up and got my balance, and we walked to the door quietly, opening it to peer out into the hall.

Everything was quiet and dark. Jimmy slipped out and along the wall towards the front, and I hobbled behind him.

When I caught up, I saw Jimmy crouched and hiding in the alcove, and I ducked as I saw two men approach the glass front door. They were locksmiths, and I watched Jimmy creep along the hall and duck into a side office.

I stayed where I was and watched them.

The men started working on the doors, and we could hear them talking. The first man said he hoped the boss didn't blow up, because they were supposed to be there the night before to change the locks, and I thought that if they had, we wouldn't have been able to get in this morning and would have known something was up and maybe could have done something about it before the cops came to arrest Louisa.

The two men seemed oblivious to us, and, after they had removed the old locks, they opened the door and came inside, obviously wanting to snoop around.

"Here we go," I thought. "We're gonna get sprung and get nicked for breaking and entering our own place!" I pulled myself back into the open office, slowly opening the door wide enough to hide myself behind it.

Jimmy pulled back into the shadows too and stood dead still against the wall in the dark.

They walked down the hall and straight past us into Louisa's office.

"Looks like we've missed all the action. Look at this place; they've taken everything except the kitchen sink," the first one said.

"According to the boss, they've been ripping off the system by millions, and they've caught this sheila red-handed with her hand in the cookie jar. They got some insider evidence, so she'll go away for a while, I guess."

"Yeah, right—six years and out in two!"

"Nah; the government don't like you ripping them off! Guy rapes a woman, and he gets six, and he's out in half the time—but you cheat on your taxes or embezzle like this chick, and they'll throw the book at you and make it stick."

"They reckon she was a big deal, with an attitude, too."

"Looks like she's got caught, so that'll shut her up."

"Shame—I thought what they was doin' was quite good, you know."

One of the men swung one of the cabinet doors shut and walked back down the hall, but as he went he said, "These things are always dodgy, mate."

The other bloke replied, "You can't let *those* kind of fullas near the money—they're all the same."

I felt my blood boil and wanted to power out from behind that door and smash him.

Jimmy slumped down on his haunches to wait and listen. I could imagine what he was thinking.

The men continued chatting as they worked on putting the new lock in and, after they were finished, got in their van and drove off.

Jimmy got up and walked to the front doors and looked steadfastly out the glass panes to the open car park, his hands on his hips.

I came out from behind the door, and I whispered, "Are they gone?"

"Yep."

I slammed my hand hard on the door I had been hiding behind and said, "Hope I never meet those pricks anywhere dark, 'cause they're really gonna have something bad to say about us after I've finished with them!"

"That'll just prove to them that they are right about us—buy 'em a drink instead, then they'll feel rotten that they got it wrong."

Jimmy tried the doors, but they wouldn't open from the inside, because they were dead-locked.

"Damn; I guess that means I gotta go back out that window!" I said.

He ignored me and walked toward Louisa's office. He stood there for a while and then pulled out his cell phone. I heard him talking to Jyly, telling her we were going down to the Cairns central police station to help Louisa.

I heard him say, "Nah...There's nothing here...There's just a mess, and the locks have been changed; looks like we're out of business for a while."

I walked down the hall to Louisa's office and looked at the disarray while he finished talking to Jyly.

"She would have been pissed about this," I said, taking a deep breath.

"Yeah—Jyly reckons we are going to have to tell the cops about the incident with your bro. She reckons this is what has started it off in the first place, and it's got out of hand from there. So we need to go back and pick her up."

I said, "Okay. We better go, then."

"Yeah. Try not to fall in the garden on the way out."

Jimmy, Jyly, and me turned up at the police station. I approached the counter first.

"We got some info on our mate that's gonna get her out of here."

"Sorry—what?" The woman was somewhat disinterested.

"You got our mate in here—picked her up this morning, and she ain't done nothing."

"I'm sorry, but if you wait over there—"

"Lady, you need to get the guy in charge out here, so we can tell him this thing is all bullshit!"

"Now, there will be none of that! You go and wait over there. If you just stay quiet, I'll find out who the sergeant in charge is—now, what is your friend's name? Was she brought in on drunk and disorderly?"

"Louisa Henderson." Jimmy stepped up to the counter, and Jyly moved forward beside him and volunteered, "Ulmarra Foundation."

"Ohhh." The woman dropped her eyes, and, without looking back to us, she said, "Well, as I said, if you wait over there, I'll see what is happening."

The three of us moved back to the chairs spread along the wall and waited.

The woman continued with whatever she was working on, and nothing seemed to happen.

Finally, a police officer entered her office area and smiled, asking her for the duty rosters.

She pleasantly found them for him and then went back to what she was doing.

He turned, looking up at us, and stepped forward. "You guys okay over there?"

I was leaning on my forearms over my knees and strained slightly to look up. "We got information to sort out a mistake with our mate."

The officer looked on with a sudden sternness on his face, as though he had heard that before.

Behind the counter the woman lifted herself slightly from the chair and said, "Oh, yes, these people are here about the Ulmarra Foundation woman. Do you want to see if Detective Bateman would like to speak with any of them?"

"What kind of information do you have?" He looked down at us, obviously wondering what we might know that would be of importance.

Jyly stood up, all five feet two of her courage with her. "We had a problem a while back—some trouble with a mad dog, and, well, it was decided that we would deal with him in our own way. Thing is, we think he has started an accusation that is completely false, and he got in touch with the TV people, and now it's blown up into a big deal over nothing, and you've arrested Louisa for fraud or something, when nothing like that has ever happened."

"Ohh-kaaay..." He looked a bit mystified. "Wait here, and I'll go and see the sergeant handling the case." The policeman turned on his heel and sauntered back to the office area. He whispered something in the ear of the woman, and she looked up and smiled mischievously.

A few moments later, another sergeant arrived, and the two walked toward the three of us.

"If you want to follow me, we will take a statement." We dutifully followed the sergeant and were shown toward a room with a door off it.

Jyly was asked, "Come through," and left the small area first.

As Jimmy followed, the sergeant put out his arm and prevented him. "If you don't mind, mate, we need to talk to you all separately."

Jimmy nodded, and I made a wisecrack. "What, you think we can't all tell the same story?"

As the door closed, Jimmy and me were left alone wondering how Jyly would do, spilling the story of her attack to an unknown white guy in a uniform none of us much liked.

She told us how it went on the way home, and I thought, "You are a brave kid when you want to be."

In the interview room, she said she had sat on the chair—"hanging on to the seat with both hands, in case I blacked out!" —and looked about the room somewhat wide-eyed.

Five minutes went by, and she began to wonder if they had forgotten her. She said jokingly, "I felt just as nervous as when they leave you in the room before the doctor eventually turns up to give you your pap smear. You know, you think, 'Shit, I don't really want some stranger looking up there and poking me with some spatula.' Then, just before you think, 'That's it, I'm going!' the bastard turns up, and you have to put yourself through it after all!"

She said, "I was just about at that stage of doing a runner, when suddenly the door swung open, and the cop came in with a clipboard in his hands, and he brightly said, "So, I guess we should see what's up, young lady!"

I said, "I ain't no young lady to you, mate—my name is Jyly Ungaru, and you can call me Ms.!"

"Ah, I see; well, that is a good start. I have your name," he said. "So, why don't you start at the beginning and tell me what you know about the whole thing, and I'll write it down, okay?"

She took a deep breath and dived in. "This all started with Wajilla's brother, Juniper Wilson, who is a real rotten-swamp type of fulla."

"Well, I can't say I have ever heard it put that way—Juniper?"

"Juniper Wilson. I went up on one of the section plant-outs about six months ago, and he was working up there too."

"Section plants?"

"Reforestation projects out the back of Mareeba."

"Address?"

"Wilderness—ex–Thompson's farm. Anyway, after the plant, we was all stuffed, and I couldn't go back to town, 'cause I could hardly walk, let alone celebrate, so I stayed at the Dongas'."

"What date was this?"

"I think it was the sixteenth of October—somewhere around then."

Jyly said she shifted in her chair, and it scraped loudly, so she clasped her hands together on the table and anchored herself there. "Anyway, this jerk must have followed me in there, and well, he jumped me. We had a tussle and he—raped me—and I kicked him in the nuts."

"And what does this have to do with Ms. Henderson?" The sergeant didn't seem even slightly phased by her revelation. She said she supposed he must have heard that a hundred times before and knew how to keep a straight face.

She looked him in the eye and said sternly, "I'm getting to that. After this, my friends asked me what I wanted to do with him when we worked out it was him, because he had my scratches on his neck and back, and I said—I just didn't want him around no more. So they took him out past Tinaroo to teach him a lesson."

"What kind of lesson—are we talking a murder inquiry now?"

"Nah! Of course not—nah, they dealt to him like the old people would have: they speared him through the calf, so he would remember not to touch a woman like that again."

"Speared him?"

"Well, actually, they did it with a screwdriver, because we don't have spears anymore."

"Ah, I suppose not. So what happened to him?"

"Well, I guess he walked home, eventually—"

"Limped home, you mean."

"Yeah, limped home, and he got out of Cairns and went down to Brisbane, and that is where we think he hooked up with this bird, Maria Ferris—you know, the lady who's been on all the news lately trying to shut the foundation down. She's part of that business group that's denying global warming and wants to get rid of the carbon tax and anything that will help to save what is left of the planet, including us."

"So you think—this Juniper Wilson has been feeding information to Maria Ferris that isn't true?"

"Yes—to get back at us for dealing to him."

"Well, you know, we don't make an arrest without evidence, so you need to know this Juniper character has nothing to do with our investigations."

"But he should be! He's made all this stuff up, and this Maria Ferris has dropped it in your lap, and you're about to make a big mistake."

"Do you know anything about the information that we have, or where it came from then?"

"What information? There is no information."

"Nothing about submissions for grants from the ministry of economic development and sustainable futures being fraudulent?"

"What?"

"So you don't know anything about these false invoices—ever see her working on invoices or payouts that never happened? Ever hear anyone talking about anything like that?"

"All I know is, it's all bullshit! Louisa is a totally honest person who's never done anything false or illegal in her life. This is just a vendetta on the foundation, and, if there is anything fishy, it is all made up."

"Well, if you don't have anything to add, I think we can conclude the interview."

"But what about Louisa? Are you going to let her go now?"

"I can't talk to you about that right now, but look, if what you say is true, we will get to the bottom of it, and if there's nothing to worry about, we will release Ms. Henderson. I really hope the Ulmarra Foundation will still be there years from now, as long as it is legit, and I hope passionate people like you are there to run it. Between you and me, I actually want nothing to be going on—because I believe in what you guys are trying to do. But if it turns out to be a sham for a bunch of thieves, I can tell you it won't just be her we will be looking for. We'll prosecute anyone that is part of that—even Ulmarra himself, because to wreck this idea with greed or corruption is more of a crime than the swindle itself."

"She didn't do nothing, you know, nothing," Jyly said.

"I am sure you would like to think that—no one ever thinks there is anything untoward happening, in my experience. That is what the courts are for, to determine what is true or not."

"Yeah, like I believe she's gonna get a fair go in court."

"Of course you will. This is Australia, not Somalia."

"Try telling Lindy Chamberlain that the bloody courts are all about 'justice.'"

He coughed slightly and replied under his breath, "You can't blame anyone for that—when she said 'The dingoes got my baby,' it must have sounded like a pretty good cover for a murder."

"You obviously never met a wild dingo."

He ignored her comment, and she went on. "So what is going to happen to Juniper?"

"Well, if what you say is true, we'll interview him and hope for your sake that he doesn't want to press charges."

"Charges? The bastard should be put inside for rape!"

"Well, you can always make a counter-complaint, if you want. If you can provide some evidence, you might have a case, but it sounds like he could have your friends for assault, at the least."

"No way! Well, I guess that's what your system likes to call 'justice.' He gets to take a case against us?"

"Yes, well, it's justice for all, including him, and administered by the Crown, not any man who thinks he wants to use a screwdriver to enforce his version of it."

"We're not 'any man'—we are the *first men* on this land. We have a right to use our own laws."

"Maybe you think so, Ms. Ungaru, but you are still part of the human race and that comes first, these days. That's what the law and the courts are for, and no one gets to opt out of that."

"Tell that to those of us who had our benefits taken away in the 'intervention' last year, or our kids taken away in the '70s. You spout 'justice for all' when it suits you!"

She said the sergeant didn't reply, but I smiled as she said it, and said, "Good on Jilly Bird. Someone's got to speak some sense."

She said he showed her out of the room by a second door, and she had seen Jimmy and me seated on chairs in the hallway and waiting.

"I don't think they believed me," she said as she looked down the hall, and Bateman appeared.

"Mr. Ulmarra, Mr. Wilson—please follow me." We looked at each other, and I whispered to Jimmy, "We might get hung trying to save the one already swinging."

Jimmy didn't reply but followed Bateman in to the office, and I followed behind.

"So, I think I have the gist of it from Ms. Ungaru. Perhaps you'd like to tell me what happened up at Tinaroo?"

"Tinaroo? What about Louisa? Shouldn't you be investigating the crap they have made up about her?"

"I'm just interested in what you've done at the moment."

Jimmy leaned forward and put his hands on the table. And I realized he wasn't keen to talk about what had happened to Jyly, so I jumped in and told Bateman everything my brother did. When I finished, I said, "Look, Juniper broke our law, and we gave the victim a say in what she wanted done about it, the old way or your way. She chose our way."

"You've committed assault, and that's a serious charge, Mr. Wilson."

"So is rape, and so is putting young black fullas in jail with criminals which is what would have happened to Juniper," Jimmy spoke up.

"I'm not interested in your ideas of justice, Mr. Ulmarra. It's not my job to write the law, just enforce it." He looked down at his hands. "I'm going to admit that what you did was probably effective in making sure he is 'rehabilitated' in a permanent fashion, but—"

"Too right!" I said enthusiastically.

"—but you committed a crime in doing it, and that can't be ignored."

"You know what we did, and I'm guessing you can see what he's done since to try and get some kind of revenge for it."

"I know that would make sense to you, but I'm not convinced about that, Mr. Ulmarra. Our evidence speaks for itself. You might not like to admit it, but that's how it is."

"It's worth looking into, isn't it?" I said. "He's gone and done something I'm sure of it!"

"And how do you propose we do that? A guy who has been assaulted is not going to say he falsified evidence, and the people who are keen to have

Ms. Henderson face these charges are not going to say they did anything but hand us over what they had in light of doing their civic duty to stop serious crimes being committed in your foundation. You're up against the evidence."

"Your interpretation of 'evidence,'" Jimmy said quietly, and Bateman ignored him and went on. "Saying it was just this disgruntled kid is not going to hold any water, I'm afraid." He paused and looked at us as though he was thinking about it privately. "Look, you need to come up with something or someone else."

We looked at the table, at a loss as to what 'else' we could come up with.

"I'm going to let you both go for now, give you some time—if you come into any further information, come back and see me, but I have to say, she lives in an expensive apartment on the esplanade, and you might not have wondered where the money for that came from, but we think we know. You might just have to accept that even if your intentions in the Ulmarra Foundation are good—there is often a bad apple where you least expect it."

"I've known Lou from the beginning—there's no way. Can we at least see her?"

"No, I'm sorry, you'll have to wait till she's been to court, and hope she gets bail."

"This has to be a mistake," I said as we walked from the room.

"I hope you're right," Bateman said but he didn't sound genuine. He looked at me. "You can wait in reception while I see whether we're going to charge you about your brother," he said, and my stomach went cold. We stepped out of the room and turned to walk down the hall and out to where Jyly was sitting, while he turned in the other direction and disappeared.

Jyly stood up immediately. "Well? Is it going to be alright?"

"Nah. They've charged her formally, and they're sticking to their guns." Jimmy looked down at his feet.

"How the hell can this be happening?" I asked.

"She's got to have made a mistake somewhere," Jimmy said.

"I bet they're going to question me again over the thing with the screwdriver. Did you hear him? We might get in trouble for that." I took a deep breath.

Suddenly a door opened at the end of the corridor, and I thought, "Here we go—I'm in for it now."

The sergeant approached us. He looked at me directly and said, "We might need you in the future to answer some more questions about your brother, so I wouldn't leave Cairns if I was you, or you will have a warrant out for your arrest."

"My arrest!" I struggled to my feet in protest, and Jimmy put his hand on my shoulder.

"Look, I'll be honest with you." Bateman shook his head and said quietly as though he didn't want to be heard by anyone else. "I don't think we're that interested in some kind of indigenous family tiff. But maybe you should learn how to 'just call us' in the future, instead of going to the trouble of using some screwdriver to make your point."

"I guess it would save us petrol—and some grief," Jimmy said quietly.

"Yes, it would, and it would save us some paperwork." The sergeant smiled slightly. "You're free to go," he said, and I thought, "You're not a bad bloke."

I looked at the others and said, "Well, I'm not waiting," and we turned and left smartly.

We three started walking, and, when we got outside, I looked towards Jyly and said, "Sorry, mate, I had to tell them everything you told me about what the prick did."

"I know, I told him too, but it hasn't helped. They say they have some paperwork. Maybe this isn't about your brother at all."

"That's what I was thinking too." Jimmy frowned. "I know Louisa wouldn't have done anything wrong, but someone has—who else could fiddle the books?"

All of us suddenly came up with the same name. "Samson Donahue," we said in unison.

"But doesn't she make all the payments and stuff?"

"Yeah, but she only goes on what he gives her," Jimmy said. "I don't know about this kind of stuff, but we had better get on to the lawyer straightaway."

Jimmy nodded, and we all got in the car and headed back home.

By the time we got to Jimmy's place, I was convinced Donahue was the culprit.

Jimmy got on the phone and was speaking with a lawyer straightaway, and I told Jyly I'd have to go and pick up Amy from John'o's work, but I'd wait till Jimmy was off the phone.

Jimmy was talking in a voice I hadn't heard before, sort of 'urgent' so I knew he was worried big time. "We have to get her out of there—they wouldn't let us see her." He looked down at the floor and then said, "So will they release her, pending trial?"

Jyly walked by, and I saw him lean forward to touch her, and I thought, "He's got it bad this time." She smiled and wriggled out of his grasp, but I could see by her face as she listened in, that she was worried for the Queen too, even if they hadn't always been on good terms.

"That's great, Mr. Cameron; at least that's something," Jimmy said, speaking to the lawyer who had helped him from the beginning of the foundation and knew him well. "I'll go and get her—when?" He looked through the leaf-shaped window and watched a parrot sail effortlessly through the air to land on an opposite tree.

"Okay. So, don't they have to tell us what evidence they've got on her—why not? I don't get it; how can we defend this if we have to wait and see what docs and signatures they've got?" He suddenly got serious, and his tone changed as he spoke into the phone. "Listen, we better ask some hard questions of Donahue—he's the only one who might have done something dodgy." Jimmy nodded as though he could see the speaker. "I know—but there has to be an answer to this." He was obviously listening to the Cameron's advice then replied, "Okay, I'll find out. I'll go get her as soon as you let me know you've talked to her, and she can come home." He listened to some instruction Cameron gave on the other end of the connection, and then he nodded and said, "Okay, 'bye —thanks, eh." Jimmy closed his cell phone and walked toward the lounge where Jyly was seated and staring at the wall. "I gotta go get Louisa. Maybe tomorrow, Mr. Cameron says. He thinks they will release her on bail."

"I have to go get Amy. Do you want to come?" I asked.

"Nah, you go." He looked across at Jyly and I realized three was definitely a crowd and I thought, "At last ... lucky bastard!"

I took off, and I never even saw the road along the way; I was lost in my thoughts about what had happened. When I arrived at the hangar, John'o was talking to a guy, and Amy was drawing choppers on a notepad he'd been given. I collected him up and waved out to John'o, who excused himself from the guy and jogged over to me.

"Is she okay?"

"Yeah—she'll be out on bail and home soon. But we still have to find out what happened. I got a pretty good idea."

"Yeah?"

"Listen, I can't talk now—thanks for looking after Amy; I'll keep you posted, eh."

"No problem," he said, and tousled Amy's hair and said he'd take him for a joyride sometime. I laughed and shook my head. I said good-bye, and John'o went back to his customer.

Amy and me had pizza for dinner, and he kept asking me about Louisa and what was going to happen. I kept reassuring him it would be okay, but, if you asked me to put me hand on me heart and swear to it—I couldn't have.

By late afternoon the following day, we got word that she could go home. Cameron had already talked to her, and he rang Jimmy and told him there was some decent evidence against her, signatures and stuff, and an investigation had been going on with the bank accounts, and it didn't add up.

I arrived at Jimmy's place, because we said we'd go down and get her together, you know, show a united front and how much we believed in her.

Jyly was sitting on the couch, and Jimmy was standing with his hands on his hips and his head down. I could see the worry on his face.

"She's going to be pretty shaken up, I'd guess—she's going to need her best mate," Jyly said.

"I know—she's going to be like a taipan that's been in a sack all day, and that is one pissed-off snake!"

"Do your voodoo on her, sing her into submission, then come back to me, and I'll bandage up your wounds. Just be back before the moon gets sleepy, or I will think she has abducted you an' put you in the sack with her an' then hidden you under her bed," Jyly said light heartedly.

"Lou isn't that bad." Jimmy looked up, and I replied with a quick quip, as I came in with my keys jangling in my hand, "Yes, she is—but she's got an excuse this time, so I'm forgiving her ahead of time!"

He smiled. "You ready to go, Wajilla?"

"Yeah, if you are."

"Well, I guess the only good news is, she'll sleep in her own bed again. It must be terrible for her in there, 'cause she won't be used to it," Jyly said, as I paused and turned around to look at us both standing opposite each other.

"Yeah—not like us, eh, Jimmy? You never forget the smell in them places." I saw him swallow, because he knew she would suffer under the humiliation, more than the smell, of incarceration. "Don't worry, she'll be okay. One way or another, we'll sort it out," I said and turned to head back out the door, with him following me.

He paused and turned back, ignoring me entirely. "Are you sure you won't come down too?" he called out to Jyly.

"But Wajilla is going."

"Yeah, so what?"

"Well, you don't need me."

"Nah—I always need you."

"What? So you're saying you don't need me, mate?" I said with false offence.

"Shut up, mate—I'm negotiating," he said, and hovered at the door waiting for her.

Jyly put down her cup, needing little encouragement, and said, "Well, all right then. Hang on; I've got something for her I was going to give her later." Jyly jumped up from the couch and gathered up a small card from the table. It was hand-painted with aboriginal designs of dots and swirls, and the outline of a dingo graced the front of it.

"Where did you get that?" I asked as she came to the door.

"I made it for her, because I sort of felt this was somehow my fault. You know, with all that stuff over that mongrel, Juniper."

"You're softer than you look," Jimmy said mischievously.

"Don't bet on it, Ulmarra! I just thought she might like to know we do actually care about her. She sometimes feels pretty alone, you know."

"Yeah, I know," he said, and nodded to his own Ute with the green-faced kid on the side. "We'll go separately eh?"

This time, all three of us walked out of the house, closed the door, and headed to the two vehicles parked in the roadway.

We arrived at the police station and stood and waited at the counter.

Jimmy told the receptionist, who was different from the one we had seen earlier, we were there to take Louisa Henderson home, because she had been released on bail until her court appearance. "If you sit over there—I'll let them know you are here," she said, and I thought, "Do they have a 'hire-only-bitches' policy in this place or something?"

Suddenly the doors opened, and she was brought out to us. The sergeant with her said nothing but handed a clipboard to her, which she signed. He took it from her, wished her good luck, then she walked forward to the three of us standing near the door.

"You okay?" Jimmy immediately clasped her arms and looked into her eyes, searching for the tell-tale fire that was normally there.

"I'll live," she said quietly.

"Hey, mate, we will sort it out; there has to be an answer to this mess," I said gently.

"He's right." Jyly stepped forward and looked up at the much-taller woman. "Hey, I made this for you."

Louisa took the card gingerly, looking down somewhat suspiciously. She opened it, and the black scrolling words of *From the much maligned dingoes of the world: "We will survive because of you—thanks!"* conveyed the girl's sentiments.

"I haven't seen you around for a long time, but I guess you're back." Louisa looked at her face, and her eyes seemed to wander down Jyly's neck and stop on her collarbone.

"Yeah; I'm sorry for not, you know—getting in touch. I was in a bad way for a while."

"Oh—well, thanks for the card." Louisa started to move forward towards the door like a sleepwalker, and we followed. I leaned past her arm and swung the door wide for her.

"So, have they opened the foundation offices for you guys, or is it still closed up?" Her voice seemed disconnected.

"Nah—we can't get in; they've changed the locks. Not much anyone can do, until we have sorted this whole thing out."

"And how do you suppose you are going to do that?" Louisa growled slightly, and I thought, "The old girl is still okay."

"First thing we are going to do is talk with Mr. Cameron tomorrow and start a bit of an investigation ourselves."

"He's told me it looks bad," she said.

As we reached the Ute, she turned and looked across at Jyly and me.

"They've got my signature on the requisitions, the invoices, the applications—hell, I could go to jail!"

"Nah, that's a joke! It's all just a wirra wirra in the desert. There's no smoke, no fire, no raincloud, no nothing, in reality. They are just fishing because some political prick is stirring them up and they are hoping to find something to hang us on." Jimmy reached out and rested his hand on her shoulder.

"Jimmy—they have something to hang us on."

"What?"

"I didn't realize, but when they showed me the ministry payouts for the farming towers against the land requisition settlements—they don't match."

"What?"

"It always has been that we make one application, but we provide maybe three invoices for the setup and then the running costs and the training."

"So?"

"So of course it should all add up, except there are three that Sam hasn't put the invoices in for, and the account has three transfers to his company trust account instead of to the contractors directly."

"I knew it," I broke in. "It's Sam—"

"Hold it, Wajilla." Jimmy put his hand on my chest to shut me up. "Let Louisa finish explaining."

She went on, all the while wringing her hands. "Somehow, the bank account number on the direct debits is different. I don't remember changing it, or maybe he just gave me the account numbers to pay it into, and I didn't check who the account belonged to. So it looks like I'm doing something with him, you see?

"Worse than that—he hasn't paid that money out to any contractors, by the look of it. According to what they showed me, it's disappeared to another account. They are accusing me of falsifying a debit on our books to the ministry, but we never made a legitimate payment. And the money doesn't add up to the requisitions we've made to the tune of hundreds of thousands of dollars. They want to know why I paid it to him and where it went and why the difference in the amount we got from the ministry, and I can't tell them."

"Doesn't he pay the contractors at each stage in a progress payment?" Jimmy asked.

"Yeah, but it looks like he's done something different, and I just don't know..."

"Isn't the foundation audited?

"Of course! Every three months—there has never been a cent missing."

"We'll have to talk to him."

"I know."

"So have you rung him?" Jimmy asked.

"What do you think?"

"What did he say?"

"His mobile is going to messages, no reply at his company office—what if..."

"He's got to have an explanation."

"Yeah—but it might not be the truth, eh!" I said.

"I know he was really worried, just before I was arrested. He came flying into the office looking for this 'notebook,' saying something about it having all the info about who was getting what, and he couldn't find it. I mean, I know he's as disorganized as anyone can get; it's just the sort of thing he would do—keep a stupid notebook. He's written a million-dollar deal on the back of his hand before today, so maybe it's just an innocent mistake?"

"Not to the tune of hundreds of thousands missing—that's no mistake." I said and Jyly looked up.

Louisa thought about it for a minute and then said in a stern tone, "Find Sam; find out what's going on—so I can get back to work."

"So *we* can get back to work." Ulmarra said and patted her shoulder.

She smiled shakily but looked like she was about to cry.

"I'll take Lou home," I said, but Jimmy looked at Jyly, and she strained to smile and said, "Don't worry about me; I'll drive the Ute back home, eh? You should both take her, and then you can talk about it—try and work out what to do." He nodded so imperceptibly I almost missed it, but she saw it and nodded back.

I said, "Come on, Lou." She turned and walked with me to my Ute as Jimmy walked Jyly to his own, with the green-faced kid painted on the side that somehow didn't look that happy either.

"It's okay, I'll keep an eye on the taipan," he said, and Jyly nodded and took the keys from him. He watched her go and then skipped over to Lou and me sitting and waiting.

When we got to her apartment, I could tell she was as wound up as I had ever seen her. She leaned against the table and sighed, and he came over and rubbed her shoulders.

"I don't know how I could have missed all this," she said as she stared at her fingers lying flat on the glass table.

"Aren't you watching out for all this?"

Louisa stood up sharply at the slight reproach. "You think I should run his company as well as the foundation and do my research!" She spun around and stared out the ranch sliders that held an amazing view of the trinity inlet. "*And* worry about where the hell you are and what the hell you're doing?"

I suddenly got the urge to make coffee and called out, "I'm going in the kitchen to get a drink. Anyone want some?" Neither of them replied, so I stood there waiting.

"You don't need to worry about me," I heard Jimmy say, and she replied, "Goddamn it! Of course I do!"

"Well, don't. You're not my mother or—"

"Your wife! No, I see that!" She swung around, slid open the glass doors, and stepped out onto the balcony. A slight wind blew the curtain in, and I thought that the time in jail had had Louisa thinking about all sorts of things, not just the predicament she was in.

I saw Jimmy reach out and hold her arm gently. "Look, I meant that I can take care of myself, that's all."

"And the protégé, I suppose?"

"Jyly?"

"What the hell is your family pearl doing around her neck?"

"Ah—now we're getting to it."

"Yes, I saw it—you didn't think I would see it?"

"Well—I guess you need to know."

"Know what? That she's your girlfriend now?"

"No..."

"Don't deny it—for God's sake, don't try and deny it now!"

"If you'd let me finish..."

"So—finish."

"We are gonna get hitched."

"What? Oh, no—I don't believe it! She's twenty years younger than you. You can't be serious!"

"You're kidding, Ulmarra!" I whispered to myself, because that was the first time I'd heard about it too.

He seemed to suck in a breath and turned away from her to stare out at the milky Trinity Inlet ocean view almost at full tide. It was drowning the last of the dugong sea grasses under its tears. I had a feeling there maybe unfinished business that was now coming on because of the stress she had been under and I sort of tried to not listen but couldn't help it.

"We—"

"Don't even go there. You are about to say something that relates to your culture, your Dreamtime, your bloody indigenous similarities!"

"No, I wasn't, actually. I was going to say, we love each other, so whatever shit people put in our way, it means nothing, and so do the people who say it."

She shut her mouth and didn't reply. Suddenly she turned and headed inside. Just as she walked into the apartment and out of the wind, she paused and called over her shoulder, "Well, whatever—I'm very happy that you think this is going to make you happy."

"Louisa, wait."

"For what? Jail, the end of Ulmarra, death!"

"For God's sake, stop that shit!

"It's all right for you—you have it all!"

"Really, and you don't?" he said as he swung his arms around the beautiful esplanade apartment.

"No, I don't. I don't have the answers for the Ulmarra Foundation, I don't have anything except this thing we're doing, I don't have—you."

"What the hell are you talking about?"

"I'm saying—that without you, I can't do this thing."

"That's not true, Lou," I said.

He walked up behind her and grabbed her by the shoulders. "I'm not going anywhere."

"Yes you are, you've already gone..."

"That's funny, I don't feel like a ghost."

"Stop that!" She laughed. She turned to face him, her eyes moist, the fear evident in her expression, her features, and even her skin. "You know what I mean. You are going to marry that pint-sized *girl*, and I will just have to hide in my work and try to forget ... When is this great wedding event going to happen?"

"Not sure—soon, I guess."

"I can't talk you out of it?"

Jimmy ignored her and turned to head for the door. "I gotta find Sam; he's got some explaining to do." As he reached the door, he turned to me. "Take care of her for a while, mate."

"I suppose you need me to talk to him too, ask him about the accounts?" Louisa said, and he replied, "No, not yet—later, I'll come back later. You'll be alright till then; Wajilla will make sure she eats something."

"Yep—and I think we'll have a drink or two, too!"

He paused and then turned slowly. "Lou, you are never alone, you know that; you're me best mate, always have been, always will be. You don't have to wear the pearl to have my magic on you."

"Does she know that?"

"Yes. She's smarter than you. She knows you don't own nothing, you just enjoy it for what it is, for whatever time you got it—anyway, we ain't a coral atoll, all on our own. We all get 'shared' with each other. Even if we don't sleep in the same beds and we don't love each other all in the same way."

"Ahh—maybe I've misjudged her."

"Maybe."

He nodded back and then, heading for the lift, turned and disappeared out the door.

She looked at me with a look of disbelief now clouding every other emotion she must have been feeling. "Did you hear that?"

"Hard not to."

"Did you know?"

"Nah. I mean, I knew they were, you know—together, but getting hitched?"

She didn't reply but stood stock-still, staring at the blank wall. Finally, she turned and looked up toward me. "I have to get through this, Wajilla—the foundation has to go on, it has to."

I think she was talking about the charges against her, but something in her voice made me think she was thinking something else. Either way, I said, "Lou—you'll get through it. He's right about one thing."

"What?"

"You're not alone. We are family."

She looked at me a little coldly and said, "Sometimes I just wish I understood what that really means."

"It means we don't abandon you or leave you alone to face your life by yourself."

"An admirable sentiment, but not very close to reality, in my experience."

"You have to give it a chance."

"Hmm—I'm a scientist, Wajilla. I prefer to look at things just the way they are, and, no matter what you say, I go to bed on my own, and I wake up on my own, and I work more or less on my own."

"But today—we came and got you, and tomorrow, if you get stuck in the mud somewhere, we'll come and tow you out."

She headed for the kitchen and said a little blandly, "Well I guess if you're right, this 'family' just saved me a taxi fare and will save me the cost of a tow truck…"

I shook my head. She wasn't called the Queen for nothing.

Chapter 14

THE NEXT DAY saw Jimmy and me in the Ulmarra Ute, speeding through a dry gravel-and-clay roadway between tall stands of ripe cane. Louisa had an appointment with Cameron, and Jyly had something to take care of with her mom and sisters, so it was just the two of us heading up to Mossman to see if we could find Samson.

When we arrived at a huge, slightly triangular structure outside of Mossman, that rose and reflected the sunshine from clear panels, we screeched to a halt. Gravel sprayed around us, hitting the spears of green with dull thuds.

Both Jimmy and me fired from the doors of the Ute simultaneously. I began yelling even before I had seen anyone.

"Donahue—get out here *now*!" I called.

"If he's here, he'll be inside," Jimmy said calmly.

"Well, he better get out here, 'cause if I find him in there, he's likely to go through one of them panes!"

"We're here to talk, mate, not wreck an IFT project."

We walked to the main entrance, and the double airlock opened to us, even though its sign read *Authorized Personnel Only* on the doorway. As we walked into the first area of the tower, I put my fists on my hips and yelled out again into the echoing building. "Hey, Donahue, get out here now!"

We looked up between the steel walkways carrying layer upon layer of plants yawning up towards the light.

A voice echoed back. "Hey, boys! What are you doing here? You come to give us some free labor?"

"You got some explaining to do, eh, mate!" I said.

Samson paused on the walkway and looked down at us. "If she's pregnant, it wasn't me!" He smiled, and then his smile faded as he saw the look on our faces. "What's the matter?"

We watched him as he walked forward and down the staircase that was connected to the huge fish pool in the center. A swath of tubes left from a pump box at the back, and the sound of humming slightly emanated from the area.

"We been trying to get hold of you," I said. "What the hell have you been up to?"

"Sorry, mate, my phone dropped in that pool four days ago, and I haven't been into town to get a new one because I'm right at the critical point with the bacterial production."

I walked up to him and stood right in his face. "Are you kidding? You were in at the office the day before yesterday. I know, because I was there, remember? Don't you know Louisa got arrested?"

"Yeah, I went in—*what*?"

"Yeah, mate, arrested! We could see you were pretty rattled, an' it looks like she got arrested on account of you straight after!"

"You're crazy! How on earth could that be? What did she get nicked for?" He shook his head. "I don't believe it! No one is straighter than Louisa."

Jimmy walked over to the pool and dropped his hand over the side." "Thought you might already know."

"Hey, mate, I'm not sure what you are talking about, but whatever it is, you had better talk plainly, because I have plenty to do."

"You let her take the fall, mate, didn't you? She trusted you." I slammed my hand down on a tray of small plants, and the whole building reverberated, and the plants scattered onto the walkway.

"Hey mate—take it easy. I don't know what's going on..."

Jimmy lifted his wet hand out of the pool and shook it. "What if—you had a company on the side, and, before the ministry payments came in, payments you alone have applied for, you sent that money to yourself and paid the contractors a bit to stay quiet and got them to send inflated invoices back in for Louisa to process. What if you managed to trick Louisa into paying your own company instead of the contractors we always pay, and you ferried all the money away to somewhere else? The whole thing looks okay on your end, as long as those contractors' invoices add up to the ministry requisition, eh? Louisa signs it all off and doesn't know she is party to fraud."

"Fraud? You're kidding me, right?"

"What if you kept a separate record of all this so you didn't forget your own bullshit, and you kept it in your briefcase?"

"Yeah...well, I do keep—"

"And what if that little prick Juniper stole that record because he wanted to get us back, because we sorted him out over him raping Jyly?"

"What? He was the bloke who attacked Jyly? I wondered about him. He buggered off real fast—"

"Forget Juniper, you bastard!" I yelled.

Jimmy broke in and continued. "Louisa is almost ready to jump off the balcony of her unit, because the cops have her pegged for a criminal."

I moved a step closer. "An' all this, because of your double dealings, you shithead!" I was steadily working myself up into a frenzy.

"You got a real imagination, mate! I might do a bit of creative accounting to cover the shortfall from the ministry, but I guarantee there isn't one cent missing at the end of the process. And I told Louisa we would be paying from a new account. Hell, don't you know what we are doing here? We're changing the bloody future with this stuff; there's no way I'd want to risk—"

Jimmy looked up from the pool. "Yeah, yeah, I know what 'we're,' doing but do you, mate?" Jimmy walked over to him and put his head down. "Look, you need to understand: you need to tell us what you've done. They've let her out on bail, but she's been charged."

"Yeah, Sam," I added. "You're out there as the best suspect for this scam! And I'd bet the spit of a camel against a smart-ass fish-feeder like you any day."

Donahue stood still for a moment, digesting what we were saying. "So you think I've scammed the Ulmarra Foundation?"

"Sounds like it's the ministry that's been scammed, but it's the foundation that is being used to do it," Jimmy said plainly.

"An' they got the cheek to blame us abos for being dodgy!" I moved around menacingly and shook my head at the tall man, who was looking shocked and puzzled.

"You have to go down and talk to the cops in Cairns and lay it all on the table." Jimmy took a step forward.

"No problem. I've got nothing to hide, nothing at all. I'll go into town in the next day or two—"

"Nah! You'll go *now*!" I yelled, and the panels of clear Perspex vibrated with the sound of my voice again.

"Hey, mate, take it easy." Sam looked from me to Jimmy and back again. "Okay, let me finish what I'm doing. I have to run the last report—and I'll head in today, since you are so hot under the collar about it."

"I said *now*, you crooked bastard." I bared my teeth and must have looked as if I had transformed into something carnivorous.

"That's enough." Jimmy stepped toward me and placed his palm on my shoulder. He turned and faced Samson, who now looked quite disturbed by the accusation and the aggression in my voice. "We can wait, and we'll take you in after— with us."

"Yeah, there's not gonna be any chance that you might make a run for it and jump a boat across the Torres Strait and live it up on some island in Indonesia."

"Oh, for god's sake, Wajilla! Whatever—do as you like. I'm telling you, there is nothing to this." Donahue shook his head and started walking to the door.

"Well, you can expect to get dumped out in on the Great Barrier Reef with a bloody big rock tied to you and half a roo for bait if there is even a hair's breadth of stealin' done by you." I moved a few steps to stand up against the tall man's chest.

Donahue was now beginning to get angry. "Look, I have nothing to hide and nothing on my conscience. Get out of my way, stuff the reports, I'm going to sort this bullshit out right now!" He stormed past us, grabbed his briefcase, some papers from the desk, and headed for the Ute. When he got there, he turned and yelled, "Well, are you drongos coming?"

Wajilla looked at Jimmy, and he shook his head at me. I was a bit surprised by Donahue's reaction too. Jimmy said, "If he's guilty, he sure knows how to blow smoke up our asses."

I looked back to Donahue leaning against the Ute door and frowned. I was now wondering if we had got it wrong because he didn't look anything like I did when I was guilty.

Jimmy whispered under his breath, "If he's innocent, he's gonna want a year's supply of beer from us both over this."

"Well let's hope he's guilty, then—otherwise we gotta look at someone else, and we're running out of candidates. God help us if it is Louisa!"

"You're an idiot sometimes!" Jimmy punched me hard on the upper arm, and I winced before grunting in Donahue's face, swinging the driver's door open to get in.

Donahue just shook his head and seated himself in the back, and we drove off down the gravel road between the cane fields.

"I tell you, you are going to owe me big time," Donahue said from the back, with more than a tinge of wounded pride.

Jimmy quietly turned to him around the side of the passenger's seat. "Listen, mate, if there is nothing to this, we are eliminating you."

"Eliminating me? Bloody hell!"

"As a suspect, I mean." Jimmy smiled for the first time.

"That's not what I mean!" I snarled. "I'm eliminating him full stop!"

"Why?" Jimmy looked over to me.

"Because if it ain't him, he's wasted my time. I had a league game to watch this afternoon, and I'm gonna miss it!"

Samson didn't reply, and we all sat in silence for the rest of the journey.

When we arrived at the police station, I jumped out, walked across to the entrance, and stood beside the doorway with my arms folded.

Donahue strode across, opened the door, and said, "Well, come on—I haven't got all day."

I smiled sourly and said flippantly, "Well, I have got all the time in the world, thanks to this bullshit—we were supposed to do a grid run this week too, but we've been shut down, thanks to you!"

"So it's my fault, then?"

"You two shut up." Jimmy swung open the door and strode in. He walked straight up to the counter and said politely, "We need to speak to Sergeant Bateman. We've got some new information."

The lady, a third one, as usual indicated that we should sit in the waiting area, and she rang through for the sergeant.

When he appeared, the three of us immediately stood up.

"There's been some kind of mistake," Donahue said confidently, "and I'm here to sort it out."

"Follow me," Bateman said.

Donahue did, and, as he went through the door, he looked back and said to me, "You better give me a lift back after this—and I'm gonna want an apology."

I just humph'd and turned to Jimmy. "God help us if this dude isn't bluffing."

"God help *you*, you mean; I only wanted an explanation. You were ready to hang him off his own IFT tower!"

Donahue had his interview and. on the way back, he told us what happened. Well, he told Jimmy what happened; he was definitely ignoring me.

Donahue said he was shown into a small interview room, and he sat down straight away.

"So let's just get under way."

"Okay. First, I need to inform you that this interview will be recorded. Are you okay with that?"

Donahue said yes, he was.

"Well, then, let's get this thing working." The sergeant switched on the machine and stated the time and date and the big man's name. He asked a few basic questions to confirm Donahue's date of birth and address, and then he stopped, looked hard into the man's eyes, and said, "So tell me what part do you have to play in these fraud allegations."

"I am the one who organizes the creation of the intensive farming towers, the IFTs. I commission contractors for supplies and the site preparation and the build. I approach the client after the Ulmarra Foundation has identified suitable land for allocation back to native forest. I also liaise with the owner of the land and the government authority as it negotiates the lease with the landowner. A contract gets prepared, and I manage the new IFT project for the client, so they can develop sustainable income from the remaining land plan that isn't replanted in native forest.

"I supervise the setup and do the training. I teach the client how he can apply for carbon credits from his leased land at year five, fifteen, and twenty-five, which is part of the deal struck with the Land Management Ministry.

"The science and system for the IFTs was developed by Louisa and myself and is an integrated system from the procurement of the land through the Ulmarra Foundation, all the way through to the production of viable crops by the landowner. The remaining leased land is replanted by the foundation and its many volunteers and connections with conservation groups, and, after that, carbon credits, and, well—world peace."

"Louisa Henderson?"

"Yeah. She does the allocation submissions and the grant-money application. I give her the invoices for the costs of everything—"

"You give her the invoices for the costs and the farmer's lease conditions."

"Yeah—I provide her with all that." He looked at the sergeant straight and said, "Look, I'm here today to tell you, if anything was not right with the money side of things, it would be me that had made a cock-up."

"So you are saying you would be responsible?" Donahue told us that the sergeant looked on with surprise because if he was crooked he was being very bold about it.

"Yeah. I mean, I am responsible for giving her all the information, so that means it is me who—didn't she tell you this?"

"Yes, she did, but not that you might be responsible; actually, she indicated that the buck stopped with her. So tell me how—" He pulled out of the somewhat fat file a number of invoices and papers and read them as he was talking. "Tell me why—first, there are such huge discrepancies between what has been funded by the government agency and the cost to the clients for the allocation of those funds?"

"Well, that's easy really. The projects happen in different parts. That is, we have the site prep and the internal pond installed first, then the towers are built, then the skin and light source computers installed, and the fish stocks, the training, the first trial crops—so the costs come together in the end."

"But aren't you supposed to pay for the projects first, then apply for the funds? So wouldn't you already have invoices, these invoices here—before you apply?"

"Well, yes, and no. We can't afford to bankroll as many projects at once as have come up. We have six going at the moment alone, and they are working on acquisitioning, I don't know—fifty more."

"So what you are saying is you are 'estimating' the cost, applying for the funds, and then managing the build from there?"

"Exactly."

"Isn't that against your obligations to the ministry?

"Well, yeah...but—"

"So how is this accounted for? Is this something that Louisa manages?"

"No—I make sure the invoices all add up. She just signs off on the application for the lump sum, and I just chip away at it as the invoices for payment start rolling in."

"So what happens if your allocation doesn't add up to the amount you have applied for?"

"Well, that doesn't happen. I've got relationships with the contractors, and well, they are fixed-price jobs."

"So this is run through one of your companies?"

"It didn't use to be but, yes—sort of."

"So is it possible that money could be, let's say, left over at the end in an account Louisa puts money in for you?"

"No, it doesn't work out that way because, as I say—they are fixed-price contracts. You have to understand, there isn't much to these things, really. A heap of tubing, and set quantities of Perspex. Just a simple computer with our program, trays, and—a bloody big concrete pond. That was the whole point when the IFTs were designed. They're supposed to be simple to erect, manage, and run, so we can get them up relatively fast and get them producing in all sorts of places. Here, and in poorer communities overseas. So the costs are very predictable."

"Seems like the ministry is paying through the nose for these 'simple' setups, by the look of these invoices."

"It might look like that, but there are all sorts of costs that are beyond the actual cost of the towers—"

"But it is possible that the landowner gets charged less than the funds that have been applied for? Or what about less than the invoices he was first charged for?"

"Well, yeah, I suppose so—but not really. I mean, that has never happened."

"And how can you prove that?"

"Well, I keep records, of course."

"And you can show us these records?"

"Ah—well, there is a little problem with that. That is, I can't find my notebook that has all the details in it."

"Would that be this notebook?" Bateman got up and walked to the cabinet and drew out a box. In it he pulled out a worn notebook bound in a blue plastic cover.

"Where the hell did you get that?"

"Someone found it, it appears."

"Where? Who?"

"I gather it was someone you know at the foundation."

"Bloody Juniper, I'll bet!"

"I'm not at liberty to confirm that, but, as you can see, it records a number of rather ambiguous deals that don't seem to be accounted for in the foundation records."

"Well, that's half right. You can see that the separate contractors have invoices owed to them, and Louisa will have her invoices to match."

"But it doesn't appear that they do match. For example, this contractor here is owed, according to your book, forty seven thousand, one hundred and twenty five dollars—but the sum transferred to a company called 'Aquatics by Nature PTY LTD'—"

"That's a holding company."

"The amount transferred is actually one hundred and ten thousand and sixteen dollars." By this time, Sergeant Bateman was sitting across from Sam with his hands locked tightly on the table, looking long and hard at a written file sitting beside the notebook.

"Well, obviously the amount transferred is for the completed job, and the amount to that contractor is only part of it."

"So where is the rest of the money? The balance of this account—is only twelve thousand?" He checked the figure on the file.

"How do you know that?"

"Well, the Crown has a large case under investigation here, Mr. Donahue. The entire foundation and any one of its employees or associates is under audit as we speak." He frowned and looked intently into Donahue's face. "I ask again—where is the balance of the account?"

"Well, obviously, other contractors will have been paid!"

"Except they haven't been, have they? The account shows funds have been spirited away to yet another account in the name of—'Donahue holdings as Trustee for the "Trust of Donahue and sons Pty Ltd."'"

"Oh, yes, that's right—that's our working account. We have a company trust to ensure that if one of these towers collapses or the setup dies—"

"Dies?"

"The micro biotic function of the relationship between the fish, the plants, and the structure—if that fails and half a million dollars of crops are destroyed or don't have sufficient yield, we don't get sued. A trust chain is just normal business practice; you know that."

"Normal business practice includes business protection insurance—not a convoluted set of 'lochs' to God knows where."

"Not in this business, it doesn't. Do you have any idea what insurance for this kind of science costs?"

"Not really; why don't you tell me."

"Well, it's too much! The world is going to burn itself out, and these ideas come along and give us some hope en masse that we can preserve land for natural cycles and still feed everyone and keep an economy going—and an insurance company says 'it's too risky.'"

"Well, isn't it?"

"Not really. I mean, you could argue that the crop choice is not altogether known if it is genetically modified, but there are dozens, if not hundreds, of modified crops already loose out there and already in our food chain. At least these towers contain them, if the owners of the IFTs chose to go that way. I guess someone would argue that the risk of contaminated water or micro bacterial adaptation might pose some kind of unknown risk. But hell, the whole world is one huge 'risk tank,' with chemicals in every part of the cycle and every soil in the world. We have already polluted everything with higher and higher levels of radiation, dioxins, and every kind of contaminate you can imagine being rained down on everything for the last fifty years, so it's a bit of a moot point."

"So you think your system is pretty safe?"

"As good as the science that designed it is, and that's pretty thoroughly proven. It basically uses a natural cycle anyway—a concentrated copy of what happens in nature."

"So, getting back to the money, you think that it's fair enough that a little profit off the top is 'justified,' in light of the huge contribution to mankind this experiment in large-scale, sustainable crop production is making?"

"No—no, not at all. There is no profit, no skimming going on. Look, here is my accountant's name and phone number. Here is a list of the contractors.

A list of all the clients and what they have been charged. The companies and trusts. Everything. Go ahead, check out every last one, every last cent, in every account connected to me, the foundation, or my subsidiaries."

Sam told me he then stood up abruptly. "If you can find a cent missing, come back and talk to me! Hell, I may have had a sausage roll or something for lunch and not kept the receipt. But otherwise, this whole thing is just trouble stirred up by people who have nothing on their minds but stopping the Ulmarra Foundation from doing what needs to be done."

"Sit down, Mr. Donahue—I have more questions."

"No, you don't; I've given you everything you need to sort this out, and, unless you have a parking ticket I haven't paid for and you intend to charge me with a crime—I'm finished."

Bateman closed the file and looked up at the door as Donahue walked to it.

"Don't leave the country, Mr. Donahue, until this is all verified."

"You can find me in Mossman. I'll be tending the set-up of tower fourteen with a bunch of barramundi fish and a load full of modified maize feeding off them."

"Sounds interesting."

"It is."

"How big are the barramundi?"

"They are only the size of tadpoles, but in a year they will weigh a kilo and have to be harvested."

"Just a year old? Why don't they let them get a bit bigger?"

"Because if they are left to their own devices, they will eat each other, grow up to 1.2 meters long, and weigh fifty-odd kilos, and that isn't economical. This is, after all, a business alternative to farming hundreds of acres with the same corn we can stack into this one tower. Gotta make the owner's bank manager happy if he's going to give all that land on lease to the foundation to replant in carbon-scrubbing wilderness again."

"Ahh—I see." Bateman leaned forward, swiped his security card, and turned the handle on the door. "Well, I hope everything is above board with you and the foundation, because I think it's a great idea. I wouldn't mind doing a taste test on a few of those barramundi beauties in a year's time, too."

"I'm sure the owner will write you an 'invoice.' We wouldn't want it to look like a bribe, now, would we?"

The sergeant laughed and showed him through the door without going through himself.

Jimmy and I stood up.

"So?" I said.

"So what!" Donahue had ignored my curiosity and nodded to Jimmy as he walked behind him and headed for the door.

"Did you sort it?" Jimmy asked.

"Well, they will have to check it for themselves, but I gave them everything they need to put this rubbish to bed."

"So it's all good, then." Jimmy nodded to himself.

"Of course it is going to be. At best they can rap me over the knuckles for putting in invoices before the damn jobs were done, but every single project is totally straight, and Louisa is completely without anything to worry about."

"Then how did they get this rubbish going in the first place?"

He didn't look at me but said sarcastically, "My guess is your brother Juniper stole my notebook and those invoice reconciliations of Louisa's that I had, because they have mysteriously got into their hands in there." Samson pointed back to the closed doors he had just passed through. We stepped outside into the car park, and he waited for Jimmy to unlock of the doors of the Ute with a *bleep*.

"They had a copy of my notebook where I keep track of the progress payments of all the contractors, and that's got the invoice numbers from the ministry in it too. If they married them up with the invoices I give Louisa from the clients, and the contractors, there would be a big shortfall—until the end of the deal. If they had used their brains, they would have realized that I was bound to be using a trust to protect us from any problems against litigation."

"Yeah, well, cops have never been known for having any brains—"

"They aren't the only ones!" Donahue replied gruffly, looking squarely at me.

"Is that why they thought money was going missing?" Jimmy asked as I frowned. "This crazy way of keeping the account information in your personal book?"

"Hey, mate—I'm not a bloody accountant! I just had to make the money stretch, so we could do it all at once, and my notebook was how I kept it all straight."

"You mean all this trouble is because you weren't keeping proper bloody books?" I replied.

"Sort of—I mean, it would have been okay if there had been only one or two going at a time, but the idea has sort of taken off. The foundation has had heaps of submissions, and more and more farmers want to have their cake and eat it too. There wouldn't have been a problem if it had all just been allowed to work itself out. It sort of got away on me a bit after we had to set up trust companies to stream the money through, because no insurance will cover us. I guess it might have looked suspicious, if you didn't know how the whole thing was going to come together at the end.

"Anyway, the cops will get their legal bean-counters together with my accountants, and they will find out there is nothing missing at all. Hell, we are honest people—you should have known that."

"Well, why couldn't you have told us all, and them, in the beginning?"

"No one asked me. I'm practically camping at these sites for a week and half at a time with no TV—and then, when this went down, I dropped my phone in the tank. To be honest, all the stuff I heard about corruption and so on, I just put down to being bullshit stirred up to discredit what we are doing. I thought it would blow over. How was I to know they were using my notebook and invoices to make a stupid case?"

"Idiot!" I let out a long burst of air along with the single noun.

"I don't think you understand. We could only have done half of what we have if I hadn't done a little creative accounting." Sam had a look on his face that was genuinely innocent.

"Well, your bloody 'creative accounting' nearly got us permanently shut down." Jimmy stated the obvious.

I was thinking about the real problem. "That prick of a brother of mine is going to get a visit. It could only have been him that nicked that stuff they got hold of."

"Have to find him first." Jimmy turned and looked out the window as though the man might suddenly be there.

"Well, just make sure you are sure it was actually him, Wajilla. You're inclined to get it wrong."

"Get it wrong?"

"Well, you had me pegged as the criminal, and you've known me for bloody near seventeen years—how do you think that makes me feel?"

"Well, yeah—I guess it was a bit rough." I looked out the window. A long, silent pause filled the vehicle as it sped up the highway towards Mossman.

Then I said very quietly, "I'm sorry, mate—I just got fired up because old Louisa has been hassled to death over this thing, an' Jimmy said the cops even searched her, and she was pretty upset. And hell, she got put in jail and charged—I know what that feels like..." My voice trailed off as I tried to hide some distant memory I would rather forget.

"Well, you still could have given me the benefit of the doubt."

"Yeah, mate, you're right." I thought about it for a minute. "Hey, you want Jimmy to stop the car, and I'll let you take a swing at me?"

"No, I don't; but you can buy me a dozen beer—"

"I knew it!" Jimmy said.

"Is that all? Hey, mate, you're a good fulla," I replied, quite surprised that was all he wanted.

"Hang on—I want that every week for six months!"

"What!"

"I'd shut up if I were you; you got off lightly." Jimmy grinned.

"Well, you thought he was the guy too! How come you don't have to go halves?"

Jimmy wasn't interested in the beer; he was staring out the window.

"The problem we now have"—Jimmy turned and looked long and hard out to the fields of cane spreading out either side of the road up to the foot of the ranges— "is how long it will be before we can get back on track. There's that new section down in the Bowen basin we need to do a grid copy on, and the last of that section to plant in G8, at Palmerton's station."

"You gotta be up north too —for the dingo release in a few weeks?"

"Yep—and that too."

"And what about you and Jilly Bird?"

"Yep—that too."

"What about Jyly?" Donahue questioned.

"Mate, you went to ground for a week, and look what happened. Jimmy get's engaged, and Louisa gets arrested!"

"Engaged—you're kidding me!"

"Nope, they're getting hitched!"

"I'm not surprised. I could have told you that almost from the beginning." Donahue looked out the window.

"Really?" Jimmy said curiously.

"Yeah. Dr. Ulmarra, you might know a shitload about the wild world, but you don't know jack shit about yourself! It was as obvious as —"

"Dingo balls!" I said.

"Well, whatever," Jimmy said with a slightly more serious tone as he looked at me. "Let's dump this bozo off, then we will head back to town and see if we can book a chopper for tomorrow or the next day, and we'll try and fit in everything we have to catch up on, so I don't miss my own wedding."

"Bozo? If I didn't like you idiots so much, I'd go walkabout and leave you to it," Samson indignantly replied.

"Yeah, right; you couldn't even walk a mile in wild country, so just keep playing with your li'l' fishy ponds and that ganja you're passing off as 'commercial hemp' growing up on the top floor, and we'll do the 'hard' stuff."

Samson shook his head, and the tiny glimmer of a smile crept up his mouth.

When we reached the shining Perspex tower rising from the brilliant green of the cane fields around it, Samson disembarked. He stood and waited for us to turn to leave. As the Ute arced around in a tight circle, it slowed, and I leaned out the driver's window with my arm exposed and my pink palm outstretched upwards.

"Hey, mate—you know I didn't mean nothing, eh?"

"Yeah, I know—but you still aren't getting off your 'beer penance,' but I might let you help me drink it."

I nodded, and a broad smile spread over my face. I turned to Jimmy and said, "Told you, nothing wrong with this guy; he's a good cobber."

Samson shook his head for some reason.

"See you, brother!"

Our vehicle sped away in a shower of stones and a thin trail of dust.

Looking in the side mirror, I saw Samson slap his hand on his thigh, and it looked like a long sigh might have escaped his lips, and then he turned to walk inside the bright and living tower.

Chapter 15

A MONTH WENT BY; Louisa was formerly released from all suspicion, and a small, innocuous comment was printed in the public notices in the Cairns and Brisbane papers saying the allegations against the foundation were groundless.

Donahue's accountants supplied a full report, and he reckoned they charged him an arm and a leg, but it was worth it to have it in the light of day. We got an official letter warning that "accounting practices must be entirely upgraded to sufficient commercial standards," and Lou gave Samson such a barracking, he promptly hired an accounts executive to make sure it all worked in the future.

Getting it straight didn't solve the finance problem with more inquiry for requisitions than we could handle, until Donahue was approached by one of the money men from a huge mining outfit that offered to payroll pretty much all we needed. They wanted to make a deal that, under the restraint of "environmental guidelines," we wouldn't raise objections to already approved future mine sites.

Louisa was militant about it and didn't want to agree, but Ulmarra said he'd be happy to plant round them, and, when they were gone, requisition the old pit sites for new lakes and waterways. He argued that nature had been blowing holes in the earth across millennia, like at lake Barrine, which was a volcano, the lava of which had contact with the groundwater and blew sky-high, leaving a perfectly round hole that filled to become the beautiful lake above the ranges. He reckoned the mine pits would pass as natural cavities, so the deal was acceptable to him.

Ulmarra was smart too. He said to me after it was signed, "Keep your friends close and your enemies closer." And he grinned that way he does and added, "Soon no one will want the coal, because the green energy is getting cheaper by the minute. Who's gonna buy it when you can have the wind and the sun for free?"

I thought he was being a bit optimistic, but I could see his point, and it was one less entity working against us.

Maria Ferris soon faded into oblivion too. She was interviewed but refused to comment on the case, returning to the usual line of "economic sabotage" by "parties" that have little to gain environmentally but a great deal to gain financially with the scheme at the expense of the rights of traditional farmers. She seemed to be spitting against that free wind and sun, by the looks of it, and hardly rated a mention after that.

The government Department for Environmental Affairs got on board too at that time and declared that the Ulmarra Foundation project was scientifically valid and only one part of the government's commitment to environmentally sound principals. "We have a social responsibility to preserve the environment, to improve it, to sustain it, or be found culpable by future generations."

We heard those clips for weeks, over and over, as they belted out the message of how admirable the government was, backing many initiatives such as education programs, recycling, and, of course, carbon-emission controls in the guise of carbon taxes.

And, I must say, it sounded convincing that the latter proceeds of which were, "Funding some of these environmental undertakings that we are so passionate about achieving, including the astounding task of restoring thousands of acres to native forest by the Ulmarra Foundation and others like Land care."

Every paper seemed to be coughing up good press on things for a while. One journo said, "In generations to come, they will liken the Ulmarra Foundation's endeavors to building the Great Wall of China; ironically, because of proceeds from the sale of coal and minerals to that same country, we can achieve the goal of a 'green' Australia."

I knew that was hardly the case, but it helped. Our money mostly came from private donations and one or two big guns that had altruistic inclinations or like the mines, could feel the tide turning, and wanted to ensure a smooth ride and their own survival.

The truth was there were only a couple of thousand volunteers, people from conservation societies and environmentalists in the whole of Australia, slaving their guts out, building this '"Great Green Wall of Australia."

Most of the rest of the population didn't really know or seem to care what was going on, I suppose, but were happy to believe whatever bullshit came their way through that damned box, and, as long as no one touched their booze or their burgers, the spin doctors could wrangle things to mean anything, and people just followed on mindlessly.

We humans weren't much like the dingo pack Jimmy was trying to save. They worked together as a family team, but we seemed more like a gang of lemmings, taking off en masse and hurling off a cliff to swim far out to sea to drown.

Mind you, we only need enough people did understand so we could get the job done. Aside from all the rhetoric, what was facing everyone was real, and even the poly's, the journos with their spin, right down to the kids at school, knew it deep down. We had to make the changes, because what was coming was serious.

So we kept getting money to carry on, and more and more people joined us.

As Jimmy always said, "just keep walking, and some will follow."

The foundation began to return to its normal routine and got on with the vision started almost twenty years before, with just half a dozen of us— only now it was a genuine movement, and it was growing.

In the time that followed, Louisa was often absent from the Ulmarra Foundation offices, preferring to work from her apartment.

Donahue hired a small team, and the shining towers grew in number up and down the Queensland and New South Wales coast.

Jimmy and me continued with the practical planning and execution of yet more grid mapping and section plants, more or less going on all the time somewhere.

And Jyly was happier than anyone I had ever seen. She moved in to the house at Crystal cascades, and the Great Ulmarra was more focused than I think he had ever been with her at his side.

On Saturday, four weeks from when Louisa and me heard the news, Jimmy and Jyly visited the elders at the Mossman reserve to tell them that they intended to get married up on the mountain in a traditional ceremony.

Jimmy told me it was supposed to be a serious thing, but he thought it was like authorizing something that had already made itself legit. He said the evidence of it and the joy of it, was already growing without permission. I didn't know what he meant by that, but I thought he was talking about her already living with him.

"So you two gonna get a real license for all that cooing and cuddling?" Jimmy told me Willy had nodded his approval even before he had heard his answer..

"Yeah," Jimmy said as he held a glass of orange juice between his hands and smiled broadly.

"And you, young lady; d'you know what you getting into if you join up with this Yidinji?"

"Yep, Uncle."

Maisy, Willy's wife, entered the conversation, and The Great Ulmarra waited to see if she approved.

"Seems to me you two are just exactly right, and there be some lovely pups coming into the world from that Dreamtime place though you. I was beginning to think it would never happen." She chuckled, and Jimmy said he breathed a sigh of relief, because their approval was important.

Jyly looked up quickly and then dropped her eyes with a little embarrassment.

Jimmy said, Maisy spotted the revealing look and sucked in a deep breath, licking her top lip.

"Maybe it's just the right time to have a 'girl chat,' eh, baby?" She swept over and lifted Jyly up by the arm. "We is gonna take some time away from these fullas, so we get to do some woman's talk, 'cause some of these things are our things, eh?"

Jyly looked up to Jimmy with a little fear on her face, but he indicated he wasn't going to rescue her by shaking his head, and then he smiled.

Willy leaned over and patted the younger man's knee. "Gotta watch out for that women's stuff, boy. They is all in cahoots, and it's us they got a mind to roping down like a stray steer."

"Yep, you probably right on that." Jimmy said he took a sip of orange juice and told me the old man had given him a reliable warning.

"But I'm pretty sure you got goanna lizard in you, so you'll just slither out of ol' Maisy's grasp—an' that young girlie is looking like she be a good 'un anyway. You is blessed in that, boy."

"Yep. She's good, Uncle."

"So you gonna say them words up where the old girl's new tree is, up on the mountain, that place you call the 'Rainforest Cathedral'?"

"Yeah. Thought you might see to organizing the festival as close as we can get to how it should be."

"Oh, my boy, that's for sure, eh! We gonna do it like it was the first and the last."

"What do you mean, Uncle?"

"Like it was when our people was here, 'first,' in them 'last' years—and now you see you are the *last* of them, so we gonna make this the *first* time it done proper in this generation."

When Jimmy told me this, I felt like a tinfoil blue Admiral Butterfly had suddenly realized it was trapped in my stomach and it turned, and turned, to get out. Willy's words often had that effect. It was like he could wish things in from the Dreamtime with what that old bloke said.

"Yeah, that's what we want," Jimmy said.

"So, you think, when? Six months, or what?"

Jimmy said he looked up and saw Jyly seated on the top of a greying stump, and Maisy intently talking to her, her hands darting about to describe whatever she was saying and then flitting to the girl's shoulder to rest occasionally, like a sun bird on a blossoming flower.

"When Jyly is ready."

Willy looked up, and he frowned as he watched his wife and her expression. Jimmy said he looked back at him with a frown. "Boy, I think you might be getting dumb to the seasons coming on. She's doing the woman thing out there with that young girl, and that can only mean one thing: she's got plans for way quicker than that!"

Jimmy said he laughed out loud, and Willy couldn't help but join in. "You better get the people together fast, Uncle."

"Yep. You gonna fly us up there in one of your choppers or we gonna have to walk?"

"We gonna go up the trail from the river. I know where it is. So you better get a few rounds in at the gym, Uncle, 'cause that's a good walk up there." Jimmy smiled as he looked up and saw Jyly and Maisy returning from the backyard. He said Maisy had her arm firmly planted around Jyly's shoulders.

As she climbed up the steps with Jyly in tow, she said sternly, "So, old man, we got a good deal to get sorted. We got wedding festival in three weeks!"

"Three weeks? Woman, are you crazy?" Willy replied incredulously, then Jimmy said he looked at him and winked.

Jimmy looked into the slightly worried and disconcerted eyes of Jyly, and his gaze softened.

"It's okay, Guli," he said gently.

"You called me Guli? How come I'm not just the pearl on its own, the Guba-Guba?" She looked at him brightly. "Why have you changed it to the mother of pearl?"

"Ohhh..." Willy shook his head and grinned.

"Yeah, I knew that ain't fat sitting on your gut." Jimmy said he smiled as he stood up and took her by the hand and lifted the pearl from her neck to caress it with his other hand before dropping it back on its chain.

Jimmy told me Maisy laughed out loud and said, "So no secret is safe from you, Ulmarra, not even women's business and new pups coming."

"I thought you was doing that talk, old woman! I could tell." Willy waggled his finger at her. "You get a look on your face that is unmistakable, girl!"

Jimmy said Willy slapped his hand down on his knees. "So we gonna get a little Ulmarra? When, young woman?"

"October, I think."

Jimmy said Maisy sighed happily and said, "Oh, my girl, it's all coming thick and fast with you, eh? We gonna have the ceremony for you two together, then we gonna have the ceremony for the new one, that's two big feeds... My mum used to say things came in threes, so I wonder what other feast we gonna have?" Maisy grinned and took a biscuit from the plate herself. "Well, that's good, eh—we get all the young ones to help an' that'll keep them out of trouble."

"Your mother and sisters, they know?" Jimmy said Willy frowned slightly toward Jyly.

"Nah—I don't even want to tell them, 'cept about the marriage thing, because all my sisters have had kids without getting hitched."

"Nothing to be ashamed of, girl!" Maisy shook her head at the implied breach in morality.

"I'm not ashamed," Jyly says somewhat defiantly. "I just want it to have its father's name on the birth certificate, and for us all to have the same name!"

"Well, that gonna be happening just as you please. We gonna get you all licensed up and saying them words in no time." Maisy swallowed hard and nodded to old Willy in the opposite chair.

"Jimmy, you gotta go to this girlie's mother and give some gifts for her, you know, 'cause that's the custom for us people."

"Yep, Aunty—I know."

"She gonna agree to this? She the mother, an' she have the rights over this little one."

"Yep—she'll be pleased to get me paid for." Jyly smiled. "But if she doesn't, I will have to start a new custom."

Willy smiled at his wife, and his gaze stayed on her rounded face and aging eyes. "It's a good thing happening. It's a good thing, old girl."

Jimmy said Jyly stroked his arm and said quietly, "One more Yidinji up the ladder."

He nodded knowingly.

They stayed for lunch. Other people in the village area were told as they wandered from house to house being congratulated and welcomed, but by midafternoon, they were ready to head home.

Maisy leaned into Jyly as she went to get into the car and whispered, "After this ceremony, I got to talk to you some more about the birthing. It's secret stuff just for us, so you come up here without him, an' I'll tell you the old ways, so this baby got all his inheritance on this land and all them Dreamtime spirits working for him right." Jimmy said he heard her and at that moment he was glad he had brought Jyly up there. Such things even he didn't know.

Jyly nodded, kissed him on the cheek, and the couple set off home.

Chapter 16

I WENT TO THEIR place a few days later, because Jimmy and me were going down to Eungella Reserve for a few days. It was the largest in Australia, and you could see platypus there. We had a requisition that would reach it, and a study was needed to see that our connection wouldn't introduce any problems to the existing area.

When I arrived, the sun was dancing off the front steps, and the door was open. Typical Ulmarra—he simply didn't have any idea of security.

I could hear them having bit of a "discussion," and I thought, "Uh-oh! We finally get him hooked up to a nice chick, and he's already wrecking it."

She was saying something about being confused, because she obviously couldn't wear a white dress.

I heard him say, "Jyly—I don't care what you wear. The most important thing for you is to just be authentic. Just be you. If you want to wear a sack— you'll still look like my girl."

"You don't understand," she said. "It matters to me! I'm the first one that has even got married. I want it to be perfect, and I'm scared it's not going to be."

"Follow the pull; listen to the still, small voice. You'll be fine."

"Jimmy, I'm too excited and worried for that. I don't know—I'm scared this is the one an only time I'm going to do this, and I can't just listen out for 'nothing'! I have to get some idea from someone."

"Calm down..."

I walked in and yelled out, "Oi! Ulmarra...Jilly Bird, where are you? If you're doin' the wild thing, you better get decent."

Jimmy called back, "You're early."

Jyly smiled at me as I turned the corner, her eyes sparkling, her face lit like a candle.

"How is the bride-to-be?" I asked.

"Confused—I have to decide what to wear; I mean, a white dress ain't gonna fit the scene, you know."

"True."

"I want it to be traditional, but—"

"The first Yidinji didn't wear nothing—I mean, I don't mind if you go that way! Maybe not Ulmarra, though, and definitely not us guests!"

"Wajilla, forget it. She's for my eyes only." Jimmy slapped my shoulder.

"You ready?" I said as I turned to him.

"Yeah, but we got a bit of time."

"Then I'll help sort out this dilemma for your girl here."

"You?"

"Yeah! I know a bit about fashion, you know."

"Bullshit!" Jimmy shook his head and walked off to the kitchen.

"Okay—start with the 'elements.'" I grabbed the pen and started drawing on the back of a white envelope. "Tits, hips, legs—now, what's your message?"

"Ah—new life. Our new life."

"Okay...something green ...something black, something like the bird you are." I sketched something. She frowned and poked out her tongue. I liked it, anyway, and thrust it to her. "Okay, that's that problem sorted. Anything else?"

"Catering?"

"See Maisy."

"Lighting, decorations?"

"Natural; see Maisy."

She smiled and shook her head.

"This is all women's business, eh?"

"Nah—the body painting, the music, getting the meat, that's Jimmy and me...seeing Willy!"

I looked at her. She was just like a veil of white clematis draped over the trees in spring. Ulmarra was her tree, and she was his beauty. No man could touch them flowers, or they would literally die there on the vine, and, at that moment, I realized she was already a married woman, and we were all just catching up.

She caught me looking and she said, "You're wonderful, Wajilla—my best mate, after him, and my best councilor ever."

"I know," I said, "I'm the best! With everyone else's girl 'cept one of me own."

"Poor Wajilla! Must be you are made for something more important."

"Right. Well, that'd be okay if I could tell my, you-know-what to play dead."

She got up, and she looked down at me and said gently, "You know, sometimes I feel sorry for you men."

"Oh, me too—so, you got a girlfriend you gonna hook me up with?"

She was now looking like a pretty piece of carved volcanic glass in the light from the door. Her cheekbones shone, her shoulders looked like her creator had molded and smoothed them with his own two hands, and she was perfect. Inside her, the newest member of our family was being knit together, and I thought when life got disappointing, every now and then, there was something that made it worthwhile, and here they were, in front of me.

"Okay, time to go, mate." Jimmy appeared, and he had a small glass of water with him. He handed it to Jyly and said, "Drink more water."

"I'm not thirsty," she said.

"Water the plant, or it won't grow," he said as he grabbed his bag.

I laughed; she was going to get good care from him, and I guess caring for her was part of his reason for being.

We headed off down the steps after he had kissed her good-bye and I had hugged the little girl and left her with her glass of water and her plans for the wedding in the Rainforest Cathedral.

As we got in the Ute, I said to Jimmy, "So, is Louisa coming?"

"I asked her, but she said she would be working."

"You can't leave it like that."

"Nah—I should. She has to get her head around it, because we got a history that is gonna go on for a long time yet. Anyway, I know her. She'll come through in the end."

"She's not gonna get round it, Jimmy—she's got her heart all tangled up in her head, so she is gonna need some help to get untangled."

"Then you help her."

"Dump it on me, why don't you!"

"What would any of us do without you?" He laughed.

"Dunno, actually...dunno," I whispered as I thought about Louisa, and we drove away.

When we got back, I had to give Louisa some of our data that we had collected and the survey map of the reserve that showed the distribution of plant species, watercourses, and topography of the whole area. We could see why the area worked so well already, and both Jimmy and I were quite excited to have some evidence of what large tracts of natural land could do for localized climate and water conservation.

I took the info to Louisa at her apartment.

When I got there, she was at her desk in the office she now worked at most of the time.

"Lou, you are like a platypus, in your hole all day an' only comin' out for a feed morning and night. I haven't seen you for weeks. How are you going?"

"Okay."

"Okay? Is that it?"

"Yeah...okay."

"Lou...how 'bout I get you a coffee, and we take a break from the Ulmarra Foundation."

"No, I'm okay; I got things that have to be done."

"No, Louisa Henderson—you don't. You're coming with me. We are going down to the Red Barron, and I'm buying you a drink!"

"But it's only eleven thirty!"

"So what? When you need it, you need it!"

"Well—I guess you're right, there." She grabbed her bag, and I grabbed her, and we set off.

When we got to the pub, they were setting up for lunch, so we took a table right at the back, and I got her a red and myself a Four X beer.

"So, Lou, you know about the wedding."

"Yep!" She took a swig of her wine, sighed, and looked up. "You know, he invited me; can you believe it?"

"Of course I can; he's been a mate of yours for years. What did you expect?"

"What I didn't expect was for him to finish with me because of her and run off into the sunset and get married half a minute after me."

"Come on, Lou, you know the heart wants what the heart wants. You and him were never gonna work out."

"Why not? Why ...bloody...not?"

"You want a list?"

She took another swig of the red and then downed almost the whole glass.

"Lou, you can't change this thing. Those two are like...I don't know, like—"

"Two peas in a pod?"

"One pea."

"Ahhh—can't fight that."

"Nah; can't fight that!"

"Why don't you take the last few months, throw it in a hole in the back of your mind, and say 'That's it, it's over, and I'm gonna start a new story'?"

"Easier said than done."

"Lou, I've had a few things that have rocked my boat too. Not the least being my kid brother. Hell, I also can't find a woman that'll have me for more'n ten minutes. I could get all sour and bitter too, but I don't want to be like that. It's a choice that you're gonna accept things and then choose what you gonna do about it.

"I mean, you can't stop them two being happy—nor stop the pricks that come at us to stop us, or the idiots that screw us over, but you can control *you*. You can say, 'Shit, I don't have enough life to waste on being miserable or hurt. I gotta find something happy for me.'"

"Well I do—I work!"

"Nah, Lou—you hide."

"Well, maybe, but I don't have a bunch of guys to just call in on or go to the pub with. I don't want to be one of those women who comes in here and sits alone and drinks away an hour then goes home alone or worse, a ten-minute wonder."

"Join something. Contribute to something. Enjoy something. Meet people for the hell of it. And keep meeting them till you make a friend or two."

"Wajilla—you make it sound easy."

"Who said it was easy? Nothing in the world is. You have to move yourself or just die in the hole you're in."

"Okay, I'll try."

"Good on you, girl—so, the wedding?"

"No."

I shook my head and said, "It'll be easier for you if you go."

"No."

"Stubborn, eh?"

She didn't reply. After a few minutes, she completely changed the subject, and we talked for about an hour on the merits of manipulating plantings to create optimized rain and water catchment.

At the end, I looked at her, thinking I might give it another go, but her eyes flashed at me in that way that tells you, you don't have a hope in hell. The only thing I got past her was she did ask me to drop her off at the foundation offices, and I thought, "Well, at least she has been pried out of her apartment cave."

With Louisa, you had to realize that if anything was going to happen, it was always going to be her choice and her decision and in her own sweet time.

Twenty-ninth of June, I got up and roused Jimmy from my spare bed.

"Get up, mate. Time to hitch up the wagon and head down to Gordon Vale for them words you been itching to say.

"We gotta pick up Jyly! Did I sleep in?"

"Nah, it's early, and Willy's bringing her down from Mossman, remember?"

"Oh shit—I dreamed I missed it."

"Come on, I'll get you breakfast. You go an' have a shower."

I turned and walked to the kitchen, and then I yelled out, "By the way, your 'suit' has arrived."

"Did I order one? Shit, I forgot about that."

"Jilly Bird did."

"Uh-oh!"

I got on with the essentials of any man's wedding day: a good breakfast of bacon and eggs on toast after a night out on the 'orange juice' with the boys until about three in the morning.

"Breakfast is ready—you coming?" I yelled out.

He had had his shower and appeared in the kitchen with a towel wrapped around his waist. "Have you seen this?"

"Yeah."

Jimmy held up a brand-new pair of khaki shorts with stitched pockets on the side that were pressed to perfection. "There's no shirt."

"No, Willy's gonna paint you, so I told her not to bother."

"What do I wear until I get to the top of the track?"

"Don't worry, I got a shirt you can borrow, at least till we get up there."

"Shorts to a wedding—an' no shirt," he said with amusement.

"Yeah, she said you told her she had to be authentic, so she told me she assumed you had to be authentic too."

"That girl—"

"I know, she's my pick as a winner too." Jimmy held up the shorts and smiled.

We took the Ute and drove to the base of the mountain at ten o'clock. I wasn't looking forward to the walk and said, "You could have picked a spot up the Kuranda range, so we could have taken the sky rail to the top."

"Yeah, but what would that have meant?"

"It would have meant I might have enjoyed it a bit more."

"Get your ass moving, or we'll be late."

The opening to the track off the road had a bower over it and white flowers. A table with cold water and fruit drinks were close by, and two young aboriginals were walking around and offering them to people preparing to go up. A few of our gang were hovering around, waiting at the entrance.

"So, we gonna do this thing?" It was John'o. He smiled broadly and patted Jimmy on the back and said, "Next time you want some kind of festival up on this damned mountain, I'm going to fly the chopper up there and drop all of us off."

"With your landings, I'd rather walk!" I said sternly, and looked up the track through the bower, wondering if I meant that.

The boys from the planting team had already cleared it, and I could see there were some rails erected and a few steps cut for the old people.

I looked around and said to Jimmy, "You reckon old Willy will make it up there?"

Just as I said that, Willy pushed through and called out, "Wajilla, I'll be up that track and sitting at the top waiting for you by the time you get to the first zigzag!"

Jimmy smiled, went over to the table erected at the top of the roundabout, and picked up an orange for himself and one for Willy. He walked back looking like his mind was elsewhere.

"Well, boy, I reckon this will be the making of you."

"Yeah, Uncle, it feels right."

A man walked over and interrupted them and said, "You got permission from the council and the reserve managers for this. I'm impressed." One of the farmers who had joined the foundation and leased two thousand acres of inland scrub for reforestation and management stepped forward and shook Ulmarra's hand.

I said, "They were happy to oblige, since it's our people that have the title to this part of the Lamb range. And it looks good for their 'sensitivity.'"

"Well, I must say it's the most unusual wedding I've ever been to."

"It's not quite a wedding, mate, it's a festival. They might be paying for the license and some kind of minister to make it legal, but we are having the celebration, and this one starts with a long walk up into the rain forest, a night of festivities, a sleep, and a long walk back. If you live, you'll never feel better in your life."

"Well, when are we getting started?"

"You ready, Uncle?"

"Yeah, the women are coming in the bus from Mossman. We left in our bus half an hour before them, so we better start, or they will be trying to take the lead up that old track, and that'd be bad! You know you can't let a woman get too much of a head start, or she'll keep on leading for the rest of your life!"

Ulmarra replied aimlessly, "Depends what kind of a leader she is, I guess."

"He's gone, Uncle, completely gone. We had better get him up there and over this in case he never comes back to his senses."

I could see the cars parked all the way down the road, and I took a deep breath and put my hand on Jimmy. "You're running out of time to make a run for it, mate."

"Done all the running I wanna do. Let's get up there."

We turned, and, amid much cheering, slaps on the back, and last swigs of drink, we headed to the track opening.

A boy stood at the entrance, and he leaned down into a huge crate and handed a bottle of water to Willy, who would lead at his pace.

I was next; Jimmy followed.

When Jimmy got to the gate, the boy thrust out a bottle of water for him. Jimmy stopped and looked up at the mountain and down to the boy. "We going back to some old ideas for all you young ones to have as your direction; you understand?"

"Yes, Dr. Ulmarra. I know all about the forest. We been learning at school."

"Learn about your people's ways, too, because those ways were designed for us 'specially, and they are good for us."

The boy smiled.

"And drink water, not coke, okay?"

"Yeah okay..."

Jimmy started to walk, and behind him the stream of men followed up the path and into the jungle.

It was one thirty when we got to the top, and, I admit, I was wheezing like I had no oxygen left for the last hundred yards. We had rested the old man twice, and Willy was being pushed from behind by two of his nephews by the time he made it to the strange feature of the mountain. Jimmy was fine, of course, and had already found the minister, Pastor Tommy Campbell, who made it up without mishap too, because he was an ex–marathon runner and was as fit as anyone there.

When the track opened to flattened canyon cut from the solid rock by some ancient rockslide, on each side, the Rainforest Cathedral floor had been covered with scattered woven mats, and a pile of them sat at the edges, ready for the guests to use. Wild vines and flowers had been draped at intervals and decorated the scene. A veil of vines flowed from an outward bow of the great tree and spread out to the ground in the center. Flowers were twisted into the vines, and below, a woven raffia mat was spread out ready for the words to be said. Petals had been strewn over the area, and they balanced on grass sprigs like snow that had fallen delicately from some invisible heaven.

A few people were setting up food that was wrapped in tinfoil, and three spits were rolling in the corner closest to the cliff-face. Cairns looked far away.

I headed for the drink table, downed two pineapple juices, and sat on the corner of one seat with my forearms resting over my knees as I recovered from the walk. I would have killed for a beer, but Jimmy wouldn't have alcohol up there.

Willy had already gone and spoken to the minister, who he knew well. He was seated on an actual chair that had been unfolded for him under the shade of the tree, and then he stood up and walked to the boys.

They were seated in the grass, already passing around wooden bowls of black, red ochre, and white lime clay, and dipping blunt sticks in it to paint one another's shoulders and backs.

Willy looked remarkably well for the hike up, as I sat where I was, puffing and feeling like I had done ten rounds in the ring. The old man stripped off his shirt and got someone to roll out a section of log for him to sit on. He held up a mirror and began to paint his face.

Jimmy had been talking with the minister too, then he smiled, shook the bloke's hand, and sauntered over, and slapped me on the shoulder. "Come on, we're next."

"Okay..." I said with a lackluster tone. I mean, I didn't mind all the traditional stuff, but it had been a long time since I had been to a corroboree or done an "increase" ceremony. I was happy enough with my shirt on, and even happier that it covered my somewhat padded body.

"Don't be shy," Jimmy said. "This is a taste of the past coming back to this mountain."

"Yeah, but it's not exactly accurate, is it? Why go to the bother of making ourselves all pretty, if it means nothing?"

"I know we aren't the old Yidinji or Djimudji, Wajilla. We're new. Some of what was is just about *remembering* where we came from and laying it down in the bottom of the hole in our souls and building the present on it, knowing the present is all different from the past. But, hell, we have to build on something!"

"Why bother? Half these guys wouldn't know what was right anyway, and, without the old spirits tagging along, what does any of it mean nowadays? The only spirits they know is Jack Daniels."

"Wajilla, where's your heart, mate—your soul? Why read a 120-year-old book? Why look at an eight-hundred-year-old painting or some twenty-thousand-year-old rock art, unless you're thinking about them that lived then and what they believed when they did it?"

He looked at me seriously. "Even if the 'old spirits' are dead in a bloke now, whether he means to or not, he brings them back out in himself today when he sees there was real power and meaning that motivated them back then to do great things. If they just live for the crap they're all trying to sell you down there on the plains"—he pointed to the gap off the mountain— "you're living for what? Clothes, cars, booze, travel, houses, just stuff you think you like? Maybe some bloke might live for a family—if they can hold on to one for longer than a year or two. But even people don't last forever.

"The old girl who started all this Ulmarra stuff," Jimmy said. "Margaret wasn't an abo, but she understood like one. She said, 'What does it profit a man if he gains the whole world—and loses his soul?'

"That's what makes a bloke live properly: bringing back his ability to believe in something more 'n himself."

I knew Jimmy and the "old girl," as he called her, were right, of course. I knew most of them young guys, and their parents and even their grandparents sure had lost it and someone had to point them back to it.

I watched the young blokes sitting painting one another, and I realized that when they put on those old designs Willy was teaching them, they were painting "wishing magic" onto themselves like they were a cave wall or a shield, and it could make them live for more than the modern stuff that had ruined them. Jimmy was right: we were bringing back *believing*, even if we weren't exactly, perfectly, authentic.

Jimmy looked at me and tipped his head on its side, leveling the question to me. "You gonna *believe*, mate?"

"Mmm—I guess so. Well, come on. Let the painting begin. Them spirits will be wanting to dance an' they gonna use my body to do it!"

I walked with Jimmy to the area, stripped off my shirt, and sat down. We got busy dotting and striping and plastering white all over our faces.

I looked across to the white fullas that had been invited and thought how easy it was for them. All they had to do was put up the odd Christmas tree or hide some Easter eggs, or maybe sing a few songs in church. You didn't have to bare your body and get painted.

It was almost as if Jimmy had heard me thinking. He knocked me with his shoulder and said, "They gotta go back too and pick up the things that are real. We all got the same need and the same composer, just comes out a bit differently. They gotta find the spirit for themselves too."

I shook my head and said, "Well, tell 'em to rip their shirts off and start looking by joining us! Why should we be the only ones trying to believe, — and naked too?"

Jimmy sat for a minute and looked over to Willy diligently painting black lines on the back of a boy of about twenty. Jimmy got up from his cross-legged position and walked over to the old man, leaned down, and whispered something. Willy looked up in utter surprise, and I thought he was going to have a hernia, and then he smiled very gently and nodded.

Ulmarra whispered to me as he walked past, "Sometimes you have good ideas, for a drongo!"

Within an hour, he had all the male guests stripped to the waist and lined up. Every one of those men, black and white, had the marks of Yidinji or Djirinbal on them, depending whether they lived south or north of the Barron River. Them white bellies were soon covered in dots and lines and a few handprints, and their faces had white clay smeared all over.

As they finished and sat waiting for the festival to begin, they were laughing and cracking jokes and really getting along well.

When I was finished, I hung around where the music and sticks were, and I watched Jimmy as he waited. He may as well have been on his own. His eyes were fixed on the entrance to the Cathedral as he watched and waited for her.

Suddenly I heard some distant singing, the echoing vibration of those female voices sounding out as they breathed in the cool air and kept their rhythm along the path.

Jimmy looked up and pointed, and all the men turned towards the opening where the track came up to the clearing.

The voices died away for a moment, as the singing rebounded off the mountainside and could not reach us. Then I heard them again, loud and clear, the song of the spring rains ending and the burning of the plain so the wallaby would breed in greater numbers for the tribe.

Then, there they were. Old Maisy being pulled up by a younger one—I think it was one of Jyly's little sisters—her skirt made of cotton and a top of reeds and fabric sewn together, with her large, round shoulders shining and a handful of long grasses, woven together, swishing left and right to clear the way. All the lead females—Jyly's mother and her two sisters, and Jyly's female friends—followed and were tightly packed together. Some of them were hitting hardwood sticks together rhythmically to the tune of the ancient song.

I couldn't see Jyly anywhere, as they had surrounded her.

Willy walked to a bark bowl under the tree and picked up a long, straight stick burning at one end. He blew it with his breath and it glowed brightly, sparks scattering in the shadows, then he walked out and began dancing left and right, his painted arms and body taking on the movements of our totem spirits.

The boys all spread out along the sides of the area, and the women poured in like molasses. Somewhere in the center was our girl.

Willy stopped and stood facing them, and Jimmy stood a little behind.

Finally, the song ended, and Maisy moved up to meet her husband.

"You made it, old man."

"You might live an extra year or two doin' that walk, old girl."

Then she looked up more seriously and spoke out loudly, "We come to give this woman to a good man. Where is he?"

Willy spoke up and said, "We elders agree to this, and we got that man here."

They stepped aside, and a group of us began dancing, and the didgeridoo howled out its growling sounds, and the sticks chimed in tune with the chants on our lips. We moved in unison from the back of the clearing under the tree towards the women and the light of the edge of the cliff. My brothers and I stamped the grass beneath our feet and jerked the movements of the goanna, and behind us Jimmy danced with us.

When we reached the women, they stepped back, and each one moved aside, until at last, I caught a glimpse of her.

Suddenly we all stopped, and Willy waved Jimmy on, and he walked through to stand behind his elder.

Maisy smiled at him, but Ulmarra's eyes were fixed on Jilly Bird hiding behind her elders.

She was dressed in finely roped raffia cords hung from a sandy-colored, cotton-bodice dress underneath. It stopped high on her thighs and the mass of long cords fell in sandy strings and stopped on her bronzed calves. Her hair had been plaited tightly with shells linked in the threads, and around her neck the gold chain with the giant, peach-colored, Ulmarra pearl glowed on her chocolate skin. I can't describe how she looked, really. There aren't words for that kind of beauty that comes on a woman who is loved and is in love, the way creation meant it to be. All I can say is I'm glad she didn't take my advice on what to wear, because what she chose was perfect.

Maisy said, "We give this woman to you..." and she turned and pulled Jyly forward as the other women pushed her gently from behind.

Willy nodded, and he took the glowing stick with its smoke twirling from the top and leaned down. He jammed it into the ground between the man, Ulmarra, and the woman, Ungaru, and stood back.

"Here is your fire stick." Maisy looked up to the young woman, and she lifted up the girl's hand. "You got his light now..." I saw a tear in old Maisy's eye, and her voice cracked slightly.

Jyly leaned down and pulled the stick from the ground, her eyes never leaving Jimmy's.

Jimmy walked forward and caught up the small girl's hand. They just looked at each other, and I thought, "This ain't a traditional ceremony! In the old days, they would have just walked to the buru he had prepared for them, gone in, and done the fun bit."

But here and now, the moment of these two pulled us all in to the deeply spiritual joining amid the forest surroundings. The birds punctuated the moment as heralds, the cicadas rose and fell like a holy choir in the background, and the shiver of leaves made it feel like God himself, the author of the Dreamtime, watched from behind the curtain.

After a few hushed moments, Ulmarra turned and led Jyly towards the tree, and, as he did, everyone burst out in cheers. The women hurriedly found their way to a mat to sit cross-legged and the men also. The dancing men followed the two to the tree and then seated themselves in the grass.

Finally the two stood together on the raffia mat in the shadow of the offshoot of Margaret Stanford's tree. Willy stood on one side and Maisy stood on the other, and Pastor Tommy appeared from the shadows.

He greeted us and said happily, "This is by far the most memorable and meaningful wedding I have ever presided over." He looked up to everyone: men naked to the waist, painted and smiling, and women decked in their various dresses of cotton or plaited grasses, looking across to their men in amusement.

"So it is good for me to say that this joining is not a light thing. It is done here, in the center of God's creation, which is fitting, and it is done here in the midst and sight of friends and loved ones. We're here to join these two in a way that is more than just an agreement to live together and love each other. God designed man to join and become one with his wife. This is a mystery, and it's a shadow of what man is to become with God himself. As we see here today, it's naturally demonstrated by these two." He looked up with a smile.

"If anyone doesn't think there is a legal reason why they should be, they should say so now."

No one spoke.

"So, Jyly Clarisse Ungaru, do you agree to join with this man? To give him what he needs, be willing to follow him and offer your support and guidance, be his champion and faithful to him alone, his ever-steady, second self, for all of your life, no matter how it turns out?"

My little Jilly Bird looked up into Ulmarra's eyes and said, "Yeah, I do."

"And do you, James Ulmarra—" He didn't get a chance to go on.

Jimmy turned to her and said, "Jyly, in the time before now, men and women sometimes came together to have kids and be company for each other, but this isn't what you and I are. We come from someplace where there is no time. We are from a Dreamtime place. Our spirits were always meant to be joined back together, and that's what has happened. If you fight with me, you fight with yourself. If I hurt you, I hurt myself. We are two bodies with one spirit joined together. We don't know what our future is, but I know this one thing: we were made to be this way, and we've made that known today to all these fullas. My love for you is my sacrifice of myself, and you're doing the same. Short or long, the life we'll have left is now for each other and whatever our purpose is. It starts with right now and will never stop, and the author of the Dreamtime, the creator of all this—he comes with us. Not just two of us alone now, but three. Jyly, I love you and always will."

"Me too..." she whispered.

"Well." Pastor Tommy smiled. "I guess that says it all! I'll add just one thing: as it says in Ecclesiastes 4:12, *'A threefold cord is not quickly broken.'*

So with that rather positive phrase confirming your own heart on the matter, I pronounce you man and wife!"

All of us clapped, and some of the boys cheered. The singer's voices rose as the instruments clacked and whooo'd, and the singers moved into the center and began to dance.

I got up and joined the circle, and then Pastor Tommy took Mr. and Mrs. Ulmarra across to a small table, and they signed the contract.

Willy and Maisy added their witness, and it was done.

We shifted the mats around and made a rain-forest restaurant picnic on that mountainside.

Willy called everybody's attention and said food was on, so we started to drift over to the tables and help ourselves to banana leaves and filled them with corn cobs, potatoes and roast roo, and pork and lamb carved from the spit. There was damper that someone from the reserve had made, and a pile of Lamingtons, those magical sponge-cake squares covered in melted chocolate and rolled in desiccated coconut, spilt in half and filled with jam and cream, and whose invention was still being argued about between New Zealanders and Aussies. They didn't look quite right amid it all, but I was glad someone had thought to bring them. Several bowls of banana prawns, as big as your hand, which one of the boys from the fishing boats up at Port Douglass had brought, didn't last long. Sweet potato had been roasted with herbs and bowls of okra and flat beans and heaps of other stuff to feed an army. Like a band of green ants, we devoured most of it.

Jimmy and Jyly sat on the mat under the tree, and we all fed in the afternoon sun in the scattered shade as the sun moved over the mountain crags. Occasionally a big cockatoo or rainbow lorikeet would fly over, heading down to fruit trees lower down or to raid an odd seeding eucalyptus in one of the parks below.

Willy got up and spoke about tradition and why it was important.

I had to say something too, and I had been thinking about it for weeks and couldn't decide, so I was unprepared when I got up and just winged it.

"So we finally see Ulmarra hitched! I guess I should say something good about him. Ah—what can I say?" I paused mischievously. Everyone laughed.

"Nah, there's a ton I could say, but he's my mate, no need to say anything about him. He's my *best* mate. That says it all, and old Jimmy, he always says that silence is underrated, so I ain't gonna say anything about him."

The crowd sat quietly watching me, and I felt like I was really under the gun to say something better than that.

"But Jyly, Jilly Bird—now, she is someone I can really say something good about. She's like a dewdrop on a day in the dry season. She's got the kind of dew that makes you wanna gather her up and keep her from evaporating. She's got that kind of water that when you have it, you never get thirsty. She's a natural, like him, and they are a reminder that we all have that innocence in us, and we can go back and get it and not be too complicated about how we live..."

I was about to think of a joke when I saw, from the top of the track, a familiar face. I stopped, and the pause, along with my stare, made several people turn to look also.

Jimmy stood up immediately.

"You forgot to invite me," the voice called out mischievously.

Jyly put her hands over her face, and Maisy immediately frowned and stood up.

"What's going on, boy?" she whispered to Jimmy, whose hackles had risen.

I stormed down the slight slope towards my half-brother with my fist up, ready to knock that idiot off the side of the mountain.

Jimmy skipped over the mats, and, just as I got to Juniper, he grabbed my fist and pressed it to my side. He didn't say anything but just looked at him.

"So, you got my girl in the end—you're a bit of a cradle snatcher, aren't you, Ulmarra? Bit of a dingo, stealing a young one from the tent!"

I lashed out, "You evil...shithead from hell—"

Jimmy pushed me back, gently but firmly, his hand open on my chest and smudging my paintwork as he did. He looked at Juniper hard in the eye, and I noticed that some of our boys had stood behind us and moved forward, waiting.

"So—nice day for it; any food left?" Juniper moved a step forward, but, as he did, Jimmy moved to match him and bar his way. It was a subtle move, like a cat shifting when the mouse flicks a whisker in a different direction and then freezes. Juniper started to look uncomfortable.

I cursed myself for not finding and pounding Juniper into a full confession weeks ago, when Sam thought it must have been him who stole the accounting book and gave it to the coppers. I wanted to yell; I wanted to pick that miscreant up and slam him into the ground, but Ulmarra was still staring at him, and no one could move.

Suddenly, Jimmy crouched down very slowly, his left hand out to his side like he might have held a spear in it and his thighs bulging under his weight. His eyes never left the man in front of him who now looked totally unnerved by Jimmy's reaction to his taunts.

Jimmy picked up something out of the grass. As he slowly rose, Juniper frowned, and his eyes momentarily flicked to what was in Jimmy's hand. It was a burnt chicken-leg bone that had laid in the earth from some fire on the edge of the clearing long time past. He rolled it in his fingers slowly, until the earth had dropped from it, and then slid it out through his fingertips and raised his arm.

I saw it and knew what he was doing. He lifted the bone and pointed it in front of him directly at Juniper.

I shuddered. We were taught as kids never to do this ritual.

I saw Juniper's eyes flicker, and his hand beside his side began to shake.

Behind me, I could feel the boys moving behind me as one by one they picked up a stick or a fish bone from our meal, anything, and all stood and pointed them at my half-brother. Right at the back, a couple of the boys started beating out a rhythm on the sticks. Someone was blowing into the didgeridoo, and it vibrated its hollow, surreal sound that seemed like it had found its way out of the rocks of the mountain itself, and it sang power into those bones and sticks in an ancient language of portent and curse toward Juniper.

Juniper stood against the backdrop of the ocean and the cane lands below. He was dressed in a T-shirt and jeans and began to stutter. "Wh-what? You gonna p-point the bone at me? You think—" He began to choke as though the old chicken leg Jimmy held had got stuck in his throat.

Suddenly he turned and dashed down the track, almost like he was a felled brush turkey.

I rushed forward to the edge and saw him running and tumbling down the track as fast as he could go.

Jimmy walked forward and looked too. Then he turned with a smile on his face. He tossed the chicken bone over his shoulder toward the path, and he began to chuckle.

I walked back to him as the other boys all started to laugh too, dropping their sticks or bones into the grass and slapping each other.

Jimmy grabbed me around the shoulders and walked me back to the festivities, grinning broadly. Just as he showed me to my picnic spot, he leaned over and whispered in my ear, "Some people will believe anything, mate—anything."

I shook my head and seated myself. I reckon Jimmy was being naive about that. Even though it's 2012—some of these old things are not to be played with, and believing or not doesn't seem to matter. A guy can still die if the bone gets empowered and ends up in your face.

Jimmy walked over and sat next to Jyly. She looked a bit upset. I saw Jimmy hand her a piece of meat and kiss her on her cheek, then go on with eating something himself.

Maisy was busy grilling Willy for information, but he just shrugged and began eating too.

Looking out at the scene, I couldn't help but scan the gap where the track comes up. Juniper didn't return, but I knew then he was back, still living near us, and I wanted to talk to him and find out if it was him who had stirred up trouble for us after all. I guess I already knew but made a promise to myself that I would find him, and we would have a heart-to-heart talk. Somewhere down in me, I wanted to give him one more go, before I gave up and let the tree be cut down.

Chapter 17

AFTER THE WEDDING, Jyly and Jimmy had a honeymoon at a lodge in Kakadu, the most ancient waterway and wildlife reserve in the world. It had been almost spring, and the water lilies were out, the green growth was shrouding the glassy rivers where wild crocs and white herons stalked the edges, and a blizzard of birds began to nest and feed for the beginning of the next season. Red-tailed black cockatoos took their roosts in high, hollow trees, and the land throbbed with new life everywhere, some of which was as old as time.

By the time they got back, I had already found Juniper.

He had cloistered himself in the center of Centennial Lakes Park. Using a blue tarp slung over a low bow, disguised in brush and leaves, he stayed hidden from anyone who might be looking for him. He had a twenty-buck portable gas hob from Burning's and a pot. A sleeping bag and a beer crate full of clothes showed he had got as low as you can go.

I tracked him in there by following the trails the bums leave in the undergrowth when they need to sleep off the booze, and, even if he had covered his tracks, I could feel him in there. When I found him, he was sitting cross-legged and looking pretty worse for wear.

"The spiders under here don't bother you?" I asked, and he began to scramble to his feet at the sound of my voice but couldn't quite make it up, probably due to the empty bottles of whiskey scattered around his den.

I said, "Forget it, mate, I'm past wanting to kill you."

Juniper sat again and seemed to stare off into the undergrowth, as though he might have been at that point when someone could finally get through to him.

I asked him plainly, not wanting to waste any more time. "Did you steal Sam's notebook and give it to Maria Ferris to discredit the foundation?"

He looked blankly at me.

"Come on, mate, clean your act up, start again—I'll forgive you, and we can start fresh, maybe get you some money and a place to stay."

He looked at me as though I had thrown him a lifeline, and then he started slowly. He soon began spilling his story with relish, and I frowned because there was too much glee in it to be about starting again or making a fresh start.

So I sat cross legged and listened to the whole damn thing.

As soon as Juniper had licked his wounds that we inflicted with the screwdriver, he went straight to the river city, but not before he had helped himself to money from the office and a few other things that he worked out would enable him to get revenge.

He told me it wasn't hard to find the people he would use to exact his "justice," as he put it. He had also seen the television story back, when the cyclone that didn't hit, on the foundation, just as we had seen it, and that gave him the idea. He knew that bitch Maria Ferris would pay anything to get something on us to do us damage. Remembering the broadcast, he said Louisa looked "hot," and he almost wished he was still up here, just so he could see her, though he didn't mind volunteering, "She can be a bitch—but I reckon I could have tamed her." I realized my baby brother had something in him that would never be cured when it came to women, and it made me sad and angry all at once.

Juniper said all he had to do was ring Maria Ferris's office, say who he was and what he had, and they sent a car for him and took him to see her.

He said Maria was standing by the edge of her desk when he came in, and she frowned when she first saw him. He gave her the notebook and the pile of invoices with their ministry-fund applications that he had stolen from Samson's briefcase and Louisa's office. He reckoned she had made him wait while she, and some guy with her, read page after page. She didn't seem to care that he was sitting there, waiting for ages; he thought that was rude. I thought, "You can judge!"

I looked at him seated in the dust and leaves, and I thought to myself that he should have been named Judas instead of Juniper by his weird, half-baked mother. It looked to me that maybe her genes were real strong in him as he told his story like it was something clever he had done.

Juniper said the man, who Maria called Russell, was seated at another desk, leaning over the papers and scratching his scalp from time to time.

"These numbers are crazy!" The man spoke and looked up at Juniper. "How the hell did you get this?"

"I got a mate who knows how to unlock things, and he taught me, eh, an' I was looking for stuff, and I thought, since they had upset me, and they wouldn't let me work there no more, I might need something to bargain with."

"Well, you sure as hell have a gold chip here."

Maria looked up over her red-rimmed glasses. Her jet-black dyed hair was cemented in place with hairspray so she looked like a Nazi Juniper said.

"So this is supposed to be from the Ulmarra office?" she asked Juniper.

"Yeah—some of it, but it's all stuff that is to do with them."

Russell stood and walked over to Maria Ferris. "This is the reimbursement from the Conservation Minister. This one, and this one, and this one—I guess that is the last section they requisitioned off this farmer, Stephen Blunt. This one is something to do with a proposal to requisition land, but when you look at the remittances, there is a hundred thousand added to this one against this internal copy, and something like forty-five on this one. They're skimming."

"Dangerous stuff. You would think there wouldn't be any records of that going on. Makes you wonder if the farmer is getting a kickback to stay quiet. Surely they can't think they'll get away with it."

"Well, you know they have got used to their 'mistakes' being 'excused,' because they are 'indigenous.'"

"Yeah, that'll be the truth," Juniper said the man had replied snidely, and Maria looked across at my brother. "So what's in it for me?" Juniper broke in. He had already decided to demand double of whatever they offered.

"Well, I think we could say—five thousand dollars," the woman said off-handedly.

"Five thousand! You've got to be kidding. I gotta go away for a long time, and disappear. That's gonna cost a bit—Nah, I want fifty thousand!"

"Forget it. This is only worth what I am prepared to pay for it—and since you'll certainly go to jail for a long time for stealing this, I think, let's say...ten thousand should be enough."

"I want it now."

"Next week, come back. I don't have it in the office."

"Nah—now! Get your EFTPOS card, and we're gonna get it now!"

"Russell, you do it, and make sure you don't get seen giving anything to this guy. Drop it in a bin or something."

"Very cloak and dagger," Russell replied.

"Maybe—but I don't want this person coming around again."

Juniper said she looked up with that arrogant, weasel-eyed expression. "Do you understand? You ever open your mouth, and you will go away for a damned sight longer than a year."

Juniper nodded but was already heading for the door with a fast limp, because he said he didn't care about the bitch, he just wanted his money.

As the door closed, he heard her say, "I got you now, Ulmarra." He saw her pick up the phone. I'll bet that was when she called the nine network news people and the police.

Juniper said he had caught the drift that he had managed a decent blow against us when the news started announcing that charges had been laid against Louisa and that the foundation was under investigation.

For a while, he said he was happy. He had money to spend from selling the information, and he had got us back. But after a while, the novelty wore off, the money dwindled, and the news changed its tune to show all charges had been cleared, and he realized we had somehow got off the hook. It never occurred to him that the foundation might be totally legit.

He said he'd been doing nothing for weeks and was "bored shitless," when suddenly his cell phone had rung. Looking at the number suspiciously, he answered it.

"Hello?"

He heard a voice that sounded something like that Russell guy from Maria Ferris's office.

"We need to see you."

"What for?"

"It's important—we need something."

Juniper was quiet for a moment, thinking what to do, then replied cagily, "Okay. I'll meet you by the bus stop on Adelaide Street next to the fire station." He smiled to himself, downed the last of the glass of beer in one swallow, and dropped it heavily onto the table. He said to himself, "So they want more info—well, that'll cost 'em."

He said when he reached the bus stop, he leaned on the aluminum wall that protected the seat and lit a cigarette.

Within minutes, he saw a green vehicle, parked on the opposite side of the road, turn around and stop a little way away up the street from him.

He said curiosity made him walk toward it. The window went down, and Russell's voice called out.

"Get in, she wants to talk to you."

He opened the back door after flicking his cigarette away. Maria Ferris was seated alone in the backseat of the car.

"You got some money for me?" she asked with an acid tone. The car started up the moment he got in, and Russell began to drive down the street.

"Huh?"

"My money—you got it, I want it back!"

"You want your money back? You're kidding, mate! What would I do that for?"

"You gave me bullshit. Turns out everything you said and implied was complete rubbish! Turns out they were squeaky clean. Sure, a bit disorganized, maybe, but there was nothing in it. You made me go out on a limb in public, and now I look like an idiot."

"Well, that's not my problem, lady. I gave you what I had. You didn't have to do nothin' with it. That was your choice."

"Where's my money?"

Juniper said he had laughed and said, "Gone!" He looked out the window and ignored the silence.

"Thomas, drop me off at the river, and I'll get a taxi. You can take this one to the 'correction' warehouse."

Juniper said he suddenly turned his head towards her with some instinct of fear.

"You ain't taking me nowhere."

"No, I'm not," she replied, as Russell slowed down for her to get out. "One way or another, you are going to pay."

After spitting out her parting shot, she dived out of that car so fast he could hardly believe it. The door slammed and locked, and he said he could see her walking off.

"Hey, let me out, you bitch!"

Juniper knew he couldn't dare let them take him anywhere, so he fired himself over the front seat. The door on the passenger side was locked, so he scrambled over the driver, who was now punching his torso and grabbing him by his jeans.

The car screeched to a halt and jolted forward a few feet, and his shoulder hit the windscreen.

Onlookers stopped and gazed with interest and concern as the two big lumps in the front seat fought tooth and nail, Juniper squashed up on the steering wheel and Russell's lap as he scrambled to find the door release.

He could hear the car's horn starting to blast in a continuous *waaaw-waaaaw-waaw*, and his hair flew in a loose mop over his spitting mouth, and he couldn't even see the man he was fighting beneath him.

Finally, he caught the driver's door handle, and, when the door opened, he spilt onto the roadway.

Russell grabbed at one of his legs and held him, but Juniper reckoned he fought "like a Thai kick boxer" until he was free.

Maria Ferris had seen the ruckus and looked around for a moment but then quickly disappeared into the gathering crowd.

Juniper scrambled away from the car as the man began to climb out after him, leaving the car door open.

A car screeched to a halt as he crawled then jumped up to his feet to run across the road. He said he automatically skipped across the bonnet like a feral cat and slid to the other side, dodging a car coming the other way.

"Russell must have realized I was being seen by everybody and that I'd practically escaped. He yelled out to me, 'We'll find you, mate!' then he turned and jumped back in the driver's seat, slammed the door, and drove off." I looked at him, frowning slightly, and wondering how the kid I had grown up with had become this kind of man.

"It was lucky I got away right then, eh? Who knows what they would have done to me?"

He grinned like a smart-ass kid and I thought, "You idiot."

He said when he arrived back at his shared unit on the outskirts of the city, he gathered up his things and bundled them into a diving bag. Without even checking that he had everything, he left the house and was on the road. He hitched his way back up the coast, stopping at Kalloundra, Noosa, Bundaberg, Gladstone, Mackay, and Townsville, but was inextricably drawn back to Cairns.

When he was through telling me his story, he started packing up. He was shoving his clothes into a supermarket trolley and tearing down the blue tarp

"Where are you going?"

"None of your business but if you must know, someone has told them where I am."

"Sot, we'll deal with it—"

"Piss off!" He yelled at me before I had much time to say anything more.

"Look, whatever has happened, it can be sorted and you can get on with your life."

"I can sort it myself—and my life is none of your business."

"Well, it is my business. I'm still your brother."

"Right!"

"Well I am—I just want you to pull your head out of your ass and make something decent of yourself."

"Well, luckily for me, other people are willing to give me a bit of a hand, and I've got a way out of being broke and under the gun that doesn't include you or your stink foundation."

"Who?"

"None of your business!"

"Well, let me drop you off."

"Nah. Anyway, I can guess you are the one who told those bastards in Brisbane where to find me."

"I didn't tell anyone anything."

"Well they've come to Cairns looking for me, eh, and if I don't do what they want—I'm likely to go missing for good, eh!"

"Well, come back to my place, and I'll sort it out."

"No need, I got a good place to go, and a mate that can be trusted. Anyway, I got a plan, just gotta swing one thing—"

"Well, just tell me how I can get in touch with you."

"I said before, piss off! I don't need you! You understand? I don't need your bloody controlling shit. Have you forgotten what you did to me? Just leave me alone."

"Juniper, bro—"

He picked up an empty bottle by the throat and smashed it on the side of the trolley. It shattered in a sparkling spray of golden glass pieces, and then he rushed at me.

"I said—leave me alone!"

His face was twisted and dark. His eyes flashed with something I couldn't recognize. It seemed like he was some kind of ghoul that had risen up out of that lake and walked with so much hatred that it had sucked all the life out of him. I was thinking maybe them bones and sticks that had been pointed were doing their magic on him after all.

"Don't you know you dog shit—I hate you!"

I put up my hands in submission, got up and backed away.

He stood stiffly and scowled, his jaw grinding and his hollow cheeks billowing like sails as he puffed hard in rage.

"You know where I am if…"

Juniper didn't reply.

I turned and began to walk back.

Before I dropped low to go under the fringe of trees, I turned and called back, "I'll always be your bro—no matter what happens."

He raised his fist and fired the bottle at me. It hit the tree and shattered all around me. I swallowed hard and ducked through the undergrowth until I reached the path that led out.

The lake was still that day, and the purple lily flowers rose from the mirror-glass water, waving gently. Shiny red dragonflies darted and hovered over the carpet of floating water plants. It was a scene that belied the sadness and confusion I was feeling.

I walked to the car and got in, and sat with my hands looped over the steering wheel and my head hung low. I couldn't think, and for about half an hour I watched the path, hoping he would come out. He didn't, so finally I started the Ute and drove home.

They say time heals all wounds. I'm not sure it does, but about six months later, I almost had normal days. I only thought about Juniper occasionally, but didn't get that churning stomach I used to after he had run me off.

He may as well have been dead, because he seemed to disappear, and no matter who I asked, or where I went, I couldn't find him.

Those early days were like a huge, stormy sea lived in me, and it whipped me, day and night. All I could do was hold on to the sides of my dinghy called sanity and splutter my way through it. Sometimes I thought I wouldn't survive, drowning in the tempest of regret and sorrow that never let up.

Then, little by little, those unforgiving waters slowly lowered their fury, and I could almost manage to row my way through a day, a week, a month, until I was surprised six months had passed.

One day, I woke from a good sleep for the first time since he had disappeared. Somewhere in that drifting sea of my dreams that night, I must have decided to risk swimming back to shore to begin a life that didn't include the memory of him.

I guess that's what happened, because I began to laugh and get on with things again, like I used to. Amy was probably responsible for that salvation.

His mum had shacked up with some bozo, and Amy, who was a handful at the best of times, really played up with her new guy, and he started hanging around with some wild kids and getting into trouble.

I took him, because I could see what was going to happen, and I hired a woman to come in and help out three days a week after school, and the rest of the time he'd come with me.

He began helping out in the nursery and loved any excuse to go out on surveys or section reports—anything that put him in the wild. I thought to myself that maybe this was what renegade kids needed, to get out into the trees and the open spaces, if Amy was anything to go on.

Seeing him settle down and becoming a real little mate to me held me together just long enough for me to come out of that tornado I'd been in after Juniper had done what he did and turned on me. I just wished I'd known that a dose of wilderness could have changed him like it had Amy. Sometimes, we learn okay—but it's all too late to make a difference.

One Saturday, I called into Ulmarra's place. Jilly Bird was seated on the couch, heavily pregnant. She looked a picture of happiness, and it was easy to smile about it.

"Wajilla! Stand up for me!" I shook my head in surprise.

"What for?"

"I am determined I am not having my baby in that damned hospital."

Ulmarra was skipping down the stairs to meet me. "Woman, it's your first child, my first child—you're not taking any risks." He looked at me quite sternly and said, "Tell her!"

"So—you gonna have it at home with a midwife?" I said, feeling a bit unsure how to say anything to her. This was definitely woman's stuff.

"Nah," she said with a smile that had a certain seriousness behind it.

"She's got this idea that she is gonna have it the old way, out in the rain forest on a birthing stone somewhere." Jimmy sounded incredulous.

"Ah—what's a birthing stone?" I said, because, even being an abo, I didn't know what that was and then I said, "That wasn't how my boy Amy was born."

"A birthing stone is a natural, hollowed-out stone they had in a sacred and hidden place on our land. The women would go out there and put red dirt and dry grass in it, and then the woman in labor would sit up, with the midwives helping, and she'd give birth there. Then they'd bury the placenta out there too—"

"Whoa, Jilly Bird—too much information!"

"Don't you know anything, mate?" She scowled at me as though, just because I was a dad, I should know this ritual.

"Some things, I don't wanna know!" I said and shook my head toward Jimmy.

"Well, it's what I want, to give birth in the sacred place. So the baby can have all his inheritance, the way it is supposed to be. Otherwise he's not really part of things properly."

"She's been talking to Maisy, I'll bet—bloody women's business! Should be banned!" Jimmy said, walked past, and then picked up a pile of photos of various vegetation we had been studying.

Jyly turned a little to face me, and her stomach seemed to follow her around. "Our people had to have their babies on their own territory, or they weren't fully part of the tribe with a proper inheritance, and I just want our child to have a part of the rain forest like his ancestors would have had."

"He's still got his part, even if he comes out in Cairns Base Hospital!" Jimmy was clearly annoyed.

"Jilly Bird, maybe you should think about what is gonna be the safest thing. You're not as tough as those women back then. And the baby won't be either—it's not meant to be hiked through the forest in your stomach, spat out among the spiders and the germs, and then what? How the hell are you gonna walk back!"

"I've got some ideas —there's a place."

"No. That's the end of it." Jimmy tried to put his foot down.

"You don't say no to me, Ulmarra!" Jyly erupted. Her pregnancy hormones had lit the fuse, and her fierce will fanned the flame. "I'm not property you can order around! Some things are not to do with you. Even the women back then were free to do their own thing about this—so there is no way you are going to take that away from me now!"

"Jyly, please, calm down..." Jimmy tried to put the firestorm out.

"No!" She stormed off, stamping up the stairs like a baby elephant making a run for it and determined to have its own way.

"Jesus! Who ever thought a woman with child was a sweet Madonna!" Jimmy ran his hands through his hair, and the curls bubbled up over his knuckles.

"Best you leave her for a while," I said. "She'll come round. Maybe you should talk to Maisy and see if she can convince her to be sensible."

"Yeah, right," he said sarcastically, "I got a feeling Maisy is gonna be on her side, mate. Seven reservation kids have been birthed out at that place."

"You kidding me? You know where it is?"

"Nah—big secret."

"Can't you find it?"

"Probably."

"Then find it and have a chopper on call."

"Are you kidding?" He looked at me quite seriously. "That place is really sacred. If Maisy and her sisterhood didn't get me, them Dreamtime spirits would finish me off."

"Now who's the one who'll believe anything?"

"Nah—some things are meant to stay sacred. That birthing stone is one of them."

"So what are you gonna do?"

"Stop her somehow—or maybe not." He looked up with some confusion passing over his face, and I'd never seen that in him before.

"You better talk to her GP."

"Yeah. So you ready to go?" He changed the subject.

"Yeah—need to see Louisa; I got the survey for the inland Arnum extension. We gonna have to do a controlled burn-off; there's eucalyptus over the whole thing.

The ranch had a thousand Brahmans on it, but the owner has no kids, so it was on the market to be sold and it's had no cattle on it for a year—been sitting fallow, and scrub has already taken over. I think the trust couldn't get a decent price, so it took the requisition deal just for the carbon credits, so they ain't gonna run any IFTs."

"It's remote—is there a house an' sheds?"

"Nah—been a land only holding. The owner is in an old folks' home now in Rockhampton, and the manager was over in Weipa."

"Okay, we should look at a plan. Can't burn near our favorite dingo pack."

"Should do it in small patches. Burn, plant, burn—what do you think?"

"Yeah, that'll be safe. Anyway, if we clear too much, we can't plant it all at once anyway, and the scrub will just come back at the first rain. You can't kill eucalyptus by burning; they come back from the roots."

"We shouldn't burn too much anyway. Not exactly clean—gonna release a lot of carbon."

"We ain't got time to clear by hand, and that land has always had a natural burning cycle anyway," I said convincingly. If I had to be honest, the thought of hacking and painting stumps with some chemical killer in forty-degree heat left me with a good inclination to go with burning, even if there would be a bit of smoke.

We chatted all the way to the office. Jimmy was excited to have a chance to prove his theory that we could transform inland arid areas by strategic planting and that section was the one to show it.

When we arrived, Louisa was quiet, as she often was these days around Jimmy. She was professional as usual, never missing a beat, but the fun had gone, and now there was just work.

It had been a bad time for us both, and I nodded to her politely, but there was nothing in those eyes that smiled back at me.

I stood watching the two of them, and I seriously wondered if our time as a group was coming to an end and who would take over.

We hardly saw Donahue these days. He was setting up IFTs all the way down to Sydney. He'd put on a new guy to coordinate, and a new trainer had joined his crew. It looked like his business was growing, but it was like he wasn't one of us anymore.

Finding enough manpower to prepare and replant the land that Louisa identified as available for requisition was also a problem and not something Jimmy or me wanted to have anything to do with, really. Louisa had started appointing leaders to coordinate planting groups up and down the country, and we didn't do all the grid copies anymore, either. Hell, I didn't even know a tenth of the people who called themselves part of the Ulmarra Foundation. Lou was so busy, I wondered how she could keep it all going, and all that work distanced her from us too, quite apart from her feelings about Jimmy and his new wife.

Jimmy didn't seem to care. He had his visions and told me, "You don't know Lou like I do; she'll come to the party when it counts. No matter what her personal feelings, she'll get over them or bury them or something, 'cause she's strong, stronger than anyone, including me."

Whatever her feelings actually were, Jimmy concentrated on what he wanted to. He steadily worked his way through the plan he'd had since he was a kid, to reach some vision he'd got of the future.

Even with the baby coming, I could see his mind was as focused as ever on those first dreams we had had in the beginning. The extension replant inland into Arnum land was a chance to prove his long-held theory that it was possible to see more than just the linked sections of reserve along the outer edges of our huge continent grow and become a solid wall of green; we could manipulate the growth into its fringe interior as well.

It wasn't that far-fetched. Australia had once been lush and forested. Huge rivers had flowed in the Jurassic and Paleocene eras. Rich grasslands had spread out like a vast smorgasbord for dinosaur and later marsupials alike. The scars of its Amazon-like rivers still showed, and you could see them on any flight across the continent.

When the oceans had been high and the poles warm, an inland sea had flowed from the Gulf of Carpentaria all the way to Victoria. Australia was almost two islands.

Everything had begun to change when the slipstream, high in the upper atmosphere, had moved toward the equator as the water in the atmosphere was sucked north and south to be stored in huge ice caps.

The drying air and the lack of rain had left an arid Mars-scape in the interior that had extended as the clearing of native forest left nothing to prevent the evaporation. Now there was only 5 percent of the whole continent left green, and the monsoon, ruled by the slipstream overhead, never got low enough to water the desert.

Jimmy still held true to his first plan: restore those precious trees that had once been thick and natural and drag inland the water-laden air from the fringe forests. One day it might be possible to get rains to form on the replanted inland, where water had been thin on the ground for over a hundred years or more. The extension to the northern Great Dividing Range sections was more than just another area to replant for Jimmy. This area was the most likely land structure to create the "rain trap" but also the most likely place not to see a difference if his theory wasn't correct. It was a test, like walking on water. Belief was half of the equation, because none of us would live long enough to see if we were right.

The following week, Jimmy and me went up to see Maisy and Willy. Jimmy could hardly speak, and old Maisy said, "Jimmy, love—what's aching in you, boy?"

"He's, ah—worried about Jilly Bird. She's got stuck on the idea of having the kid in the forest."

"Hmm... It's okay for her to do that Jimmy, perfectly safe."

"She's small, Aunty, an' this is my first kid, an' she's—"

"I don't think there's another person in the world for our Jimmy, Aunty, so he's scared shitless that she'll get in trouble and, you know, die or something."

"Oh, boy, it'll be okay. Look, I tell you, that stone, it's not far in the forest an' we can laways get her out if it goes wrong. Long time back, we put that thing close to the road, and I don't tell our women that I ring the ambulance people so they come an pick up the new babes and mums and take 'em into the hospital afterwards."

"How do you get away with all this, Aunty? Don't the GPs and child protection people say you can't do this?"

"My boy, we don't tell no one about it. The GPs book 'em into hospital, but when the time comes, we don't go! Them girls, they just have their babies real quick and too late to go in to Cairns base. We just say, 'Whoops, we is good birthers out here, you missed getting to us again.'"

She turned and looked at Willy, and a little frown appeared. "But, I gotta tell you, we got a little, little problem, Jimmy, to do with your Jyly."

"What?" Jimmy looked up sharply.

"Well, your girl got it in her head that you the last of the Mallanburra, and she is adopted to your people, you know."

"Yeah, I know she is Mallanburra too now."

"Well, she got it in her mind that her babes, they gonna have to be born down there up by the Mulgrave where you showed her your people used to camp." She shuffled around and looked to Willy as though he might give some answer. "See—I don't know that place or them people. I got no one I can ask, neither, and I don't know where that stone for them people might be or even if it is there."

I looked at Jimmy, and I don't know what made me say it, but I said, "Look, I'll take Maisy down there, and see if we can find it, and you tell Jyly if it can't be found, she will have to compromise and get a bowl of that dirt and put it under the bed in the hospital."

Jimmy shook his head. "That's not gonna go down with her, I can tell you. She'll wanna dig a hole somewhere in the forest instead—Maisy, give it a go, and see if you can find the stone at Mulgrave. I don't know what I'm gonna say to Jyly if it isn't there."

"Need be we gonna have some help from some of our spirits. I guess it'll be there somewhere. We just gotta find it in time."

The following day I went and picked up Maisy, and we went down to the field at Gordon Vale by the river. I knew where the camp had been. Jimmy and me used to walk along that river and talk about what had happened there.

When we got to the cleared area, we parked, and Maisy and I walked up through the cane. At the top, the trees fringed the field, and the mountain climbed up behind.

"Aunty, shall we go down to the river first, because at least there are rocks there?"

"Nah, boy, you stay here an' wait for me. I gonna have a quiet talk an' see what the old ones have to say 'bout what we lookin' to do."

I told her to be careful, because if she fell and broke a hip or something, I wasn't sure I could carry her out, because she had put on the beef over the years.

She gave me a look that was enough to stun anyone into silence and disappeared quietly down the hill towards the river. An hour and a half later, I was beginning to think I had better go in after her, and I wasn't sure what kind of reception I'd get if she was alright after all. Just as I was tossing up what I should do, she appeared. She was puffing hard and leaning on her knees from time to time, and when I called out, "Aunty—need help?" she shook her head and eventually climbed up the path from the river to meet me.

"Boy—not a whisper in this place. Not a whisper. Them spirits might have gone walkabout 'cause of what happed here."

"Any sign of a stone?"

"Nah..."

"Like looking for a frogmouth in a paper-bark tree: everything looks the same."

"Yep."

"What shall we do?"

"Come back tomorrow."

I raised my eyebrows but you didn't mess with Maisy so I took her hand and walked her back to the vehicle.

We came back the following day—and the day after that.

Maisy walked up into the forest, along the back trail, and along the river. She just couldn't find any sign of that stone. It wasn't likely to be a long way from the camp, because the pregnant girls couldn't go far in labor, but it was gonna be hidden, and it had been a long, long time since that stone had been used.

Day four, Maisy came back and she said, "Don't know, boy—could be, we not gonna find it." She turned, and, in a very rare moment of frustration, she yelled out to the mountain, *"Gunaga, murooba yetti djiabulla Mallanburra bama!"*

I wasn't sure what she said, but as she did, I saw a huge white cockatoo float down on a draft off the mountainside. I watched it sail effortlessly over the rain-forest giants and land in a big fig tree up on the side of the hill.

Maisy saw it too, and she looked at it curiously, and then she whispered, "Come on, old man, show me where my babies be born..."

I heard it scream, and its yellow crest flicked up, and he swung his head from side to side.

Suddenly, he lifted off, and his brilliant white wings spread, and he flew down and across the field to land in a tree there.

"Boy, stay here!" she said, and hobbled off down the side of the field toward the bird. I saw it take off and fly up the river toward the big tree in the corner, the one hanging on to the side of the river between huge boulders. That tree was the one that the first Ulmarra had taken a sapling off to mark the grave of Margaret Stanford, and it had survived just about everything going.

I lost sight of Maisy and the bird, although I heard it squawk a couple of times.

About an hour later, Maisy came back. She was worn out, but she managed a smile as I lifted her around her shoulders, and we slowly headed back to the car.

When we got there, I helped her in, tucked her skirt in the door, and closed it quietly.

I jumped in the driver's seat and said, "So?"

"We gonna have a bub in its right place. The stone was half covered by a slip, maybe in a flood or something."

"Where was it?"

She slapped me. "You can't know that boy—that's woman's business!"

So the new Ulmarra Mallanburra child would be born on its rightful land, and Jimmy made a deal with Jyly that he would take her from that place straight to the hospital, and, if there was any trouble, she had no choice.

The day it started, it was 1:45 p.m. Jimmy rang Maisy, Willy, and me. Although he was trying hard to be calm and sound like his normal self, he wasn't convincing anyone.

"Wajilla—she's gonna hatch!" Jimmy's voice was breathless.

"Okay—has her water broken? How much time have we got?"

"She started getting a gut-ache, and she thought maybe the five Granny Smith apples she got a craving for yesterday had given it to her, but I had a feeling..."

"So how often are the contractions, mate? Come on, focus!"

"Um—twenty minutes, I guess."

"Shit—we gotta get going! Sure she shouldn't just go to the hospital?"

"Are you kidding? Death by tiny abo woman is not the way I wanna go!"

"Okay, you gonna ring Willy and Maisy, or shall I?"

"You better. They had better hurry though, mate, or the kid is gonna be born right here in our lounge. She's sitting there trying to hold it in, but I got a feeling this kid has her own mind already."

I suddenly felt like it had been announced that a meteor was heading straight for us, and I had an hour to be with my nearest and dearest, so I didn't even say good-bye but clicked off and dialed Willie.

"Willy—it's started, eh... Twenty minutes apart, shit, Maisy and you better get to Jimmy's fast."

"Oh—got ya, I'll put the pedal to the metal, meet you in less than an hour."

"Hey, Willy..."

"Yeah?"

"Don't get stopped by a cop or a tree."

"Mate—I been driving for years, an' I don't have a single ticket."

"That just means you didn't get caught, mate, and that ol' jalopy of yours can't get up to a speeding speed."

I said good-bye to him and grabbed Amy, and we headed for Jimmy's.

In the car he said to me, "Is Uncle Jimmy gonna have time to go an' do stuff, you know, out on walkabout an' stuff, when the baby is here?"

"Sure, son, why not?"

He didn't reply, and I could tell something was on his mind.

"I still do stuff with you, even though I gotta work."

"Yeah, but..."

"Spit it out, son."

"He's gonna do that with—the new kid."

"Ahh... Don't worry, you is still his best mate under four feet tall, an' nothing changes about that, no matter if he has fifty kids."

Amy smiled. Knowing you'd always be "best mates" with Jimmy was something I understood and cherished too. I looked at my son, and I realized even though he had no blood connection with Ulmarra, they had a special bond, and for once I wasn't jealous about that; instead, I thought that it's the kind of luck you want your kid to get.

When we got to Jimmy's, the front door was wide open.

Jyly was lying on the big Balinese couch downstairs. She had a bag of stuff sitting on the floor, and Jimmy was squatting on his haunches, stroking her arm, and they were whispering together.

She looked up and said, "Amy—honey, looks like you're gonna have a new li'l fulla to play with soon."

"What if she's a girl?" he said quite cheerfully, and I watched him as he ran up, and they linked arms to hug.

"You can still play with a girl," she said. "But Uncle Jimmy says it's a boy." Anyone else would have questioned that certainty, but Amy just smiled and nodded.

"Willy and Maisy are on their way," I said, and I added, "We could take you into Cairns base—you know, if you think this is gonna happen fast." I barely got the words out. She looked up at me with such a piercing scowl, I quickly turned towards the kitchen and said, "Um—I need a drink, in case we don't get one down at the Mallanburra bama camp..."

The fifty minutes that went by before Willie and Maisy arrived went fast. Jyly had some pretty strong contractions, and Jimmy may as well have been feeling every one of them. His face looked drawn, and sweat had beaded on his forehead. Amy was happy watching TV, even though it had been turned down low so as not to disturb Jyly.

When Maisy rushed in the door with Karla and her daughter with Willy following up behind, it dawned on me we were really going to do this.

Maisy and Karla soon made us go outside, because some women's business needed to go on so Maisy could see where Jyly was up to and make sure everything was going to be okay.

Willie walked straight up to Jimmy and greeted him with a hug, and they turned and followed me outside.

Maisy shut the door on us, but not before saying, "We be just a minute or two, and if you need to pee—too bad, hold it in, 'cause you come in here for any reason, and I'll make sure you never pee again!"

We stood on the sidewalk in front of the house and fidgeted, walking back and forth with our hands jammed in our pockets and our minds not far from what was happening in there.

"So, boy, you got just a little while to go, an' you be putting another foot on that Ulmarra ladder."

"Yep, Uncle—been a long time coming."

"Boy, one thing you will learn, life goes faster than quick, and today will be long, long way back in a minute or two. Hell, it were yesterday, an' I was breeding and as young as you are now! So you best suck it up, every moment, because this is one of those events that is like a star bursting: it lights up the dark, and is a wonder you gonna remember, even after your baby is grown and making stars all of its own."

Jimmy smiled; I guess he knew what the old man's advice meant, just like I did. I looked at Amy and remembered my own little star coming in from the Dreamtime, and a tear suddenly formed.

"Okay—we ready to go, boys. She's all good." Maisy and Karla and her daughter appeared at the door, holding Jyly between them.

Jimmy panicked to get his keys and dropped them on the pavement, and I said quietly, "It's gonna be okay, mate."

He looked up, rested his hand on my shoulder, took a deep breath in, and blew it out slowly. We opened up the Ute, and Maisy squeezed in the back; Karla, Amy, and me went in my Ute, and Willy and Karla's daughter went in the old Ford.

We set off like a camel train and headed down to Gordon Vale, and, as I watched Ulmarra carefully turn into the main drag, I just hoped she didn't spit it out in the car on the way.

When we arrived, our three vehicles turned into the clay roadway under the trees beside the river. The cane was almost full-grown, and fluffy, soft mauve flower heads swayed in the breeze in the direction of the river, while the mountain sat waiting quietly.

"You okay, Jilly bird? It's still not too late to turn around and head for the hospital. Ten minutes, we'd be there," I asked her again as I got out of the Ute and skipped over to her standing beside the car. But it was really me that wanted to go to the hospital, I can tell you.

"Nah..."

"Sure you don't want a nice, pain-relieved, birth in a proper—" I never got a chance to tempt her further. Jimmy spoke up.

"Baby, it's okay if you want some help. But if you want to go ahead, you got the old ones helping, and it's natural, just as you say. I'm proud of you. What do you want to do?"

She smiled, and Maisy waddled around the front of the foundation Ute, equipped with towels, a bag, and an Eveready torch hanging from her arm.

Karla and her daughter had got out and had cloistered around Jyly, as they got ready to go to the special place not used for maybe 130 years.

Maisy gently stroked her hand over the girl's forehead. She crooned, "We gonna get you to the place, girl. You can walk okay?"

"Yep, Aunty. I can—how far?"

"Not far, lovely; we'll help you."

The two other women looped their arms under her shoulders, and they quietly began to walk up around the edge of the field.

Maisy turned and came back. "You boys, you wait here. You don't come now, you understand? Willy, make sure your phone is on. We gonna get this over in a few hours, I think. Looking like round dusk, maybe. She's a good girl; it'll be alright." She reached out and grabbed Jimmy's hand. "You gonna be a daddy soon, boy—'tis all planned for this day."

"Aunty—make sure you ring if anything is wrong," he said quietly.

She nodded and turned to catch up with the others.

Amy looked up at me and asked, "How come we're not allowed to go near?"

"'Cause it's an old thing, son. The women look after themselves 'cause they know all about themselves, and they don't want us men seeing them all in pain and—you know, like that."

"Did you see me when I got born?"

"Yeah, son—and I think maybe these women got a better idea. Your mum wasn't too nice doing that—only good thing was, I got to know you first off."

Jimmy added a comment as he watched them. "Amy, there's different ways for different people, but this is the Yidinji way, and Jyly and me have decided—this is our way too."

As Jyly and the women walked slowly away and began to disappear from our view behind the cane, Jyly stopped, turned, and looked back to her husband.

She nodded with a shaky smile.

He simply nodded back, and whatever passed between them was as deep as time, though not one word was said.

All afternoon, we men waited under the trees, the vehicles parked facing the river.

Willy and me chatted about the old days, and Jimmy stalked the area like a cat with a bellyache. He walked away, looked toward the mountain, and then would walk back. Eventually he sat some distance away from us on the boulders by the river and watched the water flow by.

Amy built himself some kind of castle from rocks, and I noticed he planted little stalks of leaves all around it. He was happily corralling a tiny skink and blocking off the holes, so it couldn't get out. He'd found a coke lid and filled it with water for it, but it didn't look like the lizard was the least bit interested in taking a drink.

At about five o'clock, the usual flock of cockatoos that fed in this area swept down and began finding seeds on the ground further along, toward the road.

I was getting hungry, and I said to Willy, "I'm gonna go down to Red Rooster and get some tucker. Want some?"

"Yeah, boy—is fierce hard work, waiting for women to do whatever they's doing. Build's up a man's appetite." We both laughed loudly, and then I walked over to Jimmy to see if he wanted any.

Just as I got to him, a scatter of wallabies fled from around him, where they had been feeding on shoots between the boulders.

"You're like a bloody magnet!"

"No, mate, I'm just quiet—unlike you!"

"I'm going to get takeaways; you want some?"

"Nah."

"It'll be dark after six; we gonna light a fire?"

"Yeah—maybe."

"Okay, I'll go an' get some food now."

He didn't reply but looked back to his hands where he had been plaiting some grasses together and then unplaiting them to start all over again.

I took Amy, and he couldn't wait, and he ate his burger in the car and downed the orange juice faster than a thirsty emu.

After we got back, Willy and me ate two boxes of the Big Red while sitting on the ground around a ring of stones the old man had collected, along with some dry sticks he hadn't yet lit. Amy sat with us after having collected another lizard, playing with it in his hands because the first one had indeed escaped while we had been away.

I was enjoying my chicken when I heard a vehicle crackling the stones as it drove down from the main road toward the unofficial rest area.

I looked over my shoulder, and my heart jumped.

"Shit!" I said, as a police car slowly came to a stop beside ours.

The two officers didn't get out right away, as they were probably checking out the reg'os on our cars. Finally, they got out and closed the doors behind them, and walked over.

I got up slowly and wiped my hands on the back of my jeans.

"What you doing here guys?" the first one said quite pleasantly.

"Ah—well, me mate over there has a pregnant wife, and she just had to, you know, take a leak, so we're takin' a rest and waiting for her and our women."

"Okay. You know there's no camping here." He looked at our stone circle.

"Yeah—we're not camping, we're waiting."

"Is that your mate over there?"

"Yeah."

"Is she over there too?"

"Nah—she's very private, you know how it is, eh."

"These your vehicles?"

"That's mine." Willy pointed to his old car.

"Okay, can I see your licenses please—"

Suddenly Willy's phone rang, and I jumped.

Jimmy heard it too and literally jumped up from his seat and ran over towards us.

The cop looked to his mate, and I nodded to the phone. "That'll be her..."

One shook his head and the other cop frowned.

"Yeah? Ahh—that's good, Mum, yeah...I'll tell him." Old Willy grinned and put the phone in his top pocket.

Jimmy appeared. "Is everything okay?"

"They're coming out..."

"Uncle! Is everything okay?" he said with real panic in his voice that I had never heard in him.

"Lot of worry over a rest stop..." The first cop frowned as he commented to the second.

Willy slapped Jimmy on the shoulder and said, "You is a dad!"

Amy dropped the lizard and bounced around as though Christmas had been declared early.

"What's going on?" The second one asked me as I grinned from ear to ear.

"Seems—she's ah, had the bub."

"What?" the first officer said in surprise. "She's had a baby?"

"Yep, an' it be a girl!" Willy nodded happily.

I burst out laughing. "You were wrong, Ulmarra," and I turned to the first cop and slapped him on his shoulder as I said, "So he's human, after all!"

Jimmy was smiling broadly, and his white teeth sparkled against his cocoa-colored face shining with a light sweat. He walked over to me and reached into his pocket, slowly bringing out a carved message stick painted in dots and swirls. On one side, it had a blank space for a name, and on the other, it had a message.

He handed it to me.

It read, *Daughter, today you came through us to this world, and you'll find a way back to the Dreamtime when you finish your work, after us. You'll look back and see all of us, and we will look forward to all you are meant to be...and be proud.'*

"Yeah, right—you got one to a son as well?" I said disbelievingly.

"Nah. Only one. I been waiting a long time for her."

The first cop had walked a little away and was speaking into his intercom, "Seems we have an indigenous lady here, that went for a pit stop and has, ah— had a baby. Have an ambo standing by, but sounds like she's okay, so we'll bring her in." He finished his report and turned back to his mate and said, "Come on, we better go get them."

"Nah, can't do that!" Willy and me yelled in unison.

Jimmy smiled and walked up to the cops. "It's okay, mate, she's got her ladies with her, she don't need us. This is women's business. We all got a short life if we go interrupting that."

The first cop shrugged his shoulders and looked at the second. They went back to the car for instructions and were told by their base to respect indigenous protocol. After that, they walked back to us and together, we chatted about the happy event, the foundation, and the future like we were all mates.

About an hour later, just as the mountain began to shade us from the dying sun, we heard happy voices singing from behind the cane somewhere up along the edge of the field. We all watched and waited, until at last, the four women appeared.

Maisy was carrying the baby, and Jyly was half walking, half being lifted by Karla and her daughter, toward us.

Jimmy rushed over and met them, and the cops and me followed in hot pursuit. Willy was on the phone and making up the rear.

We walked them to the vehicles, and the cops asked Jyly if she, Jimmy, and the bub would go with them so they could rush her to Cairns Base Hospital.

She shook her head, so we gently showed her to the Ulmarra Ute.

Maisy put towels down on the seat. She gingerly sat on the passenger seat, and then Maisy gently passed her baby. Ulmarra leaned in with Willy and the two police officers, peering over his shoulder, and Amy dove under all of us to pop up like a rabbit out of its hole right beside her. I jumped around the bonnet of the vehicle and opened the driver's door. I leaned in to see our new arrival under the glow of the interior light.

Jimmy pulled the wraps slightly from around the baby's face and smiled so wide that his face might have cracked and split in half. He kissed Jyly, and she smiled gently.

"I gotta go to the hospital now, Jimmy—okay?"

"Yeah, baby..." He turned and fumbled a little, looking for the cops. "You wanna be our escort?" he said, and the policemen grinned happily and headed for the police car.

I looked at the baby wrapped and held in her mother's arms.

"Jilly bird—you done good; she's beautiful."

"Yeah."

"What you gonna call her?"

"Margaru—Margaru Ulmarra."

Jimmy immediately looked up and smiled.

She looked up to him and said very calmly, "It's a good name—she can remember she is as valuable as the pearl, and she can remember she's got all our people in her and a few extras watching over her." She looked down to the little bundle and smiled. "Even the future will be looking back, egging her on."

"I didn't know you read the diary?" Jimmy said as he swung himself into the vehicle.

"Yep—*Days of our Lives* was too boring," she said as she rested her head back and closed her eyes for a moment. "And I know what my purpose was now..."

"Yeah?" Ulmarra looked up the field through the windscreen to the place where the Mallanburra bama had lived and died.

"It was to bring her back here. I guess we opened the Dreamtime place and let her touch the soil of her own land again." She sighed heavily. "And it was a bloody hard work!"

I closed the car door on Ulmarra as he laughed at her remark and said she did good in a way that told me he had returned to his normal self. He wound down the window, and I said, "We'll follow you and the cops, eh, mate?"

"Thanks, mate. See you," he said, and started the Ute.

"Drive real carefully!" I said. I walked across to Willy and the women, who were getting into their vehicle, said my good-byes, and got into my own with Amy.

I watched the procession head off down the road, away from the old Mallanburra camp. Ahead, the little family of Jimmy, Jyly, and Margaru began again the last of those people that came from the message man and Margaret Stanford. They headed off to civilization, encased in the cabin of the Ulmarra Foundation Ute with the green-faced kid on the side, who seemed to smile more broadly than ever before. I know I was.

Chapter 18

T HE NEW MUM and bub did really well. I loved seeing them become a family. Jimmy was as happy as I had ever seen him, and that made me happy.

Louisa stayed clear. I felt sad for her, actually. She had never had a child or even a love affair that meant anything. She had so devoted her life to her research or the foundation, that no man ever got within a long pole of her, and the boys would often sling off at her and say that her ovaries must have long since shriveled up and maybe her—you know, private parts—had grown over. That stuff was tactless, in my opinion. She was just dedicated and maybe a little proud, and it had cost her the normal life that the rest of us take for granted.

I asked her, "You gonna at least visit the baby?"

"No, Wajilla—I am not. I am far too busy to waste time with little families that I can only merit with the notion that they are helping to save an 'endangered species'—namely, the rain-forest aboriginals—and they don't need me to do that."

"Louisa! The last thing you want to do is turn yourself into a stone!"

"Why not? I'm treated like one."

"I don't believe that."

"Believe it or not—who cares? Now, if you don't mind, I really do have work to do. If you want to do this extension of the Great Dividing Range Reserve, someone has to organize everything. Are you going to go up with them, or are you still doing the grid copy north of Sydney? Because I'll have to get your flight booked down there if you are going."

"Nah, you got people down there that can do that one—I'll go out with Jimmy, since this one is his pet project."

"So the protégé is going to stay home with baby. How sweet. The great hunter goes out into the wilderness and leaves his little woman waiting at home."

"Yeah, I guess so, mate. I'll leave you to it, then..." I was a bit annoyed with her attitude.

She didn't reply, and I left feeling like my prediction of the end of the Ulmarra Foundation as we knew it was growing more imminent than ever.

About a month later, we had teams organized and ready to go to begin the process of transforming a strip that extended the present reserve inland by some twenty hectares.

Jimmy and me were going to go out on the far side of the section and take some samples and some data on a particular land formation that led to the big dry. This area was probably the best section we had to prove that we could alter rainfall patterns inland by strategic planting. Karla's daughter, Andrea, came down to live at my place to take care of Amy while I was away, and about two weeks after, we said he could come out and camp with us for a week, then I'd be back a month after that.

When I said good-bye to him, he said, "Dad, can't I come out now—I could help Auntie look after little Margaru!"

"Yeah, right, son; I can't see you changing nappies—an' it's real dry and wild out there. You're bound to get bitten by a snake or something, and we'd have to evac. you home, and we got no time for that. This is an important project this time—you are gonna come out in a week or two anyway, and we'll be back in no time after that, eh?"

He had taken it, but I could tell he was disappointed.

"Next time—I promise you can stay the whole time, and we can do a walkabout, but somewhere nice, eh," I reassured him, and he looked at me and waggled his finger at me.

"A real walkabout! Next time, Dad—you've promised." I smiled and scuffled his hair.

"Dad?"

"Yeah."

"Be careful, eh."

I nodded.

The land at the back of the range was very arid, and it was original, meaning it had always been as dry as it was from after the extinction event and the period following. There had not been any clearing or unnatural burning there, as the land was bone-dry anyway, so no one had ever taken a torch to it. Even cattle had not been run on that block, so we were sure that a measurable result could be gained by planting through the valley closest to the reserve with our own tree selection.

Our hope was the moisture would be sucked through the area by low inland air pressure, and water vapor would form and alter the dynamics of the arid land. Our best hope was that we might see grass appear where right now there was mile upon mile of red sand and scrappy brush.

Jimmy said he wanted to get out there before the burning crews started on the northern areas, but we hadn't been able to organize it.

By the time we were ready to go, the burning team was well under way, and the planting crew was following up a few weeks later. Airlifts had dropped pallets of plants, pumps for water irrigation, and a temporary camp facility kitset. We had groups of fifty planters sectioning out the ground and starting the main plant pattern. It was a military-style exercise, and, at one point, we even had the military on the job. Soldiers stationed at Darwin came down in aero quoits to volunteer, so before long there were large sections of little blue screens with the Ulmarra Foundation logo on the side spread out everywhere over the blackened ground.

When we were ready to go up, Jimmy told Jyly it would be about six weeks before he could get back, and she wouldn't hear of that. He held his ground, because the baby was still very small, but she played the "I gave birth on a rock in the jungle, so don't tell me I can't set up in a camp in the wilderness!"

He didn't really want to be separate from her anyway, I suspect, so we loaded up a pile of stuff for a camp and a bassinette, enough nappies to sink a ship, and off we went.

Me and Jimmy got John'o to take us up there to dump the stuff off so we could get a camp under way, and a week later he flew the helicopter back and picked up Jyly and the baby.

The area we chose as our base camp was on the high side of a low-sloping valley that ran from the lower end of the gorge on the inland side. The native dingo pack was well over fifty kilometers north, and the new arrivals were on the far side of the gorge, so we were pretty much on our own with only the odd echidna and a population of roos as our company.

The valley had dry eucalyptus that shaded the ground, but it was pretty thin. White-bark or black-bark trunks looked like the most sadistic hand of all had created them and then had tortured them, and the floor was thick with dry leaves and broken twigs. Little or no grass could get its head up, and only a few scrappy shrubs gave any hint that there was some diversification happening here.

Jimmy told Jyly to be careful walking around, because there were bound to be some death adders hidden in the leaf litter. They were dangerous, because they were not "runners." They were "stay still and hide"-type snakes, so it was easy to step on one without seeing it. Jimmy always knew where they were, somehow, and when we cleared the area for the camp, he picked one up by its tail and shifted it. Spiders were a bit of a problem too, so Jyly had the bassinette completely covered in netting, and the screen door of their tent was always closed, and she had laid contact insect strips along the edge.

Our water supply was a dry creek bed at the bottom of the valley. Jimmy and me took a drill down there, and he walked along till he thought the groundwater was high enough to get something out of it. We sunk a short bore in and attached a pump and set up a collection container, because what came out was the smallest trickle you'd ever seen, and you would wait all day just to get a bucketful.

Jyly and the baby settled into camp life, but the first few nights I was woken twice to the sound of crying at three o'clock and again at five thirty, so I shifted my tent further up the slope. They laughed at me and said I should get used to it, but there was no way that was going to happen.

While we went out and collected samples from the valley during the day, Jyly kept busy with camp life, and she was good at it. We had some good meals up there, and it was like we were a real village, complete with woman and infant.

We also took night readings, and Jimmy would disappear for hours but never tell me what he'd found or what he was doing. We kept in touch by UHF radio, and Andrea had taken Amy down to the foundation offices, and I talked to him just after we arrived. His mum had demanded he go with her to visit his grandmother in Brisbane the following week, so we postponed his flight up to our camp until after he came back. He didn't seem worried; I guess he was excited about getting to see his grandmother and being showered with all sorts of stuff too sweet for human consumption.

Day six, the chopper flew in with more supplies and to take our samples. John'o landed up on the top plateau, where there was a good clearing where we'd pulled the scrub up for him, and we walked up with a trolley to get our "groceries" and hand over our data.

"Hey—how you goin'?" John'o's voice echoed across the sand and dissipated in the searing heat.

"We're still alive!"

"Good ta see you, mate." Jimmy grasped John'o by the hand and shoulder and shook him vigorously.

"You too, mate—I got something for you to eat, so you don't have to raid the termite mounds." He pointed to the tall red piles spread out all around.

"Saw a bilby the other night." Jimmy smiled and reported the occasion with enthusiasm, because he knew John'o was keen on the small animal that was severely endangered and as cute-looking as anything in the world.

"No kidding?"

"You didn't tell me that?" I scowled.

"You too busy snoring."

John'o laughed and looked over his shoulder. "Looks like they are getting through the grid quite well. When I flew over, you could see the smoke plume bent over and trailing inland for about fifty Ks."

"Yeah, lucky the wind is going that way."

"We got some changeable weather coming on the radar. They will have to stop burning."

"They're only doing small sections anyway. If the wind gets up, they just switch over to marking or planting."

"Right."

"Well, I guess you should come down and get a cup of tea, and then you can get back," Jimmy said.

"Sure, mate, come on down; Jimmy has cleared the snakes, mate," I added, because John'o had a real aversion to anything without legs these days.

"Mmmm... I got water in the cab, so I don't know that I need—nah, thanks. Anyway, I gotta get back. They got me busy ferrying in guys or taking them back."

"Okay, we'll see you next week, then." Jimmy excused himself and started pulling the trolley down the track."

"I'll bring the box of nappies." I skipped over to the pile and lifted them from the top where they were teetering. Jimmy carried on, and I walked back to John'o.

"I got your little extras in the cab." John'o smiled and walked over to the chopper and opened the passenger door. He handed me a carton of cigarettes and some Moro bars stuffed in a plastic bag.

"Hey, John'o—meant to say, thanks for this, eh. They don't let us bring cigarettes out here in case of fire, you know, but I got my little extinguish bottle to make sure we don't have a mistake. See?" I pulled an empty Marmite jar out of my back pocket. It was filled with water that had gone black with successive dunking of my finished cigarettes. "Gotta be careful!"

"Yeah—hey, I forgot, I brought your brother up in one of the crews a few days ago. You back on speaking terms?"

"Huh? Nah, mate, I didn't know about that. I ain't seen him for months. I thought he must 'ave died."

"Well, he's working, and doing a good job, as far as I can tell. He's due to go back next week. I know he thought you were south in Sydney, doing a grid copy down there. He'd be surprised to know you're here."

"I was going to go south, but Jyly came in with Jimmy, so they needed me to help, you know, with the camp."

"Do you want me to bring Juniper down for a visit while he's up here?"

"No way, mate. Jyly would crack a fit, and Jimmy would probably spear him on the spot."

"Well, I can take you up there on the next delivery, if you wanna organize it."

"Maybe—let me think about it. Amy was supposed to be coming up in a day or two for a week, but it's been postponed, so they're bringing him up next week, Thursday. I don't want my kid brother around him..."

"Be good to get it sorted, mate—he's not a bad bloke. I've seen him a few times, and he's really pulled himself together, eh. Been working for some chick, apparently, and then I heard he was all keen to volunteer for this latest project."

"Yeah—I'd like to sort it. After all, he is my bro."

"Well, it's no trouble for him or you to hitch a ride. Meet in the middle if you like."

"Thanks—I'll let you know, mate...I'll let you know."

He said good-bye, and I watched from the edge of the ring as the chopper lifted off and red dust blew into the blue sky to scatter and settle on the brush for a hundred yards.

Hearing about Juniper made me feel like a camel had spat at me. I was wondering how it had happened after the way he was when I saw him before. I felt a bit pensive about seeing him again, because I didn't think I could take another drama like the last one.

I decided not to say anything to Jimmy, not that he would do anything. But he'd probably tell me to leave the kid alone and let him get on with it, and I didn't want to hear that either.

I walked off through the scrub with the box of nappies balanced on my shoulder.

By the time I got back to the camp, Jimmy had already unloaded, and Jyly was working out what she had and where she wanted to store it. I must have looked a bit down or distracted, and maybe he thought it was because he hadn't told me about finding a bilby.

He yelled out to me, "Mate, I'll show you where the bilby tracks are, if you like."

"What? Oh, yeah. If you want. Should mark them out on the map, anyway, and keep disturbances well away."

"Yeah. Come on, get your drink and" —he grinned and pointed to the bulge under my shirt— "You better have a Moro bar or two, and then we'll head sou-west. It's only about three Ks, so not too hard for you."

"Thanks, mate—only three Ks in blazing 40-degree heat, no cover, dry as Mars and three Ks back!"

"Wajilla—you could stay here with me an' feed an' change Margaru!" Jilly Bird said mischievously.

"Jimmy, I tell you, that woman is in cahoots with you, I swear!" I grabbed up my canteen and walking pack and turned to face the track back up to the plateau. "Come on, Ulmarra, let's go walkabout and see if we can get back alive by nightfall. And bring the radio, in case I have to get John'o to come and get us."

Jimmy grinned, and we set off in silence.

We didn't see a bilby when we got to the area Jimmy had found, because they would have been asleep in their holes. But there were tracks everywhere, and I collected some droppings in a sample bag. There was no doubt at least two or three of them were living in a small area.

As we came to the chopper clearing on the way back, I looked up at the smoke trail that was some forty or fifty kilometers away. Against the lowering sun, it was glowing scarlet and looked like someone had poured blood into the sky.

"Look at that!"

"Yeah—not good!"

"We got some rain on the way, so that'll clean it up."

"Not over there, it won't. Rain only happens once or twice a year on that inland area."

As we were watching it, I saw the distant speck of a chopper, which I presumed to be John'o. It was lifting off some three or four Ks away to the north.

"We got someone over there?" I asked, and frowned.

"Not that I know of. Louisa has a co-coordinator sorting out stuff, so maybe it's an advanced party looking around."

"You better get in contact and make sure we get enough time to finish our stuff before they come in and burn it off."

"Yeah," he said with a slight frown. "Seems these days we hardly know what's going on."

We walked down the track, and Jyly already had something she called "special fried rice" in the pan. I lifted the lid, but it looked a bit like "special fried glue," and when I made a face, she said, "Eat it or starve."

I replied quick-smart, "Hey, Jyly—it looks good, really it does! Anyway, I could eat a horse and chase the jockey!" That was true; a six-K walk had burnt off plenty, and I was starving.

Jimmy appeared and also lifted the lid and pulled a face. He looked up to me, and I shook my head and looked toward his wife and then back to him with my finger pressed to my lips in warning.

He took a deep breath and let it out before saying, "Looks good! I'm hungry, babe—got some bread or something to go with it?" He grabbed her around the waist and kissed her neck, and she smiled.

That was enough for me, so I left her and Jimmy being "friendly," and I walked down to the water-collection point with a small bowl in my hand to have a wash.

As I reached the bore, I could see the collection bucket was on its side and had rolled a few feet down the creek bed. The trickle from the hose was pouring on the ground and disappearing instantly into the sand as it went back to where it had come from.

"Shit!" I thought it was probably a big roo that had come down for a drink and tipped it over. I propped it up again and stacked some stones around it, and the trickle started to gather in the bottom again. I filled my bowl patiently, and, just as it got half filled, I heard a noise.

Turning, I scanned the bush looking to see if the roo was there, but nothing moved. The sound of a dry, cracking bow on one of the tall eucalyptus trees echoed out from the tree line, and my eyes were instantly drawn to the sight of it free-falling and landing with a thud on the ground with a swish of leaves and twigs.

"Dry as a bone," I whispered, and I thought how in a few years this place might look a lot better with our trees planted here instead. Hell, there might even be some water in the creek.

I walked back to the camp and said to Jyly, "Water was tipped over—have to wait till morning if you want to bathe the bub."

"How did that happen?"

"Roo, I guess."

Jimmy stood up and walked to the edge of our camp area and stood with his hands on his hips, staring across the valley.

"What is it?" I said as I dished out a plate of Jyly's special fried glue. I sat down on a log a little away from the tent.

Jimmy turned. "Dunno..."

"This is quite tasty, Jilly Bird." I nodded to her as I downed the food, and I admit it wasn't bad. It was a bit like risotto crossed with mashed potato.

"Thanks." She smiled and dished out some for Jimmy.

He shook his head. "I'll have it later; I need to go and have a look around."

"No, you won't; you're already as thin as a stick insect. You walked miles today, so you sit and eat now!" She sounded bossy, and it would be a brave man who would have resisted her.

He took one more look at the trees, and then he turned and humbly accepted the plate from her.

When night fell, we sat around as we usually did, talking about the various things we were uncovering with our research.

Jimmy was certain the results supported his theory, and he wished he could live for a hundred years more to see if it really worked. Throughout our conversation, he would look up and scan the trees, even though there was no sound or movement that couldn't be allocated to a simple bird roosting or a tree cracking.

I was tired and said I'd have to go to bed early or I might never make it out of my sleeping bag the next morning.

Jimmy nodded, and Jyly had already gone into the tent to see to the baby and go to bed herself.

I walked up the hill to my own tent and zipped myself inside. I didn't take more than five minutes to get comfortable, and I was soon dozing.

A little while later, the zip sang out, and Jimmy's head peered in. "Mate—you awake? Wake up, I gotta talk to you."

"What…"

"Get up—something isn't right."

"What's going on?" I grunted and pulled myself up with my hands rubbing my face.

"Something is really wrong, mate."

I wriggled out of my bag and stood up and stretched and then walked to the door. Jimmy stood aside, and I stepped out into the night air beside him. He moved forward a step or two to stand a little way away, staring out to the trees.

"What the hell is—"

"Shh." He pointed and stared in the direction of the top of the valley where the plateau began.

"What is it?"

"Animals are not moving."

"You are kidding me. You woke me up after a six-K walk today to tell me the animals ain't moving?"

"We got a visitor up there."

"What kind of visitor—a Yeti or something?"

"Don't know what's going on, but I want you to radio and tell 'em we want to be out of here tomorrow."

"Tomorrow? What's going on, mate? You been secretly smoking some herb I don't know about, and you've finally lost it!"

"Wajilla, I want Jyly and the baby outta here first thing. You understand?"

"Yeah, mate, of course, whatever you say—I just don't understand."

"Neither do I, mate, but there's a small voice telling me to go now."

It was the first time and the last time I would ever hear him refer to that strange practice of listening and knowing the voice of something bigger than ourselves. It scared me to hear him, because he kept a lot of things to himself.

"I'll radio now. Does Jyly know?"

"Nah—she's asleep." He turned away from me and stepped into the darkness. "I'm gonna take another look around."

"Okay, mate, I'll get on the air and—"

Jimmy was gone.

I looked about in the darkness, but I couldn't hear anything nor see anything, though I felt Jimmy's distress and turned quickly to go down and get on the radio.

"Just when I was getting to enjoy it out here."

I got in touch with base and ordered an evac. for the morning, and then I climbed into my bed, reassured that we would be out of here in the morning, and fell into a deep sleep.

About three thirty, the zip opened again with a loud rip. It wasn't the nice polite kind of opening that comes from someone who knows you're asleep and doesn't want to scare the living daylights out of you.

"Wajilla! Mate, get up fast! We're in trouble!"

"What's up!"

"Fire! Get up, mate, the place is a tinderbox. Not much time," Jimmy yelled.

"Where—" I flew out of my bag, jammed my legs into my jeans, and fell through the doorway. I could faintly smell the thin thread of smoke, but so distantly, it was almost drowned out by the night mists rolling down the length of the valley.

"You sure? Maybe you can smell the fires up north. The wind has probably turned."

"Nah—the animals have started running. I can hear them and feel them. They're on the move, and we had better be too."

"Jimmy!" I heard Jyly's voice as she called from their tent. "Jimmy—where are you!"

"Come on, we better go down and tell her what's up."

We ran down the slope to the light of a torch and arrived at her tent. She was wide-eyed and looking strangely disjointed, and I wondered if she could sense the fire too.

"Jimmy, we gotta go. I don't feel good, Jimmy. I'm scared."

"I know, baby—get Margaru and put her blanket in the bottom of the big cooler box, and we'll carry her."

"Jimmy, are you crazy—she'll suffocate in that! Why can't I just put her in my backpack?"

"No, if we have to outrun it, she could—get injured."

I heard a distant hum begin to fill the evening sounds, like a train was coming from a long way off. A bird screeched and tumbled from its roost, looking to fly through the dark branches and get into the open space of the night sky.

"What is it, Jimmy?" she asked with a shaky voice.

"Over on the plateau, a fire's been lit. It's running this way."

I heard a loud crackle, and I said, "That's not on the plateau. Look, on the other side, what's that—is that smoke or mist?"

"Smoke!" Jyly began to frantically empty the cooler bin and threw butter, meat, and all manner of cool goods onto the floor of the tent. She grabbed a small blanket and thrust it in the bottom. I watched her as she carefully lifted the baby, who was deep in sleep. She roused and stiffened slightly as she was lifted in Jyly's hands. Jyly laid her in the cooler, and the child blinked slightly as though fixing a last gaze on her mother, and then she fell back into sleep. Jyly wet a tea towel and laid it over the lip of the box, and then closed the lid so that it could not seal.

"Jyly you gotta shut it—"

"Not yet, Jimmy—I'm not gonna shut it tight yet."

"Come on, let me carry it." I quickly indicated she pass it to me.

Jimmy skipped into the tent and grabbed some blankets. "Here, you carry these, Jyly."

"Jimmy—there's fire showing on the ridge behind us on this side too," Jyly said nervously as a warm glow showed against the tent canvas.

"Wajilla, we gotta go down the creek line and head for the gorge."

"Gotcha. How fast is that thing gonna move?"

"Faster than you can outrun it, mate, so move yourself, it's coming this way."

As he said this, I saw a glow appear on the plateau edge. A rolling flow of grey smoke began to pour through the trees in a line. The breeze now carried the strong burning eucalyptus scent with it, and I began to race through the scrub toward the creek.

When we got to the pump, the fire was visibly running down the hill. Huge trees simply exploded with massive crackles and hissing sounds, spraying burning shards into the tinder-dry debris that began to burn like a thousand furies had lit matches to it as well.

Jyly looked back and said, "Jimmy, it's burning right along, I can see flames everywhere."

Jimmy threw the blankets in the collection bucket and frantically pushed them down to soak up the water. He threw one over Jyly and the other over me. He said loudly, "We gotta run. There's only one way out, down the bottom."

We sped down the riverbed, stumbling and crashing through the uneven ground.

Jimmy caught up with me and grabbed the cooler that was banging against my thigh and helped by grabbing the handle and lifting it away from my side. From within, the baby was crying loudly, but we kept on as quickly as we could.

"Jimmy, it's coming real fast—I can feel the heat." Jyly said.

I was panting between lunging steps into the torchlight that Jimmy thrust ahead of us, and we jolted over the brush and leaves in our path. He was almost pulling me along as he replied to her.

"Yeah, baby I know—we gotta get out the bottom and get to the stream in the gorge."

"That's miles—we can't do it!" Jyly cried out from behind us.

"Stop thinking and run!" Jimmy yelled as he sped over the stones and twigs at his feet.

"What's that?" I slowed and pulled him back a little as I stared directly in front of us.

"We got a fire starter—he's lit a ring." Jimmy was panting as we saw ahead more fire.

Smoke began to curl around us and show in the light of the torch. I could hear movement to our left, and immediately three kangaroos bounded over the creek bed and swung off in different directions with their eyes wide and their nostrils flared in fear.

"What can we do? Look, it's over that side too," Jyly was whispering, as though to speak of it would bring it on even faster.

"The wind is coming down the hill; we gotta go in the direction of the wind, and we'll run into that line of fire in front of us. It'll burn out ahead of us."

"What about your feet?" Jyly said frantically. "You can't run on burning ground!"

The baby was now screaming its lungs out, and another tree high up in the valley behind us exploded like a canon had blown it to pieces.

Jyly screamed, and even I jumped and turned to see a fireworks display of the dry timber forest going up like a torch against the smoke-filled night sky.

"Jyly, my feet are like rhino hide. Don't worry about me, come on!"

Jimmy grabbed up the handle of the cooler and swung around to hurry on towards the fire now showing below us at the base of the valley in front of us.

Just at that split second, I saw something move in the leaves. It slid so fast, I barely had time to register before it appeared further on; its bright brown eyes caught the light of the torch, and it was almost between Jimmy's legs when I yelled at the top of my lungs, but he turned and stepped forward.

"Jimmy! *Don't move, mate!*"

How he didn't see it before me or know it was there, I don't know. Maybe being focused on Jyly and the baby screaming threw him off, but he stepped down right in the center of the snake's back as it fled at full speed under him.

He immediately jumped off like lightening. The cooler rocked in his hand as he lost his balance and struggled to get his legs away from the big brown that would have been at least five foot long.

I grabbed for his arm and wrenched him away at the same time, and the cooler dropped and landed on the rocks.

I shot out and caught it before it could tip over, but the snake had lightning reactions. It spun around, raised its head, and struck with full force, sinking its fangs into Jimmy's calf as he jerked his leg through the air to miss it.

I pulled the cooler away as he jumped back and sank to his haunches.

"I'm hit," Jimmy said quite calmly.

The snake didn't even stop. It carried on with renewed speed and disappeared in front of us like a rocket as he too fled the oncoming firestorm.

"Jimmy! God, no!" Jyly panicked and ran to his side.

We spun the torch light onto his leg, and there the two puncture marks shone ominously, and a small drip of blood was oozing from the wound.

"Not a dry bite," I said breathlessly.

"Nah—he got me good."

"Jimmy we have to move! The fire—" She looked up the hill.

"Nah —if I move, I'm dead; gotta stay still."

"I got nothing to bind it with—Wajilla, give me your shirt," she ordered, flustered.

"No, Jyly, leave it—take my T-shirt and use that."

"Mate, I can carry you."

"No, you can't, not and get Jyly and the baby out."

"No, Jimmy, we're not leaving you! Forget it—we're *not* leaving you!"

He ignored her. "Mate, quick, dig out the stones a bit and lay me in it. Put the wet blanket over me, and chuck some sand on top, and then you gotta run like the devil. Go down that way." He pointed below us. "Follow the creek. At the end there's a bit of a drop, so take it easy and get down the incline to the stream—"

I was already obeying his command.

Jyly had pulled off Jimmy's T-shirt and was twisting it around his leg to try to immobilize the poison from spreading up through his skin, but I was pretty sure it was already in the bloodstream.

His voice was already slightly off, and, as I frantically dug the shallow protection from the fire, I hoped I was not digging my friend's grave.

He grabbed Jyly's arms and held them. "Be brave, little girl. I can survive this—the fire will go over the top of me, and, if I stay still, I got twelve hours or more before that bite kills me. You and the baby get out and get help. You know where I am, so you come back to me. I'll be waiting, okay?"

"Jimmy —I can't leave you."

"You have to. Margaru is everything—you have to. Anyway, there ain't enough room in this bunker for both of us," he joked, and a smile curled up his lips, and I could see his white teeth shining in the torchlight.

"I'll come back—I'll get Margaru to the stream, and I'll come back for you."

"Yeah—it's okay. You get out..." He closed his eyes and leaned back.

I helped him shift into my shallow ditch. I grabbed the wet blanket and started wrapping it around his feet, resting rocks around him and scooping sand over the blanket.

Jyly cried and leaned down, wrapping her arms around his head, kissing him. "I love you!"

"I know, Guli."

I worked my way up his body, hurrying, as I could see the fire pouring down the incline toward us.

Jyly gently laid two sticks over the sides of the depression, so there would be a gap between his face and the blanket, so he could breath, and then she wrapped the blanket over his face and weighted it either side with rocks. She called out, "You okay—can you breathe?"

A muffled voice came from beneath the blanket. "Yeah."

We piled sand over his chest and two rocks balanced over the sticks. Jimmy disappeared into the ground, but I heard him yell, "Get out of here now! I can feel the fire coming. Run!"

I grabbed the cooler, pulled the tea towel out, and locked the top shut, and the cries of the baby became as muffled as her father.

Jyly scooped up the torch, and we took off.

"Wait!" she said as she turned to look for the last time, lighting the stones and sand where Jimmy lay. "I'll come back, I promise!" she yelled. "You hear me, Ulmarra? I'm coming back for you!"

We didn't hear him reply, but I yelled at her. "Jilly Bird, get moving—we gotta run!"

We literally threw ourselves through the undergrowth and the pathway of the creek. Several times, we saw animals fleeing in the dark. The heat of the fire surrounded us, and my hair felt like it was going to ignite. We began to run through smoking, blackened land, where the bottom fire was already a long way in front of us. I was choking, and so was Jyly. The smoke was so thick, we could hardly breathe, even as we covered our faces with blanket and wrapped it over our heads. I could see the creek dipping down fast, and I was scared I was going to come to the cliff and run straight over it.

Just as I thought it was a given that we would be overcome by the fire, I saw a small wallaby leap in front of me through the smoking sticks of the burned landscape. She was blackened herself as she flew in front of us and suddenly dived down and away from my view.

"Jyly, stop! The cliff—it's just there." I stopped and pointed a little ahead.

We walked forward and Jyly cried out as wood embers burned the soles of her shoes and the heat seared her underfoot.

"Come on, we gotta get down. I'll climb, and you pass the baby down."

"Stop—I gotta look at her." Jyly grabbed the lid and opened it slightly. Smoke began to pour in, and the baby coughed. In an instant, Jyly grabbed the Ulmarra pearl from around her neck, kissed it, and threw it into the cooler with the baby, as I began to climb down where the creek stopped on a five-meter rock-face of broken ledges before it hit the floor of the gorge.

The sound of the fire was like a freight train, and the hot wind was buffeting us.

"Hurry, Jyly, pass her down."

She lifted the cooler over the edge, and I raised my arms up so that I could receive it. I put it on the ledge I was standing on and scanned to see where next I could get down. Below I could see the stones of the stream, and a sandy island lay in the center. The fire was pouring red floating shards over the edge, and new fires were burning all around us.

Suddenly, I felt the blast of hot air momentarily pause and blow cool. I saw Jyly tip her head over the edge, "The wind has changed!" she yelled and looked back over her shoulder.

"Yeah, that's good—come on."

"The wind's changed—I gotta go back!

"Jyly, no! The heat will cook you on your feet!"

It was too late—she had disappeared

I looked down, deciding. I knew I had to get the kid down to the gorge floor and onto the sand in the middle of the stream, and then I could climb up and go after her.

I stumbled along the steps of the rock face, and, piece by piece, made it most of the way down with the cooler in my arms.

At the bottom, a sharp drop of only a meter or so stopped me. I was considering making a jump for it, when a tall tree blew up above me on the left. It sprayed burning bark and twigs down on the stones below, and then I heard the shriek of cracking timbers and the whoosh of bows as it fell.

It would have missed us, low on the rock face, but it twisted in midair and crashed down near me, and a thick bow swept me from the ledge. As I toppled, trying desperately to hold the cooler and little Margaru in my arms, I thought, "This is it—we're gone."

As I hit the ground, the torch spun out and landed with a clatter, caught in the crook of some rocks. Its beam shone out over the stones, and just on the edge of that weird light, the cooler tumbled. It landed upside down with its lid open and the blanket with baby piled in a heap on the sand under it. It was pinned under a bow, and she was screaming. All I could think was, "Thank God she's yelling like a stuck pig, because it means she is still alive."

I was half under the bow on the stones, and it was burning. I grimaced as I felt the heat through the blanket on the middle of my back. My hair was burning, and I screamed as it ate into my scalp. Frantically, I tousled it with my hands, and as soon as they were free of the blanket, I felt my forearm burn, and the smell of hair and flesh filled my nostrils.

I crawled like a madman under the burning branches with only one leg that would work, the other searing with pain. I forced myself along the stones and into the stream water, rolling in its extinguishing relief.

I felt dizziness invade me, but I pressed it away, searching in the strange beam of light from the torch for the cooler and little Margaru. The tree was now burning to its top, and the last bow was smoking, propped over the box with the baby still screaming under it. The flames were licking the aluminum, and she was crying with a breathless squeal of pain and fear. I couldn't get to her, though I dragged myself over the stones with all I had. My back strangely tingled, and my left leg was trailing.

Just as I thought I would die of grief at the sound of her screaming, a fast shadow darted over the stones. I saw it break the beam of light and I stopped, panting in terror.

Suddenly a second golden shadow appeared, and I realized dingoes were flashing over the sand and rocks, cautiously poking their snouts in the air, sniffing and circling.

I yelled as loud as I could, *"Get away, you mongrels!"*

Then there he was. I recognized him as soon as I saw him: Ulmarra's big dog from Frazer. He stepped forward, not even fazed by the fires on the hills all around the stream. His coat was dusted with soot and his jowls dirty. He immediately trotted over to the cooler and leaned forward, sniffing cautiously.

I knew what he had on his mind, and I screamed and struggled to crawl and then picked up a rock and threw it. It landed only a few feet in front of me with a thud, and I picked up another one as I watched the dog dodge the burning bow above the cooler, his ears curious at the baby's agonizing screams.

I swore at it and continued pelting the ground with rocks that came nowhere close.

Suddenly, the dog used that clever mind of his, and I saw him grab a mouthful of the blanket and begin tugging it from under the cooler and the tree. The bow dislodged slightly and burning embers sprayed to the ground, and the dog let go.

For a second the baby's cries muffled as the blanket tightened over her, and then the dog grabbed it again and dragged it over the sand. When it was some distance from the fire, the dog let go. I could see the baby's limbs kicking at the blanket, and the movement sent spears of long shadows out over the stones. The dog leaned into the blanket and sniffed, and I knew what he wanted to do, and I screamed. *"Piss off, bastard!* mongrel, piss off!"

Two other dogs came in, and, as though in slow motion, I knew they were going to tear her to pieces in front of me. I screamed and cried, covering my head with my hands, then bursting forth again to find any stone I could throw.

The dog momentarily backed back as his pack came in, and he growled, obviously guarding his prize. They bolted into the shadows and continued to circle me. Then I saw the big dog drop to all fours and crawl forward. He sheepishly moved forward to the blanket and I thought, "You bastard, you're gonna play with it first."

But he didn't. He leaned into the blanket and began licking the baby. I could hear her cry interrupted by his wet tongue washing the salt from her face. I could hear her little fits of displeasure as the big dog tasted her tears.

The dog stopped for an instant and looked up quickly beyond the circle of light.

I looked up, and suddenly my focus drifted to a much larger shadow standing just on the edge of the light.

It was a man who had skipped over the streambed and now stood crouched a little, his eyes fixed on the dog. Then he flicked his gaze to me. I recognized him immediately.

It was Juniper.

He stared long and hard at me, and I saw him slightly shake his head and lower it. I knew right then, he had been the one who had done this to us. I dropped my head and wept, and, as I looked up, I saw him turn to leave. All seemed lost, and my tears left me, a cold inevitability filled my soul, and I sank to the sand and lay still as though I could ready myself for the horrors that would take Margaru and me to the Dreamtime.

Suddenly, I heard his voice yelling and the thud of stones hitting the ground. I looked up to see him with his arms raised and flailing overhead, trying to frighten the dogs away from us.

The big dog suddenly stood, and, if a dog could frown, that one might have. He stood, shoulders squared off to face Juniper, and he barred his teeth and growled with a guttural, deep rumble that told all he meant serious business. He flashed his eyes around the stream and would not move from the position between Juniper and the baby.

I guess he was reading my brother as another dog trying to steal his kill, but to this day, I like to think he knew that little kid was Ulmarra's, and he was standing his ground to protect her.

I'll never know, but immediately, from behind, another dingo flashed in and snapped Juniper in the back of his knees. He dropped slightly and turned to see what had hit him. As he did, two others dived from the dark and pulled him down. One clamped on his arm, the other scrambling for his throat. I heard him screaming and yelling with every bite. Three others seemed to come from nowhere and dived into him. One tore at his stomach, and I screamed, yelling from my heart, but nothing deterred them.

The big dog moved a step or two forward when the deed was all but done. He looked back at Margaru, who had kicked her way free of the blanket, her little arms and legs flailing in the night air, and then he stalked over to the kill to join in the feed, and I felt my head start to spin.

Shock took over, and, without a breath of strength to stop it, and with the sight of clothing being torn away and the smell of blood mixing with the smoky streambed, I left the world and sank into silent unconsciousness.

The morning came, and a certain stillness encompassed me. Groaning as I roused, I looked around and could see the dog prints everywhere, but no sign of the dogs remained. I was lying still and aching, but I lifted myself as best I could and looked across to where Juniper had been but could barely see what remained of him. Blood was scattered on the white stones heating in the morning sun. I shivered for a moment because the cold under me, and my injuries, had done their work.

I looked up to where Margaru had been, to see the blanket still on the sand in a pile. It did not move.

I sniffed, sucking back a convulsion of tears, and dropped my head to the sand.

Suddenly, the sound of thudding rotors echoed off the walls of the gorge, but I could barely register that they came my way. Soon the wind threw debris everywhere, and the thunderous craft landed a little way upstream. I heard people yelling out to each other and movements all around me.

"Mate, tell me where it hurts."

"Everywhere...Ulmarra and Jyly are up the streambed...gotta find them..."

It felt like people were swarming over me like ants as a blood-pressure device wrapped my arm, clothing was stripped away to reveal my bruises and burns, and someone listened to my heart. A needle was put in my arm, and someone said, "Do you know what day it is?"

I groaned and said, "First day in hell, mate."

"Can you wriggle your toes?"

"Can't move my left leg."

I was soon hitched up to a backboard, and I groaned slightly as they rolled me and strapped me down with a silver sheet wrapping me. I could see two guys over where Juniper was. One was standing with his hands on his hips, looking down, and the other had crouched on the ground and was pointing into what remained.

As they lifted me and turned to walk me to the chopper, I said in a daze, "The baby..."

"What?"

"Over there...gotta bring her back..."

"Mate, where—" I didn't answer, because I faded into the silent world again, but I heard them as though in a dream, calling to each other over the sound of the rotors starting up, "Guys! There's a baby out here, start looking around—there could be a baby!"

I heard someone call out in shock and surprise, and then the distant sound of Margaru fitfully crying, and then all sounds mixed and tangled together, and I was gone.

A day later, I was lying in a bed in Cairns Base Hospital. I'd suffered a dislocated hip and had some decent burns, but the worst damage had happened in my heart and my mind. No one knew my sorrows, and I just lay there like someone had sucked my spirit out and left me empty.

Andrea brought Amy up to the hospital, and I grabbed my boy and hugged him like I was a drowning man. He cried, and so did I, but my tears were filled with relief that I hadn't been tempted to take my son up there because his holiday had got postponed a week.

Louisa came to the hospital several times that day. She appeared around the door and smiled shakily.

"Lou—the baby, is she okay? Where's the baby?" I woke to look at her standing at the foot of the bed with her white hands clamped over the edge like a perched stork.

"She's fine. Some superficial first-degree burns, but not too bad. She's in the children's ward. I've been up twice to look in on her."

"It was Juniper who did it."

"Yes, we know. He had incendiaries in his pack—the dingoes had dragged that off."

I looked away, and a tear formed in the corner of my eye, and I couldn't look at her.

"Wajilla—they found Jimmy and Jyly."

"Is he dead?" I turned my head and stared at her, daring her mouth to say the truth.

"He's in intensive care—"

"They made it!" I let out a long sigh as though every bit of air in my lungs was emptied in one go, so that the terrors of the night could be emptied with it.

"Wajilla—he's in a really bad way, and Jyly didn't survive."

"Oh, no!" My heart sank, and my breath stopped. Cold seemed to spread through my stomach, and I cried, even though I was in front of Louisa.

"I'm so sorry, Wajilla. There's nothing I can say," she whispered, and moved to the side of the bed and sat down in the chair. She put her hands over mine lying on the white sheet.

"They found her over his body, and that's why they found him so fast. She had used her blanket to cover him, and she was burned completely"—Louisa's voice broke slightly, before she pulled it back so as not to distress me more than her news did— "but he was alive because of the sand and stones covering him, and the ground took his core temperature down, so that slowed the spread of the venom." She swallowed hard, almost trying to sound positive. "He's got some burns to his hand and arm, because he had it out from under the blankets and was holding her hand."

"Is that all he got? Just them burns?"

"Some of his face, and one foot is quite bad too."

"But he'll live, right?"

She seemed to take a breath that shivered. "Wajilla—they're not sure. They administered anti-venom, but the shock and the time it took to get him...he's still not doing too well from the bite."

"Bloody snakes, I hate 'em." I stared at my arms, one wrapped past my elbow. "You need to get Willy and them to pray, get the spirits to help."

"I know." For once, she looked at peace with something indigenous, as though what I had said was as clear to her as all her scientific knowledge, but I knew there was something more. It was all over her face.

"Wajilla—they've collected the remains of your brother. We need to know about the funeral arrangements after they've done the autopsy."

"Burn him! Burn him, and I'll throw his ashes in the can and flush 'em to hell!"

In the afternoon of the third day, they let me out. I felt like a truck had hit me, and the pain from my burns was only kept at bay by a pile of painkillers, but I was otherwise okay.

Louisa came and got me. In the car, she said Jimmy's lawyer had contacted her. Jimmy had named her and me legal guardians for the baby, and she didn't know what to do about it. Two social workers had already visited her, and she thought they would soon visit me. After that, we could decide what was best. She looked at me with something akin to terror on her face, and I said, "It's okay, Lou—we'll do it! Jimmy's kid is as good as my kid. Don't worry, Margaru will be safe with you or me."

She had swallowed hard, and I knew she was struggling to find a way to face Jimmy not recovering, apart from the thought of Margaru being her responsibility.

She said I would have to stay at her apartment until I was back to full strength, but I think she was bringing us close, like I was a familiar blanket to raise her confidence. She had called Donahue, too, and he was flying back.

"What is happening about—" I whispered, not wanting to say her name, because she was deceased, and we aboriginal don't speak or look on a dead person's image, in case their spirit won't leave the earth like it is supposed to.

I knew that one wouldn't leave, anyway, because of Jimmy still being here but I still wouldn't say her name.

"The family won't do anything until—Jimmy instructs them."

"Right." I frowned at the thought of her being kept on ice somewhere. My heart dropped into agony at the thought of my little friend no longer laughing at my jokes, no longer telling me to stop smoking. I wondered what Jimmy would want for her, and I pushed the thought of a funeral aside, not able to bear it.

That evening, Louisa took me with her to see him. We went into the intensive care ward, where he was hooked up to monitors and tubes. His face was covered in gauze, his left arm wrapped to his shoulder, and his left leg was elevated with large gauze covers over the burns on his foot.

"Jimmy," Louisa whispered in his ear, and he seemed to rouse.

"Lou...is that...you?"

"Yeah, it's me... How you feeling?"

"Not too good."

"Wajilla is here."

"Mate." He struggled to speak. "You okay?"

"Yeah, mate—Margaru is okay too. We're gonna pick her up and take her to Lou's place till you get better."

"We gotta be buried up on the mountain." I shuddered, 'cause I was thinking, how did you know she was gone?

"No, Jimmy, no...you're gonna fight to make it, okay?" Louisa shivered, and tears flowed from her eyes at his shocking directive.

He looked to me and said, "'Member, bro...the cathedral, under the tree... together."

"Okay, Jimmy, but you gotta try, for little Margaru's sake—you hear me? For your little girl."

"Yeah, mate, yeah..." He faded off, and the nurse, who had been hovering, came in and said it was best if he stayed quiet. I asked her was he going to get over the bite, and she said she would get the doctor, and he could talk to us.

We waited a long time out in the hall, and eventually the doctor arrived and said we should come with him to the family room so he could tell us what Jimmy's progress was.

When we got in the room, I felt like I had been called in front of the principal at school, and Lou and I sat still, tight-lipped and terrified.

"It's Louisa and Wajilla, isn't it?"

"Yeah," we answered after each other.

"Okay if I call you that?"

"Yeah, no worries. Doctor, tell us how he's doing."

"He's in a bad way..." He almost whispered. "His kidneys are failing, and his blood pressure is falling." He looked at his hands. "This was a bad bite, and the snake that did it was a big one. It administered a large dose of venom straight to his bloodstream. He should already be dead, really. I heard what you did in the streambed, and that was good thinking, immobilizing him and making sure the fire didn't get him straight off. If we had got to him within a few hours, maybe..."

"He's gonna die?" I said incredulously.

The doctor just nodded, and then he said, "You need to prepare yourselves. We can't do any more for him."

"So we just gonna watch him slip away?"

"Yes; it will happen in the next twenty-four to forty-eight hours."

"No!" Louisa burst into tears and then swallowed, as though, even here, she couldn't let go of control.

"He's gonna die in there—like that?" I pointed in the direction of that white room with Jimmy plugged into the grid like something out of *The Matrix*.

"I'm afraid so."

"Do you know who this man is?"

"Well...yes, of course—"

I broke him off. "He can't die like that!"

"We can't—"

"We're taking him home."

"We can't let you do that."

"Yes, you can—we're indigenous. It's our cultural right to follow our customs. He's not staying here!"

The doctor looked at his hands, and I could see he was thinking. "I guess we could shift him and give him some pain relief at home..."

"Good man! Arrange it now."

Two hours later, Louisa and me picked up Margaru from the children's ward, because she was released to us to go home.

We fed her at Louisa's apartment, and then we got the call from the hospital that Jimmy was going to be moved, so we went in and then followed the ambulance to Crystal Cascades.

I rang Willy and Maisy and said, "We're bringing him home." They said they would make arrangements.

When we arrived behind the ambo, the street was full of cars and people from the reserve, and all kinds of people who knew him were standing in the street. No one talked; they just stood together and watched. The ambo officers carefully carried him inside on a gurney, and we showed them upstairs. I stood at the door with Margaru asleep in my arms. The front door swung on its hinges, and I was almost going to shut it when the sound of a didgeridoo began to howl and sticks rhythmically clicked out an ancient pattern. Women began to sing a vibrating song I'd heard years ago as a kid, calling up guides for Jimmy's soul, and I nodded to them all and opened the door wide.

I could see neighbors and people coming out of their homes to look. An elderly man riding a mobility scooter, his wife, and two men walked up from the bottom of Zanzoo Close, and one of them asked what was going on. The old man stared at the door as if he knew the moments were counting down, and he pursed his lips together and nodded slightly.

The baby sighed in her sleep, so I turned and walked up the stairs.

They took him from the gurney and carefully laid him in their bedroom on the low bed, almost on the floor. The twisted-vine wood carving, surrounding the corners of the bed, was the only natural-looking part of the scene; everything else was about us hanging on—us intervening.

He was out of it. Louisa hovered around him to see that everything was being done the way it should.

I stood back while the nurses plugged in his monitor and hung up the drip lines and checked them. One of them took his blood pressure, and then she whispered instructions to Louisa. Moments passed in hushed tones, and then they turned and left us alone with him.

All that afternoon he slept. Louisa sat on the floor beside him, holding his hand. She checked his blood pressure from time to time and wrote it down on the clipboard. The drip emptied twice, and she changed it.

I took the baby downstairs and changed her, gave her milk, and carried her about. The songs continued all day, even into the night. Different people came and went, and curious onlookers left for their homes, I guess hoping to hear his death announced on the news or something. Jimmy kept them waiting.

At about quarter to one in the morning, he roused. The sound of the music and the singer's voices quietly drifted in through the front door and funneled up the stairs.

I had walked into the room and was burping the small one after giving her, her late feed.

Louisa was asleep, lying over the edge of the bed.

I saw him struggle, as though he wasn't sure where he was, and then he groaned, "Mate—what time is it?" I told him, and he looked down at Louisa, her dark hair flowing over her forearm and her eyes hidden under her other arm. He lifted his arm shakily and placed his hand on her head and stroked it gently. She started to wake.

"You're good when you're—quiet." He smiled slightly toward her.

He looked up to me, and I knew he wanted to see Margaru, even though he said nothing. I took her over, and she was gurgling in my arms, and warm, full, and clean. She was set to play even though it was the middle of the night, and she should have been put back in bed.

"Here she is, mate—happy as can be. She's gonna be like you when she grows up, stalking round in the night somewhere."

I lay the baby in the crook of his arm. She wriggled, turned over, and rested her arm on his chest, and then she reached up and grabbed his chin.

He swallowed and smiled. For a good half an hour he watched her, though I could see it exhausted him, and he struggled with every breath to hold her. He started to strain to breathe, and I leaned down and took the baby from his arms, and he nodded to me to come close.

I leaned in and he said, "Take her on walkabout..."

I said I would.

The baby started to get restless, and I walked to the other side of the room but found I couldn't leave. I could hear his lungs filling with fluid, and he wheezed and choked slightly. Louisa was frantically checking the drip and flustering with the blood-pressure meter, but he swept it away and grabbed her gently around her neck and pulled her close. He whispered something into her hair, and she said, "Yes I will."

He said something more, and she began to cry. She buried her face in the sheets on his chest, and he rested his hand on the back of her neck to comfort her.

I cradled the baby and rocked her, my eyes fixed on the Great Ulmarra.

He lifted his hand shakily from Louisa's hair, raising it to reach for the open window in the ceiling, then he sighed a rattling sigh, and his arm dropped.

Louisa looked up and frantically leaned over to see if he was breathing. She shakily touched her fingers into his neck, and then through her tears she said, "Good-bye, my dearest friend—go to the Dreamtime, where you belong... and wait for us."

She picked up his arm and rested it at his side. Then she placed his hands over one another on his chest and turned to me. She never said anything but got up from the floor and walked slowly to me. Her eyes were red and her cheeks wet, but she smiled and lifted her hands up to take Margaru.

I let the baby go, and she clasped her little, fat arms around her new mother, and Louisa walked from the room to go and put her in her cot, because it was time she slept too.

I stood in the room with my best mate lying still in front of me. I was swallowing and thinking whether I could bear the world without him, and tears flowed as though they had a mind of their own.

A curlew called outside with his haunting cry like a herald declaring something important. I looked at Ulmarra, and somehow I knew what he would say: "He's telling you the times of the new Yidinji are just beginning. All you have to do is listen for the small voice and—keep walking.'

Chapter 19

I WALKED AROUND IN shock for days. I kept expecting him to ring and say, "Hey, mate, I'm going to Rocky, wanna come an' do a survey?" The call never came, and somehow I had the same feeling you get when a girl rejects you because you're fifty pounds too heavy or twice her age. I felt rejected as though he had left me, turned off his phone, and wasn't speaking to me. Ever again.

The pain was coupled with another part of my heart that I couldn't look into. I couldn't even dare to think about *him*—our Judas, our torment, our disgrace—but as much as I ignored him, the more my heart grieved for my nine-year-old companion who I had made Vegemite-and-chip sandwiches for as soon as we got home from school. My heart grieved for shame, and pity, and in a fury, with all those thoughts you have when your dog has killed your neighbor's prize lamb and you've had to put it down and apologize. I burned with some kind of rage that was directed only at me, because he too was dead and couldn't hear me scream, "What have you done?"

Strangely, Jyly's death didn't make me feel these horror-filled and unknown feelings, but instead, when I thought of her, I felt warm and loved, and I knew she was always with me. She had tried to save him, done everything she could, sacrificed herself, and it might have worked if they had gotten to him sooner. I cried, but it was more like the sort of wonder you have when baby ducklings waddle up the grass and they are peeping as they walk in a line. Jilly Bird would rest in peace, and I couldn't begrudge her that.

Louisa was very quiet; she seemed to come to life only when she fed, or washed, or played with little Margaru. I stayed at her apartment for a few days but couldn't stand it. She was wrapped in some private bonding session, and I felt out of place. She was so organized, I knew it was only a matter of time before I outstayed my welcome, so I went home.

Feeling lonely and dark, I returned to drink beer, eat, and watch TV mindlessly.

Donahue rang me, and he came over. I guess he knew that my world had been ripped apart. He was actually pretty helpful. I mean, I felt better afterwards. He brought a copy of Margaret Stanford's diary with him and said it was time I read it. I couldn't see why, and I didn't feel like it—but I did, all that week.

After that, I helped Louisa sort out what we were going to do for the funeral. It was a difficult one. Willy and Maisy did a huge amount of organizing, and we got a dispensation to bury them up at the Rainforest Cathedral, together, just as he wished. The council agreed because the man was the focal point for real animosity against all things environmental, and we argued his grave needed special protection and to be free from defilement and should be "accessibly difficult," and they agreed. We took that as a sign of respect and acknowledgment of our Yidinji heritage as custodians of that land.

We decided to have a service at Cairns for anyone who wanted to come, and Jimmy's lawyer had instructions where it was to be held, and that really surprised me. For a man I knew to ignore any details except for those of the moment, it seemed strange that he had his death all mapped out.

We decided that after the service, John'o would fly their coffins up onto the mountain for their final burial.

About a week after he had gone, we had the funeral.

That morning, I didn't want to get up. I was going to bury my mate whom I knew and loved privately since we were kids, but today I was summoned to join with everyone else who loved him. I felt like I wanted to say, "Nah—I'm not going. You think you can leave me like this and expect me to like it? You think you can get everyone to come and mourn at your feet like you have us by the short and curlies, an' we can't do anything about it? Nah! When you come to your senses—an' come back—then I might forgive you for being such an idiot, and I'll worship at your feet all you want."

Stupid, eh? The stuff you think when you're like that...

Anyway, I got up, had a shower, and got dressed. I wore the shirt that I'd lent him for his wedding and stared at myself in the mirror, almost as if I was imagining him looking back at me. I smiled to myself like I was smiling at him, knowing I had to let go, so I took a deep breath and looked into his eyes in the mirror, though they had turned from green to brown.

"Alright," I whispered, "I'll do this for you, but I'm not keen 'bout it, mate!"

Willy came and picked Amy and me up. He said, "You okay, boys?" And I said, "Sure, Uncle, it's okay."

Amy wasn't saying anything, and I looked at him. "You okay?"

He didn't reply; he just looked down at his hands. He had taken it hard.

We went to the church in Freshwater for the service. The hearse arrived and Donahue, four others from the foundation, the university, and me carried Jimmy into the auditorium. Behind us, six others carried Jyly, and we set them in the center on a solid stand. The aboriginal women from the church stacked up flowers and laid a wreath on each coffin.

The church was packed, even in the foyer. I sat up front with Amy between Louisa and me, and Donahue sat next to me on the other side. The baby was in her pushchair and was being rocked back and forth on the space in front of the pulpit. Various notables had come to pay their respects and to honor the work my amazing friend had spearheaded, and they all sat looking this way and that, waiting for it to start.

Louisa and Amy couldn't take their eyes off the coffins, and I leaned down and gave Amy a handkerchief that he shyly dabbed at his eyes. I put my arm around my son and waited out the torment of the whole thing.

Jimmy had wanted a Christian service, which kind of surprised me a lot, since he was pretty quiet about what he believed, and he had some kind of "religion" all his own. Pastor Tommy spoke about the hope of a resurrection, and he talked about how he had known Jimmy and how the church had supported the work of the foundation. He made the point that the work was almost a sign of how to be at peace with that God they believed in, our way of acknowledging that we could not mess with the laws laid down before we came, and we were doing something that cooperated with healing and would help many, many people, and this pleased Him.

The pastor then read something out that really helped me make sense of what had happened:

"John 12:20: *The hour has come that the Son of Man should be glorified. Most assuredly, I say to you, unless a grain of wheat falls into the ground and dies, it remains alone, but if it dies, it produces much grain. He who loves his life will lose it, and he who hates his life in the world will keep it for eternal life. If anyone serves Me, let him follow Me, and where I am, there My servant will be also.*"

I realized that the shock of Jimmy leaving us would make many move to take up the work he had left, and that we would pull together and press on for ourselves, resting that terrible responsibility on our own shoulders instead of his name alone.

As I listened to the pastor speak about Jimmy, I could hear his genuine closeness and sadness. I guessed Jimmy had probably followed old Margaret Stanford's advice in her diary and discovered "the Great Captain's" message as he listened for that voice he taught us about. I was glad I had read the diary at last, and I understood a lot more about my friend because of it. I had never thought of him as religious, but I knew he had a deep sense of spiritual things. I knew he had found "something" in his long walkabouts and in his silence, but it hadn't occurred to me that he might have found "Him," the big fulla, on the way.

Whatever ... it was a nice service.

We talked for a while around the entrance afterwards, and then someone called out and said that if we could all move to the grass field in front of the car park between the Christian school and the main road heading for Cairns, we would have the farewell.

Donahue, the others, and me carried Jimmy over the grass. Behind us, Jyly's casket and bearers followed, and the church funneled out with a huge procession behind us, and we walked on a path strewn with flowers to the sound of aboriginal songs, the sticks, and didgeridoo. The sound of the weird dirge was dancing between us all as we lifted them onto the stand that had been prepared for them in the center of the field. Some of the women quietly gathered up huge bunches of flowers and stacked them around the base. Other people began to drift in and lay their own, until there was a mountain of them.

Willy had arranged for the men and women of the reserve to do a traditional farewell dance and to sing for the sake of the non-aboriginal people who had come. As they were singing, I heard John'o's chopper in the distance, coming through the gap in the range and the mountain-sheltering freshwater.

Everyone looked up as it finally hovered high overhead, our clothes blowing and hair flashing about. The flower petals spun off and spread over the grass, and the crowd was politely moved back in a huge circle around the coffins. John'o dropped the winch cable, and four men gathered the cables and net under the stand. It took a few minutes before they had hooked it all up. Then, while we watched, Jimmy and Jyly were lifted from the stand on the field, and a cascade of flower heads and petals fell like rain all around us. They soon rose high above us and began to fly away.

People watched for some moments until the coffins were far in the distance and then turned and walked back to the church. A few of us seemed to be hooked to that chopper too, and we just stood, our hearts flying with them, while our feet stayed anchored to the spot. Finally, that invisible thread between us and the chopper seemed to snap, and we too walked back to the church.

The pastor welcomed everyone and said over the loudspeaker that anyone who wanted to stay was welcome to join in a drink and some food. He said the Ulmarras would be flown to a special resting place of their choice, and he asked us all to join with him in prayer. I bowed my head, and if that strange God that knew my mate was there at all, I prayed I would one day see them again and the agony I was feeling would bugger off, because I could hardly bear it.

Louisa turned and hugged me so tight and for so long I felt every bone of her rib cage and might just as well have felt her heart pounding fast underneath. She told me to say good-bye for her; she would take the baby home, because she didn't think she could stay awake any longer, and when she was older, we could take her up to where her parents would finally rest.

I nodded and said good-bye, and shortly after that, we got in the cars and headed off to Gordon Vale. A bus had been provided for our people from the reserve, and we all followed it in a long procession all the way through Cairns, down the main road south that the first Ulmarra had gone on in his mother's cart with his fresh, new birth certificate.

We drove to the base of the mountain just as we had a few months before for his wedding. I saw the chopper flying high over the range, skirting the city of Cairns, heading for the first section ever planted in the hinterland, so they could fly over it one last time before John'o brought them back to the Rainforest Cathedral.

We arrived before the chopper and, once again, we climbed the track behind Willy and Maisy and all the reserve people, the foundation members, and some of the notables who had been invited to attend. The men and women weren't separated this time, and the mood was somber. Only the rain-forest birds chimed out, and the sounds of the forest, that kept on living, lightened the mood.

We arrived at the clearing puffing hard, and ahead of us, a large hole had already been dug, and woven mats covered the ground beside it.

Around the clearing, mats were strewn about, and we all sat down to wait for the chopper to arrive. The sticks and music started as the group sat under the big tree, and everyone joined in the song that the singers began.

Finally, the chopper arrived. The coffins were lowered into the clearing, and ten of us added our weight to them to get them in the right place. John'o did a fantastic job and was helped by a magnificent clear day with not a breath of wind. The coffins landed gently on the grass.

When the clips were removed, John'o lifted the winch and spun off the mountainside out into the free air of the plain, and we watched him as he dropped to the bottom to land.

We lifted them to the burial site. No words were said. With men leaning their weight against them, we let them slide on their straps until they reached the bottom. Above them would have been the last window of azure Queensland sky peeping from behind the forest canopy as they lay ready to say good-bye.

Painted warriors danced like cranes around the site, and the women wailed and sang. The forest shivered, and the birds and animals would have stopped as they listened. If they didn't already know, our voices and the music told them all, that the only human who truly understood them was going back to the earth.

I was numb from head to toe and, utterly blank faced, as I stood with Amy.

Suddenly Willy motioned everyone, and the singing and the music stopped. We were left alone with the silence of the mountain and our reflections.

I heard a siren distantly on the plains below, and it made us feel even more separate, more alone up there, as we waited for Willy to speak.

Finally, he coughed and began. "I knew this fulla from very young... Yeah, he was a son of mine. Flesh from me, he wasn't, but spirit of my spirit, he was. He said good things all his life. Things that are obvious, but we find hard to do, unless we had someone like him to follow. He found a way to be at peace with the creator of everything and how to cooperate." He dabbed his finger to his eye.

"We can't say nothing that can change this good-bye we gotta make—he and his wife have gone into the mountain together and under the offshoot of his ancestors' tree." He looked up, his big, wet eyes, brown and piercing, staring over us all. "You know, I thought about this thing, his life an' his death, and I got an understanding that came to me in the night.

"Them trees—well, there are three of them. The tree of the Mallanburra people; then the English lady that joined with them people, her tree at the place she named Ulmarra and gave that name to the first of his line and where she's buried—and this one, his tree, the Ulmarra Tree.

"Seems to me that this old writing says something about it: *'And there are three, that agree on earth: the Spirit, the water, and the blood.'*

"Yeah, I know who them words are talkin' and agreeing about, because I know that way, too. I think our boy an' these three trees was a sign pointing way, way back, and then a long way forward—to the right way. Them trees is a sign of those deep things that writing is talking about too. Them three things came to me while I was dreamin' on my bed. Yeah, the Spirit of things, the water of things, and the blood of things. What them dreams was showin' me was, 'The Spirit of the Mallanburra,' agreeing with the 'flesh of that one that bore the first Ulmarra'—and the 'blood of our boy,' having left his life behind, hoping that what was started way back in that past, through to his work in this day, can carry on tomorrow, until it is finished.

"That Dreamtime voice was telling me something to tell you, to comfort you. It was saying that this plan was set out so far back we couldn't know it, 'cept that old woman wrote it down, and that means we're standing here today, as part of that plan going so far forward, none of us will ever see its end 'cept if we get to rise up."

He shook his head and choked a little. "I got only this one thing I can say now...and I can hardly say it. My boy—son, we know you is waiting for us in the Dreamtime with that Great One that organized all this. You did your work in your time, as much of it as He knew you would do, and you showed us stuff we didn't see for ourselves. We will miss you...we will miss you..."

Amy suddenly tugged at my elbow. "Dad—I wanna say something too; he was my uncle, even if we wasn't related..."

I looked up to Willy, indicating the boy wanted a turn, because, as is the custom of the Yidinji, he is allowed to speak. Willy smiled and nodded and then waved him forward. The boy stepped forward cagily, and I couldn't have been more proud of him. Old Willy put his arm round his shoulder and we waited.

"Um...my Uncle Jimmy...he, um, taught me lots about the forest and the wild things. Um... He took me on walkabout to the secret places of the really old ones. Back then, I wasn't sure if I was Yidinji at all, because me mum is a white woman, and I've got sort of grey-blue eyes, and I got, you know—lighter skin. But he told me I was something new, that fullas like us…are the 'new Yidinji.'

"He taught me that it's in your *heart* that you are what you are, not the customs or the traditions you follow nor even the color of your skin, you know, your genes—it's in your heart, and that makes sense to me, because otherwise the rules of things would keep everyone good out of stuff they are meant to be in.

"So, everyone here that does what Uncle did because they 'love this land and have it in their bones' is one of us Yidinji. Maybe not an 'owner'—but a part of us, like us. You know?

"I don't own a house or nothin', but I'm still Australian, so I'm thinking, a lot of you guys that don't have no legal paper for this forest, you're still Yidinji if you love it and wanna protect it like we do.

"Yeah…I'm one of them new Yidinji, an' I know'd he meant *all* of us." He paused, and we all waited to see what else would come out of the mouths of babes.

"And that's something else I know I'm gonna do. Yeah, when Uncle and Auntie's baby, Margaru, is old enough, we gonna take her on walkabout, even though she's a girl an' that. I'm gonna show her stuff Uncle showed me, and we gonna teach her too … 'cause the Yidinji way is something you gotta learn from someone who knows it. But if you don't got it *inside*, it won't *never* get know'd, no matter how much teaching you get. That's what Uncle showed me by being who he was, you know, a real special guy. I'm gonna miss him bad … but if you are what you are in your heart, and he's in mine, he's still around … cause I … I … loved me Uncle, eh? I got him always in there and maybe I can be like him too an' plant me own tree that starts something off…" He looked sheepishly at the ground. "Um …that's all."

The crowd clapped and cheered, and I knew Jimmy and Jyly would have smiled big-time. I knew I was.

Willy told us to each say our good-byes in our own way, and we started to move toward the grave in a slow procession.

People kneeled on the mats, and many tears flowed, and whimpering sporadically came up from women holding each other or the men standing arm in arm.

It was time. Some of us walked up to the graves, and I picked up a shovel and started to cover them over. A few of the other boys pitched in, and the music began again. By the time they were inside the mountain and resting in it like they should, the dirt was piled up, and we laid covers over them and weighted them all over with stones from the Mulgrave River, right near where the old camp had been.

The mound shone white in the sun under the big tree, and, as I looked on at it, I couldn't bear what I was seeing. We moved back, and many sat and spoke of him or chatted about what this meant for the foundation, what they could do to help. Maybe Amy's speech had got them thinking.

I walked over and sat on a boulder looking out to the sea with my forearms over my knees. I got out a cigarette and put it in my mouth to light it. I stuck a match. Looking at the flame wavering in the slight breeze, I blew it out and put the dead match back in the pack.

John'o came from somewhere in the crowd, and I looked up as he walked over to me. He stood side-on and looked out to the view. "I practically ran up that track; I'm sorry I missed it... But I brought up a stone from down there, and I added it to the pile."

"Yeah—that was good, you flying them in like that."

"It kills me to think that was one of the last things I said to him—you know, at the wedding—that I'd fly them up here next time. I didn't realize..."

"He would have said, if you look back, you can see all the pieces of the puzzle coming together like it's been planned and is on autopilot, so it don't matter what you said."

"Yeah—well, that's why I gotta speak to you."

"What about?"

"Well...I'm sorry, eh. I feel responsible."

I looked up in surprise. "How's that, mate?"

"Ah...your brother. He asked if they were there. He said he wanted to apologize for upsetting them at the wedding. I offered to fly him down—you know, to make amends. He didn't know you were there, and I didn't tell him. I thought maybe if you saw him trying to do the right thing, you guys could bury the hatchet. I didn't know he was playing me. I had no idea, mate...that he was gonna do what he did. I couldn't believe it."

"We saw your chopper—that explains it."

"I've been to the police. They're making enquiries to see if he did it alone or someone else put him up to it. He told me a while back that he had been working. He never said who for, so who knows what was going on. He'd certainly cleaned himself up, had some money in his pocket—I dunno."

"Yeah, who knows—let the cops sort it out."

"I heard he saved the baby from the dingoes; is that true?"

"Not sure; it looked to me"—I pointed to the white-rock mound—"like 'his' dingo saved the baby. But maybe...he had a change of heart before they dished out his punishment."

John'o nodded. He could see I was struggling to talk about it, so he said sorry again, and I said it was okay, and he walked off aimlessly.

I knew John'o was a good bloke, and it was weighing so heavy on him, he was in the wrestle of his life. As I watched him go, I thought, "You're okay, mate," and I made a note in my head to take him for a beer and help him understand he was just one part of the show and there was nothing he could have done about it. Thinking that, I realized there was nothing I could have done either.

The sun was warming me, and I was about to move, maybe find Willy, when suddenly I saw someone appear at the top of the track.

It was Louisa. I sat up and watched her as she made her way to the grave site, ignoring the stares and looks that came from people who noticed the well-dressed woman who had been our boy's best right hand. She carefully approached the grave, and I almost got up to walk over to comfort her, but I caught the inkling of her moment with them, and it was a private one.

She bowed her head and then walked up to the base of the mound. I watched her as she kneeled down on the mat, and I could see she had things to say, and tears were falling. She reached out and placed both her hands on the stones to the left, over him.

Then, without lifting her head, she raised her right hand and slid it over the stones to her right, and rested it over Jyly. One on him and one on her—it was the greatest gesture of reconciliation I had ever seen of her, and, at that moment, I realized she was entirely worthy of my friend's confidence and trust.

After about ten minutes, she got up and walked back towards the track, not stopping to speak with anyone and none rising to speak with her. I saw the divide, and I rushed over and grabbed her by the shoulders.

"Lou, you made it!"

"Yes..."

"This is where they wanted to be, and it's a good place, eh?"

"Yeah, I should have come here before now..."

"Come and meet Willy and Masiy—I guess he might have told you about them?"

"Oh—well, if you think it's okay?"

"Of course it is—we're family!" I looked deep into her eyes. "Lou, you're one of us. An important one of us."

"Thank you, Wajilla—thanks."

I stood looking across the group, wondering where Willy was, and as I searched I asked, "What did he say to you...you know...at the end?"

"He told me to tell you, 'Listen to the small voice, and...keep walking.'"

Instantly I knew he had been with me even after he had taken his last breath. He had turned on whatever spiritual phone those fullas use, and he had called me after all and spoken thoughts right into my mind. I shook my head and laughed, a flood of relief passing over me, any shred of rejection left in that very moment. I said in my heart, "Good on you, mate, wait for me—good-bye, eh, good bye..."

"And what made you cry?" I said.

"He said, 'You'll make a good mother for Margaru...I'll call you 'Guli' now.'"

I smiled at her, and a glimmer of smile touched her lips also as we stood with our backs to Cairns city, warmed by the afternoon sun and looking toward the Ulmarra Tree.

"Where is our Margaru?"

"I got a babysitter, so I can't take too long up here—but I guess she can do without me for an hour or so more... After all, she's got me for the rest of my life."

"Yeah...well, when we get back—the work really begins; you're going to have to juggle the foundation and being a new mum. How are you going to do it?"

She looked at me gently and put her hand on my shoulder, "With your help, Wajilla—you and Amy, Donahue, John'o, Willy and Maisy and all the others who believe in this... But most of all, with you..."

At that very moment, a huge cockatoo screeched for all he was worth. rose from the upper canopy, and sailed off the mountain, riding the wind all the way down to the ground below.

Louisa looked up and I saw Maisy, laughing and crying loudly and pointing to it. Willy slapped his thigh and tousled Amy's hair and pointed to it too.

I didn't say anything. I just smiled, my white teeth rivaling the stones of my greatest friends lying in the mountain's mantle in the place they called their real home: the Rainforest Cathedral.

THE END

www.ingramcontent.com/pod-product-compliance
Lightning Source LLC
Chambersburg PA
CBHW070332030726
47505CB00004B/1171